DESPERATE MEASURES

Kathleen H. Nelson

DRAGON
MOON
PRESS

DESPERATE MEASURES

Kathleen H. Nelson

For information, contact Dragon Moon Press: www.dragonmoonpress.com.

ISBN 978-1-897492-74-1

Printed and bound in the United States

DEDICATION

This book is dedicated to Les. You are a day in the sun and a candle in the dark. You gave me strength on the worst of days and never despaired. Thank you, thank you, thank you, my love. You want wine with that?

ACKNOWLEDGMENTS

I'd like to give a big shout-out to the Space Studies Institute, the National Space Society, and NASA for their detailed, public speculations on space colonization and off-world manufacturing facilities. Their heavy-lifting made it easier for me to visualize a place like Farside. I'd like to thank my editor, Fanny Darling, for her succinct, spot-on recommendations, and my publisher, Gwen Gades, for welcoming me back to Dragon Moon Press. There's no place like home.

On a rather more personal note, I'd like to thank Christopher Camilleri, DO, for delivering me from the grips of an auto-immune disease that was slowly squeezing the life out of me. If you've never had an auto-immune disease, you can't imagine what it's like. One moment, you're running plays as usual. The next, you hit a wall and everything goes flat. After that, you start to slide. You keep on sliding until someone finally figures out that whatever's going on isn't all in your head. I cannot tell you how good it feels to be going up again instead of down.

Finally, I'd like to thank my family and friends for sticking with me while I was trapped in auto-immune hell. If I never have another stitch of good luck in my lifetime, I'll still consider myself the luckiest woman ever because of you.

I was watching
when the sky first formed a mouth.
I thought it would
eat the stars like zyl.

—from "Poems of The Q"

CHAPTER 01

N<small>IJI HAD JUST SETTLED</small> into its burrow for jaza, the-rest-state-that-follows-feeding, when the ground began to quiver. The sensation did not alarm niji, for seismic disturbances were as common as ice mites and usually just as harmless. But because usually was not always, and exceptions could kill the unprepared, niji monitored the activity anyway. The tremors seemed unremarkable at first: a series of feeble shockwaves, the well-traveled residues of some distant land-shift or slide. But instead of dissipating or growing stronger, the vibrations held steady. The irregularity intrigued niji. It shifted out of its compact, heat-conserving jaza configuration and plunged an array of sensory tendrils into the ground surrounding its burrow. The immediate influx of information was mundane—ambient temperature, the regolith's tastes and textures, the proximity of an eroding rock formation. Then it began to sense details about those shockwaves: direction, frequency, origins. To niji's surprise, they seemed to be coming from the surface. It pursued that peculiarity, directing its sensors topside though a mixture of coarse sand, particulate ice, and mineral-laden rubble. Ground-break came with its own impressions: cold-gray-still, which was no surprise; nazza often rested while darkness was away. But while there was no wind, the air was not unoccupied. Niji could feel vibrations—sound-waves, not the ground groaning as it sometimes did when it shook, but rather a mild, cyclical thrumming. Could the sound and the quivering be connected? Niji was inclined to think so, for it had knowledge-from-experience that curiosities usually schooled together. But niji was zervarz, an evolving intellect, and zervarzi did not slake their selves with theory when they could hunt for facts. So even though niji's digestive vacuoles were very full and it was chemically primed for drowsing, it retracted its outstretched frani, realigned its body mass for traveling, and then dislodged the burrow plug that it had so recently wrestled into place.

The regolith beyond niji's burrow was cool and loose—and still quivering. Under hungrier circumstances, niji would have plunged headlong into the oncoming shockwaves and tunneled directly to their epicenter. But the intensity of those vibrations was likely to increase as niji neared their source, and that could agitate niji's distended vacuoles. Too much stimulation could provoke a premature burst. That would leave niji's protoplasm full of partially digested *zyl*. Extruding their hard-shelled carcasses would be a slow, unpleasant process, one that would stud its outer membrane with *crustules* and make reconfiguration difficult. Niji preferred to keep its outer membrane supple and smooth, so it went topside and followed a series of its own markers to the top of a nearby outcropping. There, niji squeezed itself into the wind-polished crack that it occupied when it studied the sky-mouth. The rock was much colder than regolith, but it offered superior support for lengthy watches and protection against nazza's sporadic returns. Niji could not sense the ground quiver from its roost, but that strange thrumming was still discernible so it reorganized several clusters of frani into a trio of far-sensors and then extended them toward the flatlands. As it did so, it glanced skyward. The sky-mouth was not there. Niji was not surprised by this, for niji had seen the mouth swirl shut during its last watch, and thus far, the mouth stayed shut for several watches before opening again. But when better to look for an unexpected return than when curiosities were swarming?

A flash caught niji's attention. Its oculi focused on the light immediately: it was white like starlight but much, much closer. Had there been a sky-fall? Niji did not think so. Such an event was usually accompanied by a terrain-shattering explosion, not a pleasant thrumming. And afterward the air was always filled with scorched ozone and water vapor, neither of which was present now. But while niji did not believe that a piece of sky-stuff had come to ground, it had no doubt that something extraordinary had happened. For in addition to that delicate little light, niji could sense heat—not the white-hot flare of a lava upwelling, but dull red residues, remarkably self-contained. And there, on the peripheries of those residues—was that movement? Niji tried to strain more resolution from its oculi, but the only thing that it managed to discern was a shadow where no shadow should be. It was boulder-like in its dimensions, boulder-like in its density, too. But it was not pitching or rolling at the ground's whim as boulders often did during a seismic disturbance. It was moving. And—its movements seemed deliberate, as if the shadow was in pursuit of some purpose.

Zhee! How could this be? Only varzi frequented the surface. Only varzi moved with purpose. But no varz, not even the greediest of nijiti, grew to even a fraction of that shadow's size. There was no advantage to such excess. The mystery intrigued, delighted, and excited niji. It could not resist the urge to investigate further. That meant getting closer—an exciting prospect. It expressed its intentions in an *azrum*, then evacuated its roost and made its way down the outcrop. When it was free of the rocks, it oriented itself in the direction of the pernicious quiver and took off.

Niji started the journey underground, half-tunneling and half-streaming through the regolith. Such activity generated *zuna*, the-warmth-that-came-from-friction, and niji had a weakness for heat, especially after idling for so long out in the open. But as soon as the chill in niji's protoplasm abated, niji surfaced again. The thrumming began to acquire a plasma-tingling intensity. Zhee! That sensation alone would have been enough to entice niji away from jaza, but to its wonder, other novel stimuli were cropping up: hints of humidity, inklings of heat, and even exotic traces of burnt metals and hydrocarbons. Maybe there had been a sky-fall after all, a kind with which niji was not familiar. Maybe the stuff that had come aground was vibrating from the fall. Niji re-shaped its oculi, hoping to refine its impressions. Before niji could start gathering information, though, nazza came tearing across the flats. The shadow-boulder and its delightful emanations disappeared within a cloud of swirling, seething grit. Niji had no desire or reason to suffer the wind's fury, so it sank back into the regolith and resumed its hunt. The quivering grew stronger and then stronger still. Niji's excitement grew apace. It had never encountered such an intriguing collection of—

A warning from niji's leading edge displaced the thought: ice-mass, front-side. Niji immediately sent out additional frani to assess the mass's dimensions and density. Most varzi could cross a large patch or puddle without ill effect, but only a nijit would risk freeze-drying its memory strands by attempting an entire icefield. A zervarz with no memory was an evolutionary dead-end, good only for eating. Niji had grander ambitions. So if the mass proved dangerous, niji would find a less direct path to the shadowy not-varz regardless of curiosity's cravings for a straight line. As it happened, though, niji did not have to put caution before intrigue. The mass was a mere frost heave, neither broad nor deep. Niji tunneled under the frozen lens and back into normal regolith. The subterranean quiver grew steadily more intense. Niji's still full vacuoles began to vibrate, too. The feeling unsettled niji, so even though the digestive process was well underway now and the chances of a burst were diminishing, it decided to return topside.

Niji breached the surface warily, expecting to be buffeted by the wind. Instead, it was assailed by a confusion of other sensations: thrumming, humming, pounding, scraping, humidity, hydrocarbons, exotic dusts, molecules of airborne metal. Zhee! Niji had never experienced such an overwhelming influx of new stimuli, not even as a bud fresh from the split. And, there was more: shafts of light, movement, several sources of heat. The shadow-that-was-not-a-varz was very close now. It was tearing into the ground with a clumsy, oversized appendage. Was it digging a burrow? Why else would it need such a massive hole? Niji loosed an azrum, declaring its fascination. If another varz happened this way before the marker deteriorated, that varz would know that niji had encountered something that it did not understand and intended to investigate. That varz would also know that niji's curiosity was more potent than hunger and more seductive than heat. Niji simply had to know what was happening here; no other option sufficed.

But as fascinated as niji was, niji was still a zervarz and not entirely without caution. So instead of closing in on the not-shadow-not-varz, it stayed where it was and began accumulating information for eventual digestion. The *ulvarz* was easy enough to observe. Indeed, much about it seemed designed to attract attention. It beamed pale white light from its front and rear sides. It made many, many noises. It possessed multiple thermal profiles, all small and compact except for one that spewed heat into the air along with carbon residues and exotic gasses. It had a front end and a back end and two middle segments. The first segment was long and mostly flat. The other was boulder-like and seemed to be turning on an axis—slow, ponderous revolutions that produced a loose, semi-liquid sound. Niji did not understand what it was sensing, but at this point, it did not care. It was mesmerized; exhilarated; transfixed.

The ulvarz's appendage lurched to a stop. Several sounds and vibrations stopped, too. Zhee! Was the burrow finished? Would the ulvarz now slip into the hole and go to sleep? That was what niji would have—wait! What was this? The ulvarz's front-side had just pulled free of the ulvarz's main body! Now it was moving of its own volition. Niji was astounded. Had it just watched the ulvarz replicate? The offshoot was smaller, faster, and more flexible than its progenitor— just like a varz budling! Niji's excitement swelled to intoxicating levels. This was rapidly becoming the most singular event in niji's long experience.

The offshoot began removing long, narrow objects from the progenitor's long, flat middle-segment—strips of ulvarzi shell, perhaps? Niji could not sense the nature or purpose of these objects from this distance, but it grasped their destination easily enough. The offshoot was hauling them over to the hole and placing them within—in a specific, predetermined order! But why? The only thing that went into a varz hole was the varz who had dug it. And while one varz might abandon a burrow for another to find and claim, no two varzi, related or otherwise, would even think of working together on an excavation. There was no evolutionary advantage to such collaboration. But the ulvarzi did not appear to know that. As soon as the offshoot ran out of objects to put in the hole, it dislodged a large tube from the progenitor's revolving middle-section and positioned the terminus over the hole. Then the progenitor began excreting a substance like cold lava into the hole. Niji could not believe its oculi. Why would the ulvarzi dig a hole only to fill it back up? What possible purpose could such a not-burrow serve? The strangeness did not stop there, either. As soon as the hole was filled, the offshoot returned the *ul-lava* tube to its former resting place and then reunited with the progenitor. Where once there were two ulvarzi, there now stood only one.

And now the ulvarz was starting to move away!

Niji flushed, a conflicted display. Niji wanted to visit the not-burrow and ascertain its nature. It also wanted to see what the ulvarz meant to do next. Both options had their appeal, for one was as novel to niji as the other. But of the two, niji was likely to learn more from the ulvarz than the not-burrow—and more was always better when it came to learning. Furthermore, since the not-burrow was not going anywhere, niji could always return to it later. That bit of reasoning agreed with niji, so it commemorated its decision with an azrum and then started its pursuit. To its amazement, the ulvarz was already disappearing over the horizon. How could anything so big move so fast? But niji did not need to see the ulvarz to track it. All niji had to do was follow the gradient of cooling hydrocarbon chains and—zhee! Niji tumbled into a strange depression in the ground: wide-shallow-compacted, with smooth side-walls and an intricately ridged bottom. It ran in a seemingly straight line with no obvious beginning or end. Varzi left similar impressions when they traveled topside, although not as big or as straight, so it was reasonable to assume that this trail had been made by the ulvarz. Such a gratifying find. Now niji would not have to rely on gradients for its bearings. Now it could retract its sensory frani, streamline its body mass for speed, and race these impressions to their end. The ulvarz would be waiting there. Of that, niji was certain.

Rut-racing immediately agreed with niji. The highly textured bottom offered plenty of purchase for niji's motion frani, and the side walls provided just enough resistance to generate zuna. The taste of heat made niji giddy, which compounded its excitement. The unimaginable awaited! Niji could be chasing a chance to evolve! But just as niji was about to breach for joy, it encountered the flattened remains of an azrum. The marker tasted of confusion and a *pervarz's* panic. So niji was not terribly surprised when it discovered the varz's collapsed remains a little further down the trail. The ground had already swallowed up the contents of per's nucleus, and without a final memory to analyze, niji could only speculate as to why the ulvarz had killed the pervarz. It had probably not been hunting; otherwise, it would have eaten its catch. Possibly, it had not sensed the much smaller pervarz. Possibly, it had been going too fast to stop. Possibly, it had expected something so clearly inferior to get out of its way. The third possibility seemed most likely to niji. And regardless of the reason, niji considered the pervarz responsible for its own demise. The first thing any forward-thinking varz had to do was learn how to neutralize its panic chemistry. If per had done so, per would not have gone frozen-stupid in the ulvarz's path and had the life pressed out of it. The lesson-from-experience came too late for the pervarz, but niji derived something from it: a reminder that mysteries were often hazardous things. And so it resumed its chase with more sobriety.

The trail outlasted niji's last feed. Hunger began to slow niji down. Niji was not inclined to deviate from its path to go hunting, so it fed along the way on the dead and dying ice mites that it found trapped in the ulvarz's track. The catch offered minimal sustenance, but it was enough to keep niji going and had the additional benefit of not inducing jaza. Niji sped up again, intent on—wait, what was that? A subterranean quiver? Yes! Niji knew that sensation. And the tremors were soon joined by a delectable, airborne thrumming. Niji dispatched a cluster of frani, hoping to get a clearer sense of the ulvarz's location. As it did so, a thin beam of red light, narrow-band-wavelengths-all-in-phase, came streaking out of the gloom. It was traveling close to the ground, and appeared to be following the ulvarz's trail. And—as quickly as it appeared, it vanished. Niji had no doubt that the beam had come from the ulvarz, but—what purpose could it serve? Was it a defensive discharge like a zyl panic sting? Or was it a form of communication, not stationary markers like azrumi, but more like the electro-magnetic pulses that varzi used to convey specific thoughts to specific recipients. Or—maybe the ulvarz was trying to communicate with niji! Maybe it desired contact, the kind that did not involve crushing.

Zhee!

If there had been a wind, niji would have dove into it in an attempt to reach the ulvarz faster. But since nazza was still elsewhere, all niji could do was press on with more motion than sensory frani and hope that the ulvarz did not take umbrage at the wait. Niji had never traveled so fast or so blind. It did not enjoy the sensation, for zervarzi were thinkers, not thrill-seeking nijiti. But niji was willing to endure all manner of discomfort for the chance to learn more, for the ulvarz was like nothing that niji could have ever imagined. Also, some opportunities came and went and never returned. Niji had no intention of missing this one.

Blind as it was, niji knew it was closing in on the ulvarz, for its vibrations grew steadily more intense and complex. Then, without warning, the ulvarz's trail disappeared. Frani-beats later, the ground vanished, too, and niji went plummeting into a hole that tasted of humidity and freshly turned grit. It fell a long, long way, and then flattened into a semi-senseless splat as it hit bottom. As niji struggled to overcome the shock, darkness entered the hole. Dazed as niji was, it could not discern the darkness's nature, only that it was broad, jagged-lipped—and closing in on niji. Niji thought to flee, but could not yet coordinate such an effort and so contracted itself into a protective knob instead. The jagged lip dug into the bottom of the hole, scooped up a mound of regolith, and then tipped back. The mound slid into an iron-sided hollow, taking niji with it. Alarmed now as well as disoriented, niji slipped toward the onset of *dwaza*, the chemical cascade that resulted in frozen-stupid. Be calm, niji urged itself, as the hollow began to rise out of the hole. Stay aware. Panic is for the unevolved. But just as niji began to regain its composure, the hollow came to a stop and its bottom-side gave out. The next thing niji knew, niji was airborne. It contracted again, anticipating another stunning landfall and more panic-chemistry. Instead, it landed on a hill of fresh-turned regolith along with the newly excavated mound. As soon as niji realized that it was capable of moving again, it shifted into traveling form and tunneled its way to the top of the hill. There, it shaped itself a set of oculi only to be baffled by what it saw. There were two ulvarzi again! The progenitor was digging a not-burrow. The offshoot was preparing to fill the hole back up.

What peculiar behavior!

Niji realized then that there would be no understanding of what the ulvarzi were doing unless niji acquired some understanding of what they were first. That meant getting closer and taking samples. That meant making contact. The thought thrilled niji. It could not even begin to imagine what it was going to find, but fully expected to be amazed. It started down the side of the mound in the progenitor's direction. Although larger and likely less dominant, that ulvarz was the less active of the two and therefore the more accessible. Neither ulvarz seemed to notice niji's descent. Niji wondered if it was too small for their sensors. Or—perhaps niji was too inferior to them and unworthy of notice? The thought troubled niji, for while niji could change its size, there was nothing it could do immediately to make itself more evolved.

At the bottom of the hill, niji slipped into a familiar-feeling track. Soon, it was within frani-reach of the progenitor. The ground was trembling. So was niji. It had never encountered such a fabulously complex, self-contained mystery. Curiosity urged niji to rush in and start collecting samples as fast as it could, but niji resisted the greedy impulse. It was on the cusp of a destiny-shaping event—even a heat-drunk nijit could sense that. If it acted like a heat drunk nijit, it might offend the ulvarz and be rejected—or crushed. Niji did not want to lose an opportunity that might not come again. It did not want to be flattened, either. So it proceeded with respectful ceremony, depositing an azrum that declared its status and desires in front of the progenitor. The ulvarz did not respond to the introduction—no acknowledgement, but no challenge, either. Niji interpreted that as permission to continue and so extended several clusters of frani toward the ulvarz's base. A whirlwind of impressions followed contact: the taste of frozen, cross-linked hydrocarbons and metal residues, the feel of impacted grit, gaseous traces, even an echo of heat. The hydrocarbons formed a rugged, slab-like membrane that bore a pattern on its surface—the same pattern that niji had sensed on the bottom of the ulvarz's trail. Therefore, this membrane must have something to do with motion. The deduction pleased niji. It had not expected to make such immediate progress.

The membrane curved upward. Niji followed that bend until it flattened out and then was drawn toward a gritty, metallic overhang. The metal was an amalgamate of some kind; niji did not recognize the taste or texture. As niji explored its dimensions, niji discovered an inner space. This space was underground-dark, cavernous—and warm. Zhee! Niji adored heat. Heat made everything feel new. Niji wondered if the ulvarz had come to a stop over a lava tube, but no—the air did not taste volcanic. Therefore, the source had to be somewhere within the ulvarz. Curious as to what besides magma could create such a pleasant temperature without destroying everything in the vicinity, niji ventured further into the space. Combustion residues coated every surface. Carbon dioxide flavored the air. And what was this huge tangle of strange-metal and hydrocarbon membranes? Was it one thing with multiple segments? Or had several heat-liking things converged on a warm spot like nijiti around a geyser? Niji loosed another azrum—a bid for the tangle's attention. When the tangle did not respond with a challenge, niji felt free to stay and explore. So it settled down on a deliciously warm-but-not-too-warm stretch of strange-metal and extended its frani in all directions, probing every cranny it could penetrate. A dazzling array of sensations came streaming back: hydrogen, water droplets, a magnetic field? What use would an ulvarz have for—

Wait, what was that sudden influx of gaseous petrochemicals mixed with air?

The vapors ignited. Somewhere nearby, a small explosion ensued. Everything in the ulvarz's inner space leapt to loud and urgent life. Some segments contracted. Others began spinning, racing, shaking, thrumming. Niji recoiled, a primitive reaction, but many of its frani were caught in the crannies that they had been probing. One was being smashed, over and over again. Another was wrapped around a fast-spinning something. And the stretch of strange-metal that niji had settled on was rapidly changing from warm to hot. Zhee! Niji tried to free itself, but to no avail. Apparently, the tangle objected to niji's presence after all! Niji issued a hasty azrum, acknowledging its inferiority and offering to withdraw. To its surprise, the tangle responded—first with a tendril of acrid steam, then with a snap and a series of frantic flaps. A long strip of membrane went flying past niji. The tangle shuddered, then went silent and still. But its grip on niji's trapped sensors remained unyielding. The implication was clear: niji could withdraw, but the offending frani would have to stay. Regret crystallized in niji, cold and grainy like ice. Shedding sensors was energy-consuming work. Its outer membrane would be scarred, and scars complicated reconfiguration. Still, what choice was there? It could either lose a few feelers now or wait until the tangle took further offense and maybe lose everything. In this situation, less was definitely better. Niji expelled another azrum, recognizing the tangle's forbearance, and then began to produce the enzymes necessary for shedding.

Niji's chemistry was still in the process of shifting when a large hole appeared in one of the ulvarz's sides. Gloom streamed in through the gap only to be mostly eclipsed by a shadowy something—the offshoot? A beam of red light narrow-band-wavelengths-all-in-phase shot into the ulvarz's inner space, swept across the length and breadth of the tangle, and then disappeared. Frani-beats later, a tube tipped with what looked like overgrown feelers entered the inner space. The feelers attached themselves to a piece of shredded membrane: the one that had gone flying by earlier, niji realized. The shreds, niji noted, were covered with azrum-residues

The tube withdrew, taking the membrane with it.

Then it returned and seized niji.

In less than a frani-beat, niji's trapped sensors were stretched beyond their limits and then torn from niji's body mass. Niji had never experienced such pain, not even when it was budding. Its thoughts swirled. Its protoplasm went cold with shock. A lesser varz would have lapsed into dwaza. Niji squirted free of the offshoot's grip instead, and chanced to land in an opening in the offshoot's outer membrane. It fled inward, oozing plasma. An acrid smell rose up in its wake. Niji continued to flee until exhaustion set in. Then, oblivious to its surroundings, it drew itself into a compact mass and fell into *fwaza*, the deep-sleep-that-heals.

The next thing niji knew, niji was being hauled out of fwaza by a metallic, many-tipped something. Dazed and only half-healed, niji lacked the capacity to react. Before it knew what was happening, it found itself out in the open and plunging toward the ground. Landfall came quickly. The impact jarred niji back to full consciousness even as it broke its scars open. Nazza pelted the wounds with sand—a most unpleasant sensation. Niji knew that it should retire to an out-of-the-wind hole so it could rest and heal. But it did not want to return to its burrow—not when the ulvarzi appeared to be rousing. So niji decided to take shelter in the offshoot's underside. It would be out of the wind's way there, and hopefully, out of that many-tipped something's reach. From there, it might also be able to get a better sense of what was going on.

But first niji had to find the ulvarz—a difficult proposition in its abused state. Some of its frani were numb. Others were hindered by scarring. Eventually, it managed to shape itself an oculus, but that too seemed to be compromised-by-injury, for it registered three ulvarzi in the vicinity instead of two. Then the would-be mirage loosed a tendril of heat and niji realized that there was nothing wrong with the sensor after all. There was a third ulvarz! And—it seemed to be conjugating with the offshoot!

The observation excited niji. In spite of its fatigue and oozing scars, it could not resist the urge to investigate further. So instead of returning to the offshoot, niji started up the newcomer's backside. This ulvarz's outer membrane was deliciously warm. As soon as niji tasted the heat, it found itself wanting more. The higher niji climbed, the stronger that craving became. The next thing it knew, it was invading the newcomer's inner. As it searched for a place to rest, it loosed a series of azrumi, assuring the ulvarz that it would only stay until it was healed. The ulvarz responded with an acrid smell and went to sleep.

That was when niji made the connection: that miasma signaled the onset of dormancy in the ulvarzi! The realization encouraged niji to speculate: if one smell signaled their dormancy, then maybe another would signal their awakening. It seemed a reasonable theory. All niji needed to do now was wait and see.

CHAPTER 02

AN ILL-TEMPERED WIND HOWLED across the plain, churning up clouds of grit and particulate ice. The grit scratched at Awinita Johnson's face-plate like something small and mean that wanted in. The ice melted on contact and re-froze in feathery micro-patterns, making the already cruddy visibility even worse. Awinita loosed a howl of her own, a private burst of fury laced with yearning.

She was supposed to be going home, dammit!

Yet here she was, tramping around in an off-world sandstorm trying to get a fix on some MIA seed-stuff—as ridiculous a proposition as trying to find diamonds in a copper mine and infinitely more exasperating given that she didn't want to be mining at all. Her gaze strayed toward the heavens, or at least what passed for the heavens in this part of space. The skies looked familiar enough at first glance, like something she might have seen on a cold winter night way back when she and her parents were living on the TSC compound in Flagstaff, AZ. On second glance, however, the differences became all too apparent. There was no moon in this sky, no blinking satellites or cis-lunar installations or air-traffic, either, just a smattering of windblown stars that had never been named or mapped.

Not by humans, at any rate.

Awinita scowled, self-reproach for letting her thoughts stray into territory that was best left alone. No point in picking at a scab, her father used to say—unless you want it to bleed. She was usually more disciplined. Had to be the fatigue. Remote Site Fever. She needed to return to Terra, not just to visit but to reconnect. It had been over eight years since her last LTL. And she had already been on her way, dammit: boarded, debriefed, and shown to her quarters. She'd felt *The Bonhomie*'s engines begin their slow climb to power. She'd heard the cruiser's crew going through their pre-flight preparations.

Then Shingo had requested the pleasure of her company.

She should've suspected that something was up as soon as she heard that the Chief of Space Operations wanted to see her, because she'd already been interviewed by one of his underlings. That suspicion should've ripened into a sense of impending doom when he had her brought to his private quarters rather than a ready room. And she should have flat-out known that she was SOL when he offered tea and then served it himself a la an elaborate, old-style Japanese ceremony, because she'd heard it said on more than one occasion that the CSO used tradition like some people used a zap. But Awinita had been fresh off a double stint on Io: a frigid, relentlessly tedious gig that had left her mentally, physically, and emotionally spent. It had never occurred to her that her host might have anything other than genuine, Terra-grown tea leaves up his sleeve. Indeed, she'd had RSF so bad, she'd actually imagined the humorless son of a bitch was joking when he first broached the subject of reassignment.

"We did not receive a signal from Farside when the APW opened up this time," he said, as she basked in the fragrant steam that was rising up from her teacup. "We are sending a team to do a site inspection and revive the seed if necessary."

"Poor bastards," she said, enjoying a moment of *schadenfreude*, and why not when she had spent the last eight plus years drinking powdered commissary swill instead of fresh-brewed oolong. "Who'd you tap for the lead?"

"You."

Ha-ha. Who wouldn't have laughed? But he remained closed-off and unsmiling, her first chilling clue that this was no laughing matter. "Sorry," she said then, going as straight-faced as he was, "but I'm going on long-term leave. Tap someone else."

"There is no time," he said, with a shrug that gave nothing away. "The APW is due to close within the week, and TSC wants a crew on the far side before it does. This cruiser is closest to the jump-point. You are already on board. And no one does what you do better."

"Sorry," she insisted. "I'm so fried, I'm surprised you can't smell it. I need some serious downtime on Terra before I take on another project."

"You will only be there for one interval," he said, and the lack of inflection in his tone made it clear that he was dictating terms rather than trying to persuade her. "Your main objective will be to get that OMF up and running. We must have a reliable source of hydrogen fuel on that side of the wormhole ASAP. You would sacrifice three months for homeworld security, wouldn't you?"

"Certainly," she said. "Just not the next three. Because like I said, I'm fried."

Shingo breathed in a tendril of scented steam and then exhaled it like a sigh. "TSC regrets the imposition," he said, "but these are desperate times. Desperate times require desperate measures. TSC will compensate you for delaying your LTL."

Bastard. He must have known that she was too tired to fend off such unrelenting pressure. He must have known that when push came to shove, the only thing she could do was cave. "If you're going to force me to do this," she said, when she finally folded, "then at least make it possible for me to do it right. Shuttle me back down to Io so I can draft a seasoned seed crew. That'll only take a day or two."

"There is no time," he said, with the creepy, pre-programmed consistency of a hologram. "The crewmen of *The Bonhomie* are a capable lot. I'll have my LT assemble a dozen or so of the most able bodies and you can pick your team from their ranks."

She had almost swallowed her tongue at the thought of working a remote site op with a crew of Johnny Rockets. Not that she had anything personal against spacemen. In her younger days, she had wiled away plenty of interplanetary flights in the company of off-duty Johnnies. But as a rule, they didn't do well on solid ground unless they were medicated or well into LTL. The gravity differential left them clumsy and easily fatigued. And away from the well-marked warrens of their star-ships, they tended to get lost. She would've had to look pretty hard to find a bunch of candidates who were less suitable for remote site field work. But since Shingo didn't see the problem and there was no going over his head, all she could do was screen his LT's short-list for the most obvious rejects and have the rest of them chipped for RSO basics. She toyed with the idea of conscripting Shingo, too, turn-about being fair play, but decided to forego the pleasure because that kind of man was only good at making more work for others.

"This sucks."

Her thought exactly. But had she said it out loud? She wasn't sure. She talked to herself sometimes, mostly when she was tired. And sometimes, other voices kicked in—her mother's mostly, Meli the spirit-guide.

"I hate this place."

This time, she saw the ID window in the upper right corner of her face-plate pop up. Definitely not her mother. The speaker's avatar was a leering holo-spider. She rolled her eyes, wondering what she had been thinking when she OK'd this whelp. He was fresh out of training, an apprentice Johnny working his first deep-space tour. Shingo's LT had picked him precisely because he was so green, arguing that he hadn't had time to lose his conditioning and land-legs. But while there was no denying that the hatchling was in phenomenal shape, his post-adolescent need to assert his individuality irked her, as did his volumes of often inappropriate energy.

Or maybe RSF was turning her into a grouch.

"What's up, Spider?" she said, in a curt but still civil monotone that deteriorated into a near-snarl when she had to repeat herself. As if it were the rookie's fault that she had made a rookie's mistake and forgotten to cue her mic before she spoke.

"I'm trying to set up the guide-line network around base-camp like you wanted," he said, "but this friggin' wind keeps trying to blow me off-course."

"Install the posts leading from the pod to the garage first," she said. "Quickset 'em point six meters deep at one point eight meter intervals."

"I did that already."

"Did you use the BTS to map out your lines?"

"Yes."

"And recheck each post as you strung it?"

"Yes."

"Then you're doing everything right, and there's no need to worry."

"But the wind—"

In another time and space, she might have cut him a little slack for being put out about the current situation for it really did suck in every imaginable way. But she'd been hijacked, too, and not from her maiden voyage, brimming with energy and excitement and memories of the mother-world. She was worn out, tired down to the last molecule in her body, and she hadn't felt the sun on her skin in almost a decade. So TFB if the poor little earth-boy wasn't thrilled with his work environment.

"The wind is something you're going to have to learn to ignore just like everyone else," she said. "Quit your bitching and get back to work."

A pause ensued, and then a snide, "Yes, Mother."

"That's 'Chief Johnson' to you, Johnny," she snapped, and not just because she didn't appreciate the comparison. On a job this extreme, no one was allowed to challenge her authority. Insubordination could put the op's success—and quite possibly their lives—in danger "And if you lip off again, I'll pound sand so far up your ass, you'll still be shitting it out when *The Bonhomie* pulls back into orbit. Are we clear on that? Or are you campaigning for a load of intestinal grit?"

The link fell silent again. This time, it was the chastened sort of lapse that often accompanies a slap to the face. Then Spider cleared his throat and said, "Sorry, Chief. I was out of line. It's just that I—I can't believe the CSO left us here!"

In the innermost chamber of her heart, she felt the very same way: abandoned, marooned, stranded on the dark side of a wormhole. But she couldn't tell him that any more than she could let him get cheeky with her. The first link in the chain had to be the strongest.

"What choice did he have?" she asked, reminding herself as well as him. "TSC needs this installation up and running ASAP."

"Like three months is going to make that much difference," Spider groused.

Again, she felt the same. Again, she counter-punched with a TSC sound byte. "The longer it takes us to establish a presence on this side of the APW, the longer Terra remains vulnerable to attack by the Un. Now shut your trap and get back to work."

But apparently the boy lacked the capacity to suffer in silence. "The least Shingo could've done was let *The Bon* stick around for a while. You know, until we got settled. I mean, what are we going to do if something goes wrong?"

"Nothing's going to go wrong," she hastened to say, trying to slam the door on that thought before it could get loose and prey on her already weakened concentration. In three or so months, ninety days and counting, *The Bonhomie* or some other cruiser would be back in orbit around this miserable rock with supplies, personnel, and relief.

"You don't know that," he said.

She clenched her teeth against the urge to snap, then thought screw it and went after the SFB for not knowing when to quit. "You're right," she said. "I don't know that. In fact, given where we are and how we got here, there's a better than average chance that I'm terribly wrong. But that doesn't matter. You wanna know why?" Before Spider could respond, yea or nay, she shoved the answer down his metaphysical throat. "Because in the words of my favorite twentieth century philosopher, 'The needs of the many outweigh the needs of the few.' And we, Johnny, are the few. Now for the last time, dummy up and finish that network."

"Yes, Chief."

But silence wasn't the respite that Awinita had hoped it would be. All it did was crawl into her head and incite sadistic games of what-if. What if their ride didn't come back? What if the wormhole stayed shut? What if their food ran out or their reclamation unit failed or—wait. Her scanner was flashing. Finally. The promising, neon-green blip was slightly off the grid template, but so far, everything about this op was screwed up, so why not this, too? She squinted in the specified direction and then swore as a reef-like series of mounds hazed into half-view. Stupid POS. She was looking for transponder towers, not an outcropping of boulders. She re-entered the profile—not the easiest trick in a thick-fingered habitat suit. When the read-out continued to point to the outcropping, she cursed again and then cocked her arm, meaning to pitch the scanner into the wind. In mid-throw, though, she held back because even though it was a make-do instrument that didn't always get the job done, she had nothing with which to replace it. She added that to her list of reasons to hate Shingo. Not only did he expect her to pull off a full Lazarus op, he expected her to do it with re-purposed equipment and a crew of Johnnies.

Unfortunately, there was no quitting some jobs.

The thought had an odd, calming effect on her. Her irritation dissipated. Her grievance against the CSO gave way to dogged resignation. She could handle anything for three months, she told herself, as she closed in on the outcrop. Three months was nothing. And after that—

"Well, I'll be damned."

She looked again, but her eyes weren't deceiving her. The boulder that was emerging from the swirling sands wasn't a boulder at all, but a half-buried fix-it. "I wasn't expecting to find you here," she said, as she came to a stop alongside the 'bot. "Let's have a look." She brushed the worst of the blow-over away from its chassis. "Wow," she said, as she brushed the worst of the blow-over away, "you've been out here for a while, haven't you."

The 'bot was badly scored, which was no big surprise given the intensity of the wind. It wasn't a big deal, either, since fixits didn't need to look good to function. They did, however, need a certain degree of internal integrity—and this fix-it's boot had been sprung. She peered into the exposed compartment. Ugh, sand everywhere. Cleaning that out was going to be a bone-deep drag. She slapped a locator strip to its front as if she were slapping some junior miscreant upside the head and said, "What were you doing out here in the first place?"

The answer loomed just a few feet away in the form of two more mounds. These turned out to be 'bots, too—a small, unplugged op-'bot and a hulking APC with backhoe and c-mixer attachments. Both were wind-scored and seized up like the fix-it. Both of their boots were sprung, too. Crud. She was going to need help getting these suckers home.

"Anyone free to make a pick-up?" she said, using a PA channel. "I've got a fix-it and a tandem APC here, all disabled."

A cartoon image of Johnny Rocket from the original DGV series popped up in her IDW almost immediately. She rolled her eyes. Didn't anyone use a standard issue holo-photo as an avatar anymore? "I'm pulling into base-camp AWS," her caller said. "As soon as I secure my load, I'll head your way. What's your location?"

"Fifik," she said, which was short for fuck if I know. "Somewhere off the nonexistent path. I activated a loca-strip. Follow the signal."

"Roger that. LT out."

The IDW went blank. She switched her comm link to standby and then resumed her field inspection. Who knew? Maybe there were other disabled 'bots in the vicinity. Maybe there were other things, too—things that knew how to spring a man-made boot. She slammed the door on that avenue of thought. Recon had declared this miserable piece of rock devoid of intelligent life. That was good enough for her, and whoa—what was this here just beyond the backhoe? A pit filled with rebar spikes? Booby-trap, the paranoid voice in her head gabbled. And: told you so! But as the initial shock and thrill of a close-call subsided, she noticed a c-tube hanging over the hole, and came to a very different conclusion. This wasn't an ambush. This was unfinished business, the base to a transponder tower, probably. The tandem must have just started the pour when the APC malfunctioned. See? Mechanical failure. Nothing sinister about that. But part of her still wanted to blame it on the Un. After all, that's what had brought humanity to this side of the APW.

The Unknowns and their wormhole were by far the biggest mysteries to ever hit the Terran solar system. And of the two, people were more accepting of the wormhole, probably because it came and went at predictable intervals, and could be studied from all angles and both ends. In contrast, the Un remained a colossal enigma. No Terran had ever seen one in the fifty-something years since the wormhole had started swirling open and shut in the dead zone beyond Pluto. No Terran had ever heard one, either—at least not directly. But for many years, the radio telescope array on Mars had picked up a stream of mysterious, murmur-like transmissions whenever the APW opened. Un-fuzz, the radio astronomers called it, and insisted that it was too structured to be a naturally occurring phenomenon. People of every stripe and persuasion set out to decipher the signals but none succeeded. Their endeavors became something of a running gag for late-night talk shows and tabloids: Researchers say Un-fuzz is Voice of God, Pope disagrees.

Then the wormhole went quiet. Fifteen years later and still counting, it remained quiet. A few Terrans took that much silence as a sign that the Un were dead, wiped out by an even more formidable alien race, and theorized that the fuzz had been a last-ditch appeal for help or maybe a warning. But the vast majority interpreted it as the calm before an intergalactic storm, a pre-invasion hush from a civilization advanced enough to exploit and possibly even manipulate the comings and goings of a wormhole. Hence, the rush to establish an outpost on the far side of the APW. Better in their backyard than in ours, TSC liked to say. Before this assignment, Awinita hadn't spent a lot of time worrying about the Un. Their coming fell into the same apocalyptic category as Terra's sun dying and the Milky Way colliding with Andromeda. Sure, it was going to happen eventually, but not in this eon or even the next, so why sweat it? But now that she was camped out on what could be the front line, it was harder to ignore the what-ifs. What if Recon had missed something? Scouts were under tremendous pressure to find exploitable worlds—

The ground bucked and then began to quiver. The temblor bounced Awinita out of her worries and back to her first encounter with Kisin, god of earthquakes. She'd been playing in the shade of a coconut palm. The first jolt tipped her over. The second jerked the palm halfway out of the ground. Coconuts began raining down around her. The ground was shaking so hard, it made everything seem blurry. Her father burst out of the beachfront bungalow that he had given to Meli for their ten-year. Meli followed on his heels, shouting, "Nita, run!" She tried to get up, but even though the ground had stopped shaking, everything felt like it was still moving and she fell down again. The next thing she knew, there was sea-water everywhere, gritty and warm and powerful in ways that a nine-year-old child could not comprehend. It collapsed the bungalow like a wrecking ball. An instant later, it swept Awinita inland. She hit her head on something hard in passing and woke up on the bottom of someone's dinghy almost a quarter-mile away. The world smelled like low tide only worse and there were dead bodies everywhere.

"Yee-haw! Anyone else feel that?"

The excited query pulled her out of the memory but could not save her from the benumbed, orphaned feeling that always rose up in the tsunami's wake.

"Everyone OK?" she asked.

All reports came back thumbs-up. The good news should have come as a relief, but she was still caught in the flashback's undertow and couldn't regain her focus. How could a memory hold that much power over her almost forty-five years after the fact? Was it because search-and-rescue had never found her mother's body? Meli had so loved the ocean. Maybe it was better that she had gone that way, carried out to sea like a Greek goddess in reverse rather than battered into fish meal on the breakwater like her father. "It's a good thing TSC chips its executives," people said to her at his memorial back in Flagstaff. "Otherwise, you might never have known." But knowing wasn't all that great, either.

A distant flash of blue-white light caught her eye, inspiring a microburst of fear. Aliens! Then she sneered at herself for being such a twitch. Of course it was an alien. A warm-blooded, fur-bearing, biped with opposable thumbs—and a lead foot, judging by the rate that headlight was bouncing across the horizon. She issued a correction immediately.

"Throttle back on that crawler, Johnny," she said. "It's the only one we've got."

"Begging your pardon, chief," LT said, easing up but not by much. "This old girl needs to be opened up every now and again to keep her valves from sticking."

She harrumphed to herself. What would he know about old girls?

The sleigh's high-pitched whine began to weave in and out of the wind's bluster. The sound reminded her of the mosquitoes that used to invade the bungalow at night and buzz her out of her sleep before going in for the kill. Melancholia crept through her like a low-grade malarial flare-up. She glanced skyward again, and then forgot to look away. That's how LT found her: head tilted back, lost in thought.

"Chief?" he said, tapping into her private channel. "You OK?"

And she was so far gone, she didn't even care that she'd been caught unawares. "Yeah," she said, from that faraway place. "I suppose."

"What're you looking for?"

"Canis Major," she said.

"Any particular reason?"

"My mother's ancestors believed that those two stars were dogs that guarded the path to the land of souls," she said, remembering the night that Meli had first shared the myth. There had been more bugs in the sky than stars, but they had just returned from E-li-si's funeral and Meli, moderately drunk, insisted on staying outside and star-gazing. "They buried their dead with food so the deceased would be able to bribe their way past the guardians. But if a soul messed up and fed the whole bribe to the first dog, that soul was screwed because the second dog wouldn't let it go forward and the first wouldn't let it go back. It was stuck in limbo forever."

"Grim," LT said. "And you're thinking about this now because—"

"I'm afraid we forgot about the second dog."

As soon as the words left her mouth, she regretted them. And her regret was like a sharp slap to the face. What was the big idea, letting her guard down like that in front of a crewman, especially Shingo's 'ling?

"Don't worry, chief, they'll be back."

Which wasn't the point. Or was it? Crud, she was so tired, she couldn't follow her own blather anymore. But at least she kept that thought to herself. "We can leave the c-mixer here for now," she said, as if they had been talking about that all along. "The flatbed can stay, too."

"It's loaded," he said, sneaking a peek under the auto-tarp. "That make a difference?"

She cocked her head at him. "Where's it going to go?"

He acknowledged the point with a snort and then began prowling around the rig. She trailed after him, wanting to see how well he sized the job up. "Looks like the mixer froze with a load of wet cee in its belly," he said, at one point. "If I were you, I wouldn't bother hauling it all the way back to BC. It's toast."

She shrugged his advice aside. "There's no telling what might come in handy on a job like this. 'Waste not, want not,' my father used to say."

"Mine used to say, 'Wipe that smirk off your face or I'll do it for you.'"

She waited for a mitigating gesture or look that would blunt the starkness of that remark, but it never came. He ducked in to uncouple the mixer from the backhoe and then resumed his prowling as if nothing at all had been said. If she hadn't been so tired, she might have been intrigued. And if he had been an ordinary Johnny, she might've tried to draw him out a little. But he was Shingo's LT, a long-time 'ling who had undoubtedly signed on as her second to make sure that the CSO's objectives were met. She had no intention of getting chummy with a man like that.

"OK," he said, when he was done with his prep-work, "we're good to go. I'll bring the crawler around and we can get this show on the road." He was backing up, looking at her when he should've been watching where he was going. She saw his danger and lunged after him. "What the—?" he said, as she grabbed an arm and then, "Ow!" as she yanked him back onto solid ground. "What'd you do that for?"

She pointed out the pit. While she couldn't see through his gold-tinted face-plate, she would have bet her retirement fund that he turned pale. "Thanks," he said, absently rubbing his arm. "I didn't see that."

"That's because you weren't looking," she said.

If he took offense at her snappishness, he didn't let on. Instead, he continued to stare into the hole. "What's it supposed to be?"

"Platform for a transponder tower," she said. "Unfinished, of course."

He smacked himself upside the helmet. "So that's what that was."

"What what was?" she asked.

"There's a loca-stripped slab of concrete about a half-click north of here," he said. "That was the first signal I locked on, so that's what I followed. I must admit, I freaked a little when I got there and didn't see you. My TD kept pointing to the ground. I thought you'd had an accident and been buried alive or something, so I started digging. The slab was just below the surface."

At last—a tiny bit of good news. A very tiny bit, to be sure, but like Meli used to say, anything was better than nothing, and it was one less thing she'd have to get done in the next three months. And speaking of which—

"Go and get the sled already. And watch where you're going this time."

He was gone and back in a Johnny Rocket flash. "I'll attach 'em," he said, as he climbed down from the cab. "You reel 'em in."

Technically, it should've been her telling him what to do. But she'd been on her feet for almost six hours straight already. Her low back ached, her reconditioned knee was stiff, and the thought of more bending and stretching and squatting made her want to cry. If her second had a craving for grunt-work, she'd be more than happy to indulge him. So she retired to the lee-side of the crawler without a word and watched as he got the backhoe ready for loading. No doubt about it, he knew what he was doing. His file said he had a handful of master certifications, including several in engineering, but that didn't always translate into capability in the field. Knowing he was the real deal was a definite plus.

Too bad he belonged to Shingo.

They loaded the backhoe onto the crawler's flatbed without incident. The tandem core went next, and then the plug-in. "I see what went wrong with this one," LT said, as he prepared the fix-it for loading. "Its boot popped open."

"It's the same with the rest of them," she said. "I'm guessing the latches weren't designed for such a harsh environment. TSC was in such a hurry to establish a toehold on this side of the APW, it deployed a stockpiled seed instead of assembling a new one to suit host planet specs."

"Practically guaranteeing some degree of launch failure," he said, and then gave his head a world-weary shake. "Why do something once the right way when you can do it half-assed twice."

Her father used to say that, too—in that same tone and cadence. For one bittersweet, out-of-body moment, she pretended that it was him down there in that habby giving her a thumb's up. He would have approved of her choices: a life in space, more work than play, always putting the needs of the many first. Her mother, however, would've been appalled. *No family? No child? No earth beneath your feet? What kind of life is that?*

And right about now, Awinita had to wonder.

"Chief," LT prompted, when she didn't respond to his thumb's up, "are you OK? We're good to go."

"No problem," she said. "I was just making sure the plug-in was secure. While I'm running the winch, slap a loca-strip on that flat-bed—just in case." She added that last bit to be funny, but the joke tripped over her half-buried concerns and fell flat. "As soon as the fix-it's secure, we're heading in. You can drive if you want."

That suited him just fine.

The crawler's cab was as bare-bones as the rest of the op: no heat, no padding, and no leg-room on the passenger side, just a plastic bench and a milky, shatter-proof windshield. But Awinita didn't care. She was happy just to be sitting down and out of that infernal wind. How pathetic was that?

"What's that, chief?" LT asked, as he powered up the sled. "I didn't hear you."

"I think I'm done," she said, not realizing that she'd gotten to that point until she blurted it out. "I think I'm going to retire after this."

"No kidding." The crawler skirled to life. LT waited until he had a full charge at his disposal and then hit the accelerator. The crawler lurched forward, straining against the weight on its back. Moments later, it surged forward. As soon as he was sure of the sled's momentum, he activated the auto-pilot and then resumed the conversation. "Where's that going to take you?"

"I'm going to return to Terra and buy myself a little island in the Caribbean," she said, planning out loud. She could do it, too. She had a lifetime of credit stashed away. "I'm going to live on the beach and swim in the ocean and sleep in the trees."

"Meh," he said, projecting revulsion. "Why would you do a thing like that? Terra is a pisshole: hot, smelly, and teeming with disease. There are more bugs on that rock than people."

"That's always been the case," she said.

"Never more so than now," he said.

But she didn't want to hear it. "You do a few tours in the Oort-back without shore leave between trips and then talk to me about Terra. I bet you'd synthesize an entirely different tune."

"Really? What do you want to bet?"

"A sack of oysters," she said, inspired by her daydream.

"What's an oyster?"

Her first impulse was to laugh, ha-ha, very funny. Then it occurred to her that he actually might not know. Terra's oceans were warmer than bathwater these days. And oysters were cool-water animals. It wasn't beyond the realm of possibility that they had gone extinct while she was gone. Thousands of other species had disappeared. Some things just couldn't take the heat.

"I like the runner lights," LT said. "They remind me of my great-gran's front yard at Christmas-time."

She started out of her thoughts to see a constellation of red lights glimmering on the horizon. The sight lifted her sagging spirits, which was exactly what it was meant to do. Shingo hadn't wanted to give her the runners. Frivolous, he had called the request. Unnecessary. But he had never done time on a raw remote-site. He didn't know how oppressive such a stint could be: shift after shift after shift of extreme otherworldliness, often cold and usually dark, with virtually nothing to do but work. Most of the time, that splash of home-grown cheer at the end of a long day was only enough to trigger a smile or a sigh. But every once in awhile, it was enough to stop a chronically sensory-deprived man from saying FIA and walking off into the wilderness. And that was why she had insisted on having them.

The lights grew closer and then closer still. She immersed herself in their thin glow as she had once immersed herself in the glow of a gas log on a snowy Flagstaff winter's day. *Look, 'Nita, the fire's making faces at us.* Then the crawler veered to the right and a mountainous shadow compelled her attention. This was the seed, 200 tons of raw materials, modules, and equipment waiting to be deployed. It should have been gone by now, broken down and recycled. There should have been a command center in sight, a bunker for the outpost's cyber-brains. She should have been able to see a power station, too, and beyond that, an up-and-running wind farm. And just a little further down the nonexistent road, there should have been a fuel manufacturing facility going up on the skyline. But once they were past the seed, all she saw was wasteland and windblown runner lights.

"Damn," she muttered, forgetting that her mic was on. "A near-total failure to launch."

"C'mon, chief," LT said. "It could be worse."

Technically, he was right. Their situation could have been a teeny-tiny bit worse. One TT platform had already been poured. The pavers had managed to dig and grade foundations for the command center and the power station before crapping out. But the ticks in the minus column vastly outnumbered the ticks in the plus column, and she was too tired to see anything but negatives so she just changed the subject.

"Who drew KP tonight?" she said. "I'm starving."

"Me, too," LT said. "Habby juice might keep a body going over the course of a shift, but it's got nothing for the soul. I'd give anything for a plate of Gee-Gee's fried potatoes and onions right now."

"Gee-Gee?" she asked, thinking lover or wife.

"Great-Gran," he said. "What's your default craving?"

"Pinto beans in gravy, brown rice, slow-cooked pork, and slices of avocado all wrapped in a steamed corn tortilla," she said. Another memory that could still drop her after forty years. "My mom made amazing burritos."

A silver-skinned Quonset hut appeared in the crawler's headlights—their new garage, she presumed. It looked like a standard-issue modular pop-up except for the astonishing double-wide bay door that had been built into the leeward broadside. "Whoa," she said, pointing. "Is this a new model?"

"Negative," LT said. "I had Azu expand the single-wide for better access. He's an ace with liquid metal modifications. Wait till you see the work he did on the inside."

"Is it stable?" she asked.

"Azu says it is," he said. "And it did just fine in the shake that rolled through here a little while ago."

"Lucky for you," she said, in a prickly tone. For while she appreciated initiative in a second, this Johnny had overstepped his authority by a lot. Good call or not, he had no business ordering modifications for a structure that they couldn't replace. At the very least, he should've consulted her first. She needed to have a word with him—and soon. Right after she ate. She was so hungry, she could barely keep a straight thought in her head.

"Any chance we can leave the sled loaded until the start of next shift?" LT asked, as they closed on the garage. "I'm starting to fade big-time."

She thought about insisting on finishing the job now—payback or punishment for ignoring the chain of command earlier. But unloading heavy equipment wasn't work for tired people. One lapse, mental or physical, could get someone crushed. And she was in far worse shape than he was.

"Yeah, sure," she said. "Safety first."

"Thanks," he said. "I always forget how much a little gravity takes out of a body."

"The first few shifts are always the hardest," she said.

The middle section of the double-wide scrolled open. LT drove the crawler into the garage and then killed the engine. For one moment thereafter, she remained seated in the cold, cramped cab, savoring the absence of wind and flying grit and their associated noises. Then her stomach growled. Big guts eating little guts, her father used to say. The memory followed her out of the crawler. LT offered her a hand as she made her way down the ladder. Leastwise, she thought it was LT until she noticed the leering holo-spider that had popped up in her IDW.

"Oh hey, Spider," she said, extracting herself from his grasp in what she hoped was a casual manner. "How's that network coming?"

"All done, Chief," he said, and then offered LT a private greeting as he joined their ranks. Without her IDW, she wouldn't have been able to tell the two apart because everybody looked the same in a habby. Everybody but her, that is. She was a head shorter, and a lot smaller in the shoulders.

"You want a tour of the place before we head out?" LT asked.

"Later," she said, and headed for the pedway. Both crewmen followed on her heels.

They emerged from the garage to cold, still darkness. In the wind's absence, the sky was clear. "Look!" Spider said, and pointed overhead. "It's Shingo's Butthole." She saw what had caught his eye then: a pinkish trumpet-flower of light radiating from a 3-D opening in space. "I still can't believe we're on the other side of it."

She supposed she ought to discourage the kid from referring to the wormhole as that part of Shingo's anatomy. It was bad form, disrespect for a superior. But on a job this miserable, you had to cut your guys some slack somewhere or risk an uprising so if he wanted to abuse that son of a shogun, then so be it. And if her second wanted to put that in his report, then she'd take full responsibility with no regrets.

"*The Bonhomie* should be closing on the jumping-back point right about now," LT said.

Spider affected a shiver. "Creepiest ride I've ever taken."

LT responded with a good-natured sneer. "Where's your sense of adventure, Junior? Shooting the tube is a FCT."

His attitude appalled Awinita. Shooting the tube? First-class-thrill? You'd think he was talking about zip-diving the marine parks of Manhattan rather than traversing a galactic singularity.

We shouldn't be here, we're not ready.

The thought rang so loud and clear, she was afraid she'd said it out loud. But if it had slipped out, her crewmen didn't let on. They were already securing themselves to the guide-line that Spider had just finished installing. They probably could have found their way home without it since the wind wasn't blowing at the moment, but spacers were used to moving around on a tether as a safety precaution. She wasn't quite so conditioned, but she hooked herself up anyway because there was no telling when the wind was going to kick up again and besides, with a line, she didn't have to think about where she was going. All she had to do was walk.

The next thing she knew, she was standing in front of a half-buried class twelve transport: home for the next three months. The vessel had a sharp nose, a deep chest, retractable wings, and a sturdy, compact body. Sunk in the sand like it was for stability and insulation, it looked like a giant guinea hen sitting in a dusty nest—or a roasting pan. Her stomach squealed, broadcasting impossible cravings. She punched the hatch release as if it were Shingo's jaw and then crowded into the airlock beyond with Spider and LT. There, they were scanned for hitchhikers because it was SOP and better safe than sorry. As soon as the all-clear sounded and they were admitted into the main cabin, she unlocked her face-plate and flipped it up. The switch from gold-tinted light to regular spectrum made her dizzy. The rush of unfiltered smells made her sneeze.

From the catch-all space that functioned as their galley, head-work room, and lounge, someone said, "Gesundheit."

"What does that mean, anyway?" Spider asked, to no one in particular.

The Johnny who had blessed her was hunched over a hand-held at the central console. His long, thin Afro-Cubano face was drawn into a scowl that seemed at odds with the bluesy tune that he was humming. He had been humming pretty much nonstop since *The Bonhomie* departed. According to her second, that was his way of coping with stress. "When he gets really nervous," he added, "he'll start singing instead of talking." She'd read about that psychological quirk in his personnel file, but that hadn't stopped her from tapping him for the op. He was in good shape and had field experience. As long as his idiosyncrasies didn't impact his work or drive the rest of the crew crazy, he could be as OCD as he had to be. And personally, she'd rather listen to his nerves jangling than hers. The sounds he put out were deceptively soothing.

"*Danke schön*, Stanley," she said.

The humming sheered off into silence. He glanced up from his hand-held, met her gaze for an instant, and then looked down again. "Please, Chief," he said, in a voice that was equal parts velvet and gravel, "call me Singer. Everyone else does."

"OK," she said, "*danke schön*, Singer. How'd the inventory go today? Anything turn up missing?"

"I'm crunching the numbers now. I should have them for you shortly."

Then he started humming again: Chief dismissed. Awinita didn't mind. She wasn't much of a talker, either—not like Spider, who found babbling as easy as breathing. He was standing in front of the sanitizer unit at the moment, and chattering at LT like a howler monkey on speed. As she watched him through her lashes, the kid slapped his padded thigh and let out a raucous hoot.

"Valentine?" he said. "For real? What possessed you to pick a name like that?"

"I didn't pick it," LT said. "My mother gave it to me."

"Why?"

LT shrugged. "Apparently, my father was a cheap bastard."

"You should've had it legally changed when you left home," the kid said. "That's what I did."

"Seriously?" LT said, happy to give as good as he got. "You paid to take the name of a bug that shoots stick-um out its ass?"

Spider sputtered like a sucker-punched schoolboy. But before he had a chance to compose a suitably trenchant comeback, Azucar emerged from the SU wearing a hip-hugging sarong. He was so fine-looking, he couldn't help but commandeer the room's attention. His body seemed to be chiseled from mocha marble. His face was heart-shaped thanks to a rakish widow's peak, and his long, straight hair was dark as space. Yet despite the abundance of pheromones that he giving off, the first thing that popped into Awinita's head and out of her mouth when she saw him was, "Crud, Azu, aren't you cold?"

"*Un poco*," he admitted. "But after being in a habby all day, a little exposure feels nice. Besides," he said, with an almost shy smile, "the memory of the woman who gave me this wrap keeps me warm."

"Yeah, well, I'll bet she's keeping someone else warm AWS," Spider said, and then ducked into the SU.

LT cocked his head at Azu. "You going to let him get away with that?"

Azu flashed him a wink and a grin. "Not really. I'm cooking tonight."

LT groaned, then shot Awinita a long-suffering look and said, "I hope you like your tofu spicy."

"You don't?" she asked.

He loosed another groan—mock dismay this time. "Great. Another fire-eater. Did you get that from your mother's ancestors, too?"

Confusion swirled through her hand-in-hand with suspicion. How did he know about her mother? Then she recalled her little slip in the field. Figures he'd remember that. He probably remembered everything. That could be a good thing—or a very bad thing. Either way, good to know.

"My father was the one who liked spicy food," she said. "He used to put Tabasco on everything. That so offended my mother, she said she stopped trying to make food taste good for him. He maintained that it was a chicken-and-egg thing."

He laughed. "Was it?"

"Some of it was kind of bland," she admitted. "Especially the traditional stuff that she and E-li-si used to cook for special occasions. Even I reached for the pepper sauce on feast days."

"If nobody liked it," LT said, "why did they keep on making it?"

"Because they were proud of their heritage," she said, "and they wanted me to be proud of it, too. They tried everything to foster a connection in me: traditional foods, traditional name, traditional dances and stories. But I guess I'm more like my dad."

If LT heard the disappointment in those last seven words, he didn't let on. "You have a traditional name? Really?" he said. "What is it?"

She didn't usually share such details with her crew, for they were the only family secrets she had and she liked to keep them close. But today she found herself ridiculously forthcoming. Had to be the RSF. "It's Awinita," she said

"Juanita?"

"Ah-wee-nee-tah," she said, breaking it down for him. "It's Cherokee for 'fawn'."

"Nice," he said. "Can I call you that?"

"I prefer AJ," she said. "Or Chief." *Definitely your father's daughter.*

"AJ it is then," he said, as if she hadn't offered him a choice. "Call me Val."

"Sure," she said, although she didn't think she would. LT had better margins. And she liked her space. Liked her spaces. Distance was good. Distance was...

"Damn!"

The exclamation blasted Awinita back to wakefulness. Crud! How long had she been out? She'd only closed her eyes for a moment. Eyelid inspection, her father used to call it. Just checking for holes.

"I feckin' love being out of that suit!"

She blinked back a haze of sleepy tears to see Spider posturing in front of the SU door. Without a habby to disguise and contain it, there was no ignoring his youth. His demeanor was impossibly spry. His smirk was immortal. He wore his dirty blonde hair in long, retro-slacker dreads and cultivated a tiny patch of chin-hair. His skin was so bronzed as to be almost orange—a trademark of bootleg melatonin implants. The color made his blue eyes stand out like shuttle-port runway lights.

"Checking me out, Chief?" he asked, striking a comical body-builder's pose in his red flannel cozies. "You never know, a younger guy might just be the jump your battery needs."

The thought of him and her together was so utterly ridiculous, she laughed aloud. Val laughed, too, and then invited her to use the SU ahead of him. She didn't give him a chance to change his mind. "Thanks," she said, as she strode past him. "I owe you one."

As soon as the door closed behind her, she began stripping, a process that felt more like disarmament. The helmet came off first—carefully, because it was loaded with communications and data retrieval systems. The utility belt went next with only slightly less care because it was loaded with equipment that could not be replaced. After that, she capped the feed-line to her juice bag, cracked the helmet's support collar, and then tripped the habby's releases. The suit dropped to her ankles. She stepped out of it and then hung it in the decontamination closet for sanitizing, grimacing along the way because the damn thing was heavier off than on. By now, every muscle in her body was stiff or heading that way. Her knee ached as if it had never been reconstructed. She needed an extended lay-over at a rejuvenation spa, the complete joint and connective tissue package. *TSC regrets the imposition.* Damn that Shingo. Comparing a wormhole to his rectum was an insult to the wormhole.

She wiggled out of her insulated, super-absorbent undergarment. As she did so, a swarm of rancid body odors enveloped her in that sinister, eye-watering way that only miasmas have. The stench reminded her of the old days, when unders hadn't been so reliably self-contained. The inside of a field-op's habby had been a truly noxious place. By comparison, a little birthday suit BO was nothing. She tossed the used garment into the recycling bin, and then hit the shower. The spray that came out of the shower-head wasn't water or even liquid, but it was warm and tingly, and on a bare-bones op like this, that qualified as luxurious. She reveled in the low-grade sting until she finally felt clean, then shook herself off and relocated to her locker. There, she smeared heavy-duty moisturizer on her moisture-starved skin, ran her fingers through her short-cropped salt-and-pepper hair, and chewed a mango-flavored dento-tab. Meli would've been appalled by her grooming habits. *That's it, 'Nita? That's everything?* But really, what was the point of doing more? She donned a fresh pair of unders, a Mars-red cover-all that an old lover had given her as a joke and then accessorized with a muffler that she had bought on her very first Olympus Mons layover.

"It's what all the space-girls are wearing these days," she said, in response to her mother's imaginary scowl. Then she cleared out of the SU. "All yours," she said to Val in passing. "Much obliged for letting me go first."

"*De nada*," he said, with a dyspeptic half-smile. "Good luck with chow."

The main cabin smelled of man-musk, hot starch, and cumin. Spider, Azu, and Singer were all seated around the center console, shoveling food into their faces. The only sounds to be heard were sporks scraping plates and open-mouthed chewing. Music to her ears, she thought wryly, and headed for the microwave. There, she found a bowl heaped with rice, tofu nuggets, and bits of rehydrated pepper waiting for her.

"That's yours, Chief," Azu said, before she could ask. "There's more in the micro."

"Thanks," she said, thinking that she could probably gobble up their entire stockpile of provisions right about now and still be hungry afterward. She rummaged through cold storage for a packet of mango-flavored water—her favorite drink and another frivolity that she had insisted on, just because. Then she grabbed the nearest seat and started shoveling. The first mouthful tasted of garlic and cumin. The second was all habanero. Tears welled in her eyes. An instant later, her nose began to run. She didn't mind. After a steady stream of flavorless habby juice, any kind of seasoning was welcome.

"Good job with the rice, Azu," she said, when her vocal cords recovered from the scorching. "It reminds me of summers on the Yucatan."

"Thanks, Chief. I've pulled my share of shifts in *The Bon*'s galley."

"A lot less people to feed here," she said.

"A lot less space to do it in, too," he said.

"That's for sure," Spider said, looking up from his bowl with a sweat-slicked scowl. "If we were packed in here any tighter, we'd have to take turns breathing. Why can't we move into the seed and spread out a little, Chief? That thing's gi-mungous."

"For one thing," Awinita said, "seeds don't have built-in life-support systems like heat and air and SU's. For another, it's going to be swarming with 'bots as soon as the transponder network is up. You want to try sleeping through nonstop construction traffic?"

"Oh," he said, "I guess not. I didn't think about that."

"That's OK, Johnny. How could you know?" she said, and then returned to the remnants of her meal. But now that the worst of her hunger pangs had been silenced, other things started to clamor for her attention. There were reports to read, information to digest, a course of action to compose. So she snatched her handheld from its cradle in the wall and began to multi-task. By the time she was done eating, she had a knot in her belly that had nothing to do with hyper-spicy food.

"Anyone have enough left in the tank for a little OT?" she asked.

"What do you need, Chief?" Val asked. He was puttering around the console in a fresh pair of unders—cleaning up after supper, she realized. Removed of his habby, he looked like someone's uncle or dad. He was tall and stocky, with grizzled half-jowls and a butter-sugar Johnny Rocket buzz-cut. An old scar bisected his right eyebrow, giving it a permanent arch. His mouth was a little off-kilter, too. "Want me to dig out the stim?"

Her body responded to the offer with an emphatic pang: ooh, yeah. So what if it was false energy? So what if her adrenals would take a hit? It would be so nice to feel a little electricity in her veins instead of sludge. But as much as she craved that charge, she knew it was way too early in the op to be going for it. They hadn't even scratched the surface of depleted yet.

"Not this time," she said. "If any of you can't run a few more hours on your own juice, then go ahead and turn in. I won't hold it against you."

Val trained that scarred eyebrow of his on the other Johnnies, but she couldn't tell if he was assessing their fitness or daring them to show less grit than a burned-out, middle-aged woman. When no one withdrew, he made a satisfied noise deep in his throat and said, "We're all in, Chief. What do you need?"

"I want someone to look up the transponder network schematics and figure out how long it will take to do the installation manually," she said.

Singer stopped humming long enough to say, "I can do that."

"Good," she said. "I'm thinking it's going to be a two-man job, but break it down for one man as well. The necessary materials are already clear of the seed. You'll have to locate another c-mixer, though. The one in the field is ruined."

"Got it," Singer said, tapping at a handheld that she hadn't seen him grab.

"Spider, you've got recycling this shift," she said, and then stared him down when he started to complain about being stuck with laundry and garbage. "When you're done with that, report to the garage. Same goes for you, Azu, when you're done with kitchen detail."

"What about me?" Val said, in a half-teasing tone.

"Suit up, Johnny," she said. "It's triage time."

[∗∗∗]

"So, what do you think?" Val asked, proprietor-proud as he showed her around the garage.

She couldn't figure out why he was so excited. Aside from the double-wide door, this garage didn't look much different than any other garage that she had ever seen. The floor was graded regolith—a slightly crunchy, slightly slick surface cluttered with broken 'bots, transport crates in various stages of disembowelment, and packing detritus. The liquid-metal walls were a drab shade of gray and the domed roof was crisscrossed with low emission light fixtures.

"Looks OK to me," she said.

"Oh yeah?" He pointed to the wall adjacent to the double-wide and said, "Matrix On." The wall flickered and then burst into color, an eruption both startling and intense. The colors coalesced into a panorama of tropical trees and dense brush. The projection was so exquisitely detailed and clear, she thought she caught a whiff of humidity spiked with vegetal rot even though she was sealed up in her suit.

"What do you think now?" Val said.

"I'd forgotten that there were so many shades of green," she said, unable to look away. "I'd forgotten—" So much. The feel of sunshine, the smell of rain, the taste of a papaya plucked ripe from its tree. Her mother used to say that longings were memories in reverse. Awinita thought they were one and the same.

She heard Val say, "It has sound, too," and then, "Audio On." An instant later, a cacophony of jungle noises filled the air: howler monkeys barking, macaws squawking, thousands of hungry, horny cicadas screaming. The sounds fit perfectly with the holo. She could've been standing in the middle of the Belizean nature preserve that she had visited on her last LTL. "For the complete experience," Val quipped, "just add malaria."

"How is this possible?" she asked, still transfixed.

"Azu took one of those pocket holo-gens that are the all the rage back on Terra, tweaked it a little, and then—don't ask me how—fused it to the liquid metal matrix in that wall. And the best thing is, it runs on mini-rechargables. Shingo left us with a decade's worth of those."

She might have breathed a sigh of relief at that, for even though she had only been in the holo's thrall for a few minutes, she already felt different—better, saner, refreshed. The knots in her belly were loosening. Her fatigue seemed to be retreating a little, too, although she supposed that could be the carbs from chow kicking in. And while she still resented Shingo for shanghaiing her, at least now she remembered what he was trying to protect and preserve.

"It can run just about any kind of recreational chip," Val was saying now, "so we'll be able to listen to music while we're working or take in a flick or short course on our down-time."

"You really think you're going to have enough spare energy to learn something new?" she asked, from somewhere deep in her private jungle. "Or that much free time?"

"Probably not," he said. "But this is going to make whatever breaks we do get much more pleasant."

"Agreed," she said. Then, because she could not force herself to look away, she added, "But I think we should turn it off for now and get some work done."

"Sure thing, Chief. Matrix off."

Just like that, the jungle noises fell mute and the wall went liquid-metal grey. The sheer bleakness of their reality made Awinita want to cry. Three months, she reminded herself. She could bear anything for three months.

"So where do you want to start?" Val said, calling her back to day one.

"You're the master mechanic," she said, "so you get to diagnose all the 'bots that crapped out. Start with the pavers you brought in. While you're doing that, I'll off-load the crawler."

"Roger that," he said, and then tapped his face-plate. "OK if I pop my top? I'll be able to get a closer look at more things that way."

Technically, the answer was 'no,' because technically, this was an unsecured area, and all TSC personnel were required wear full protective gear when operating in hostile or unsecured environments. Hell, he was Shingo's right hand, he probably knew the rules as well as she did. Was he was setting her up then, thinking to make her look bad in that ongoing secret report of his? The possibility irked her until she recalled that she didn't care. And she could foresee a time in the very near future when she might want to go topless, too.

"Go ahead," she said. "There's nobody here but us chickens."

"What's a chicken?" he said.

"Something that crosses things that it shouldn't," she said, and then went to work.

[***]

Unloading the crawler was a simpler, faster matter than loading had been, mainly because there was no swirling wind to complicate the process. Three strokes of the EM boom and boom, she was done, on to the grittier task of unpacking. Women's work, her father would've said, and Meli would've agreed—*because men were better at imposing order than creating it.* AJ smiled, remembering how affronted her father had been by such statements and how Meli had teased him for it. Would you have been happier if I had disagreed with you?

"Hey, AJ."

She started—once at the sound of Val's voice and again when she realized that he was standing right next to her. He must've mistaken her surprised recoil for the first stage of a stroke because he grabbed her by the arm and said, "Whoa, are you OK?"

Mortified by his unwarranted and unwelcome concern, she pulled away from him with a sharp and possibly punitive jerk. "I'm fine. What's up?"

"Good news," he said. "The paver shut down because they ran out of juice. Tune 'em and charge 'em and they should be right as rain again."

"Great," she said. "Anything else?"

"Yeah," he said. "Would you mind vacuuming out the APC we brought in? It's full of sand, and I can't see jack."

"Sure," she said, and then set off to find the shop-vac with a forced spring in her step. Anything to prove that she wasn't as feeble as he seemed to think she was.

The vac was an industrial-sized relic that had probably been gathering space dust in *The Bonhomie*'s maintenance depot since the cruiser's maiden voyage. Not only was it ungainly and old, it also sounded like a cat in heat when switched on. The noise set her teeth on edge at first, but then triggered a memory of her mother dancing a vac through the Flagstaff living room and singing an old Cherokee song. "What's it mean, mama?" Awinita remembered asking. Meli had smiled—a look like sunrise over a glassy ocean. "It means I love you, baby-girl. It means I'll love you forever."

"Hey, AJ," Val said, shouting over the SV's caterwauling. "Is this weird or what? Both the plug-in and the fix-it have damaged motherboards. And both boards look like they've been partially melted or something."

"Yes, Val," she said, irked at him for chasing Meli's ghost away. "That's weird."

"What do you suppose caused it?" he said. "Bad batteries?"

"I don't know," she said. "And at the moment, I don't particularly care. All I want to know is if the 'bots are salvageable or not."

"Got it," he said, and sounded like he meant it. But just a few minutes later, he loosed a garbled curse and hey-AJ-ed her again.

The irritation that she had been trying to dead-head became a toxic bloom. She rounded in her second's direction, meaning to chew him out in earnest, only to lose her momentum as he appeared in her crosshairs. He was inching his way toward her with his right arm stretched out in front of him as if it were on fire. There was a giant splotch of stringy brown goo on his forearm. Her first thought was that it was some kind of fix-it gunk, axle grease clotted with sand maybe, but then some of the stringy bits moved and she knew.

She was looking at a native.

"Shit," she said.

The alien waved several thin, hyperactive tentacles or tendrils in the direction of Val's face. He craned his head the other way and then shot her an urgent, wide-eyed look. "Jesus, AJ," he said, "do something."

Acting on pure, shock-laced impulse, she turned the vacuum nozzle on the alien. It clung to Val's arm for what seemed like an eternity and then lost its grip all at once. With an ungodly thhwwuck, the SV sucked it up.

"Shit," she said again.

CHAPTER 03

DARK-WINDY-COLD DID NOT AGREE with niji. Like most varzi, niji preferred lighter, calmer conditions, and a modicum of warmth. Like most varzi, it usually migrated to a more temperate place when The Season of Storms returned to this region. This season, however, niji had chosen to forego migration. This season, it had a reason to stay. That reason was the ulvarzi. They were still sleeping, oblivious to their surroundings and the wind that was filling their inner spaces with grit. Niji visited them regularly, always on the hunt for the taste or smell that might herald their awakening, but thus far, nothing. And niji was starting to grow anxious.

What if they never woke up?

What if they were dead?

What if niji had already learned as much as it was going to from these beings?

These were the thoughts that came to niji as it poked and probed the ulvarzi for signs of life. It wondered if its desires were unreasonable. It wondered if it should give up and move on. There could be other, non-dormant ulvarzi in the area. Maybe niji could find one or more of them who could teach niji teach things that niji did not know how to imagine. The possibility was quite seductive, especially when nazza was blowing hard and cold. But temptation came with its own set of questions.

What if these ulvarzi were the only ones of their kind?

Why would they come here just to dig a few holes and die?

What if they were not dead, and woke up after niji moved on?

So far, patience had always managed to reassert itself. Better to wait too long than not long enough. Some losses were worse than regret.

After its latest visit with disappointment, niji retired to a compartment in the newcomer's upper reaches. The space was full of ulvarzi matter, most of which was either pointy or scratchy, but it also had a patch on one of its walls that was like ice only clearer and niji could see through it. Usually, all niji could perceive was cold-dark-windy, but during a recent rare calm spell, niji had caught sight of the sky-mouth and a fleck of star-stuff. Ever since then, niji had been taking its rest here instead of its old burrow. Doing so made niji feel less aggrieved.

As niji waved its oculi this way and that in front of the patch of clearer-than-ice, it caught a flicker of motion close to the ground. What was that—nazza playing tricks? The wind did like to fool with oculi. But no, there that flicker was again. Not only was it moving against the wind, it also bore a fragment of pale white light. Niji flushed, an excited display that turned into joy as that flicker shaped itself into a strange new ulvarz.

Zhee!

This ulvarz was different than the others: smaller and faster, with a curiously upright orientation. It had two sets of appendages, one upper and one lower. The lower set served as transports. The upper set appeared to be sensors of some kind, for the first thing this upright ulvarz did when it came upon the newcomer was touch it. By then, it was close enough to the clearer-than-ice for niji to discern details: a richly textured outer membrane and a gold-banded top-nob. Satisfaction swelled within niji. This was its reward for patience.

As niji congratulated itself for its perseverance, a dull metallic clank echoed through the newcomer's inner-sides and the wind went strangely quiet. Niji was quick to deduce what had happened. The upright had shut the newcomer's outer membrane flap, depriving nazza of easy access. In doing so, the upright had deprived niji of an easy exit. Niji was not concerned at first, for it knew other, more convoluted ways out. But then the upright disappeared from view, and niji went rigid with dismay. It could not bear the thought of losing another opportunity to learn and possibly evolve. It had to know where the upright was going! It had to follow.

Propelled by that thought, niji immediately reversed its orientation and tried to evacuate the compartment. But niji was scarred, and clumsy with urgency. The compartment was packed with pointy, scratchy ulvarzi matter. A sharp jab to niji's outer membrane shocked niji out of its greedy panic and roused a zervarz's sensibility. Slow is the surer way to go, it reminded itself, as it struggled to suppress conflicting urges. It might never catch up with the upright if it punctured itself first. But niji's anxiety persisted. What if the upright went away before niji caught up with it? Or: what if it went to sleep?

The latter possibility unsettled niji, for there was no denying that ulvarzi were prone to going dormant. But niji had the feeling or perhaps just the hope that this ulvarz was different. Different or not, though, slow was still the smarter way to go. If the upright was going to go to sleep, there was nothing that niji could do to stop it. And if the upright was going away, then it was most likely gone already. But niji wanted to believe that the upright was visiting the other ulvarzi and would still be doing so when niji finally emerged from the newcomer.

So niji modified its attitude as well as its orientation and then began its evacuation once again. As it worked its way through a maze of nooks and crannies and gaps, a familiar vibration impinged on its sensors: thrumming! Zhee! Niji's half-submerged anxiety dissolved, melted by an ecstatic flush. The ulvarzi were waking up! Frani-beats later, its delight was flattened by the memory of what it was like to be caught in a waking ulvarz. Suddenly, haste no longer seemed like such a bad thing. It retracted its far-sensors immediately and began a half-blind race for the exit. Too late. The newcomer shuddered loudly, then began to jiggle and twitch like something in the throes of wakefulness. Niji loosed an azrum, urging the ulvarz's forbearance. The ulvarz responded with a massive lurch. Niji clenched itself into a protective knot against an onslaught of hard noises, frantic activity, and heat. Instead, it sensed upward movement, a short drop, and then—nothing. As niji tried to make sense of what had just taken place, a whole new swarm of activity broke out, all of it on the ulvarz's outer sides.

Confusion coupled with curiosity in niji. They formed an impulse to investigate—now. Once again, zervarzi restraint dictated otherwise. Too much movement could be a dangerous thing when it came to the ulvarzi. Niji would investigate, but only when conditions were less tumultuous. Until then, it was going to find itself a safe place to hide and wait.

[***]

Intense thrumming. A sense of forward motion. An irregular series of sharp jolts that made it seem as if the newcomer were breaching. These were the dominant sensations that niji gathered in the interval following its retreat to a recess in the newcomer's underside. Niji liked the thrumming, but found the jolts excessively thrilling. So niji willed itself into a drowse that deflected sensory input and eventually slipped into a deeper sleep. When niji roused again, the thrumming was gone and all had gone still. It extended a single fran to gather more impressions. The stillness tasted different, slightly stagnant like a plugged burrow. And there was no trace of nazza anywhere, not even in the distance. So niji had either slept through the Season of Storms or niji had found its way into an ulvarz burrow. And it did not think that its sleep had been that protracted.

Niji marveled at this most unexpected of developments. Fond as they were of sleeping in the wind, niji never would have imagined that the ulvarzi might dwell anywhere other than in the open. But now that niji knew better, it could not wait to begin exploring. Zhee! What wonders this place must hold!

Pulsing with excitement, niji detached itself from its hiding place and then let gravity pull its mass to the ground. The regolith felt different, hard and compact like ice but not slippery. Niji could still dig into it, but doing so took more effort: a detail that niji was happy to know. Its frani were going wild now, collecting samples in all directions. But most of the impressions that they registered belonged to the newcomer's underside. Niji was already familiar with those tastes. It was ready to experience something new-new-new! So niji streamed its way toward the ulvarz's outer edge. There, it began to shape itself a set of oculi. As it did so, it sensed a rumbling in the distance. Before it could react to that, darkness gave way to dazzling whiteness.

Instinct dragged niji back under the newcomer and urged it to tunnel to safety. But even though niji started to dig, it knew that doing so was futile. That falling star-stuff was too close. When it landed, niji would either die from the massive shockwave or the equally massive wave of heat. Niji's only consolation was that it would die with the ulvarzi that it had so wanted—

Wait.

The star-stuff should have slammed into the ground by now. There should have been an impact tremor. The ulvarz burrow should have been vaporized. And darkness should have returned. Yet—none of that had happened. The whiteness was still everywhere, and the only impact tremors that it had sensed were tiny— and ongoing. Indeed, they seemed to be coming niji's way. Zhee! Niji was terribly confused. It did not know if it should keep digging or start looking for the source of those tremors, so it decided to compromise and take refuge within the newcomer instead. It had been safe there during the last upheaval. And—if it made its way back to the patch of clearer-than-ice, maybe it could get a better sense of what was happening.

So niji began streaming toward that upper compartment. It was so intent on getting there, njii did not sense the unexpected obstruction in its path until niji collided with it. Immediately after contact, niji was all over it, collecting impressions. It was another multi-tipped something, thicker than the last one, soft-shelled rather than metallic—and fast! Before niji could disengage and retreat, the thing hauled niji out of the newcomer—and into sensory disarray. That dazzling whiteness was everywhere. And while nazza was not present, nothing was still. The ulvarz on the end of the multi-tipped something was making strange noises as it off-gassed. When niji tried to sample the exhaust, it began to twitch so violently, niji had to tighten its grips or be tossed into the whiteness. The noises it was making had a deliberate feel: GeeZuzAyJayDooZumZin.

The next thing niji knew, something circular was attached to its body mass and a strange, localized turbulence was tugging at niji. The pressure was intense and relentless, like nazza only in reverse. Niji struggled to maintain its hold on the multi-tipped something, but its grip slipped once and then again. And before niji could generate new frani-holds, niji was sucked into a long, narrow tunnel and swept away.

CHAPTER 04

AJ GAPED AT THE vac's nozzle in dumbstruck horror. Had she really just suctioned up a *bona fide* ET like an overgrown daddy long-legs? Or had it been a fatigue-induced hallucination? Which would sound better in a report? She hadn't meant to turn the vacuum on it. Leastwise, she wanted to believe that she would have done something more inspired if she had had a moment to think. But—damn. That thing had been all over Val, creepy-crawling up his arm and reaching for his face with dozens of flailing, whip-like tentacles. *Jesus, AJ, do something.* The memory raised every hair on her body.

"What was that?" Val said, looking wide-eyed and pale and on the verge of barfing up his habanero-laced chow.

"How would I know?" she asked, resisting the urge to snap but only by a little. "An alien, I guess." She wondered if she had killed it. She wondered if she could honestly say that she regretted its death.

Val loosed a sigh that sounded like, "Shit," then raked his fingers through his sweat-slicked hair and said, "What are we going to do now?"

"Fifik," she said, still trying to shoulder past the shock. "Give me a minute to think."

But nothing came to mind—nothing but a stream of denials and profanity. Shit. This shouldn't be happening. Recon had classified this planet as uninhabited. What was the point of having scouts if they weren't going to do their jobs? Dammit. This should be Shingo's problem, not hers. He was the one who had the hard-on for meeting aliens on their own turf. Bastard. He shouldn't have left her and the Johnnies here.

"So," Val said, "what's the plan?"

"Call everyone back to the boat," she said. "We need to have a meeting."

"What about—" He grimaced in the vac's direction. "That?"

"Leave it in there for now." He cocked his head at her, clearly wondering if she had lost her mind. And who knew? Maybe she had. Everything certainly seemed a little unhinged. "Why not?" she said. "We have to keep it somewhere."

"*Au contraire,*" Val said. "What we should do is kill it, dispose of the body, and break out the zaps." In response to her disapproving scowl, he said, "That's what Shingo would do."

And who would know better than the CSO's right hand man? She appreciated the reminder. This 'ling was only on loan to her. And ultimately, he was here to protect his master's best interests—even if that meant killing locals. Lucky for the locals, she had a different set of priorities.

"If Shingo wanted a say in this RSO's SOPs," she said, "then he should've stayed on this side of the APW. Since he nicked off, I'll be calling the shots. And I say 'no' to killing natives just because they aren't supposed to be here."

"Natives?" Val said, stressing the ess. "You think there's more than one?"

"Stands to reason," she said. "There's never, ever just one."

"Then what's one less?" he asked. When she refused to dignify the question with an answer, he pressed his case. "C'mon, AJ. These things could be dangerous. My guys shouldn't have to worry about being attacked while they're in the field. The next three months are going to be stressful enough as it is."

Resentment flared within her—a dull red bloom that added texture to the tension headache that had invaded the space behind her eyeballs. Couldn't he see that she didn't need more pressure on top of the shock of a lifetime? Wasn't it obvious that she was running on adrenaline and borrowed time? All she wanted to do was web herself into her bunk and fret herself to sleep. But before she could do that, she had to conduct a meeting. And before she could do that, she had to set Val straight.

"Oh yeah, and here's something else to think about," he was saying now. "That creature was hiding inside the fix-it. What if it was the reason behind all those popped boots? What if it sabotaged the 'bots to prevent the seed's germination?"

In another time and space, she might've mocked him for trying to blame a 200-ton seed's failure on a ten pound blob. Here and now, however, she didn't have the energy to spare. Instead she offered him a point-blank glare.

"Are you finished?" she asked. "Because if you are, I have a few things to say." He folded his arms across his chest: grudging permission to proceed. Grrr. "One," she said. "While they're on this rock, they're my guys, not yours. I'll take all necessary measures to keep them safe. I will not, however, start with the most drastic measure. Two: I don't need you to tell me how stressful the next three months are going to be. I know it's going to be hell. I also know that whipping the guys into a xenophobic frenzy won't improve the situation. We're here for one reason and one reason only—to get this seed back on track. The more focused everybody is on that, the better." Val opened his mouth to say something then, but she wasn't done yet and kept on talking. "Three: we're the aliens here, not them. And we're trapped here until *The Bon* returns. So it would behoove us not to piss the locals off—especially if they're smart enough to stop a seed from germinating.

"You roger that, Johnny?"

He stared at her for a long moment as if he were contemplating mutiny or murder, then deliberately unfolded his arms and shrugged. "You're the boss," he said. But it sounded a lot like: You'd better know what you're doing, lady.

Which was exactly what she was thinking, too.

[✶✶✶]

"No shit?"

That was Spider. His shocking blue eyes were wide-open and throwing sparks. "You found an HTG alien?"

AJ nodded, a minimal response designed to conserve her strength. The bulk of her brain was screaming for sleep. The rest of it was determined to resist the call. Her crew seemed much less depleted, and part of her couldn't understand how that could be. They were the Johnnies, not her.

"What do they look like?" Spider asked, with surprising relish.

This time the nod went to Val. He glanced down at his forearm as if to cue the memory, and then obliged with a description. "The object in question was on the small side," he said, "ten pounds maybe with sandy markings and lots of thin, hyperactive tentacles. It looked gooey, like a blob of whale snot, but wasn't actually sticky or slick."

"Did it have hands?" Spider asked.

"No hands or legs," Val said. "No face, either, as far as I could tell."

"Then how did it hold on to you?"

Val started to say something, only to cut himself off with a scowl. "I don't know," he said, in a suddenly testy tone. "It just did. And it had a damn strong grip, too. Chief had a hard time getting it off me."

"Did you kill it?" Azu asked, in that soft, sweet voice of his.

"No," Val said, a flat denial that felt like a slap in the face.

"Why not?"

"Because I told him not to," AJ said, before Val could get off another shot. "That has to be our last resort, not our first."

"Why wait for trouble?" Azu said. "The OIQ attacked first."

Ugh. More resistance. This was what came of using Johnnies in the field. A real seed crew would have trusted their chief. But an instant after the thought asserted itself, she had to qualify it with a giant 'maybe'. Most Terrans were hardwired to fear the unknown. And they tended to kill what they feared. If it were Val asking her to disregard her instincts, would she do so quietly? Not likely. So she scraped the bottom of her brain-pan for one last crumb of patience.

"As far as attacks go," she said, "it wasn't much of one. Could be it wasn't an attack at all. We have no way of knowing one way or the other at this point." Azu scowled, deflecting her sensibilities. Aliens simply had to be hostile. Like the Un. "We also don't know how many OIQ there are," she said, "or how they'll respond to violence. I'd rather wait for trouble that might not happen than go out and maybe stir some up."

Because there's no point in picking a scab unless you want it to bleed. Right, Dad?

Her father hummed something in reply, which was weird because he had never been musical. Then she recognized the bluesy tune and realized that she was listening to Singer. And he was getting louder with every measure.

"You got something to say, Singer?" she asked.

He tapped the cleft of his chin three times and then burst into song. "This is so not my scene. Nobody mentioned monsters when you asked if I was keen."

"The OIQ aren't monsters. They're—" She groped for nouns that did not exist and then gave up the hunt with a shrug. "They're just aliens."

"Se-man-tics," he sung. Then he closed himself up like a fan and started humming again.

Spider hooted. "What a bunch of candy-asses! Can't you see? This is the opportunity of a lifetime!"

"Oh yeah?" Azu asked, shooting the kid a supremely skeptical look.

"Hell yeah!" Spider insisted. "Who else in the galaxy can say they have an HTG alien for a mascot? We're going to be freakin' legends!"

"Are you out of your skull?" AJ said, with more force than she thought she had in her. "We know zip about the OIQ. They could be poisonous. They could be infectious. They could be dangerous in ways that we can't even imagine. So we're all going to treat them with the utmost caution and respect. This means no hunting, no handling, and no harboring. Got that?" she asked, looking straight at Spider.

"Yeah, I got it," he said, sounding disappointed rather than truculent. "You want us to stay away from them. But what if they come to us?"

"If you find yourself in a situation like the one LT was in," she said, "just stay calm and issue an SOS over the PA. Your habby will protect you until help arrives—if your suit is intact." She glanced at Val, and while it could've been her imagination, she thought she could still see a trace of get-it-off-me in his eyes. "So if you absolutely have to pop your top outside the boat, take the time to make sure your area is secure before you do so, OK? And if you can keep your lid on, well, all the better."

Nobody said anything for over a minute. AJ was inclined to interpret the silence as an adjournment—and not a moment too soon! But as it happened, the crew was only regrouping.

"And then what, Chief?" Spider asked.

Crud! It was always something with that kid. She felt like kicking his ass. She growled at him instead. "Then what what?"

"What are we supposed to do when help arrives?" he asked.

She drew another partial blank—a memory lapse that both frustrated and embarrassed her. And to make matters worse, Val stepped in. The bastard was trying to show her up in front of the crew!

"Chief wants us to catch the OIQ," he said.

"How?"

That was Spider. Again. The urge to punish him intensified even though part of her recognized the legitimacy of his question. She answered before Val could. "I don't know yet," she said, grinding out the words. "If the one we caught today survived the vac, we'll use that. Otherwise, we'll think of something else. I don't particularly care how we catch them," she added, before he could ask, "so long as we don't cause them lasting harm."

"And then what?"

Don't do it, she commanded herself. It wasn't right to blast him for asking questions. Oh, but releasing the fireball in her belly would feel so good, like a nuclear orgasm and to hell with the awkward silence afterward. Don't do it, she thought again. She could stay in control a little longer. "After we catch it," she said, "we'll transport it back to the wild and release it."

That raised three sets of eyebrows and the volume of Singer's humming. She met their dismay with a clenched-jaw scowl, daring one and all to give her an excuse to explode.

"You're joking, right, Chief?" Azu said, in a semi-pleading tone.

And that was it, ignition. "There's no fucking joke here, mister. If I tell you to do something, you will do it, and that includes bussing ETs back to the boondocks. Otherwise, I'll bury you up to your head in the sand and let the OIQ do what they will with you." The words shot out of her like projectile vomit. Val looked shocked. Singer looked as if he wanted to wipe his face. She continued to spew. "We did not come here to kill these creatures. They have done nothing to warrant being killed on sight. So unless one actually breaks into your suit while you're in it and starts chewing on a body part, you're to behave in a civilized fashion—"

"And suck them up with the vac."

For one out-of-body moment, she thought the words had come out of her own mouth. Then she saw Val elbow Spider roughly in the side and realized that the kid had said it. Was he mocking her? Or just—sucking up? The pun tickled her. She laughed out loud. The next thing she knew, her thoughts were sliding down the side of her skull and her vision was starting to go dark. Was this what a stroke felt like? It really didn't seem all that bad, just a bit—disorienting.

"Meeting dismissed," she muttered. "I've got work to do."

But for the longest time, all she could do was sit there and daydream of tentacles.

Jesus, AJ. Do something.

CHAPTER 05

THE TUNNEL EMPTIED INTO a small, dark space filled with swirling sand. There, the wind-in-reverse tumbled niji round and round like an airborne ice mite and then abruptly disappeared. Niji crashed to the ground amid a blizzard of sand, dizzy but unharmed. As soon as its thoughts stopped spinning, it began to access its new environs. There was no mysterious bright white light here, only familiar and comforting darkness. Was this then where darkness had come to hide, or had the wind-in-reverse sucked it up as it had sucked niji up? And how could a world's worth of darkness fit into such a small space? Zhee! Questions multiplied faster than zyl when it came to ulvarzi things!

Other impressions registered: tastes, shapes, textures. The space had smooth walls and a flat, seamless bottom-side that tasted of grit and dissipating heat. The upper-side was arched and had an opening that had been plugged but not sealed. Niji had explored the inner sides of enough ulvarzi to recognize another when it sampled one. But up until now, niji had had to find its own way in. Why had the wind-in-reverse brought niji here? Was it trying to be helpful? Or was it like nazza, random in all things? Under other circumstances, niji might have chosen to stay here and try to discern wind-in-reverse's nature. But niji had had its fill of ulvarzi insides. And there were other, more intriguing mysteries awaiting niji elsewhere. So niji excreted an azrum for the wind-in-reverse, an expression of respect and regret, and then dedicated itself to dislodging that upside plug.

Shortly thereafter, niji found itself at the mouth of that long, narrow tunnel. The space beyond was stale-dark-still. Niji was relieved to discover that the darkness had likewise escaped. That mysterious brightness had been much too exciting. How could light be that intense and yet so cool and harmless?

As niji emerged from the opening, it sensed a sharp drop in the immediate beyond. So it anchored its far end to the tunnel's rim and then allowed gravity to carry its globulating mass to the unseen ground. Its leading edge began taking samples as soon as it touched down. The floor was compacted, just as niji remembered. It was also cluttered with curiosities! Here was a span of ulvarzi metal tipped with a hook. And here were sheets of compressed organic matter smeared with petrochemical residues. And what was this—a container filled with ice-melt? How curious! Niji did not try to make sense of any of these discoveries. That would come later, while niji was resting. For now, niji was intent on exploring. Here was a coil of organic fibers twisted together! And here was another span of ulvarzi metal!

As niji was fondling everything in its reach, nazza burst into the burrow, accompanied by a dazzling flash. Just like that, the darkness was gone. And though nazza departed a half-gust later, the brilliance remained. Niji was both baffled and stunned. When had the wind developed the ability to blow darkness away? And why did that glare persist in the wind's absence? And—wait. It was sensing something else now: two sets of vibrations, soft-shallow-slow, one of them slightly out of phase with the other. Both were traveling in niji's direction. Niji loosed an excited azrum: a greeting for the ulvarz. Then, because it was not sure how that greeting would be received, it went streaming toward the nearest overhang. There, it shifted its coloring to match the shadows and then shaped itself an oculum. Compound sensors processed light more efficiently and offered better perspective, so they were better for observing things from a distance. They were also better for observing things from protected spaces.

The vibrations were drawing closer. Eager to see what sort of ulvarz was causing them, niji extended the eyestalk beyond the overhang. The whiteness blinded niji at first. Then, as the sensor adjusted to the wavelength, the glare shimmered into an array of heretofore unimaginable colors. Such a spectrum would have been a singular discovery for any zervarz, but to niji's joy, there was more. Those incredible colors solidified into shapes which then coalesced into objects that possessed dimension and definition, details that got lost in the dark. As uncomfortable as it was, this wind-borne brightness was proving to be exquisitely helpful.

Then niji caught its first glimpse of the approaching ulvarz. Niji knew it for an upright immediately, for it had that orientation. This one had two top-nobs and multiple appendages and a distorted central mass that split apart just as niji started to focus on it. Zhee! That was not one upright. It was two! The realization prompted a surprised azrum. Uprights traveled in swarms? That made no sense to niji. Swarming was nijiti behavior. Nijiti were inferior. It seemed more likely that niji had just witnessed a budding.

As niji puzzled over what it had seen, the uprights came to a stop in front of an ulvarz whose most prominent feature was a long, wrinkled tube with a peculiarly shaped tip. That was, niji realized, the ulvarz that niji had recently vacated. Niji wondered if the uprights had come to visit the wind-in-reverse—or perhaps rouse it. The second possibility caused niji to retreat a little deeper into the shadows. Even so, it saw one of the uprights rap the top of the ulvarz with one of its upper appendages. And as it did so, it made a strange sound.

"RedEeOrNotEeeTeeHereWeKum!"

The other upright made a sound as well. "LezGoBakDoodCheefzGonnaKillUz."

The sounds electrified niji. They were softer and less resonant than the noises that the other ulvarzi made. They were also more complex, and possibly—

purposeful?

"CheefzNotGonnaNoUnlezUTelerAzoo."

"SezU."

"KmonAwlIWantIzaLook."

"YerKawlButIfEeTeeGozFerUUrOnUrOwn."

Niji flushed a triumphant shade of red. Yes! Niji was sure of it now. These uprights were communicating with each other. But instead of depositing their thoughts on the ground, they fed them to the air. That seemed like a rather transitory way to express a thought, but what did niji know? Sense to a superior being was not always sense to the lesser evolved.

The upright who had rapped the ulvarz now separated the ulvarz's top-side from the rest of its body. Niji expected the wind-in-reverse to come swirling forth from the opening. The two uprights must have had similar expectations, for when the wind remained in hiding, one of them grabbed a span of ulvarzi metal and began poking at the ulvarz's insides.

"ZeeIt?"

"NoItzNotHere."

"ChekThaTrap."

"IDidDamitItzNotHere."

"ZhitCheefzGonnaKillUz."

One upright slapped the ulvarz's topside back into place and then began to withdraw. The other started to follow only to come to an abrupt stop and let out an emphatic, "WatTha?" Then it bent one of its lower appendages and cocked its top-nob at the exposed bottom side. "WatzThizZhitOnMyBoot?"

"Dunno," the first said, after doubling back for a top-nob cock, "ButItzDuzntLookGud." Then it grabbed the span of ulvarzi metal that it had used to poke the ulvarz and started poking at the other's exposed bottom-side. Niji did not understand what all the excitement was about until bits and pieces of a viscous silica polymer began hitting the floor. The droppings were gibberish, scrambled scraps of a ruined message, but there was no mistaking the underlying chemical signature. That was one of niji's azrumi. Apparently, the communiqué had offended the uprights.

"ThaGooAytHafwayThruUrSohl," the upright said, when it was finished with its poking. "ItChewdUpThaCrowBarToo."

"IGottaGetBakToThaBohtStatAnPutThizThruDeeCon."

"DamStraytLezGo."

Both uprights rushed off in the direction in which they had come. The last sound that niji heard them make before they passed beyond sensor range was, "CheefzGonnaKillUz." Then nazza blew in and back out, taking the light with it. That left niji in the dark to contemplate all that it had just absorbed.

CHAPTER 06

AWINITA WAS FLOATING IN warm, flat-as-glass sea-water. She felt good—weightless in a full-gravity sort of way and relaxed as an oil-slick. The sun was ozone-hole hot, but she had no fear of burning as she was wearing an ultra-SPF and had had her summer-package nano-booster. "That little tingle tells you damage is being repaired," Meli said, as she floated next to AJ. "That little tingle is protecting you from skin cancer and wrinkles." A flock of white, seaworthy birds with split tails and dapper black caps began to circle overhead. "Roseate terns," her mother said, because she always knew. "This is the wrong season for them. They must be on vacation, too." A feather drifted out of the sky. AJ plucked it from the water and stuck it in her hair, Indian-style. "Look," she said. "I'm a chief. Chief Johnson."

"*Washte*," Meli said.

"Chief!"

Her mother's face blurred. Her form began to fade away. Awinita made a grab for her, but—too late. Meli vaporized. The ocean shrank into a coffin-sized glory-hole. A sponge-orange human head occupied the entrance to that hole. It was gazing at her with electric blue eyes. "Sorry to disturb you, Chief, but—you need to hear this."

The last vestiges of Awinita's dream dissipated, leaving her stranded on the rocky shores of wakefulness. Her knee ached; her heart felt leaden. How could she possibly feel so depleted after eight hours of rest? She shifted in her webbing to get a better look at the person who had intruded on the patch of faux-privacy that she insisted on calling her own. It took her a moment to put a name to the face.

"Spider," she said, and then scowled because he looked so damn young and refreshed. "What's so important that you had to cut my sleep short?"

Spider swallowed hard and then blurted, "He's gone."

Awinita's heart stutter-thumped, instigating adrenal jihad. Suicide and accidents ran neck and neck as the leading cause of RSO deaths. "Who?" she asked, as she scrabbled out of her webbing and onto her feet. "Singer?" He'd been having a hard time getting settled, sure, but he hadn't struck her as manic enough to do a walk-off. Had she misread him—or overlooked the signs? "Did anyone try to get a fix on his chip yet?"

Spider's expression froze for a microsecond and then capsized. "Whoa," he said, "major mash-up. You're thinking human. I'm talking Q. Sorry."

"Talking Q?" she said, spiraling from alarmed to confused. "Sorry?" Was he messing with her head? "Is Singer OK or not?"

"He's fine," Spider said, scowling as if she was the one who wasn't making sense.

Her panic spun to a stop like a spent cyclone. But the aborted adrenaline rush was already starting to smell like an Armageddon headache. Just what she wanted for breakfast. She glared at the kid, wondering what had possessed him to jack her up for no good reason. Was he trying to prove something to her or the rest of the crew? Or had Val put him up to this? She meant to flay the truth from him, strip by fleshy strip. But even as she sharpened her tongue against her teeth, the gist of what he was trying to tell her finally sunk in.

'Q' as in OIQ. Crud. The alien had escaped.

Part of her wondered: but how? At the same time, the rest of her figured out why the kid was so twitchy. "Dammit, Spider," she said. "What did you do?"

"Nothing!" he said, raising his hands as if to ward off a blow. Which was, perhaps, a reasonable expectation given that her hands were clenched. "It was already gone when me and 'Zu—" He lobbed her an exquisitely uncomfortable look—reluctance to incriminate his partner in crime perhaps, or perhaps himself. She prompted him to continue with a raised eyebrow. "We went to check on it. You know—to make sure it was OK. We thought it might need water or something. But there was no one home when we cracked the canister."

"Are you absolutely sure about that?" she asked, remembering how elastic that blob had been.

"We gave that canister a first-class going-over," he said. "If it had been in there, we would've found it. 'Zu thinks it escaped out the intake valve and up the hose. LT has him modifying the flow-trap so that can't happen again."

"Val knows about this?" she said, unable to keep her tone from arching.

He responded with a hang-dog nod. "He caught 'Zu stripping down in the airlock."

"What?"

"'Zu stepped in some kind of semi-corrosive goo while we were looking for the Q," the kid said. "He didn't want to track it into the boat. LT basically caught him with his habby down and wanted to know what was going on. As soon as we got done telling him, he sent 'Zu into the SU with a bunch of chemicals and me in here to tell you."

She couldn't fault Val for that sequence of events, but something else started niggling at her—something about Val catching 'Zu in the airlock. What was everybody doing up already? Were they still on cruiser-time? Or was Val stealing time from the crew to put his own agendas into play? She found her hands clenched again.

"Chief?"

"That mistake is going to cost you, boy," she said, although she wasn't really talking to him.

"But it didn't get away because of us," Spider said, half-arguing and half-pleading, an irritating combination. "It was already gone when we got there."

"Not the point," she said flatly. "I explicitly told you to stay away from the alien. You ignored me. That's the point. So the waste management detail is all yours until further notice." He opened his mouth to protest. She cut him off with a withering look. "If you'd rather, I can log this incident into your permanent record. Crewmen who disregard direct orders aren't offered a lot of jobs on star cruisers. Do you really want to spend the next couple of decades out in the Oort-back trying to get rid of a bad rap?"

He had the decency to look mortified. "No, Chief."

"Then grow up and take what you've got coming with a little class," she said. "And just so you know, this is a one-time-only option. You flout my rules again, and your next RSO will make this one look like Nueva Vega. Are we clear?"

"Yes, Chief."

"Then get out of here."

A heartbeat later, she was alone with her thoughts and a stress-induced headache.

Time to hang up the ol' habby, she thought, as she began to get ready for the day. She was getting too old for this shit. She tossed back the usual complement of supplements plus extra E and B-12 for the throbbing in her frontal lobe and then a stim from her personal stash. Everyone took stim on a RSO sooner or later, for human bodies could only be pushed so far before they began pushing back. But this was the very first time that AJ had felt the need for a boost at the very start of a job. Definitely time to retire. She chased the supps with a dento-tab, then combed her fingers through her buzz-fuzz and headed for the common area. There, she fixed herself a bowl of instant oatmeal spiked with flecks of dried mango. Most of the time, breakfast went down without her really noticing or caring what it was. Today, everything about it offended: the rubbery texture, the glue-y taste, the preservatives. The first thing she was going to do when she got back to Terra was buy herself a whole crate of fresh fruit and eat her way to the bottom, cost and bellyache be damned.

The presence light over the hatchway flashed red. Minutes later, it switched to green and the hatch swung open, admitting one of her crewmen. He nodded in her direction—a courtesy that she returned. Then, as the hatch closed behind him, he flipped his face-plate. The tune he was humming was already in mid-verse.

"Looking for duct tape," he said between notes.

"Spacer's best friend," she said, because that was the traditional refrain. "Top storage unit, next to the charger." Then, because she could not stop herself from marveling out loud, she said, "I can't believe you're all up and out already. I'm usually the one who wakes up before the alarm."

"Yeah, well." He looked away just as she tried to make eye-contact. He did that a lot. "You were up pretty late."

Crud, another nursemaid. She feigned a renewed interest in her breakfast, but what little appetite she had had was gone now, banished by her crewman's seemingly casual observation. Was everyone watching her? Why? Did they think she was losing it in some way? Did they have a pool going? And was it her, or was Singer's humming getting louder? She scowled, trying to block the noise. He upped the volume again—as if he were deliberately trying to annoy her. She locked on his position like a gunboat turret. Before she could get a shot off, though, he met her gaze and said, "LT set your alarm ahead by six hours."

Her thought processes stalled for a moment—vapor-lock brought on by surprise and fatigue. By the time her synapses started firing again, Singer was out the hatch and gone. That was just as well, because there was no way that she could have stopped herself from blasting him for Val's treachery, and she would have regretted that loss of control later. She dumped the last of her breakfast in the recycling bin and then stormed into the SU, fuming all the way. Damn that Val . He had snaked a full half-shift from her. No wonder the crew felt free to ignore her. Their precious LT was doing his best to undermine her authority. She should have gotten those black-market implants when she'd had the chance. Because she'd love to able to shoot lightning from her fingertips right about now.

As soon as she was suited up, she accessed the central log for Val's location. His avatar was parked in the garage. Hers, she noted, was still in bed. Her already foul mood deteriorated further. She flipped her face-plate down with a gesture that could've passed for obscene and then started on a manhunt. Outside, near-white-out conditions prevailed. The wind was so violent, it nearly blew her away before she had a chance to clip herself to the guide-line—and for a second, she considered letting the wind have its way. *Screw you, Val, just try to get the job done without me.* But she wasn't that spiteful, not yet anyway, so she clipped up and then bulldogged her way toward the garage. The wind's helmet-muffled howling reminded her of Singer's humming—this is so not my scene. She wondered why he had spilled on Val. Did he want something—an extra hour of downtime maybe or a promise of hazard back-pay? Whatever it was, she was inclined to let him have it just to keep him on her side. How embarrassing was that?

Everyone needs friends, 'Nita.

The garage loomed out of the grit-filled darkness, almost in front of her nose. A step later, the pedway's motion-detector flared green. She switched clips, then opened the door and let the wind shove her inside. She could hear music playing— some retro ditty about cheeseburgers and paradise. It was louder than it needed to be, especially once the door closed again and cut off the wind. The matrix was on, too. At first, she thought a soft porn chip must be playing, because all she could see was scantily clad bodies. Then the cameras pulled back to reveal a beach volleyball match in progress. Go figure, she thought, and then ordered both audio and video off to flush Val out. But quiet was the only thing that ensued.

She checked the log again. Val's avatar hadn't moved. She pinged his private link and got an auto-reply: "My current location is—'bot bay." Her resentment flared like a sunspot. His next location was going to be—up Shit Creek. She went storming toward the bay muttering about her second's king-sized nerve only to hit pause as she passed the vac. She couldn't believe that the alien had escaped. No, scratch that. She didn't want to believe that it had escaped. Had that ugly little blob gotten lucky? Or had it known what it was doing? She tried to tell herself that it didn't matter either way, but deep down inside, she knew that it might.

A metallic clatter disrupted her train of thought. It was followed by a muffled groan. The first thing that sprang to her mind was Val with a writhing alien attached to his forearm. *Jesus, AJ, do something.* Had the Q had come back for round two? She broke into a run. Moments later, she came around a corner to find Val on the ground with his head under an APC. He didn't seem to be moving. Crud. Was she too late? She pinged his link. No response. She put a boot to his ribs. He grunted. Yes, still alive! She flipped up her face-plate and said, "Can you hear me, Val?"

"Sure," he said, in a slightly irritated tone. "Hang on a sec."

She went from worried to incensed without a stop at relieved in between. She kicked him again, a solid shot to the thigh that she wanted him to feel in his nuts.

"Front and center," she said. "Now."

He pushed himself out from under the machinery and then onto his feet in one nimble, pain-free move. Despite her recommendation to the contrary, his face-plate was up. The look on his face was a mix of curiosity and imposition. "What's up?" he said.

"I thought you were being attacked," she said, forcing the words past gritted teeth.

"Sorry," he said, and although he tried to hide it, the ghost of a smile flitted across his mouth.

Her concern amused him? The thought carried her past the point of self-restraint. She hooked him by the helmet-collar and hauled him down to her level so he could see the firestorm in her eyes.

"Do you have a problem with me, Johnny?" she asked. He seemed taken aback by the vehemence of the question. That pissed her off even more. "Do you think I'm incapable of doing this job?" He opened his mouth, but nothing came out. She punished him for that, too. "Or is it because I'm a woman? Are you the kind who just can't bear to let a pair of tits run the show?"

His brow furrowed into an annoyed vee. "I'm fine with you, AJ, tits or no tits. What makes you think I'm not?"

"You keep doing—things." She was so aggrieved, her verbal skills were decaying. "Things that undermine my authority."

"Like what?"

She bared her teeth at him—a feral display. "Like resetting my goddam alarm, for starters!"

But if he was impressed by the sight of her canines, he certainly didn't show it. Indeed, he seemed oblivious to the possibility that he might be in any danger at all. "You needed the rest," he said with a shrug, "so I saw that you got it. How's that undermining you?"

"You have no business making decisions that pertain to me," she said. "That's not your job. That's not why you're here."

"C'mon, AJ," he said. "I'm your second. We're supposed to be a team. Teammates are supposed to look out for each other."

Oh sure, he sounded reasonable enough. But that was probably another of his specialties. "Is that the way Shingo rolls?"

"That's the why I roll," he said, adding 'unflappable' to his list of sins. "And as long as I stick the landing, Shingo couldn't care less about my form."

"I'll bet you've never reset his alarm ahead by six hours," she said.

"You're right," he said. "I haven't. I would if I thought he needed the extra rest, though. But the fact is, he doesn't work half as hard as you do." She didn't know if that was flattery, a lame attempt at humor, or both, and so just continued to scowl at him. "Look, AJ," he went on to say, "we all know you're fried. We all know why, too. No one could come off a double on Io and not be on the verge of bottoming out. So why not spend a few more hours in the webbing before things get crazy around here? Nobody's going to think less of you for it."

She didn't want to believe him or admit that he might have a point. That would only encourage him to overstep again. "You should've talked to me first."

"Begging your pardon, AJ," he said, and there was that flicker of a smile again, "but you don't always want to hear what I have to say, especially if what I have to say pertains to you. So when I saw an opportunity to improve a situation at no cost to the op, I took it."

His self-righteousness ticked her off all over again. "Oh yeah?" she said. "What if Azu sees an opportunity next time? What if Spider decides to act first and apologize later?"

"Don't worry," he said. "I'll keep them in line."

"Like you kept them in line this morning when they went to see the Q?"

He tensed like a man stung, and the righteousness drained from his face. "I admit, I didn't see that coming. But you can rest assured that that's the last stunt that those boneheads will be pulling."

She was inclined to believe him on that score. But her faith was based on perpetual waste-disposal detail rather than anything he might have said or done. She didn't bother to say so, though. Her anger was sputtering like a fatty candle, and as it faded, so did her desire to butt heads with this man. "Fine," she said, "keep the guys in line. But remember: you work for me. You are not to make decisions based on my perceived well-being without talking with me first."

"Deal," he said. "But only if you agree to hear me out."

"Only if I get the last word," she countered.

He just smiled, coyly refusing to commit.

The embers of her irritation flickered red as if windblown, but even as they threatened to ignite again, her thoughts swirled like water going down a drain. Stress reaction, she told herself. The man was definitely a carrier.

"I mean it, Val," she said. "No coddling. Clear?"

"Clear," he said. With his next breath, he added, "Now c'mon over here and let me show you what I found."

She didn't know what she had been expecting from him—a hang-dog look perhaps or a moment of silence, some small display of remorse rather than an immediate, kowabunga change of subject. *Now that you're done throwing a fit, let's move on to something interesting.* Good thing she wasn't the sensitive type. Good thing she didn't need validation. As long as Val did his job according to her specs, she was willing to live with tactless. She could live with anything for three months. So she followed him back to the APC that he'd been working on earlier and stood quiet as he retrieved a large strip of ragged rubber from a storage bin.

"I pulled this from the APC," he said, dangling the strip between his thumb and forefinger. "It's a fan belt. Something chewed the hell out of it."

She leaned in to take a closer look at the damage. "I don't see any teeth marks," she said, talking more to herself than to Val. "I'd say heat caused this—not a fire, the pattern doesn't fit. This looks more like a chemical spill, some kind of corrosive." She glanced up at Val. "Did you find evidence of a battery leak?"

"Negative," he said, "battery's intact. But I did find some kind of dried-up sludge on the floor of the APC's chassis. It looks like the same kind of sludge I found in the other two 'bots that came back from TPS2. I haven't run any chemical comparisons yet, but my guess is that it's the same kind of sludge that Azu stepped in this morning."

"What's the status on that?"

"We saved the boot," he said, "probably because the treads were packed with sand. Whatever this gunk is, it only seems to react with off-world materials."

"So the damage done to our stuff was the result of a chemical incompatibility," she said, thinking aloud again.

"That's one theory," Val said, a rather tight-lipped concession. "But you can't rule out sabotage."

She didn't have enough data to argue the point and so simply moved on. "What else you got?"

"I checked the latches on the TPS2 'bots. There's not a bad one in the bunch."

Crud. She'd been hoping for a design flaw. That would have been an easy problem: easy to explain, easy to fix, easy to joke about afterward. *How many design flaws does it take to make a seed? I'll let you know when I'm finished counting!* But no one was going to be laughing about this.

"Ironically," Val was saying now, "by popping the boots and letting in all of that sand, the Q probably prevented the sludge from causing more damage than it did."

They, she noticed, not it. The conspiracy was expanding. Just like her headache. She wanted both to dry up and blow away. Perhaps putting Val in charge and going back to bed wasn't such a bad idea after all.

Contrary on principle, her father used to say. *Just like your mother.*

But Meli had never just given up.

"Anything else you want me to see?" she said. He shook his head—a blessing. "I want a full report ASAP, including estimates on how long it will take to get all 'bots operational again."

"Already filed," he assured her.

"Then carry on," she said, and then turned to go.

Val grabbed her by an elbow in mid-pivot. His expression was intense, a montage of creases and furrows. "Seriously, AJ. What are you going to do about the Q? They're obviously destructive if not outright hostile. Playing catch-and-release with them would just be begging for trouble."

"And exterminating them on sight would be, what—good karma?" she said. "I agree, the Q appear to be destructive—to unattended 'bots. But the 'bots aren't unattended anymore. We're here now. I'm sure we can figure out—"

A dark, amorphous shimmer just beneath the APC's undercarriage caught her eye.

"How to make them Q-proof if you—"

It could have been anything: a slick of oil or anti-freeze, or maybe a bit of debris. Yet she could have sworn that her eye been drawn to the spot by a flicker of movement. She flipped her face-plate down and clicked the magnify feature. Crud. Was that a little eyeball she saw peering at her from the shadows?

"AJ?"

She looked again. But in the time that it had taken her to blink back surprise, whatever it was that had snagged her attention had disappeared. *Now you see it, now you don't.* More likely, there hadn't been anything there in the first place.

"What's going on? What are you looking at?"

"Nothing," she said, because there was no way that she was going to tell him that she was imagining things. He'd think she was going side-out and overthrow her for sure. "I had something in my eye, is all," she said, and kept her plate down so he wouldn't see otherwise. "But as I was saying, I'd rather turf the Q out one at a time and keep them passive than kill a bunch and maybe piss off the whole nest. My way, everyone wins."

"I respectfully disagree," Val said.

"Duly noted," she said, and snuck another peek under the APC. Nada. She blamed those few extra hours of sleep that Val had forced on her. Instead of replenishing her, they had merely exposed the true depth of her deficiencies. Now her body was acting out, hallucinating, hoping to shut her down. But her dad had been right; she was very like her mother. There was no quit in her, either.

"Now if you'll excuse me," she said, "I've got a schedule to draw up."

[∗∗∗]

AJ waited until after chow to call the briefing. She thought the guys would take the news better on a full stomach. She hoped they would be less inclined to push back if they were relaxed and comparatively comfortable. But now that she had their undivided attention, she didn't quite know where to start. This outbreak of stage fright confounded her. She had thirty-plus years of experience in the field. She knew how to demand the impossible and get it without taking the subsequent grumbling behind her back personally. So why the butterflies?

What's a butterfly?

Great. Now Val's peculiar, not particularly amusing sense of humor was starting to rub off on her. She shot him a glower that he probably didn't deserve and then blurted out a summary of their situation as if it were a bad joke. "Good news and bad news, guys," she said. "Here's the good: I've figured out a way to get the seed back on track. The bad news is, we've got to bust our butts to do it."

No one complained, not even Spider. So far, so good. She tapped her handheld. A holo-schematic sprang up from the center of the table. "You'll all find this file in your in-boxes under bigpic," she said. "It's an overview of seed dynamics. Normally, you'd get chipped for this kind of stuff before you got to the job. But since chipping wasn't an option in this case, I'll just have to bring you up to speed the old-fashioned way.

"As you can see, the successful germination of a seed depends on three elements: a transponder network, operational 'bots, and a steady power source. The network goes up first to provide a grid for the 'bots. This enables the pavers to grade foundations for the command hub and manufacturing facility, the APCs to set up a long-term power source, and the fix-its to keep everything functional until central control hardware can be installed in the hub. Once the power station goes operational, MF construction accelerates and then becomes self-contained. That's the stage this seed should have reached six months ago. That's also the mark that Shingo expects us to hit in less than three month's time."

Singer started humming—a soft, nervous doggerel. She made an effort not to single him out. "I know it sounds like a wormhole-dream," she said. "But the truth is, we can do this. Our seed isn't defective, and its failure to germinate wasn't catastrophic. All three elements can still be deployed.

"That's where we come in."

She tapped her handheld again, calling up the next bullet in her holo-point presentation. "You'll find this file under littlepic," she said, as a series of images paraded through thin air. "It depicts each element's current status and what-all needs to be done to bring it online. As you can see, there's not a lot of high-tech work involved, and most of that will involve reprogramming the plug-ins. We are, however, looking at some serious physical labor. The transponder towers need to go up first—and fast. Then we've got a wind-farm to put up."

Singer's humming grew louder. Azu shifted anxiously in his seat. But Spider didn't see the problem. "What's the big deal?" he said. "We've got 'bots."

"We'll have access to one APC for installations," she said. "The rest of the 'bots are going to be dedicated to the manufacturing facility's construction. "

"But—" She could almost hear the buzzer go off as the big deal revealed itself to him. "Those turbines are huge."

"Not to mention ungainly," she said, in a tone that only sounded cheerful. "And setting them up in this bitch of a wind is going to be pure hell. According to the inventory, there are two hundred and fifty turbines packed in the seed's hold. That means we'll need to assemble and install three turbines every day. And—we'll have to pour the bases first, so they'll have time to set up."

Azu was quick to contest her calculations. "Begging your pardon, Chief," he said, "but at that rate, the power station will be done well in advance of three months."

"You're right," she said, acknowledging his smarts with a nod and a smile. "And the sooner we're done with it, the better. Because the power station has to be operational before the MF reaches c-point."

Spider made a face that even a Q could've read. Val started to respond, but then glanced at AJ and waited for her to explain. She smiled again, thinking that she'd finally gotten through to him.

"That's the point where the wall and roof modules integrate and the facility becomes self-contained," she said. "At that time, most of the on-site plug-ins will be diverted to substructures for eventual conversion to maintenance 'bots. If the MF doesn't have its own juice by then, we'll have to track those 'bots down and recharge them manually—and believe me, you don't want that headache on top of everything else you'll have on your plate. Grueling as it sounds, setting up the wind farm ASAP is the easier way to go."

Her throat was parched, sucked dry by stim and recycled air. As she paused to rehydrate, the room fell quiet except for the soft sound of Singer's humming. Then that stopped, too, and in that soft, deep voice of his, he said, "What about the Q?"

She swallowed a last mouthful of water. It felt like a rock going down a child's wishing well. If only that stupid little alien had stayed out of sight. Meli chimed in: *if wishes were fishes, we'd all carry nets*. Her father rolled his eyes and urged her to just answer the question.

"My earlier instructions still stand," she said. "If you see a Q in the field, you are to go out of your way to avoid it. If you find one in the garage, use the vac to catch and contain it. I've been told that its flow-trap has been modified to prevent further escapes. Is that right, Azu?"

"Yes, Chief," Azu said, trying not to look at Spider. She pretended not to notice either of them.

"Excellent," she said. "We'll be inspecting all active field 'bots for Q infestations on a daily basis, leastwise until the MF reaches self-containment. These inspections will have to be very thorough, because LT says these things know how to pop a boot and can work their way into almost any compartment. They also excrete some kind of caustic goo that you'll have to look out for. If you see any—or get any on your habby," she added, torturing Azu with a sideways glance, "heap sand on it ASAP. Apparently, that neutralizes the goo. It's not a stylish solution, but until we find a better one, it will have to do.

"Any other questions?"

They responded with terse head-shakes and muted, "No's." She took that for gravity rather than a lack of enthusiasm, but supposed that they were entitled either way. Attitude was optional as long as the job got done.

"In that case," she said, bringing up her last holo-point, "let me show you how our schedule's going to work. The computer hasn't finished hashing out all of the details yet, but basically, the shifts are going to be five-hour staggers."

"Now that sounds like my kind of schedule," Spider said.

His mates chuckled. AJ managed a bittersweet smile.

"We'll all work back-to-back five-hour shifts," she said. "If you're out in the field, you'll have a partner. If you're in the garage, you'll work alone. Sometimes, you'll work both shifts at the same site. Sometimes, you'll migrate to another site at half-time. That will depend on what needs doing most on the day. No one will do the same job or work with the same partner for more than five hours. That will help keep us fresh and out of auto-pilot. When your ten hours are up, you're free for eight. I don't care how or where you spend those eight so long as you pick up after yourself."

"I take it back," Spider said, in a much more dejected tone. "This schedule sounds like something out of a chain gang."

She should've been glad that he was finally getting the message. But for some reason, the thought left her tired and sad. She felt obliged to try and make amends—to him and everybody else. "Life should get a little easier after the MF c-points," she said, "but we won't know for sure until we get there. And until then, the only break you're likely to get is the next thirteen hours so I'd make the most of it if I were you."

"Wait," Val said, a surprised eruption. "What was that?"

"The schedule is set to launch tomorrow at the crack of stupid," she said, "and I'll be taking the first time-slot. So the rest of you are off until your shift rolls around. Don't worry about what time you need to get up. From here on, the boat's life support program will take care of that. If any of you are so inclined, there's a bottle of sake in the cooler. It's not great sake, so go easy and stay hydrated."

Spider and Azu traded a dubious look. Singer made a show of studying his fingernails. But Val said, "Well, all right then," and then shot to his feet as if he were spring-loaded. "Sleep well, Chief. See you on the flipside."

But instead of the cooler, he headed for the SU.

"Don't be gone too long, LT," Spider called after him. "Otherwise, me and 'Zu might snake your share of the sake."

"You boys go ahead," he said, and then half-turned to look at AJ. "I think I'm going to get a jumpstart on reprogramming those 'bots—if I can find a cheat sheet that says who and what, that is."

She could've lied and told him that said sheet was still a work in progress. She could've insisted that he spend his free time at rest as a payback for sticking his nose in her business earlier. But while these thoughts crossed her mind, she knew better than to act on them. She was too tired, and had too much to do in a very short span of time. And—he had asked first. That was the important thing. So if he wanted to rearrange 'bot modules rather than lounge with his 'lings, then he had her whole-hearted blessing and then some.

"Check the central log," she said. "Look under 'bot-mods.'"

"Thanks," he said, and then started off again.

"Just don't work too long," she called after him, because part of her could not resist having the last word. "Because as of tomorrow, the easy part is over."

"Mercy," Singer said, and started humming again.

CHAPTER 07

Niji was overwhelmed. Ecstatic. Obsessed.

Uprights were easily the most fascinating subjects that niji had ever studied. What other beings created not-beings to work for them? What other beings defied nazza and made darkness disappear? And what other beings had a burrow wall that could generate images and sounds? Niji found that wall more exciting than any other upright artifact. Not only were its displays alluring in their exoticness, they were often revealing as well. Now niji knew for certain that the uprights were swarmers and that they communicated ethereally. It had also learned that in addition to the hard-shelled uprights that frequented this burrow, there was another, soft-shelled type that lived elsewhere and liked to conjugate. These soft-shells came in two distinct forms: conjugal-tube and no-conjugal-tube. Moreover, the forms appeared to be immutable. The concept of physiological permanence shocked and unsettled niji, for zervarzi believed that evolution favored variability. The more changeable a being was, the more adaptable it became. The more adaptable it was, the greater chance it had of becoming something better. Yet the uprights, soft-shelled or otherwise, were clearly superior beings, and they were as single-shaped as zyl! What did this mean?

As niji pondered that paradox, nazza blew into the burrow—a single-gust intrusion that announced the arrival of an upright. Niji craned an oculum in the direction from which the wind had come and then flushed with joy as the smallest of the uprights came into view. GeeZuzAyJay was the hard-shell sound to which this one responded. Niji believed it to be the *zranarz*, a being superior to all others. *Zra* came to a stop in front of the image-wall, then thrust its shiny gold fore-nob to the top of its top-nob and issued a series of sounds from its exhaust orifice.

"FronAnCenyrSpyDerTymTooShiff."

Another upright came surging into view. This was SpyDer, a lesser upright. On its own or when swarming with other inferiors, the *pernarz* tended to be noisy and high energy. But in zra's presence, per was subdued—like a nijit that did not want to be noticed and maybe eaten. That reinforced niji's belief in GeeZuzAyJay's superiority.

"ZarEeCheef," per said. "EyWuzJuzTrynTooFinishUp."

"HowdUDoo?" zra asked.

Per seemed to shrink a little. EyFellTwoCownzZhort."

"JuzToo?" zra said, and then bobbed its head. "GrateWurk!" Then zra shifted toward the display that was streaming across the image-wall and said, "DohnUEvrGetTirydUvPorn?"

The pernarz cocked its top-nob and said, "UrKiddynRyt?"

"Yah," zra said, "EyGehzEyAm. NowGetGohinBeforElTeeStartzFretyn." As the pernarz went bounding toward the nearest burrow plug, she added, "May-trikzAwf."

All at once, the image-wall went dormant. Disappointment stung niji like a zyl panic pulse and then gave way to eagerness as GeeZuzAyJay moved toward the giant container that one of the ulvarzi had carried in earlier. Observing the zranarz in action was better than watching any display—although niji had to admit, it was not always easy to make sense of zra's doings. If only the uprights committed their thoughts to the ground for others to examine! An azrum might have told niji why zra was pulling objects out of that giant container only to set them in other, smaller ones. An azrum might have provided niji with some insight as to why the ulvarzi were not doing this work instead. But as far as niji could tell, the uprights did not leave biochemical markers of any kind. So all niji could do was watch and wonder as the zranarz went back and forth between containers. The objects were awkwardly shaped and obviously heavy, yet zra seemed to have no trouble moving them. This surprised niji, for it would not have expected something so upright to be so strong and coordinated. Varzi were much better situated for transporting things larger than themselves, leastwise underground.

A soft, meaty thud caught niji's attention. It popped out of its wandering thoughts to see zra hopping around on one lower appendage. At first, niji thought the upright had stepped in one of its azrumi, for uprights reacted strongly to such encounters. But then zra hopped its way over to a small, wall-mounted container marked with a red splotch and snapped it open. It snapped its fore-patch back, too, and an explosion of agitated sounds roiled forth.

"ZhitZhitZhitThaHurtz!"

The upright yanked something out of the container and slapped it to its top-nob stalk. Soon thereafter, its exhalations became less forceful. It hobbled over to an overturned container and folded its back-side into a shelf for resting. "JuzFerAMinut," it said, as if another upright were listening. "JuzTilThaPeeKayKiksIn." Then the zranarz relaxed a little and said, "LytzAwf! MatrikzAwn!"

The burrow went dark. That surprised niji, for no wind had come to drive the brightness away. But before it could figure out why the light had abandoned zra, the image-wall roused—a thrilling eruption of sound and soft-shelled body parts.

"MayriksFazForwerdTooTravelChipOne."

The conjugating uprights vanished. Niji flushed, mourning their loss, only to forget its distress as a new display formed on the wall. It started with colors—layer upon layer upon layer, hues so vibrant and intense they simply had to be alive. Then the colors fragmented into a field of separate blades and began to sway as if they were being swept by the gentlest of winds. The field expanded. The wind turned into a wave that rippled over the blade-tops. And all the while, those luscious, living colors endured. Although niji did not understand anything that niji was sensing, niji felt connected to it, molecularly entwined.

MaytrikzFazForwerdTooIlanZeekwenz."

The field gave way to an enormous span of blue-green liquid fringed with white froth. As niji watched, it made landfall and disappeared, leaving only a trail of foam behind. Another span rolled in, then another and more—a mesmerizing procession. Niji could not believe that anything other than sand could come in such vast quantities or on such a scale. It felt profoundly enriched for having learned of this liquid-in-motion's existence. It felt—privileged.

A sharp buzz intruded on the sound of liquid splashing onto land. Zer groaned and then returned zer's back-side to a flat, upright configuration. "MaytrikzAwf," she said. "LytzAwn."

Darkness vanished. The image-wall went blank, too. The next thing niji knew, zra was back to hauling things out of containers and setting them elsewhere. Niji watched the zrnarz as it worked, but niji's thoughts were still entangled with those incredible images. Any doubt that niji might have had about GeeZuzAyJay's superiority were gone now, laid to rest not by its size or its dominant behavior but by the displays that it favored. The images that the other uprights watched stirred niji's curiosity. Zernarz's images inspired yearning.

Niji had to see that rippling field of living color again. It wanted to view the images again and again and again until it had committed every last detail to its memory strands. To do that, niji would need the image-wall's help. All niji had to do was figure out how to rouse it.

CHAPTER 08

AJ WAS WALKING THROUGH a jungle of strangler figs and parasitic vines, one eye on the path, the other on the howler monkeys that were trooping through the treetops. *I want to do that.* The next thing she knew, she was up in the canopy, preparing to zip-line down the mountainside. As she donned the harness, she felt a sting in her left biceps. *Ouch.* A moment later, she got stung again—in exactly the same spot. *Ow!* The third time, she was out of her webbing and on her feet *enough already, I'm up.* But even though she popped a stim first thing, she remained fog-brained and drowsy well into breakfast. Meli had been the same way. "We're dream-travelers," she'd tell AJ. "If we're slow to wake up, it's because we have to come all the way back from the stars."

"You could try going to bed earlier," her father used to retort, when he was around to comment.

The presence light over the hatchway flared red. In another time and space, AJ might've checked her handheld to see who was inbound, but here and now, she couldn't be bothered. She would know as soon as the hatch opened anyway. And she did. Spider's lanky frame was a dead giveaway, though there wasn't nearly as much spring in his step as there used to be. She enjoyed a microsecond of *schadenfreude* only to wish that she hadn't when he flipped his plate. Because the eyes that were now looking her way were those of a working man rather than some pampered space-pup. She had to respect the change.

"Hey, Chief," he said, sounding as tired as he looked. "Sleep through?"

"Oh yeah," she said. "You down this shift?"

"Just as soon as I get something in my belly," he said, as he pulled his helmet off. "Habby juice may keep a body alive, but it does absolutely nothing for the soul."

"Careful, kid," she said. "You're starting to sound like LT."

"Want me to start humming instead?"

She rewarded the quip with a faux snarl and then returned to her bowl of muesli—not dismissing him exactly, but not inviting him to stick around and chat, either. So she was mildly surprised when he didn't make a beeline for the S-rat locker. "It's in our report," he said, in response to her inquiring eyebrow, "but LT said to tell you anyway."

That got her heart going. Or maybe it was just the stim finally kicking in. She'd bumped her dose up to two or three per shift cycle—sometimes she could get by with less and she'd only needed more once or twice. She hated the edgy, cannibalized feeling it gave her, but at this point there was no getting or staying started without it.

"Don't you want to know what he said?" Spider asked.

"Why else would I ask?" AJ said, only to realize that she hadn't—at least not out loud. But instead of calling her on it, he shrugged as if it were his mistake and said, "We didn't meet our quota this shift."

"Where were you?" she said.

"Wind farm," he said. "South forty."

"What was the problem?" she said. "You run into Q?"

"I wish," he said.. "You and LT are the only ones who have that kind of luck. In fact, if it weren't for Bob, I'd be tempted to think that you guys made that sighting up just to mess with the rest of us."

"Bob?" she said, drawing a blank.

"You know," he said, "the Q that lives in the garage."

Surprise flared within her. Everyone knew about the resident Q, of course, for there was no other explanation for the goo-bombs that turned up on the floor every now and again. But no one talked about it. Morale was better that way. Singer hadn't burst into song in days.

"You call it Bob?" she said

He shrugged. "Why not? It sounds better than blob."

"Have you seen it?" she asked. She hadn't, not since that first time. But sometimes when she was alone in the garage, she got the stim-fueled feeling that that she was being watched.

"Nah," he said. "He's good at staying out of sight. Probably doesn't want to get sucked up by the vac again." He let out a chuckle and then added, "Can't say that I blame him."

And that, she thought, was probably why they didn't talk about the alien— there was just no place to go that didn't end up weird. "So OK," she said, eager to move on, "if Q didn't hold you up, then what did?"

"The friggin' wind," he said, trading his smile for an aggrieved scowl. "Every time we stood a turbine up, that bitch blew it back down."

Ah yes, that friggin' wind. Was it so wrong of her to wish that the problem had been Q instead? At least a blob could be avoided—or removed. That wind was an unyielding misery. If she'd had the luxury of time, she would've waited for milder conditions before attempting to set up a wind farm. But that season—the one that the original launch had targeted—was still nearly two months away and well past Shingo's deadline. And while she'd built a generous pad into the schedule to compensate for wind-related setbacks, that margin was disappearing faster than anticipated.

"Sixty-nine," she said.

"Say what?" Spider said, and then arched a rakish eyebrow, not so mature or played-out that he could resist turning that number into a raunchy innuendo.

But sex was the last thing on AJ's mind. She'd been counting up the days that she had left—on this job, this rock, the side of the APW. And the funny thing was, she hadn't realized that she'd been counting until the number popped out of her mouth.

"Never mind," she said, because she didn't want him to think that she was even crazier than Val made her out to be. "And thanks for the update. The wind dies down a little on the back end of the day so maybe we can take advantage of that and make up the shortfall."

"OK, whatever," Spider said, suddenly remembering that he was tired and hungry. As he started drifting toward the S-rat locker, though, he added, "Oh yeah, I almost forgot—LT says you left the matrix on when you clocked out last night."

Did not. Turning off the matrix was part of her check-out ritual: *good night, Meli; good night, dad, matrix off.* "He must've read the schedule wrong."

"He said a nature chip was playing. You're the only one who watches eco-crap."

There was no arguing with simple fact. But she hadn't left the system on, had she? She tried to recall yesterday's highlights: a breakfast of re-hydrated eggs and head-work followed by two shifts out on the wind-farm, a third in the garage, and then a half-hour alone with the day's reports and a few highlights from her favorite travelogue. She watched the same chip every time, and it always ended the same way—in darkness, lights off, a billion light-years away from home.

"Then there must be a glitch in the programming," she said, "because like I said, I turned it off." But inwardly, a part of her wondered, right? She hated that inner voice, so paranoid and quick to doubt. She hated Spider, too, for rousing it from its turgid slumber.

"Maybe Bob did it," he said, as he rifled through the locker for something that appealed to him.

"Has Bob given you reason to believe that it knows how to activate the matrix?"

He must have caught the edge in her tone because he abandoned his foraging to look her in the eye. "No, Chief," he said, sounding tired and slightly abashed. "Like I said, I've never even seen the thing. I was just trying to be a little funny."

"Oh. OK," she said, but what she thought was whew. Because while she was obliged to ask, she didn't really want to know. Not with sixty-nine days left, and a mean wind at her back.

CHAPTER 09

NIJI RUBBED ITS NEWLY formed sound-makers together. "Mzz, mzz, mzz."

The sounds bore no resemblance to the ones niji wanted to make. Niji modified each of the new constructs, adding rigidity to the bases and hardness to the upper surfaces. The result was, "Mzz, mzzz, mzzzyz."

Better but still not acceptable. The image-wall was very particular.

Niji would have liked to make sounds the way the uprights did, but it had no wind of its own and lacked the capacity to manipulate nazza. So it had to generate vibrations externally and shape them into reasonable imitations of upright sound.

"May-zyz, may-zriz, may-zrikz."

Better.

Niji continued to experiment with modifications: thicker scrapers, multiple files, thinner amplifiers. It did not intend to stop until it found a combination that worked. Because sound was the way to uprightness. And 'MaytricksAwn,' was the entrance to that grand and glorious tunnel.

CHAPTER 10

"DAY SEVENTY-ONE," AJ SAID, recording notes in her personal log as she trudged out to the garage to start her first shift. She had the sense that she might be off by a day, but couldn't bring herself to fret over such a minuscule detail. Auto-correct would catch the mistake.

"The manufacturing facility will hit c-point within the next fifty hours." That should have been a hands-down good thing. Instead, it had the potential to become a disaster. "Despite our best efforts—" Which meant shift after shift after shift of unrelenting struggle against the wind, the cold, and their own physical limits. "—the wind farm is a dozen turbines behind schedule. To make up the deficit, I may have to scrap garage detail and triple-team the last of the north forty." Bot maintenance would suffer, but since Bob steered clear of the machinery and no other Q had turned up to mount an infestation, the risk seemed minimal. Even so, she was reluctant to chance anything because shit had a way of knowing when her guard was down. "I'll know more by the end of the shift."

AJ entered the garage to find the matrix broadcasting a jazz concert. The display showed four larger-than-life musicians bunched together on a laser-lit stage. All of them were blowing oddly shaped horns in a loud, discordant fashion. AJ silenced the display immediately, and not just because she despised that raucous retro crap. People tended to go topless in the garage, so shutting off the matrix was the easiest way to let them know that it was time to shift. But Singer did not respond to that cue. Nor did he appear when she pinged him on his private channel.

"C'mon, Singer," she shouted then. "Front and center!"

No response.

Had he left for his shift on the back forty already—without turning off the matrix? *Ha-ha, Val, told you it wasn't me!* But even as the thought happy-danced through her head, she noticed that the central log still had Singer's avatar parked in the garage. That meant that he was either ignoring her or napping somewhere. And while Singer often tuned her out after they were done with their business, he never shut her down before then. She wasn't angry with him for nodding off, not really. This deep into an RSO, brown-outs happened to everybody, stim or no stim. Even so, she meant to give him a ration of grief for not having some kind of back-up alarm in his suit.

"Wake-y, wake-y, Singer," she shouted, as she headed for the 'bot bay. "Your worst nightmare is here."

A faint scraping sound from the vicinity of the battery-charging station cut her off. She pivoted in that direction and then squinted. Was that a leg she saw next to the dock? Yes! And—it appeared to be twitching.

"Shit."

The next thing AJ knew, she was staring down at Singer. He was doubled up as if he had a spike in his belly. His face was ashen and slick with sweat. His eyes were rolled back in their sockets. AJ dropped to her knees and gently gripped him by the shoulders.

"Singer," she said, "can you hear me?" He managed a tiny, pain-wracked nod. "Can you tell me what's wrong?"

"Pigeon pox," he said, gasping each word. "Stage four."

Shit. She didn't know what 'stage four' meant, but it couldn't be good. "Are you con—" The word got stuck in her throat. She resisted the urge to snap her face-plate down. "Are you contagious?"

His head twitched left and then right. "Got a—fresh booster—on my last— LTL." His eyes rolled forward. They were bloodshot, and glazed with misery. "This shouldn't have—happened."

"When did it start?"

"Couple days—ago," he said, and then seized up as a wave of pain rolled over him. "But," he added, as the spasm passed, "the pain didn't get bad till a few hours ago."

Good, she thought—and not just because she hated the thought of him or any other crewman hurting. She would have hated herself, too, if he'd been in this much pain for days without her even suspecting that something was wrong. But a man could hide a fair amount of misery behind a habby. And if he did what he could to keep the problem to himself, then she wasn't going to beat herself up for not being able to read minds. She had plenty of natural failings.

"What about meds? Does the ICE kit have anything that might help?"

He tried to shrug but gave up halfway through. "PK maybe."

"OK," she said, bouncing back to her feet. "Back in a tick."

She sprinted over to the wall-mounted emergency box and rifled through its contents: bandages, clotting goop, skin glue, instant-ice, duct-tape. When she finally found the pain-killer patches, she pulled a bunch out of the bundle, slapped the box shut again and then sprinted back to Singer. In her absence, he had started trembling like a man in the grips of a fever chill.

"I'm going to apply the PK to your carotid," she said, "so you should feel it pretty quick." She swabbed his skin with the back of a wrapper, then stripped off the patch and pressed it to his neck. Moments later, his shivering calmed down. A moment after that, his jaws unclenched.

"Better?" she asked.

"Maybe," he said. "Got any more?"

"See how you do with one first," she said. "I can't have you so doped up that you can't function." When he didn't react to that statement, she said, "You getting what I'm saying here, Johnny? As much as I'd like to, I can't spare you. You're going to have to work your shifts no matter how horrible you feel."

He groaned, a ripped-from-the-guts zombie sound. AJ threw him the only bone she had. "I'll go and work the back forty for you this shift; you can stay here and finish the inspections. When I break between shifts, I'll modify the schedule. Until this attack subsides, all you'll have to do is keep the 'bots running. You can do that much, can't you?"

For a moment, Singer just laid there barely breathing as if he were playing possum. *What's a possum?* Then he rolled his eyes in her direction and licked his cracked, dry lips. "Yeah," he said. "I can do that."

She climbed to her feet, none too spry herself now that the adrenaline had worn off, and then offered him a hand up. He accepted her help, but with averted eyes as if he was embarrassed by his weakness. As she steadied him afterward, he said, "Thanks, Chief. You're—" He winced, fighting off another spasm, and then eked out, "You're OK."

Pain-wracked as it was, AJ felt unworthy of the sentiment and so wasted no time in changing the subject. "Where's your helmet?" she said. "You should put it on. You'll stay better hydrated that way."

"It's over there," he said, pointing vaguely, and then waved her off when she made a move in that direction. "I'll get it," he said. "You should get going before LT starts freaking."

She handed him the extra PK patches. "Use them at your discretion," she said. "If you need more before the end of the shift, you know where the ICE kit is. As long as you're careful and check in every few hours, I'm not going to keep count."

"Roger that," he said, and then went shambling after his helmet.

Poor bastard, she thought, as she headed for the pedway. Because the only thing more miserable than being on an RSO was being on an RSO while impaired. She had fractured a collarbone in an excavator accident during her first tour on Mars and been obliged to keep working until TSC found a replacement. The pain had been so bad, she'd thrown up in her habby—on multiple occasions. And the suit deodorizers back then hadn't been as efficient as they were now.

The wind slammed AJ as soon as she set foot outside, but it seemed less belligerent than usual. She wanted to take that as a promising sign—rhe tide turning, as Meli used to say. But it was hard to be hopeful when there was a man down on the beach. She released the scoot from its cocoon and aimed it in the direction of the wind farm. As it lurched forward, her mother returned to scold her for being so much like her father. *Look on the bright side for a change!* And she had to admit, the situation wasn't the absolute worst that it could be. Luckily for Singer, his affliction was homegrown rather than indigenous, and painful rather than lethal. And luckily for everybody on this rock, it was non-infectious because one of the downsides to a career in space was immune system suppression. A decade ago, an Oort Belt mining station had been decimated by a mutated cold virus. Cruisers were herpes hotbeds. And Terra had far nastier viruses up its steamy sleeves. There were naturals like influenza that had been in circulation forever. There were naturals like Dengue Fever and E-bola that had sprung from ravaged jungles and spread to erstwhile temperate climes courtesy of global warming. And then there were designers like Pigeon Pox that had been engineered to reduce the populations of pestilent species only to mutate and turn on their makers. If not for nanotechnology, very few Terrans, spacers or otherwise, would live beyond their prime. Nanos stopped infections and genetic disorders at the cellular level. Nanos prevented radiation damage, cancer, inflammation, and parasites. Every Terran was required to have at least a basic nano-package. Most spacers, AJ included, preferred maximum coverage. Even so, she had still freaked a little when she thought Singer might be contagious. New viruses were always spinning into existence. And while nanos were the best thing since penicillin, they went bad sometimes or simply didn't work.

An APC hauling a flatbed loaded with seed slabs barged across her path. It was heading toward a corona of backlit dust on the portside horizon. That was the MF construction site—a frenzied hive of robotic activity. The giant hole that the pavers had dug was long gone, floored over and overlaid with interlocking modules. If she squinted, she could just make out where the cooling towers were going up, and the holding tank. And even at this distance, with her eyes wide open, she could see that c-point was rapidly approaching. She would have to shut down every 'bot on the site to prevent that from happening, and that would cost her dearly in terms of time and lost momentum. Better to triple-team the rest of the north forty.

She veered right and sped across a desolate stretch of ice that was slated to become hydrogen fuel fodder. Not on her watch, though. She'd be digging for clams on some beach in the Caribbean by the time strip-mining commenced. Good thing, too, for strip-mines were ugly things, and not the kind of footstep she cared to leave behind.

Off to her left, a light flashed twice, went dark, and then flashed again. That was Val, signaling his position. As she adjusted her course, the scoot's headlight swept over an army of giant ovoid silhouettes. These were Darries—vertical axis wind turbines that were designed to generate electricity for dark-side outposts. They stood still, their blades locked, waiting in the wind for a chance to spin. They looked alien and oddly imposing, like the giant stone Moai on Easter Island. She wondered if the sight daunted the Q, and if that was why they stayed away.

Assuming there was more than one.

The scoot lurched as it cleared the last vestiges of the ice-field and then downshifted to compensate for the regolith's looser composition. A man-shaped shadow appeared in the gap between two turbines and waved. AJ waved back and then hailed Val on his private channel.

"Sorry to keep you waiting," she said.

The shadow's back and shoulders stiffened—a non-verbal WTF. "AJ? Is there a problem? I was expecting Singer."

"Everything's under control," she said, as she closed on his position. "But Singer's restricted to garage detail until further notice."

"Why?"

"Pigeon Pox." Then, because she knew he'd want to know, she added, "He says he's not contagious."

"Poor bastard," he said. "He must be stage four."

"What exactly is that anyway?"

"It's the dormant viral infection going active again," he said, "probably in response to stress. The original virus was designed to target nasal cavity nerve-endings in pigeons, which basically causes them to fly headlong into the nearest building. The mutated version attacks the same tissues in humans, and is reputed to be extremely painful. Somebody who used to crew for me said it felt like his head was expanding and caving in at the same time."

"How long was that crewman down?" she asked, though she wasn't sure she wanted to know the answer.

"Two weeks," he said. "But I hear some flare-ups last for months."

"Crud," she said. "I gave Singer some PK and told him to get back to work. He's going to think I'm a—"

'Monster', she meant to say, but before she could get the word out, Val cut her off with a ping. "Don't beat yourself up over things that can't be helped, AJ," he said. "This isn't Singer's maiden voyage. He knows the op always comes first—and that you cut him as much slack as you could."

Just like that, the sense of guilt that had been trying to sink its hooks into her dissolved. Sometimes, she thought, a girl just needed a little validation.

And sometimes, it was impossible not to like this man just a little.

She cocooned the scoot on the leeside of the foremost completed Darrie, well out of the APC's way. Afterward, as she was trying to stretch the feeling back into her butt, she noticed that the turbine's blades were twitching as if they were trying to self-start. She hailed Val. "This baby has a loose brake," she said. "Got any SBF?"

A minute later, he was at her elbow with a roll of duct tape. "I never did like Darries," he said, as she reinforced the locking mechanism. "They aren't as sturdy as the propeller types, especially the blades."

"True," she said, "but vertical axis turbines are easier for 'bots to erect and maintain because their gear boxes and generators are close to the ground. They're also cheaper to make, package, and transport so of course TSC adores them." She wound one last length of tape around the cuff, then stepped back to check her work. The blades were now completely still. "That'll do until we can get someone out here with a replacement cuff," she said. "What's this Darrie's address?"

"SFQ4R10."

"Got it," she said, making the note in her log. "What's the number?"

"242."

"No kidding?" At his nod, she made a happy sound deep in her throat and then gave him a congratulatory thump on the arm. "You made up some ground."

"Yeah," he said, sounding pleased. "The wind's been cooperating."

She thumped him again, just because she could. "Excellent news. Let's see if we can make more headway. You want the APC or the ground?"

"I ran the 'bot last shift," he said, "so I'll take the ground this time around."

"Deal," she said.

Normally, a plug-in would've been running the APC. But the plug-ins were all dedicated to the MF now, so the only alternative was man-power. Fortunately, big rigs like the all-purpose came with a manual option, and you didn't need to be strong or even particularly smart to work them. AJ climbed up to the cab and strapped herself into the operator's seat, then looked beyond the windshield for Val. He was standing at the base of what was to be Darrie 243 and giving her a thumb's up.

"Get a generator module first," he said. "The flatbed's at D239."

"On it," she said, and turned the APC in that direction. She couldn't see the flatbed from where she was not, but she knew it wasn't that far away. That was a nice thing about Darries—because of their design, they could be planted closer together. That resulted in bigger wind farms on less acreage: a win-win combination. That also allowed them to leave the immensely heavy attachment parked in one place until ranging back and forth for components became more time-and-energy-consuming than relocating it. Ordinarily, she would've waited until they had a few more turbines under their belt before considering a move. But with the wind as mellow as it was, she suddenly decided to put them in a position where they could work fast.

"Val," she said, "FYI, I'll be a few minutes late."

He came back with, "Problem?"

"Negative," she said. "I'm going to hitch Flat-So up to the wagon. I have a feeling we're going to cover a lot of territory this shift."

Silence ensued—him doing the math. Then he said, "I think you're right." A moment later, he added, "You really are the best at this kind of work, AJ. Are you sure you want to retire at the end of this tour?"

"Very sure," she said. The flatbed was in sight now. She angled the APC toward it. "My next and final stop is Terra."

"You got family there?"

"Nuh-uh," she said, which was short for don't want to talk about it, thanks.

"Me, either." He grunted—hopefully a work-related noise, . "Sometimes I wish my dad had lived long enough to see me now. He didn't think much of me joining up with TSA. Said I'd wind up cleaning SU's—if I was lucky."

"Nice," she said, although she was more focused on backing the APC up to the flatbed's hitch. "Sounds like he was—" There, aligned perfectly. "A big fat tool." Now for the couplings. She climbed down from the cab, grimacing at every rung because it felt like she was tearing fresh scar tissue with each passing step.

Had there really been a time when she could work whole shifts without rigor mortis setting in halfway through them?

"My mom was worse," Val was saying now, and what the hell had gotten into him to make him so chatty all of a sudden? "She threatened to strangle me the day I turned ten."

"Nice," she said again, although she'd had the same urge once or twice herself. He must have that effect on women. "My mom dropped a twelve pound pumpkin from her garden on my head when I was seven."

Crud! How had that gotten past the internal filters?

"Your mother was a gardener?"

"Not a gardener, a farmer." The censors hadn't OK'd that factoid, either. Meli must be channeling. "Our ancestors regarded farming as a sacred task. Flowers were a waste of water and therefore immoral."

There. Couplings secured. Now—ow, ow, ow—back into the cab.

"That's right, I almost forgot. You're part NA."

"Cherokee," she said, amazed to find herself possessed by the same blabber-bug. "Our clan nearly died out on the Trail of Tears, but a few of those who survived resettlement broke away from the Nation and moved to what used to be SoCal. Their descendants started out growing tomatoes and corn for hungry Angelenos, but eventually relocated to New Mexico and founded a medical marijuana co-op. My mother spent her formative summers working in the fields with her cousins. She used to say that the smell of pot made her think of sunshine."

She was heading back to D243 now. She could feel the APC straining to compensate for the flatbed's weight. It was a very strange sensation, like being held back by a shirttail.

"What about your dad?" Val asked. "Was he NA, too?"

"Nah. My mother said there was some Aztec blood in him, but you wouldn't have known it from his looks. He was a tall, stocky white guy with curly brown hair and green eyes." What she didn't say was that while she could still describe him down to the faint childhood scar that left a dimple in his right cheek, she could no longer picture him with her mind's eye. "He doted on my mother. But he didn't have much time for me."

"What'd he do?"

"TSC exec," she said. "He was on the fast-track for a council seat when he was killed."

"Wow. What happened?"

AJ didn't usually share that part of her life because the wrong word at the wrong time could still bring the threat of tears to her eyes and she needed to be strong for her crewmen. But today she felt particularly good about discussing her parents. It was as if they were glad for the chance to get out of her head.

"He died in the Yucatan tsunami," she said. "So did my mother. We were there on holiday. I was nine."

Silence ensued, which was no great surprise. Hardly anyone knew what to say in the aftermath of that disclosure. Perhaps that was another reason she usually chose to stay mum.

The POS that someone had duct-taped to the dash started to flicker—the perfect excuse to change the subject. "I'm closing in on your position now," she said. "I'll drop Flat-So halfway to D244 and then get down to business. You ready for that generator module yet?"

"Been waiting for ages already," he said, and she almost couldn't tell that his drollness was slightly forced. "So step on it."

"Yessir," she said.

The drop-off went as AJ expected—except for the extra set of ow-ow-ow's that cropped up during the uncoupling. And after six solid weeks of practice with the APC's robo-claws, she had no trouble plucking the pre-assembled generator module out of its designated bin. "This is so much easier without the wind," she said, as she carried the module back to D223. "We'd be done already if we had gotten here three months later."

"Sure seems that way," Val said.

She set the module down on its base and held it steady while he connected all the dots. When he was done, she motored back to the flatbed for the rotor module and then the structural supports.

"Now for the hard part," he said, when the turbine was finally ready to go vertical. "You good?"

"Stand back," she said, and then began to stand Darrie 223 up in its bed. Getting the turbine upright was not the issue, for VART towers were lighter than propeller types and not as top-heavy. The problem was getting it to stay upright until it was properly secured. Managing that in a high wind was like riding a mechanical bull in zero-g after drinking synthetic gin all night. But today, everything fell into place on the second try with almost no fight at all.

"Damn," Val said, when he was finished bolting the tower to its moorings. "We could set a record today. You ready for 244?"

"Hop in," she said, "I'll give you a lift."

Her headset registered a second ping-tone. The caller's avatar belonged to Singer. Checking in just like she'd told him to. "How are you feeling, Johnny?" she said, prepared for good news because of the way everything else was going this shift. But what she heard next was wet and garbled, a strangled sound that seemed wrapped around her name.

Then Singer's avatar flared red, a distress signal. Man down.

CHAPTER 11

Nɪᴊɪ ʟᴜʀᴋᴇᴅ ɪɴ ᴛʜᴇ regolith outside of the *garj*, waiting in ambush for its next feed. It did not want to be away from the uprights and their wondrous things, but fewer and fewer ice mites were turning up in the ulvarzi's slushy tread-droppings. That meant that the zyl were starting to gather on subterranean ice-fields to breed. That meant that niji had to hunt if it wanted to eat.

And niji was very, very hungry. Its appetite for learning had caused it to neglect its need for nourishment for far too long.

The super-school of zyl that niji was stalking had amassed at a depth well beyond niji's range. But niji could sense the school's growing frenzy and knew that a reproductive free-for-all was on the verge of erupting. When that happened, pods of mating-crazed juveniles would break away from the orgy and flash-surface. That was when niji would strike. Until then, all it could do was wait and try to ignore the regolith's chill. Such disregard came hard for niji, for it had grown accustomed to living warm-and-out-of-the-wind. Acclimated or not, though, it could still tell that the temperature out here in the wilderness was rising rather than falling. That meant that the Season of Storms was coming to an end. That meant that varzi would soon be migrating back to this region. Their return meant nothing to niji; it was simply what happened when nazza went away.

A shockwave of diffuse, almost fizzy pressure tickled niji's outlying frani. Faster than thought, the prey-tickle intensified and then—*zoozh*, zyl everywhere, hard-shelled flecks shooting like star-stuff through the regolith. Niji disgorged a swarm of *vytzi*—tiny, zyl-dedicated hunter probes. The pod responded with a collective panic pulse and then zoozh, plunged back into the depths. The pulse's percussive sting stunned niji, more so than usual because niji was weak from hunger. So niji was late in expressing the chemical that recalled the vytzi and not all of the vytzi returned. The loss of a few probes did not distress niji, for vytzi could survive on their own until they made their way back to niji or were absorbed by some other varz. But less vytzi meant less to eat, and niji found itself less than sated after ingesting its reduced catch. That distressed niji. For now niji would have to stay here and wait for another pod. And niji did not want to linger out in the cold. It wanted to return to the garj and get warm. It wanted to watch the image-wall and learn new *wrdz*. Most of all, niji wanted to see zra.

AyJay, the uprights called her. AyJay. AyJay. AyJay. Niji practiced the sound whenever it could, shaping it in her likeness, wanting to get it exactly right. She was supreme, the pathway to evolution, and niji would rather endure hunger than miss a chance to observe her.

The next thing niji knew, niji was on its way back to the garj.

[∗∗∗]

The first thing niji sensed when it emerged from its coming-and-going hole in the garj's compacted floor was light: an encouraging sign, for uprights had little tolerance for darkness. It loosed an azrum to mark its arrival and then streamed to the edge of the overhang that protected its comings and goings from view. There, it shaped itself a pair of oculi—*eyz*. Niji had come to rely on these compound sensors for processing light-generated impressions, but they could have been as useless as crustules and niji would have sprouted them anyway because they made niji feel more evolved—like an upright.

As soon as niji's eyz were functional, it glanced in the image-wall's direction. When zra was present, the maytriks was usually bristling with mesmerizing shapes and colors. Usually was not always, however, so niji did not get discouraged when it saw that the maytriks was dormant. Instead, it went looking for her in the usual places. But the zernarz was not tending to the ulvarzi or moving things from one container to another. She was not wielding wind-in-reverse, either, or tapping at the mysterious little slab that niji often saw her holding. Finally, niji had to admit that she was not in the burrow. Niji was disappointed, even though it knew that its expectations had not been entirely reasonable. Zra did not visit the garj as frequently as she used to, and when she did visit, she did not stay as long. It was the same with the other uprights, but niji only mourned AyJay's absence.

Niji was not without consolation, however, for niji had finally figured out how to rouse the maytriks. When there were no uprights to observe, niji watched one of their displays instead. Although AyJay's displays remained niji's favorites, it had sampled many others, some of which featured soft-shelled, non-conjugating uprights making mouth sounds. *Tawkyn*, this was called. And the sounds were called *wrdz*, each of which had meaning. Niji did not yet know the meaning of every wrd that it had absorbed thus far, but it was making progress. Not only that, but it could also reproduce some of those wrdz in its buzzy, breathless way.

Wrdz like: maytrikz awn.

The thought propelled niji toward the image-wall. As it had discovered over the course of many failed attempts, there was more to rousing the maytriz than making the right sounds. Niji had to be in the right place and at the right height as well—factors which had not occurred to niji until it considered the process from an upright's perspective. So it streamed its way to the highest point in the wall's vicinity. The uprights called this place *wrk-bnch*. Niji knew it as an elevated slab of polymerized hydrocarbons. Usually, the top-side of this slab was cluttered with bits and pieces of ulvarzi metal that tasted of combusted exhaust. The only thing that niji sensed now, however, was a strange, free-standing orb. It was a very large orb, almost as big as an upright's top-nob, and it appeared to be smooth. Niji extended a cluster of frani, meaning to get samples. But as soon as niji made contact, the orb rolled away—bottom over top over bottom, right over the slab's edge and into a container full of *toolz*. The resulting crash was very loud.

"Iz Zhat U Cheef?"

Niji flushed, an astonished display, and then flattened its mass against the bench. How had it failed to notice that there was an upright present?

"Im Zoree. I Tryd Too Keep Werkn But I—Pahzd Owt."

Even without looking, niji knew that the sounds had not come from zra. Her exhalations were sharper and higher pitched, not loud and watery. But without looking, niji could only guess at which other upright this might be—and guessing did not agree with zervarzi. So niji extended an oculum beyond the slab's edge. As it angled it this way and that, the upright known as Zyngr happened into view. Instead of moving forward in the focused, fast-paced way that was typical of uprights, he was lurching from side to side—an erratic, unbalanced gait that left him unstable.

"AyjJay? Ar U Theyr? AyJay, I Need Help—Pleez," he said.

Then he stopped moving and slumped to the ground.

Niji had seen uprights slump like that before now. It happened when they went into the little sleep that was like jaza only briefer. Niji had not, however, seen any of them slump like that in mid-stride. Niji watched, waiting for Zynger to wake up and snap back to uprightness. Instead, Zyngr twitched and made tiny wet noises. Curiosity tugged at niji like gravity. If this was not the jaza-like little sleep, then niji wanted to know what else it might be. Zyngr continued to twitch. The urge to investigate grew to irresistible proportions. So niji streamed down from the wrk-bnch and went on the hunt for knowledge.

Zyngr was sprawled flat on his front-side. His un-shelled top-nob was cocked to one side. As niji approached, he let out a shuddering exhalation that almost sent niji streaming the other way. But from this distance, niji could see that there was something wrong with the upright. His eyz were moving back and forth and back again beneath their fleshy coverings. His mouth was a rigid, half-collapsed hole. And—was that water glistening on his outer membrane? What would cause an upright to leak like that? Niji streamed closer and then closer still, abandoning caution for the taste of airborne humidity. It had never been this near to a half-shelled upright. It would never have imagined that they were so warm. Or so moist.

And what was that oozing out of the meaty, two-holed nob in the center of his face?

The ooze looked like protoplasm. But niji was not content with that impression and so helped itself to a sample. To niji's surprise, it tasted semi-molten proteins, dead and dying single cells, free-ranging memory strands that felt like conjugal matter, and even a few bits of inorganic matter. Zhee! Niji could not resist investigating further. It extended several clusters of frani into the holes from which the ooze was running. The feedback was immediate, and sensational. The holes were actually tunnels of hot, swollen membrane. The tunnels were lined with bristles that directed the flow of ooze. And what was this further up the passageways—fluid-filled cavities? Was this why uprights were so moist?

As niji explored Zyngr's inner spaces, the upright began to swat at niji's central mass and make urgent noises. Niji understood this to mean that he wanted niji to withdraw, but niji could not bring itself to do so. Its zervarzi sensibilities had been denatured by excitement and heat. Now primitive greed held sway and its only thought was, 'More!'

The next thing niji knew, it was discharging vytzi into Zynger's passageways.

Niji had not meant to release the probes, for even in a frenzy it knew that inferiors never fed on superiors. But its last catch had done nothing to boost its energy levels and all this activity had depleted them even further. So as it struggled to maintain its hold on Zyngr, it had somehow confused the upright's attempts to dislodge it with a prey-tickle and instinct had done the rest.

"Zhit!"

The sound sobered niji faster than a blast of cold air, for niji would have recognized one of zra's exhalations under any circumstances. Before it had a chance to react in any way, though, Zyngr went from front-side down to back-side down—a swift and quite disorienting realignment. It sensed another, "Zhit!" and then felt something seize its central mass. A single glance told niji that the something was an upright—AyJay! And the intensity of her grip made it clear that she wanted niji to withdraw from Zyngr immediately. But desperate as niji was to please the zernarz, it did not want to extract itself while its vytzi were still in Zyngr—not because it would suffer for their loss but because Zyngr might.

So instead of letting go, niji dug in and released the recall chemical.

AyJay continued to squeeze and tug. Niji continued to resist. But the upright was strong, remarkably so. And Zyngr's slick inner passageways offered few frani-holds. So AyJay dislodged niji, frani-cluster by frani-cluster. The next thing niji knew, it was suspended in mid-air, dripping ooze and unabsorbed vytzi. It knew it had left many more vytzi behind.

"Zhit," zra said again.

Niji angled an oculum in the sound's direction and then flushed with joy as the zernarz came into view. The gold patch on her upper shell was up, revealing her inner tob-nob. Her eyz were very round. Her mouth was pinched. Niji understood that she was not pleased to see it. Niji also understood that this could be its only chance to impress her before she summoned wind-in-reverse. So niji shaped itself a sound-maker and did its very best.

"GeeZuz AyJay," it said.

CHAPTER 12

"SHIT!" AJ SAID, AND began undoing safety catches with a swiftness born of urgency. Val slung himself into the cab just as she popped the last clasp.

"What's up?" Val asked

"I got an SOS on Singer," she said.

He reached over and killed the engine. "I'm going, too."

No way was she saying no to that. Because who knew what was waiting for her back at the garage? Singer could be OD or out of his mind from pain. In either case, he could be too much for her to handle on her own. Better safe than sorry. Plus, Val had more experience with Pigeon Pox than she did. If Singer's woes were physical rather than mental, Val might have a better idea about how to treat them.

"You got a scoot?" she asked, as she climbed down from the cab.

"Negative." He was already on the ground and waiting for her. "I drove the APC back from its weekly maintenance visit this morning."

"We'll have to double up on mine then," she said. "It's parked by 242—"

"I'll get it," he said, and took off before she had a chance to give the order. Typical. But as irritating as that chivalrous or chauvinistic habit could be when all was well or at least routine, AJ was nothing but grateful for it now. As she waited for him to return, she pinged Singer.

"Can you hear me?" she said. No reply. Shit. "Hang in there. We're on our way."

The ride back to the garage passed like a bad dream that kept looping back on itself. She spent most of the time mashed up against the span of Val's back. "Hang tight," he'd tell her, just before he jumped a bump—as if she didn't have a death-grip on his torso already. Through it all, she kept pinging Singer and listening for some kind of response. But all she ever got was static. By the time they reached the garage, she was almost frantic to be on her own two feet again and doing something.

"Secure the scoot," she said, jumping off while he was still powering down the engine. "I'll meet you in there."

He grabbed her by an arm. "Maybe I should go in first."

"If anything happens to me, you're in charge," she said. "But not until then."

Then she pulled free of his grip and dashed toward the pedway. As soon as she was inside, she tried once again to raise her MIA crewman. "Singer," she said. "We're here. Ping if you can hear me." Nothing. Shit. She flipped up her face plate, grudgingly, and tried shouting. "Sound off, Johnny! Any way you can."

Val appeared at her elbow. "Anything?" he asked.

AJ silenced him with an upraised hand. For just as he spoke, she thought she'd heard something. Moments later, she thought she heard it again: a faint, bowel-loosening whimper. It was quite possibly the last sound she ever wanted to hear again and yet she had no choice but to beg for more.

"Don't stop now, Singer. We're coming!"

They found him face-down in a twitchy heap in the 'bot bay. Relief flared like fireworks in AJ only to fizzle into cold apprehension as she noticed the dark brown, half-coagulated puddle next to his face.

"Is that—blood?" she asked Val, whispering for no defined reason.

"Could be," he whispered back. "Could be virus-related. Or," he added, pointing to an APC ball-bearing that had found its way into a box of tools, "this could've caught him in the face on its way down from wherever."

That seemed like a plausible explanation. Accidents happened on RSOs, especially when people were distracted—or out their minds with pain. And this far away from home, unfair was a relative term.

"OK," she said. "Let's roll him over and have a look."

An instant after they flipped Singer, AJ found herself wishing that Singer had caught a ball bearing in the chops. Because that semi-clotted blob wasn't blood, it was a Q—and it had a host of tentacles stuffed up Singer's nose. His eyes were rolled back in his head. His face was a rictus of horror that AJ couldn't help but imitate. This alien was larger than the last one: bigger than a puppy, broad as a plate. And it was pulsating like a flaccid heart. If Singer hadn't wigged from stage four pain, this—this invasion had to have turned him freaked-side out. She glanced at Val in the hope that he would somehow dilute the horror, but he had frozen up like a hunted thing, and his spacer-pale face had gone white. She recognized the look.

Jesus, AJ, do something.

And of course, the shop-vac was nowhere in sight.

So what else could she do but take matters into her own hands?

The Q warped like a mushy water balloon when she grabbed it and then almost squirted out of her hand. "Slippery little bastard," she growled, but boneless probably described it better. She redoubled her grip and then tugged, not too hard in case those tentacles were expendable like gecko tails but not that gently, either, because adrenaline was sizzling through her veins and this sucker had to go. As she pulled, Singer let out another gut-wrenching whimper.

"You're going to be fine, Johnny," she said, mostly because she didn't know what she was going to do otherwise. TSC chip-trained all of its field officers in emergency medicine, and over the years, she had had plenty of opportunities to transform that knowledge into skill. But she didn't have any kind of training, chip or real-time, on alien-inflicted injuries.

Or alien extraction.

The Q was resisting, not violently but in a dug-in way, like a big, throbbing tick that had embedded itself in an island dog's ear. And every time AJ tried to dislodge it, it changed colors: brown to red to grey and every angry shade in between. Could be a threat display, she thought—the final warning before the serious firepower came out. Crud. Why couldn't the thing just be scared like she was? Like Singer must be. She tugged again and felt the alien give a little. She knew then that she was going to win this contest and tried to imagine how it was going to play out. In the best case scenario, the Q came spurting out of Singer's nose DOA like an extraterrestrial miscarriage. The worst case was pretty much the same as the best case except it came out alive and was more like afterbirth. The Q gave again. She tightened her grip, meaning to press her advantage.

"You're mine now, you little—" Shit, she meant to say, but gabbled instead as a thick, bulb-tipped tentacle snaked up from the Q's underside and blinked at her. An eye-stalk? Really? Figures she'd pick now to have a psychotic break.

"Shit!"

That was Val, who had apparently returned from his Q-induced out-of-body experience just in time to see the alien bat its nonexistent eyelashes at her. She could imagine the look on his face—horror crossed with revulsion, a slack-jawed WTF.

"Get the vac," she whispered.

"Are you kidding me?" he fired back. "Look at that thing, it's huge!"

"Then get something else," she said, straining the words through gritted teeth. "A bin will do."

"A storage bin?" Val echoed, and again she could imagine his expression: bug-eyed with indignation, every hair on his face on end. "Jesus, AJ, just kill the damn thing."

"Not till we know if it did anything to Singer," she said. "If it did, we might be able to—" She couldn't think of the word, possibly because it did not yet exist. "Just go and get a bin, Val. Now!" she added, and channeled her impatience with him into a vicious tug

All at once, the Q lost its grip. Tentacles began sliding out of Singer along with an ocean of snot. The next thing she knew, she was holding a drippy, glistening blob out in front of her like an overfull diaper. As she stood there gaping, too shocked to do anything else, the Q began to rearrange its still-writhing tendrils.

"Shit," she said, and Val, still at her elbow, echoed the sentiment.

Another eyeball-on-a-stick appeared, and then a pair of bristly fifiks. And just when she thought the situation couldn't get any creepier, those fifiks began rubbing against each other, generating a series of soft but distinct buzzing noises that sounded disturbingly familiar.

She snapped her head in Val's direction and said, "Did you hear that?"

He nodded. "Jesus, AJ."

"Yeah, that's what I thought," she said, and then nudged him with the toe of her boot. "I'm still waiting on that bin."

"Oh. Yeah. Sorry," he said, in the distant tone of a man who's caught in a dream. "On it."

He disappeared, but she knew by the racket he was making that he hadn't gone far. In his absence, the now placid Q stared at her—an intense, unblinking scrutiny. Then it made that series of sounds again.

"GeeZuz AyJay."

She gave it a shake. Bad alien. Bad. "What the hell am I supposed to do with you?" she said. "What the hell were you thinking?"

It stared at her. *No comprendo.*

"Yeah, right," she said.

Val returned with a mid-sized bin with scuffed sides and greasy smudges. His face plate was down now. And who could blame him after what they had just seen? He cracked the lid open, presenting just enough clearance for her fist and its overlapping contents. She thrust the Q into the box as if it were a percussion grenade and then withdrew like she was afraid of losing her arm.

"Seal it up with SBF," she said.

"With pleasure," he said, and pulled a roll of duct tape from a pocket in his habby.

As he went to work on the container, she turned to check on Singer. He was completely limp now. His eyes were shut, his face was ashen, and his nose was free-flowing. Instinct insisted that she contain the infection so she reached down and closed his face-plate. Val noticed and nodded approvingly.

"Good idea," he said, as he topped his seal off with one last layer of tape. "There's no telling what this monster left behind." He rapped the bin with his knuckles, trying to startle the Q. But all it did was swivel its eye-stalks toward the sound. "You look like an ostomy bag with eyes and bad skin. Can you say that, Bob? Ostomy bag." Then he turned back to AJ and said, "Do you think it really understands the sounds it's making? Or is it just a clever mimic?"

"Fifik," she said. The adrenaline rush was starting to wear off now, and a great big wave of fatigue was rolling in to fill the void. The last thing she wanted to do was go another round with Val over what to do with the Q, especially since he was bound to throw this incident in her face—and then rub her nose in it. She needed a chance to regroup and organize her thoughts. "I know you want to talk about this," she said, "but let's take care of Singer first. OK?"

"Absolutely," he said. "I'll get the scoot and take him to the boat. Meet you there?"

"Negative," she said. "Bring the doc here." His head took a contrary slant—questioning her judgment yet again. And he wondered why his mother had threatened to strangle him. "He's not getting back on the boat until I'm sure he's not a threat to the rest of us," she said. "If push comes to shove, this place is expendable."

"Oh. Right," he said, and off he went.

"Doc's coming," she told Singer. "You're going to be fine."

But was he? She couldn't help but worry. What if he had brain damage? What if the Q had turned him into a Trojan horse—or an incubator? What if—? Crud, she didn't have the energy for this kind of suspense. She felt like bombed out ruins inside and out. Adrenaline hangovers were the worst. She pinged Val, but got no reply. She figured he had his top off and left a message to bring some stim back with the doc. Then, because she didn't want to get back on the what-if wheel, she gingerly slid Singer's face-plate open.

At first glance, he looked a lot better than she thought he would. His skin tone was back to normal as was his temperature. His nose was still runny, but there was no blood in the discharge and no—wait. What was that floating in the mucus? Tiny white bumps? There weren't very many of them, and they were smaller than pinhead, but she was pretty sure that they weren't normal. As she watched, one bump did a leisurely one-eighty and began moving against the flow. Crud, she thought, and closed Singer back up. Then she pinged Val again. When she was invited to leave another message, she shouted, "What's taking you so friggin' long?"

Then she turned to glare at the Q.

"Why'd you have to go and do a thing like that?" she asked. As if it knew what she was talking about. As if it were capable of explaining. As if it weren't a grotesque little monster that had just seeded her crewman's head with its larva or eggs. "You really screwed the pooch this time."

The Q was looking right at her with a calmness that belied its captivity. It seemed very different from the alien that she had vacuumed up at the beginning of this misbegotten adventure: larger, more developed, uglier, an ostomy bag with eyes and bad skin just like Val said. But in spite of the crab-like eyes and those bizarre buzz-thingies on its back, AJ had the feeling that this was in fact that same alien. And while nothing about its crustacean-like gaze suggested cognitive thought, AJ could not shake the suspicion that it was in fact intelligent. Not clever, not imitative, but possessed of an intellect. A credit to its gene pool, no doubt.

"I can't let you go," she said. "You know that, don't you? You attacked two of my people."

"GeeZuz AyJay."

"Yes. That's me—AJ," she said. "And you are Bob."

Bob turned a startling shade of green. AJ didn't know what to make of the change—or the color. It was a lush, vibrant hue that reminded her of Terra rather than this gloom-shrouded rock.

"You'd make a bunch of lab-jacks very, very happy," she said, and then abandoned her contemplation of the Q's unlikely coloring as Singer stirred. "Welcome back, Johnny," she said, giving him a gentle pat on the chest. "How you feeling?"

"Chief?" Singer said, in a wan, played-out voice. "Wha—what happened?"

She caught his hand as he reached for one of his helmet release. "I know that a draft of cool air on your face would probably feel real nice right about now," she said, "but it would be better if you stayed intact for the time being. OK?"

"Why?"

"You had a Q on your face." She did a quick-check on Val's avatar: it was parked in the boat, going nowhere fast. What the hell was his problem? "We removed it, but—" There was nothing in the protocol chips about how to break this kind of news so she decided to let him have it fast and straight. That was the way she would want it. Maybe. "There's a chance it might've laid some eggs in you."

He reached for his helmet with both hands—an instinctive reflex, get me out of here! But he managed to stop himself before he cracked the seal. AJ didn't know if she would have been as restrained in his place. And instead of humming, he lapsed into deafening silence.

"Don't worry," she said, trying to keep him from slipping into fear-infested catatonia. "We're going to take care of you. Val's going to be here with the doc any minute now."

"It's weird," Singer said, and his tone was detached, almost whimsical. "I don't feel bad. In fact, I feel almost OK—a little depleted maybe, but not wasted." He paused as if to confirm some physiological impression and then added, "The pain's going away."

"What?" She hadn't even been thinking in that direction yet. There was too much happening on too many levels. "That sounds like shock talking to me."

"I'm telling you," Singer said, regaining a measure of animation in his tone. "I feel better."

She wasn't going to argue with a claim of 'better'. But she couldn't bring herself to buy into it, either—not after what she had seen. But before she had a chance to say anything, Val finally reappeared with the doc.

"Sorry it took me so long," he said, before she could shift into alpha bitch mode, "but we got a call-in while I was at the boat and there was nobody there to take it but me."

"You could've answered my ping," she said, as she grabbed for the doc. Then the import of what he had said hit her with the flattened clang of a ringside bell. A call-in? But that could only mean—

"*The Bonhomie* is back?"

"Yes, ma'am," he said, in a lively tone.

Relief skipped through her—not abandoned, not deserted, not marooned! She thumped Singer on the chest. "Did you hear that, Johnny?" she said. "*The Bon* is back! Let's get you sorted out so we can go home."

"Yes, ma'am!" he said.

She went to enter his specs into the doc-box only to discover that Val had already done so. Nice. The man knew how to keep his junk from getting roasted, if only just barely.

"Lie flat on your back," she told Singer, "and flip your plate."

She was happy to see that his nose had stopped running. She was even happier to see that he was smiling—after all he'd endured over the course of this shift. And why not? Their ride was here. They were getting out of here!

Going home.

"This thing is ancient," she said, as she positioned the doc over his eyes and nose, "so the diagnostics will probably take a while to run. Try not to move until you get the all-clear, OK?" At his murmured OK, she hit the run button and then went to talk to Val. Because as thrilled as she was that *The Bon* was back, something about the ship's return kept snagging the backside of her brain. And now that she had a moment to think about it, she knew what that catch was. The timing was wrong. The math didn't add up.

"So how'd they manage an early arrival?" she asked. "I didn't think that was possible."

"Neither did I," Val said. "But apparently, some mega-genius in the astrophysics lab figured out a better way to predict the wormhole's comings and goings. So *The Bon* got a better jump on the current interval and caught a good wave. That put her on this side of the APW nine days early. She'll be pulling into orbit in twenty-eight hours."

"Twenty-eight hours?" she said, thinking out loud. "That's no good."

Val laughed. "How do you figure?"

"We won't be ready," she said, feeling twinges of panic. "The MF isn't due to hit c-point for another fifty hours—give or take, and you know how much taking this rock does. Meanwhile, we've got seven turbines to plant with one man down and a power station to de-bug and make operational. There's no way we can do all of that before *The Bon* gets here."

"Doesn't matter," Val said.

If she'd had a microgram of energy to spare, she might have throttled him for being so shortsighted. As it was, she had to settle for snapping at him.

"Of course it matters," she said. "If they put in early, they'll leave early. And if the job isn't done by the time they're ready to go, they'll make us stay until it is and I—" Her breath thickened in her throat, filling her with an urge to hum. "I can't do this anymore, Val. Don't you see? I'm—"

"You're done. I know," he said. "But you can relax. Shingo won't make you stay if you don't want to."

Just like that, all of AJ's long-submerged suspicions about her nemesis's most trusted LT came bobbing back to the surface like a badly weighted corpse. "You talked to Shingo?" she asked. At his nod, she glanced at the Q. It was still staring at her. "Did you tell him about our little—complication?"

"I left that for you," Val said, and while AJ didn't want to, she grudgingly believed him. "He's not going to take the news well, you know."

"TFB," she said. "Whoever takes charge of this outpost is going to need to know."

"Actually," he said, in a heel-dragging tone, "Shingo's taking command."

"What?" That didn't make sense. Why would TSC banish one of its top guns to a half-constructed frontier fueling station on the far side of the wormhole? "He must've pissed off the wrong person big-time."

"I believe he volunteered."

Well. That was disappointing. But there were still things to relish about his appointment. He would be miserable on this rock—miserable and isolated and deprived. Just try getting oolong tea here, Shingo-san! The best thing was, she wouldn't be around to see any of it. She was going home ha-ha and could not stop herself from gloating just a little.

"Maybe I'll present him with a mascot when he lands," she said, glancing at the Q again. "Maybe I'll slip it in his habby and seal them up together."

"Not funny, AJ," Val said, ever the dour-puss when it came to the alien. "That thing is dangerous, and should be destroyed before it can attack anyone else."

A tiny green ping cut him off—the doc signaling the end of Singer's exam. A moment later, it pinged again with a diagnosis. She was quick to capitalize on the distraction. "OK, Johnny," she said, as she lifted the doc-box from Singer's face. "Let's have the verdict."

A drum-roll started in her head as she scrolled past the jingo-laden list of tests run and results obtained—a beat riddled with as much dread as suspense. But when she finally got to the verdict, that rhythm acquired a brighter cadence. "Evidence of recent inflammatory response present in sinus cavities," she said, reading aloud, "but the causative agents have been denatured. Unidentified organisms present in sinus discharge, but no internal infestation detected. Samples being analyzed for ID purposes. Time until completion unknown.

"You hear that, Singer?" she said, flipping up her plate like a handful of confetti. "You're clean. You can go back to work."

He pushed himself into a sitting position, grinning every inch of the way. "Just tell me where you want me," he said.

"How 'bout we start you off with a double shift out on the farm?" she said, grinning back so he'd know that she was teasing. "After that, you can get to work on the power station."

"Anything you say, Chief," he said. "Really. I'm feeling better and better by the minute."

"Really?" she said, as in was it really that hard to tell when she was joking? She glanced at Val. He'd popped his top and was scowling at her like bad weather on the horizon. She could not resist seeding those thunder-clouds a little more as payback for talking to Shingo behind her back. "Do you suppose the Q had anything to do with your amazing recovery?"

Surprise upended Singer's grin, and then mellowed into thoughtfulness. "I don't know, Chief," he said. "It's possible, I guess. I've never had a flare-up die back this fast."

"It could have been a mild flare-up," Val said, looking at Singer like a man betrayed. "I hear those tend to die back sooner."

"If you say so, LT," Singer said.

"And what do you think would've happened if the Chief hadn't pulled that thing off of you when she did?" Val asked, trying to back Singer into his corner.

But Singer remained surprisingly neutral. "I don't have any answers, LT," he said. "All I'm saying is that I feel good enough to go back to work."

But AJ wouldn't have put him back in the field now even if she was months behind schedule with no hope of relief. That would have made her as ruthless as

Shingo, and she'd rather blow her deadline than suffer such a comparison.

"I appreciate your willingness to soldier on," she said, "but I was kidding. You're not field-ready yet. Your habby was breached and needs to go through D-Con. You should spend some time with the sanitizer, too—just in case you're still shedding 'unidentified organisms.' And once your body finishes processing everything it's just been through, I'm guessing it's going to need some downtime. So go on back to the boat and take care of yourself. Next shift it will be business as usual."

She offered him a hand up. His grip, she noticed, was surprisingly robust. "AJ?" he said, as she ushered him toward the pedway. She arched an eyebrow, encouraging him to continue. "I wanted to say—that is, I've been thinking and—" He snuck a look at Val, swallowed hard, and then blurted, "Don't kill the Q on my account, OK?" An instant later, he was off. As soon as he was out of earshot, she turned to Val and said, "Did you notice? No humming."

"Call Ripley's," he deadpanned. In an equally flat tone, he said, "You are going to kill the thing, right?"

Single-minded bastard. What was the big rush?

"I haven't decided yet," she said.

"What's to decide?" he said. "It attacked Singer. It's probably the same one that attacked me."

So. He had reached that conclusion, too. She wondered how they could think so much alike and never see eye-to-eye. "I'll admit," she said, "it certainly looked like an attack from where we were standing. But the doc says it didn't do any damage. And you heard Singer. He used to be a huge Q-phobe. Now he's on their side."

"He said not to kill it on his account," Val said. "He didn't say not to kill it for other reasons. Why are you dragging your feet on this?"

She couldn't say, exactly. It would certainly be easier to just kill the thing and be done with it. History would exonerate her—there had been extenuating circumstances, two crewmen attacked, and she had done what was necessary to get that crucial first Farside seed back on track. But was it necessary? Really?

"Well?" Val prompted.

"It knows my name," she said. "I heard it. You heard it. That has to count for something."

"Why?"

Again she found herself at a loss. She didn't have a convincing argument or even a few profound words, only an abiding sense that it would be wrong to kill the Q just because it was scary. GeeZuz AyJay.

"Because it feels wrong, that's why." When he made a disgusted sound in his throat, the prelude to more badgering, she added, "I'm not saying I won't do it. I'm just not going to do it now. And TFB if that doesn't work for you."

That wasn't the end of it; she could tell by the stubborn set of his jaw. But before either of them could launch the next round, the pedway door slid open and Azu came running in like the boat and everything in it was on fire. Her immediate thought was that Singer had relapsed. Then Azu flipped his face-plate up to expose a mega-watt grin.

"I got great news, amigos," he said, and did a quick two-step. The lights in his eyes were dancing, too. "*The Bon*'s back."

"Singer must be feeling better," Val said, in a near-grumble. "Because it sure as hell didn't take him very long to spread the word."

The lights in Azu's eyes skidded to a momentary stop. "How would Singer know? He was in the SU when the call came in."

"Wait," AJ said, trying to stay on track. "You took a call from *The Bon*?"

"Yeah," he said, "it came in while I was having breakfast. Com-officer said CSO wants to talk to you and nobody but you ASAP. He's going to keep pinging in half-hour intervals until he reaches you."

Resentment broke open in her like a badly healed scar. As if she didn't have plenty of other, better things to do than hang around in the boat waiting for his lordship's ping. And when they finally did connect, he'd probably take her to task for not being out in the field. But as much as she wanted to grumble about the nervy bastard, she was not about to give Val or anybody else the satisfaction.

"Holy mother! It's got eyes!"

That was Azu. He was crouched in front of the Q's makeshift cage. The look on his handsome face was a mixture of wonder and mesmerized horror.

"Stay away from that thing," Val said, a half-tone short of a bark. "We just got done pulling it off of Singer."

GeeZuz AyJay.

"Why don't we all go back to the boat?" she asked, uncomfortable with the thought of leaving Val alone with the Q. "We've all earned a little break, and the remainder of this shift is a lost cause anyway."

"Sure thing, chief," Azu said, still gaping. "Whatever you say."

[✶✶✶]

They were just filing in from the airlock with the comm board started to flash and chirp as if to celebrate the incoming call. AJ pulled her helmet off as if it were a certain somebody's head. She was so not ready for this. She needed energy, a clear head, a pulse to interact with Shingo. Had she told Val to bring her a stim? Had she taken it already?

"Aren't you going to get that?" Val asked.

"You pick it up," she said. "Tell your boss that I'll be with him as soon as I finish my toilette." A flagrant fiction, deliberately tendered. She wanted Shingo—and his 'ling—to know exactly how much she appreciated being summoned. He shot her a half-puzzled, half-reproachful look which she dismissed with a shrug. "Do it," she said. "I'm not doing anything else until I secure the doc."

But that was just an excuse to raid the medi-cab for stim. She left the doc on the common area pull-out because it was still processing information about the unidentified organisms and she didn't want the eventual results to fall prey to out-of-sight-out-of-mind syndrome. Then she fixed herself an instant caffeine chaser and made sure that Shingo could see the steaming container when she nudged Val out of the comm-chair. As she sat down, she said, "Chief Johnson here, reporting as requested. What seems to be the problem, Commander?"

The corners of Shingo's mouth seemed to flicker as if he were trying to contain his disapproval, but that could have been an optical illusion because his tone was as neutral as ever. "There's no problem," he said. "I simply wanted to be the first to congratulate you on the completion of your historic mission."

"Thanks," she said, but she was thinking Yeah, right. "The only problem is, the job's not done yet."

"Val assures me that you've made remarkable progress," he said. "I am most eager to get a firsthand look at what you have accomplished."

"I respectfully request that you delay your arrival by seventy hours," she said. "The power station will be operational by then and the MF will be self-contained. It will be easier for us to make those things happen within the prescribed timeframe if we don't have to deal with a distraction as exciting as incoming personnel."

"I appreciate your dedication, Chief," he said, as smooth as ice. "You and your team have done a remarkable job in the meager time allotted to you. I can only hope that the transition team will accomplish as much as quickly."

"Transition team?" she asked, pouncing on that before she had a chance to think about what she was doing. Must be the stim kicking in. "Why do you need a transition team? The MF is still three months away from completion. Hydrogen fuel production can't start until then. There's nothing to transition to."

"You would have no reason to think otherwise," he said, deadpan as ever. "But circumstances have changed. Just before the APW closed last interval, the RT array on Mars picked up an Un transmission."

Fresh Un-fuzz—after fourteen years of silence? That definitely qualified as a significant development. But was it good news or bad?

"Our scientists have determined that it was threatening in nature."

Bad, then. But even as her astonishment began to curdle into something that felt a lot like disappointment, Meli piped up. *When did our scientists learn to speak Un?*

"The council convened and voted to secure a defensive line on this side of the APW," Shingo went on. "So in addition to serving as a post-APW fueling station, Farside is going to become a personnel hub."

Which was sneak-speak for military base.

Now AJ understood why he'd volunteered for this command. Everything on this side of the APW was going to be his domain.

"But you can't do that," she said, falling prey to another stim-driven disconnect between mind and mouth. "Recon got it wrong. This planet is inhabited." Shingo's eyes went as round as O-rings, a look of raw surprise. She did not give him a chance to recover. "We believe that the dominant life-form was partially responsible for the seed's failure to germinate."

A robo-voice said, "Please hold." An instant later, the comm-screen went gray. Shingo would no doubt blame the interruption on technical difficulties when he returned, but AJ knew what had really happened. Her news had shocked the crap out of him and he had turned off his comm-screen to regroup in private. Good. The larger the impact, the better.

"Are you out of your mind?" Val said, all but hissing in her ear. "What do you think you're doing?"

She swiveled to face him. She didn't understand why he looked so angry, and so parried his scowl with one of her own and said, "I'm trying to protect the Q."

"By surprising and embarrassing Shingo?" he said, switching from anger to towering incredulity. "Jesus, AJ, really?"

"Embarrass him?" she said, ready and willing to own to surprising him just because she wanted him to know what it felt like. But she wouldn't have thought it possible to discomfit him until she realized that surprising a man who glorified composure was the same as embarrassing him. "I—oh."

"Oh," Val said, a sarcastic echo. But before he could turn the sound into a full-fledged sneer, Shingo's image reappeared on the comm-screen. All traces of distress were gone from his face. He was back to his usual inscrutable self.

"Forgive the interruption," he said blandly. "We had—technical difficulties. Now let us get back to these aliens of yours. Are you telling me that they are hostile?"

"Negative," AJ said, disregarding the image of Singer in a Q headlock that sprang immediately to mind. "Their involvement in the seed's shutdown appears to have been accidental. I do not believe that they bear us any ill-will."

"I see," Shingo said, although she was almost certain that he didn't. "And would you say that these aliens are intelligent?"

"Negative," Val said, before AJ could decide how much she ought to say. "They're sub-zero-tech, with no obvious communication or organizational skills. We're not even sure if they have brains."

GeeZuz AyJay.

"Are they going to be a problem?" Shingo asked, and again, Val jumped in as if it were his place to do so.

"Negative," he said. "They're too small and few in number to be anything other than an incidental pest."

"In that case," Shingo said, "I see no reason to cancel the second seed's deployment. Farside's transition from fueling station to personnel hub will proceed as planned."

"Wait!" AJ said, refusing to be completely muscled out of the conversation. "I agree with Val that the Q probably wouldn't have a significant impact on Terran interests. But what about the flipside—what about our impact on their interests? We don't know enough about them to predict what kind of effect our presence will have on their world. And it is their world, Commander. Let's not forget that."

"My foremost responsibility is to the people of Terra," he said. "It is them and them alone that I must not forget. However," he added, with the beginnings of a smile, "it occurs to me that I should have an expert on these Q on site until we know what to expect of them. If you wanted to serve in that capacity, I would be pleased to sign you on for a three-year. You could oversee their welfare, and make sure that we don't get in each other's way."

She clenched her teeth to keep her jaw from dropping all the way into her boots. The sneaky bastard had played her again. And oh, what an elegant play it was. On the surface, it looked like he was doing the right thing for all the right reasons. But just below the surface, this was payback, him daring her to put up or shut up. How much did she care about those ugly little blobs? And was she willing to give up three more years of her life to protect them?

Bastard! He knew she was fried.

"You'd report to me," Shingo was saying now, "but I grant the members of my staff a great deal of leeway once they've gained my trust."

She tried to catch Val's eye for a little moral support, but he wouldn't look at her. He had probably told Shingo about her plans to retire. He'd probably been the CSO's trusty LT all along. She should've known better than to let her guard down with him.

"You'd be doing your home-world an important service," Shingo went on. "I'm sure the aliens would appreciate a little help, too."

A little help? Ha! The Q were going to need as much help as they could get. Otherwise, they were going to wind up with a Trail of Tears in their history, too. But as right as she was for the position and as right as taking it would be, she couldn't bring herself to accept it—and not just because she couldn't bear the thought of being one of Shingo's 'lings. She simply didn't have anything left in the tank—mentally, physically, or emotionally. If somebody was to cut her right now, she'd bleed stim and concentrated weariness.

"Sorry," she said, instead of thanks. "But as soon as the clock on this gig strikes midnight, I'm retired."

"I do not need an answer immediately," Shingo said. "Think about it for a few days. Perhaps you will reconsider."

"Not likely," she said. Prompted by spite, she added, "LT knows almost as much about the Q as I do. Give him the job."

Shingo's gaze shifted to a point beyond her shoulder—the spot where his LT had been standing only minutes beforehand. But Val had moved to her right, beyond the comm-cam's range, and was now scowling at her like fury incarnate. The sight gave her a pang of visceral satisfaction.

TFB, 'Ling. Time for you to do a little sacrificing.

"An interesting suggestion," Shingo said. "I'll consider it if you decide not to take the job."

"I've decided that already," she said. "Now, if you'll excuse me, I have to get back to work."

But the CSO would not let her out of this awful, awkward conversation and its disappointing ripples. "Nonsense," he said, all tight-lipped munificence. "You and your crew have been working nonstop since you landed. I invite you all to take the next few days off and catch up on your rest."

"But—" *Weren't you listening, butthole?* "The wind-farm's not done yet, and the power station's still off-line. These matters need to be resolved ASAP. Otherwise, the MF—"

"As I told Val," Shingo said, "The MF is no longer a priority. C-point is to be put on hold until the transition team has settled in and installed the necessary security upgrades. The wind farm will have to be expanded to accommodate the second seed's needs and the power station will have to be relocated for logistical purposes. So you see, this project has outgrown you."

So much blood rushed to AJ's head, she thought she was having a stroke. Outgrown her? It felt more like bait-and-switch. And no matter how you phrased it, the cold hard fact was that she had spent the last three months on this rock for nothing. Three months of alien anxiety and hard labor. Three months of stress, deprivation, and stim that had reduced her to a smoldering stub. And his lordship had personally twisted her arm into sacrificing those three months for the greater fucking good. What a bitter way to close out a career. And knowing that Val had been privy to the re-org and not given her a heads-up made the end more galling still.

"However," Shingo went on, as she struggled to keep her bile down, "I am very interested in these aliens of yours. If you feel you must do something, catch one for me. I will have my science officer examine it when we get there.

"That is all for now. Shingo out."

The monitor went black. Her mind blanked, too, leaving a dozen different inner voices to fume and mutter in the dark. Then Val turned up at her elbow and started to say something. She cut him off with an upraised hand.

"Don't," she said. "I'm not interested. In fact, unless it's official business, I don't want to hear from you at all."

But as usual, he only followed her orders when it suited him. "Where are you going?" he asked, as she stormed toward the airlock.

"I've got something to do," she said. "You stay here. I mean it. If you dog me, I'll flag you for disobeying a direct order."

He shot her a half-aggravated, half-pleading look. "C'mon, AJ," he said, "don't be like that. We're done here."

"Not yet we're not," she said, and then set off for the garage.

Catch one for me.

Nope. Not happening.

PART II

CHAPTER 13

AJ STROLLED ALONG THE beach, getting in her morning exercise before the sun got too hot. As she walked, she harvested trash from the high-tide line. There was always something tangled up in the dead, washed-up turtle grass: nylon fishing line, empty bottles, decaying plastic, unpaired flip-flops, crushed beer cans. The park ranger paid her a bounty for such flotsam, but she would have collected it regardless. She wanted to live in a nature preserve, not a garbage dump. And every now and then, her vigilance paid off in other ways. Yesterday, she had found an intact lace murex shell; the week before, a striking piece of sea-glass. Free-traders gave her meat and booze for such things. She did not need to barter for foodstuffs. Thanks to TSC's aggressively generous retirement packet and thirty-odd years of hazard-pay-plus, she was set for the rest of her life and then some. She simply enjoyed the contact and the mental stimulation that trading brought.

A waterlogged coconut tumbled out of the surf. It looked as if it had been out to sea for a long time. She flipped it over with the blade of her foot, idly searching for bait crabs—or maybe a brownish blob with tentacles. Even now, almost a year since her departure from Farside, the Q still infringed on her thoughts with distressing frequency. There were reasons, of course: guilt for abandoning them to Shingo's ruthless ambitions *catch one for me* and regret for recommending his right hand man to be their advocate in her stead. AJ didn't know if Val had taken the job. She didn't know anything about him anymore—and that bothered her sometimes for reasons that refused to yield to a virtual therapist's gentle probing. *Talk to someone*, the hologram had finally advised. Which was funny in a massively ironic way because Shingo had forbidden her to discuss the Q or related matters with anyone aside from authorized personnel. "You will be arrested and charged as a threat to global security if you fail to comply," he'd told her, after she signed off on everything but the non-disclosure law-doc. "People are already worried about the Un." TSC had said the same thing although in more baroque terms when she finally arrived at Gateway, Terra's cis-lunar space complex. Then it hustled her off to this tiny spit of an island. Before the Tsunami That Changed Her Life, it had been the southernmost tip of the Yucatan Peninsula. Now it was part of the Yucatan Archipelago. TSC managed the whole chain as a Global Heritage Site, but occasionally leased parts of it to the "most deserving of its members." At first, the islet had seemed like just what the doc ordered: a place to rest and recover. But as the months went by and her mental acuity returned, she began to sense that her tropical retreat was really solitary eco-confinement. For the most part, she was OK with that. And free-trading in sea-junk kept her from going stir-crazy.

She stopped to admire the multi-faceted glint of sunlight dancing on the surface of an inter-tidal pool. As she did so, a glassy green flash caught her eye. She waded in after it, crane-like in her efforts not to stir up the sandy floor, and in doing so, spooked a juvenile reef octopus. It flushed an angry shade of red, then fired off a round of ink and jetted into a mound of broken coral. Meli had loved octopi. *Watch one sometime, 'Nita; you won't believe how smart they are.* AJ tried to find the back door to the animal's hole, but wound up finding the source of the flash instead—not sea-glass like she'd supposed, but a woman's ring. The stone was rainforest green, dark yet vibrant, an emerald perhaps, not huge but not exactly small either. The band was banged up as things that spent time on the ocean floor usually were, but it had only just begun to acquire a coral overgrowth which meant that it couldn't have been in the water for more than fifty or sixty years. Therefore it was probably tsunami swag, a souvenir from that day in '11 when the Yucatan peninsula broke into pieces and the ocean rushed in to fill in the gaps.

Run, 'Nita!

This ring could have belonged to Meli.

The rational part of AJ understood how unlikely that was. Her mother had preferred turquoise to other gemstones, and her fingers had been too slender for this piece. But the romantic in AJ wanted to believe that the sea had finally given a little something of Meli back to her after all this time. She slipped the band onto her third finger—perfect fit, she had her father's sturdy hands. He'd never worn a ring, not even a wedding band. Don't need one, he used to say. Everyone can see that I'm taken. And it was true. When Meli was around, no one else existed.

AJ's stomach growled. She went to take a sip of habby juice only to laugh, ha-ha, how long was it going to take her to break that habit? Although she would never admit it out loud, she missed her habby sometimes—especially the way it addressed certain basic bodily functions. It had taken her months to get used to eating and preparing regular food all the time. And while she had been much quicker about learning to use the toilet when the urge to evacuate hit, she'd had several mortifying slip-ups over the course of her first weeks here. Fortunately, no one had been around to see.

Her stomach growled again, a throaty squeal that sounded like mango. She hoisted her swag bag, grimacing as her right shoulder fired off a complaint. Nothing like gravity to make a body remember how old it was. Although she did not consciously alter her pace, the walk home seemed to take much longer.

Her place looked like a cross between a solar collector and an antique Airstream camper. It sat with its back to the jungle like a giant silver cigar. The technician who had moored it there claimed that as long as it was properly secured, it could survive anything from a category four hurricane to a tsunami. "Good to know," she'd said, but getting blown or washed out to sea no longer seemed like such a terrible way to go.

She shrugged her swag bag into the storage bin that she had set up next to the hatchway, shed her water mocs at the threshold, and then stepped into the 'mud room' for D-con. One by one, the pest-scan located, identified, and then removed the hitchhikers that she had picked up over the course of her walk. "Two anopheles mosquitoes," it reported, which made her glad that she had gotten a fresh anti-malarial nano-booster. "One salt-water leech." Disgusting creatures, they liked to lodge themselves in a body's dark, moist places. "Twenty-eight sand fleas." Those were the absolute worst, all teeth and reproductive organs. They would've chewed her legs into Braille boards already if one of the rangers hadn't showed her a trick to disable their bite reflex. "Scan complete. Welcome home."

Inside, there wasn't much to see—no art on the walls, no coverings on the floor, just a table, a chair, the king-sized futon that was her one indulgence, and a high-tech strip kitchen for food prep and storage. Decades of remote site living had left her with no knack or affinity for interior decoration. Besides, who needed crap on the walls when you could see a dappled tangle of deep-green jungle through one set of windows and gulls wheeling over an expanse of ocean through another? She went into the kitchen, washed her hands with water from the desalinization unit, and began to fix lunch. Today, she was having a salad made with leftover chicken and some mango on the side. She sampled the meat and mmm-ed out loud. So much better than S-rats! She didn't care how expensive the alternatives were—she was never eating tofu again.

As she was slicing the fruit, a holo-alert popped up from the countertop: perimeter breach on northwestern corner, one human following the inbound trail, no weaponry detected. She was not overly concerned. The ranger stopped by every other week or so to check on her and deliver any supplies she might have ordered. Free-traders visited on a semi-regular basis, too. But there were plenty of other, less well-intentioned types at large—pirates, smugglers, terrorists. Better to hope for the best and prepare for the worst.

"Action desired?" the keeper asked.

"Lock up," she said.

The hatchway's seals snapped into place. Liquid metal shutters slid over the windows. A body would need a fairly serious can-opener to get in now. And she had other deterrents at her disposal. But for now, she was content to have the keeper monitor the interloper's progress.

"One hundred feet and closing."

"Fifty feet and closing."

Whoever he was, he was in a hurry.

"Twenty feet and closing. Activate defenses?"

"Stand-by only," she said, and then hit the PA as a charge built up in the solar collector's main battery. "Stop where you are and identify yourself." When the person pressed on, she said, "Failure to comply will set off security measures that you will regret."

The person skidded to a halt, but could not seem to stand still. "Jesus, AJ, don't make me wait out here," a familiar voice said. "I'm being eaten alive."

WTF?

"Advance to the hatchway," she said. He ran. "Remove your shoes and step inside. D-con will begin immediately." As soon as the pest-scan started to run, she cancelled the alert. The shutters rolled back. The room turned bright. Then the inner hatch opened and Val stumbled in. He was red-faced and sweaty and supremely out of sorts.

"I swear, I will never understand your fascination with this armpit of a world," he said, rubbing at his arms. "It's filled with things that eat people."

"That's just the day shift," she said. "Wait till you see what comes out at night."

He looked up from his scratching to give her a critical once-over. By the time he was done, he'd forgotten all about his itch. "I have to say, hot and sticky seems to agree with you. I don't think I've ever seen you look better."

"That's probably because you've never seen me fully rested," she said.

"I guess," he said, in a dubious tone, and then ran a hand over the top of his own head. "Your hair is longer now, too. It looks—good."

AJ resisted the urge to run her fingers through the coarse salt-and-pepper thatch that she had managed to grow over the course of a year and instead voiced the question that was ringing through her head. "What are you doing here?"

"Do you have anything to drink?" he asked. "My throat feels like it's on fire."

She knew the feeling. It came from dehydration and breathing unfiltered, unconditioned air. "Yeah, sure," she said, and motioned him toward her only chair. "Sit down before you fall down."

"Thanks," he said. "Baggage claim lost my land-legs."

"You want water or spiced tea?" she asked from the strip.

"Water."

He drained the first glass she offered him in one long gulp and then held it out for more—a gesture both childish and disarming. The second glass vanished in a heartbeat, too. But when she tried to pour him a third, he declined, saying, "I don't want to leave you short."

"I have my own DSU," she said, "so feel free." And since it was sliced already anyway, she offered him some mango, too. "Try it," she said, when he hesitated. "It's fresh off the tree."

Shortly thereafter, the fruit was gone and Val was licking his fingers clean. "That," he said, "was incredible. It might've ruined me for the dehydrated stuff. If I get space-scurvy, it'll be your fault."

"So you're not here to investigate retirement opportunities," she said. His lips twitched, him politely suppressing a sneer. "And I'm pretty sure you didn't venture into the Terran-eating tropics for the sole purpose of visiting me." His mouth took a more ambiguous turn: him trying not to hurt her feelings. Ha. As if he had that power. "That means TSC sent you." His eyebrows arched, signaling a direct hit. "That means they want me back. I'll save you the trouble of asking. The answer is no. NFW."

"But that's just it, AJ," he said, looking supremely out of sorts again. "TSC doesn't want you back.

"The Q do."

Her thoughts swirled like something big and heavy going down a flush toilet. She didn't want any part of the stuff that was left behind. "What makes you—" The question stuck in her throat. "What makes you say that?"

"They've been asking for you," he said.

GeeZuz AyJay.

The swirling accelerated. She had to set her hands on the table to steady herself. "They? I don't understand."

Val's agitation constricted into something harder and shrewder. "C'mon, AJ, it's just the two of us here. Drop the innocent act, OK?"

Really? He thought she was acting? She couldn't help but marvel at his ongoing ability to offend her regardless of the circumstances. She also couldn't stop herself from returning fire. "Why don't you tell me what you think I'm guilty of first?"

"All right," he said. "You said you killed Bob, but you didn't, did you."

Oh. That. She licked her lips, tasting mango juice and old righteousness. "I believe my exact words were: 'I got rid of it.'"

"And what does that mean, exactly?"

Catch one for me.

She knew then as she knew now what would've happened to Bob if she had handed him over to the CSO and his science officer. Bye-bye, blob. The Q hadn't done anything to deserve such an end.

"I loaded the Q's container onto the crawler and drove out to the wilderness," she said, remembering how anger had goaded her on and fatigue had held her back. "Then I unloaded the container and removed the duct tape that you'd used to seal it up. I knew the Q would find a way out of the container eventually. But I never dreamed that it would find its way back to the outpost."

"Yeah well," Val said, "it did. And apparently it brought a bunch of friends with it because the place is crawling with Q now. And all of them seem to know your name."

Crud. Her father used to say that no good deed went unpunished. She had never quite believed it until now. What had she done?

GeeZuz AyJay.

"I can see why you turned Bob loose," Val said. "What I don't get is why you misled me about it."

Again: really? "You're Shingo's LT," she said. "You would've told him."

Now it was his turn to look affronted. "I was your second at the time, AJ. And I'm my own man. You should've trusted me."

A wave of weariness crashed over her—a taste of the bad old days. She found herself craving something to wash the bitterness away. "I need a drink," she said, "something stronger than water. How about you?"

"The stronger the better," he said.

She went to the kitchen and hauled a full bottle of vanilla flavored vodka out of the freeze. Val made a face when he saw the label, but AJ dismissed his dismay with a shrug. "It was a shack-warming gift from the rangers," she said, as she filled their former water glasses. "And it's all I have on hand."

Particular or not, Val knocked back his drink in a single swig. AJ followed suit, grimacing at the metallic taste of cheap vanillin, and then poured them both another generous round. She could feel the alcohol coursing through her empty stomach and toward her brain. It made everything in its wake feel a little padded. That sense of insulation made her brave.

"OK," she said, "I'm ready now. Tell me everything."

"Do you mind if we relocate before I start?" he asked, glancing at the futon. "I've had a helluva long day."

"Yeah sure," she said, and followed him over there. She made a point of bringing the bottle, too, and refilling their glasses. "There," she said, as she sat down next to him. "We're all set. Now spill."

He picked up his glass and stared at the vodka as if it were a window to the past. "The year started out pretty much business as usual—lots of activity and no Q. We deployed the new seed, expanded the wind farm, and relocated the power station. Then Phase Two started, and alien sightings went from zero to OMG almost overnight. The first few that turned up were singles—you know, like Bob. But then they started appearing *en masse*. They seemed drawn to the new construction sites and, strangely enough, one particular section of the wind farm. As a rule, these Q are larger than Bob. They're more energetic, too, and excitable—rowdy, you could say. The field crews freaked. Shingo had a fit. He put a rush on the perimeter fences and ordered patrols for the infested areas. My job was to make the Q we found on the premises 'go away.' We tried catch and release, but it was like trying to push back space. Every time my guys carted one bunch away, another popped up. Shingo and some of his aides started carrying zaps. 'To help with the relocation process,' he said, even though I haven't met a Q yet that's survived a zapping. At first his brutality seemed to work. Q sightings dropped dramatically.

"Then people started hearing things.

"It started in our old garage—a soft, strange buzzing noise that came and went for no apparent reason. Maintenance decided that there was a short in the matrix and disconnected it, but that only made matters worse. The buzzing gradually grew louder and then more distinct. I realized early on that the Q were making the sounds. But it took me a while to figure out that they were asking for you."

GeeZuz AyJay.

That had to be Bob's doing. Who else? But was he really asking for her? Or was hers the only name that it had managed to learn? Crud. What was that blob thinking?

"Is that it?" she said. "Or is there more?"

Val shrugged. "The buzzing spread to the other outbuildings. Shingo had another fit and sent me here. End of story."

She reached for her drink, hoping to refresh the insulated feeling that was rapidly wearing away. To her surprise, her glass was empty. So was Val's. She refilled both without a word and pretended not to notice that her hand was a bit unsteady.

"If I were you," she said, "I'd take steps to stop the Q from getting into the out-buildings. They're tunneling in, you know. But I don't think they can burrow through liquid metal."

"We put down flooring," Val said, looking both glum and grim. "It didn't do a damn thing."

"Because the Q were already inside?"

"Maybe." He tossed back his drink in a single gulp and then lowered his voice as if he were afraid of being overheard. "But I think they found another way in. I think they figured out how to work the doors."

Just like Bob had figured out how to use the matrix. The thought gave her gooseflesh, but she could not say why.

"Then I don't know what to tell you, dude," she said, "because I'm fresh out of ideas."

But he wasn't. "You have to come back. Productivity is down. Morale is low. Shingo's getting desperate."

"Like I care," she said.

"You should," he said. "A desperate Shingo is a dangerous Shingo. You have to come back and find out what the Q want."

She dug her heels into the ground, a subconscious reaction to the thought of being dragged back to a place that she absolutely loathed. She'd hung up her habby, dammit. Let someone else rise to the challenge for a change.

"Why can't you deal with them?" she asked, waxing petulant. "You've spent more time on Farside than I have. That makes you the leading expert."

Val shook his head—a slow, downcast back-and-forth that broadcast his regrets. "I've tried, AJ," he said. "But the Q aren't interested in me. They want you."

She could feel herself being cornered, boxed in by a bunch of overgrown OCD slugs and a berserker bureaucrat who didn't know the meaning of enough. She had spent most of her life in the dark, working on Terra's behalf. Was it so wrong of her to want to enjoy a few moments in the sun while she still able enough to do so?

"I won't go," she said, digging her heels in even deeper. "You can't make me."

"Jesus, AJ." At first she thought he was mad at her because of his red face and the way he was gritting his teeth. Then she realized that gravity and vanilla-flavored vodka were responsible for the grimace, and that his anger was directed elsewhere. "He said if you don't come back and finish what you started, he'll exterminate every Q on the planet."

That didn't surprise her. She'd never doubted that Shingo was capable of slaughter. No, what surprised her was that he had come right out and said so in such barefaced terms. He must be trying to impress her with his seriousness. Or guilt her—if I do this thing, it will be your fault. Or maybe this was his idea of punishment, payback for siding with those pain-in-the-ass blobs in the first place. This was what came of trying to do the right thing. And she'd learned her lesson. Honest. She wanted nothing more to do with the Q, their planet, or their part of the universe. She was home now, home after a lifetime of service, and home was where she was going to stay. The only thing stopping her from saying exactly that to Val was Meli.

Remember the Trail of Tears, 'Nita.

"Wait," Val said. "What's wrong? Why are you crying?"

She made no reply. She was too busy grieving. Because her mother was right. As much as AJ ached to stay on her island and soak up as much of Terra's degraded splendor as she could before she went to join her ancestors, she couldn't bring herself to abandon the Q to Shingo's final solution.

Meli would've known what to think of her tears *they're just spring-cleaning for the heart*, but they seemed to confound Val. He reached out and then pulled back, reached out and pulled back, and then drew her into the most awkward of hugs. The next thing she knew, they were going at it like hormone-crazed teenagers: sloppy, open-mouthed kisses with vanilla-flavored tongues, and hands all over the place. AJ thought about pushing him away, about shutting the monkey-business down before it went too far because she was too drunk, too stressed, and too damn old for this kind of shit. But the monkey in her wouldn't hear of it. If she couldn't have the life she wanted, then she was going to start giving herself permission to want other things.

CHAPTER 14

Niji emerged from a hastily dug burrow that began to collapse even as niji surfaced. Niji did not care. The hole had been a jaza stop, nothing more. And now that niji had roused from its post-feeding drowse, niji had no further need for such shelter. Niji sampled the surroundings—clear-dark-still, excellent conditions for sky-watching. According to niji's reckonings, the sky-mouth would be opening soon. A sighting would confirm its deductions. A zervarz of niji's vast experience should have been excited by such a prospect. A zervarz of niji's ambition should have been pleased to pursue it. But to niji, it was just another jaza hole. The only thing niji wanted to think about was AyJay.

Where was she?

What was she doing?

Why had she returned niji to the wild in a container?

Niji's preoccupation with zra was not simple fascination. It was compulsion, insistent as hunger. It was relentless, irrational yearning that went against the natural order of things. Lesser evolved beings eschewed contact with their superiors to avoid being taken for food. Only a nijit would be so bold as to seek the company of a supreme being. Yet here niji was, attempting to do just that. Again. Despite having been thoroughly rejected after its last attempt. Niji did not know why it felt to driven. There was no history of obsessive behavior in its memory strands. Focused behavior, yes. Fervent behavior, yes. But not a single instance where niji felt compelled to do something so contrary to its conditioning. Whatever it was that was causing niji to act this way was as new as the uprights—

Wait. What was this? A hindrance of some sort? It tasted of ulvarzi metal rather than rock, and stood so tall and wide that niji could not sense an end to it in any direction. It was also remarkably porous—a span of regularly spaced holes. How curious. Niji streamed through one of the gaps—an easy transit, no effort at all. It tried another gap and then several more. All of them were exactly the same size. The discovery excited niji, for it was obviously an upright thing and obviously made with a varz's convenience in mind. Who other than zra would do such a thing? And for whom other than niji would she do it? Maybe she had reconsidered her rejection of niji.

Or—maybe this hole-y span was some kind of test.

The thought thrilled and inspired niji. Maybe that was why zra had returned niji to the wild in that container! Maybe she wanted to see how clever niji was, how evolved. If niji could not overcome the obstacles that she set in its way, then niji was not worthy of her notice. Yes! That must be it. The zernarz was offering niji a chance to demonstrate its worthiness. And niji was going to do exactly that. No matter how hard or convoluted the journey might be, niji was going to find its way back to the upright burrow and impress zra with its worthiness. Maybe then she would consent to teaching niji the things that niji did not yet know how to imagine.

[⋆⋆⋆]

Shortly after niji cleared the holey-span, niji happened upon a fresh azrum. The marker was rife with wonder and confusion and the precursors of panic. Niji recognized the taste of first encounter immediately. The pervarz who had left the deposit did not describe the encounter or what it intended to do next, but niji had no appetite for such details anyway. The only thing that mattered to niji was that there were uprights or ulvarzi in the vicinity.

Niji had never felt more worthy.

The pervarz's marker was only the first of many that niji encountered as it pursued its still-nebulous journey. A few offered useful navigational hints, but the majority was swarm spoor—foolish nijiti babble. Niji was not surprised by the number of azrumi. The Season of Storms had passed, so varzi would be following the Season of Calm back to this region. Nijiti in particular would be attracted to the abundance of novel stimuli that the uprights generated. Niji did not begrudge the newcomers their experiences. Each to its own was the varzi way.

A glimmer in the distance caught one of niji's eyes. It was blue-white and cool—the light that traveled with uprights. Niji flushed, an elated display, and reoriented its body mass in that direction. The glimmer disappeared as quickly as it had materialized, but niji remained euphoric. It was closing in on AyJay!

Niji caught another glimpse of the light, and then another. Then it sensed something it did not recognize—a swarm of strange, airborne vibrations, each of them low-pitched and repetitive, whoozh whoozh whoozh. It was as if nazza was chasing its own backend. But there was no wind, only a mild breeze, and—wait, what was this? There were objects on the horizon now, objects so outlandishly big, they even appeared large from a distance. Niji strained its eyz to their limits, but could make no sense of what it thought it was seeing—a super-swarm of immobile loops? Some of these loops were still. Others were spinning around and around for no apparent reason. Certain that these were ulvarzi of some sort, niji shifted its course in their direction. For where there were ulvarzi, there were sure to be uprights. And if there were uprights, then zra would be somewhere nearby. Niji began to anticipate their next encounter. It would make the right wrdz and stay very calm and not try to taste anything even if it got the chance. It would show AyJay just how—

An emphatic slick of nijiti spoor disrupted niji's fantasy. The graffiti was very fresh and very excited. Apparently, the swarm was intrigued by the whoozhing ulvarzi and wanted to know more about them—and their upright companions. As soon as niji tasted that, it decided to follow the swarm. Under any other circumstance, it would have gone the other way, for niji were greedy and thoughtless and destructive in their thrill-seeking. But niji was prepared to endure all manner of unpleasantness when uprights were concerned.

So niji trailed after the nijiti and sifted through their droppings in the hope of finding some mention of AyJay. The horizon drew nearer. The whoozhing ulvarzi became larger and louder. The swarm grew increasingly excited. Then a familiar rumble tickled niji's leading edge. The sensation was shallow-cyclical-oncoming. It loosed an azrum, an expression of recognition and joy. The ulvarz called *crawlyr* was coming this way! The rumbling drew closer, then closer still. Blue-white light appeared in the gap between two spinning giants. The next thing niji knew, uprights were streaming forth from that glow and into the surrounding gloom. The uprights were all carrying rods that projected tiny bolts of lightning. They were poking these rods at the ground. Niji wondered what purpose the little lightnings might serve, but before it had a chance to go and investigate, a nijit came streaming full-speed from out of nowhere and slammed into niji. Caught by surprise, niji had no chance to prepare for an impact. Its body mass flattened. Its frani went limp. The last thing niji felt before its senses faded was a deep sense of surprise.

[∗∗∗]

The first thing niji sensed when it returned to awareness was the whoozh whoozh whoozh of the overgrown ulvarzi. It flexed its body mass to shed the chill that had started to creep into its protoplasm and then extended its frani. It sensed no blue-white light, no activity, no nijiti swarm. Niji wondered if this lack was due to trauma from the collision, but the whoozhing convinced niji otherwise. The uprights were gone. Niji had missed a chance to reunite with AyJay—because of a stupid nijit. The recollection raised an irate flush. No forward-thinking varz would race blind in the vicinity of ulvarzi. Such behavior was dangerous. But nijiti were thrill-seekers, reckless in their hunger for excitement. No doubt the swarm had been playing some foolish game and driven the uprights away.

Although irked by the swarm's interference, niji refused to be stymied by it. The uprights would have departed with the crawlyr. That ulvarz left distinctive tracks. So all niji had to do was find those tracks and follow them. Eventually, they would lead niji to the upright burrow.

The plan pleased niji. It shaped itself a pair of eyz for track-searching, but just as it set off in the direction in which it had last seen the crawlyr, it spotted a large nijit sprawled in a nearby sand dune. It appeared to be frozen stupid.

The sighting intrigued niji. Logic held that this was the nijiti that had run into niji. But if that was so, then why had it gone into panic-sleep? If anything, the collision should have sent it into the little-sleep-that-heals and probably not even that, given its far greater mass. Also, where were its swarm-mates? Niji could not sense so much as a trace of their presence anywhere. Nijiti might be greedy and they might be destructive, but they did not abandon still-living members of their own swarm. If nijit had been dead, its swarm-mates would have eaten it before moving on. Niji found these oddities too compelling to ignore. So instead of setting off in search of crawlyr tracks, it indulged in a closer examination of the nijit.

At first glance, it looked no different from any other nijit. They were all oversized and dotted with crustule scars; that was what greed did to a varz. But the sample that niji extracted from the nijit's panic residues was—surprising. So surprising that niji did not want to believe what it was sensing. But there was no disregarding the taste of one's own chemistry. This nijit was an offshoot, one of niji's own clones.

Disappointment formed in niji like ice crystals. Unlike nijiti, who replicated arbitrarily and passed little beyond protoplasm to their clones, evolving intellects like niji divided only in the aftermath of significant experiences so the memory of that experience and its evolutionary potential would not be lost. Niji did not know which momentous event had inspired this clone, but it would have inherited a then-full complement of niji's memories. And knowledge was the pathway to supremacy. Why would any offshoot eschew such a legacy and instead dedicate itself to the pursuit of transient thrills?

The nijit began to twitch its way out of its stupor. Niji waited until it was fully aware and then emitted an electromagnetic micro-pulse that conveyed its presence and status. The nijit loosed an azrum acknowledging niji's superiority and then responded with a docile pulse of its own.

Are you here to feed, zer?

Although niji was in fact starting to feel hunger, it had no intention of eating its wayward clone—at least not until it had satisfied niji's other cravings. But rather than answer an inferior's question, niji pulsed one of its own.

Why did you attack me?

The nijit flushed, a display of humility and mortification. *Such was not my intention, zer. I was possessed by panic. I had no sense of your presence else I would have tried to avoid you.*

What caused this panic?

The nijit flattened, signaling distress. Beads of sweat appeared on its topside. *I do not know how to describe the sensations, zer. My swarm was on its way to explore the whoozh when we happened upon a patch of warm-and-tingly. The sensation was very exciting. We got very high. So when the rumbling came our way, we thought the ground was playing with us. And when we sensed the light that did not burn, we wondered but were not afraid. Then we were beset by the little lightning.*

That did not make sense to niji. The uprights had been carrying the rods that projected lightning. Why would they share such a wonder with inferior beings like the nijiti?

What did you do to merit such attention? it asked.

I do not know, the nijit replied—a typical nijiti response. But there was no denying its distress. The precursors of panic were creeping back into its sweat, a bio-identical tang that left niji feeling a little anxious, too. Under any other circumstances, niji would have abandoned the nijit to break down or recover on its own. But niji had not yet slaked its curiosity and so only withdrew its sensors.

Where is the rest of your swarm? it asked.

Gone, the clone replied. *Destroyed.*

How? Why?

*Zhee! These are memories I do not wish to relive!"

Then let me examine them for myself.

The request shocked the nijit out of its panicky relapse. *You want to—conjugate? With me?*

Niji was well aware that it was an unusual request. Nijiti were not known for the quality of their memories. And zervarzi were connoisseurs who scorned swarm babble. But niji wanted to know what had happened out here in the whoosh, and why. If that meant tapping an inferior for information, then so be it.

Yes, niji said. *I wish to extract those memories from you.*

Will you give me something in return? the clone asked.

I could give you knowledge, niji said, *but why would I? Nijiti do not want to know, they want to feel.*

You know I am one of your buds, the nijit replied. *You know I am more—evolved.* There was no flattery in that pulse, and no conceit, only recognition. *My swarm is gone. Make sense of what happened here for me and I am nijit no more.*

More unusualness: a nijit propositioning a zervarz! And what an intriguing proposal it was, for reasons that had little to do with an inferior's need for insight. If niji shared what niji knew about uprights with this offshoot, then two varzi would possess the information and niji would not have to go through the long, depleting process of creating an entirely new offshoot. And, if in the process, niji reclaimed one of its own from the thrill-seekers, then so much the better.

I will have the memory of your swarm's destruction from you, niji said. *You will have the answers you seek from me. Is this an acceptable exchange? If so, prepare yourself.*

In response, the nijit shifted to expose more of its topside. Soon, a blister appeared on its outer membrane. Niji stroked the welt with a specialized *fran*, teasing the membrane thinner and then thinner still. The nucleus within swelled and softened, then rose toward the stimulus. When it touched the inner membrane, it stuck there and the blister broke. Niji immediately plunged its conjugal tube into the tear and siphoned up the bundle of replicated memories that the clone had pledged. Then it pumped a bundle of its own into the nijit.

The bundle did not contain everything that niji had learned about the uprights, because too much knowledge was worse than none at all to those who were new to thinking. Niji had, however, been generous. So when the nijit started to twitch after niji withdrew, niji was not surprised.

This is—too much. I cannot—this makes no sense!

But now that the exchange had been made, niji's tolerance for the company of inferiors was collapsing. *It will eventually,* it said, offering a last bit of advice in parting. *Sense comes with processing,*

Wait! the nijit pulsed, as niji began to stream away. *Do not leave—yet. What are these upright—things?*

The clone's clinginess offended niji. Niji was zervarz, not some foolish swarm-member! It intended to continue on its way to prove the point, but then the nijit pulsed, *What is—zra?*

Shock disrupted niji's irritation. The nijit had memories of AyJay? Niji had not meant to share its knowledge of her. She was niji's domain, niji's secret. Niji must have been thinking of her while it was assembling the nijit's bundle. Just as niji was thinking of her now.

Zra is the supreme upright. You are to zra as grains of sand are to nazza.

I understand, the nijit said. *What is—Zyngr? What is—green?*

The questions relieved rather than annoyed niji, for they suggested that the nijit's interest in zra was passing rather than specific. AyJay was still niji's domain, still niji's secret. And that was niji's idea of a thrill.

Process what I have given you, niji said. *All will be revealed.*

Then niji went in search of a place to examine its new memory.

[✷✷✷]

Wait! Nijit feels something deliciously new—a diffuse, prickling tingle. It feels like a static shock only sourceless and enduring. It feels like it should hurt but it does not. Nijit dives after the sensation, following it down into the ground. The tingling grows stronger. The regolith grows a little warm. Nijit's senses begin to dip and swirl like schooling zyl.

Zhee! The fun goes on and on and on.

Later, as nijit is lounging on the surface, resting with its mates, they sense an oncoming rumble—a playful little shockwave, or it seems. Then lights break over the horizon like grounded star-stuff minus the heat. Some of the swarm wants to investigate this curious glow, but not nijit. Nijit wants to visit the tingle again. Nijit wants to refresh its high. So nijit tunnels back into the ground. When it surfaces again, topside is a very different place. The swarm is scattered, and its spoor is panicked. The air tastes of spent lightning. Nijit is high and cannot understand why this is so.

A swarm-mate goes racing past nijit, spewing confusion and fear. It is being chased by a fast-moving crunch: the sound of heavy objects striking sand. The impact tremors skid to a stop. The fzzzt of an electrical discharge sings out, filling the air with the tastes of ozone and burnt membrane. The crunching starts up again—this way now! Zhee! Nijit must flee—

There was more to the memory, but niji already knew how it ended—the whole swarm destroyed! And there was no doubt that the destroyers had been uprights. The reason for the destruction, however, remained unclear. The uprights had not consumed any of the nijiti, so they could not have been hunting. And as far as niji could tell, the swarm had not done anything to offend the uprights. But what else could have prompted the uprights to assert their dominance in such an emphatic manner? Could that mysterious tingle be the reason? Maybe it was essential to the uprights' well-being. Maybe the uprights had been protecting it.

Maybe, maybe, maybe. Niji had hoped for something more substantial from the clone's memory strands. But as curious as niji was about the uprights' motives, it never occurred to niji to condemn them for what they had done. The uprights were superior. That made them right. Niji expressed an azrum that described the tickle as a peril and then went in search of crawlyr tracks.

[***]

The crawlyr tracks led niji through a delicious confusion of ulvarzi activity that reminded niji of its first experience with upright things. So much energetic movement and displacement, so many novel tastes and sensations! Niji was glad that it had encountered this activity before now. Otherwise, it might have been tempted to investigate and lost its way. Instead, it stayed focused and followed the crawlyr all the way back to the garj.

The sight of that massive structure infused niji with a sense of warmth. In response, the pressure that had been bearing down on niji all through the wilds began to melt away. This was relief, the sweetest of feelings. How delightful to be able to think of AyJay without feeling her impossible weight on its leading edge.

Now all it had to do was get into the garj and wait for her to appear.

Niji burrowed into the regolith, meaning to tunnel its way into the structure as it had done so often before its expulsion to the wild. But when it tried to break through the garj's compacted floor, it was stopped by a span of ulvarzi metal. Niji tried to surface elsewhere, but was repelled again and again and again. Finally, niji had to conclude that the uprights had covered the whole floor with ulvarzi metal—no doubt to keep destructive nijiti out. Happily, niji knew other ways of getting in. There were the giant duhbulwydz that the ulvarzi used. Niji could wait until one of those opened and then try to race in without being seen—or flattened. There was also the much smaller pedwhey, which the uprights used. Niji would not have to wait for that to open, for niji had learned how to make it work by watching AyJay and others. The task required fingerz and hanz, which were easy enough to shape but surprisingly hard to work. Fingerz were like frani, only thicker and clumsier. They grasped and manipulated objects. Hanz provided strength and support. Niji was getting very good at moving individual fingerz up and down and side to side, but coordinated movements like grabbing and holding were still a challenge. And niji had not yet discovered the secret to strength. Nevertheless, niji favored the idea of using the pedwhey. There were fewer risks that way and niji did not want to wait.

So niji surfaced on the garj's out-side and went hunting for the pedwhey. Nazza's absence aided its search, as did a green light that lived above the entryway. As soon as niji found what it was looking for, however, niji discovered a problem. The knob that it needed to touch to activate the hach was in a box that had been fixed halfway up the side wall. That was well beyond niji's reach, even when niji stretched itself to its limit. Niji flushed, a display of self-contempt. In its eagerness to see AyJay again, niji had failed to anticipate the difference in height. Zra would not be impressed by such thoughtlessness. She would see a varz who thought it was more than a varz just because it could shape a few upright features.

As niji scorned itself, it sensed two sets of slight, surface-based vibrations. Uprights were coming! Niji did not know what they might do if they found niji trying to use their pedwhey. Niji did not want to find out, either, so it dove into the nearest corner. The ground there was too hard for easy tunneling, but there was plenty of wind-blown sand and shadows for camouflage, so niji hid itself and waited. The footsteps drew closer. Two uprights came into view. Niji tensed, ready to flee if a commotion arose, but the only activity that ensued pertained to the hach opening and the uprights moving on. Propelled by opportunistic impulse and the knowledge that uprights did not have eyes on their back-sides of their outer top-nobs, niji followed on their heels.

Warm-bright-stagnant, was the first impression that niji collected upon entering the garj. That was just how niji remembered this place! Niji did not recognize the sounds coming from the maytriks, however. And the volume of those emissions was very distressing. Niji ducked beneath the nearest overhang to dampen the unpleasant impact that the boom-boom-booming was having on its protoplasm. As it did so, it heard one of the incoming uprights shout, "Somebody shut that crap off! The CO can't hear himself think!"

Excitement dispersed niji's discomfort, for it was very familiar with the upright who had made those sounds. He was the one whom AyJay called Vahl. For reasons that niji had yet to grasp, zra seemed to prefer that upright's presence more than the others. So if he was here, then maybe she was, too. Maybe she was the other incoming upright. Zhee! Could that be her? Niji could not tell from where it was, the angle was wrong. And now the two uprights were moving away. Niji moved, too, streaming from shadow to shadow as fast as it could. The blaring noise was gone now and niji could sense lots of activity in the area, but it could neither slow down or exercise more caution because it simply had to know if it had found the zranarz.

The uprights came to a stop in front of a large container. ElTee cracked the container's lid for his smaller companion—was it her, was it her? Niji still could not tell, for that one's top-nob patch was down. The smaller upright glanced at the container's contents and then pressed the lid back into place.

"Yes, I know there's only one live one in there," Vahl said, and then paused. "Yes, I know the report said there were more." He paused again and then said, "They don't do well in captivity. Some of them go all glassy and die. I think the survivors eat each other. And then, of course, there's your science officer."

The smaller upright tensed and then brusquely pushed up its top-nob patch. Elation flared within niji only to fizzle when it saw the tight, pinched inner face. Not her. Not her. Not her.

"How are we to understand these creatures if he does not study them?" the not-AyJay said.

"'Study' and 'dissect' aren't interchangeable, you know," Val said.

The not-AyJay's mouth crimped at one corner. "More squeamishness, Val? I'm beginning to think Chief Johnson slipped you a white-knight chip in your sleep."

"Ha-ha," Vahl said, which was a sound that uprights made when they were happy about something. Niji wanted to know what these two were saying so it could be happy too. "AJ might have been a little over the top about protecting these buggers, but I think she mostly had the right of it. You're not going to figure out how they tick by cutting them up."

"So you say. I believe the jury is still out in that regard. Therefore you will continue to give Guzman access to the catch-and-release bin."

"Actually," Vahl said, "I'm thinking of phasing out the catch-and-release program. It's not particularly effective and my guys have better things to do."

The not-AyJay rolled its shoulders—*zhruggyn*, this was called, and it appeared to have many meanings. "I would not object to that," he said. "There are certainly easier ways of getting rid of them."

"Zapping them isn't the answer, either, Shingo," Vahl said. "In fact, it's inhumane."

That stream of wrdz prompted another zhrug. "We have neither the time nor the resources for more of your 'humane' methods. In case you have not noticed, we are no longer dealing with one or two aliens. There are hundreds of them now, possibly thousands. We could be overrun at any moment."

"Oh, please," Vahl said. "They're overgrown slugs, not mujahideen. And even if that wasn't the case, being outnumbered shouldn't be a license to practice brutality."

"Desperate times call for desperate measures, Val," the not-AyJay said, in a soft, almost amused tone that clashed with the enduring hardness in his eyes. "If you cannot accept that and act accordingly, then perhaps I should find a new second."

"Perhaps you should," Vahl said. "But if you do, I want the record to show that my resignation was a matter of conscience."

Now it was the not-AyJay's turn to make the ha-ha sound. "And to think that I actually suspected Chief Johnson of chipping you. You are the same stubborn throwback you have always been. Who cares about honor as long as you get the job done?"

"I do," Vahl said, infusing the wrdz with a surprising rigidity.

"Yet despite your old-fashioned proclivities," the not-AyJay said, "I have never had a more reliable second. That is why I am going to relieve the regulars of their zaps and leave the matter of alien relocation strictly up to you."

The bony jut beneath Vahl's mouth dropped a notch and then immediately realigned itself. The slip seemed to please the other upright for he made the ha-ha sound again. Then he said. "A man by the name of Oscar Wilde said, 'When the gods wish to punish us, they answer our prayers.' Consider your prayers answered."

"Shingo," Vahl said, "I don't—"

A loud beep from the maytrick cut him off. "The XK5 facility inspection team will be departing in five minutes. All team members not yet assembled at DW2 are requested to do so now."

"That is me," the not-AyJay and then thumped Vahl on the shoulder. "Send the alien in the holding tank to Guzman. He is to have access to any others that you take into custody. If you wish to discontinue catch-and-release, you may do so. But know this, Val: if you do not rid this compound of aliens in very short order, I will be forced to exterminate them and that will be on your head.

"Now, if you will excuse me, I am late for an inspection."

The not-AyJay began moving back toward the pedwhey. Niji wanted Vahl to depart, too, so it could start processing the exchange it had just absorbed. But the upright remained where he was, and as long as he was in the vicinity, niji felt compelled to watch him. He stroked that bony jut below his mouth as if he were trying to raise a conjugal blister and then abruptly made a loud, piercing wind-noise. Another upright came hurrying over from out of nowhere and said, "What's up, LT?"

"Grab me a sock so I can catch that Q for the SO," Vahl said. "After I net it, I want you to forklift the container out to the field beyond the junk-heap and fill it halfway with fresh sand. Maybe if we keep 'em cooler, the little bastards won't croak as fast."

The other upright darted off only to return frani-beats later with a long, sinuous tube that appeared to be attached to an even longer pole. "Anything else, LT?" he asked.

"Yeah," Vahl said, as he claimed the tube. "As far as everyone else is concerned, you're junking the tank. No one needs to see you filling it. You roger that?"

"Sure thing."

The other upright darted off again. As he did so, Vahl cracked open the large container that the not-AyJay had been so interested in and thrust the tube into the gap. The action intrigued niji. It could not figure out what the upright was trying to do. As niji watched and wondered, an ulvarz with a pronged front-end came rumbling into view. The ulvarz was moving quickly—too quickly, it appeared, for as it rounded a corner, its back-end clipped a tall stack of containers. The stack rocked and then buckled. A series of calamitous crashes ensued. The next thing niji knew, uprights were converging on the collapse from every point in the garj and Vahl was directing the flow. Niji had never seen so many uprights working together. The behavior was profoundly un-varz-like. It was also profoundly effective. The only way the detritus could have disappeared faster was if the floor had swallowed it whole. Niji tried to imagine varzi cooperating like that—and was struck by a most amazing idea.

[∗∗∗]

Niji was experiencing a novel sensation: impatience. It was sprawled in the shadows of a rock, at rest but not resting as it waited for a response to its azrumi. It had deposited the markers in strategic locations: by the garj, near construction sites, amidst the whoozhing ulvarzi. In each message, niji had expressed its status and desire. It had also included an unprecedented bit of advice: uprights have no tolerance for inferiors so avoid contact with them. Not that it expected the advice to be heeded. Intolerant or not, uprights were irresistible. Still, niji had this idea about sharing and offered the warning as an introductory taste.

As niji waited, it deflected its restlessness by contemplating the nearby ulvarzi and their whoozhing. Clearly, the uprights wanted them to create turbulence. But why? They did not seem to care for the turbulence that nazza generated. So perhaps they were creating turbulence to force something else out of the air. But what? Water molecules? Oxygen? Static? That last possibility reminded niji of the little lightning that the uprights had used to destroy nijit's swarm. And that reminded niji of the other mystery in this area: the tingle. Perhaps that was what the ulvarzi were driving out of the air! That would explain why the uprights were so protective of it and—

Niji's outlying frani registered oncoming vibrations: no crunching or thrumming, just the sibilant rustle of a streamlined body-mass displacing regolith. A varz then. Good. Its plan seemed to be working. It loosed an azrum that contained an impression of eyz and hanz, then fell back to see how it would be received. The oncoming varz went flat as soon as it sampled the marker and then issued an azrum of its own: respect-curiosity-suspense. The response pleased niji.

You have progressed, it said, flavoring the micro-pulse with approval.

Niji's clone acknowledged the praise with an azrum that tasted of pleasure and pride. It seemed calmer, more thoughtful, and smaller since their last encounter. *The infusion was most instructive,* it pulsed back. *Will you give me another for following the azrumi that you left for me? Doing so was scary-new for me. You could have been hungry.*

With that, the clone revealed how limited its progress had been. For only a nijit would try to bargain for an another infusion before it had thoroughly digested the first. Only a nijit would treat a second bundle of zervarzi memory strands as casually as a catch of zyl. As off-putting as the clone's assumptions were, however, niji could not reproach the pervarz for them because niji had in fact drawn per here with such an offer in mind.

I would consider a second conjugation, niji said, *if you agree to do something for me in return.*

Anything, per pulsed.

I want you to join me in finding zra.

The clone turned a distressed shade of gray. *Collaboration is nijiti behavior. I no longer swarm."

What I want from you is not swarm behavior, niji said. *It is upright behavior. They are superior beings. Their ways are superior, too.* When per continued to struggle with the fear of backsliding, niji added, *Think of this as an experiment. We will try it and see where it takes us.*

What will you give me to do this?

Niji suffered another pang of annoyance mixed with contempt. This pervarz might have given up swarming but per still embraced nijiti habits—always wanting more of what it had not earned. If there had been another, worthier clone in the area, niji would have left this one to grow or die on its own. As it was, niji had no choice but to endure per's unbecoming greed so it could go forward with its plan.

I will give you upright knowledge and skills, niji said.

The clone flushed, a triumphant display. *Finding zra will be very exciting,* it said. *Where would you have me search first?*

I do not want you to search for her, niji said, augmenting the pulse with a memory of uprights and tiny stabs of lightning. *Better that she comes looking for us.*

Why would she if she has not already?

Because, niji said, *we are going to demonstrate our worthiness.*

CHAPTER 15

SOS, AJ THOUGHT, AS she bounced down the shuttle chute and into a patch of windswept semi-gloom. Same Old Shit. Those little blobs had no idea how much they were asking of her. Neither did TSC.

"Save our sanity?" Val said, as he touched down behind her. At first, she wondered if he was going psychic on her. Then she realized that she had spoken into an open mic. Oops. And no one who had the slightest sense of what was going on in her head at the moment would have said what came out of his mouth next. "C'mon, AJ, it's not that bad, is it?"

"It's worse," she said. "And it's going to be hell for you too if you don't ditch the cruise director sim in a hurry."

"If you didn't want a sunny second, you shouldn't have picked me for the job."

"That was just my way of shooting the messenger," she said, which might've been a little true when she first added him to her list of non-negotiables—*pull me out of retirement, will you?* But the fact was, she liked having Val around. Even now, when he was played out from weeks of traveling and ornery as a bear with a bellyache, she liked knowing that he was right behind her, at her back. She felt secure.

That would have freaked out the old AJ, the one who had made a career of keeping other people at a distance so she could demand the impossible from them without feeling bad. But over the course of her too-brief retirement, the ocean had stripped her of that emotional armor-plating as surely as it had stripped the flesh from her mother's bones. And the funny-sad thing was, she didn't miss that shell, not even a little, for once she sloughed it, she saw it for what it was: dead weight, the weight of her dead gone wrong. Meli would've wanted her to have friends. And her father would have at least wanted her to live fully.

No guts, no glory, kid.

"Yeah, well," Val said. "Next time find a different target."

"There won't be a next time," she said. "You can bet the farm on that."

"What's a farm?"

A pair of habbies came striding toward them with the programmed aggressiveness of heat-seekers. "MPs," Val said, and sure enough, the avatars that popped up on her ID window were TSC standard holo-IDs. So nice for a change, AJ thought, and then sneered at herself for sounding so incredibly geriatric.

A query came over the PA. "Special Envoy Johnson?"

She stepped forward, a courtesy when conditions forbade the flipping of face-plates. "That's me," she said, and then gestured at Val. "This is my second, Valentine Fox."

"We know the lieutenant. Welcome back, sir."

The taller of the two men stepped forward. His avatar was young and buzz-cut, with a square jaw and Asian eyes. "I'm Sergeant Kim. This is Sergeant Chavez," he added, gesturing toward his counterpart. "We have the honor of being your escorts. Come this way, please." He motioned them toward a familiar-looking crawler that was idling just beyond the cyclone fence. AJ arched an eyebrow at the fence, finding it rather superfluous, and then snorted out loud when she saw the sign that been welded to its links: No Unauthorized Personnel Allowed.

"What?" Val asked.

"What idiot would want to trespass here?" she replied.

The climb into the crawler was harder than she remembered it. That first rung seemed a lot higher off the ground. "You're just tired," Val said, as he gave her a discreet leg-up. "You'll be back to your old self in a couple of days."

"Now there's something to look forward to," she said.

The two MPs bounded into the crawler like fleas on steroids. Kim claimed the driver's seat while Chavez joined her and Val in the back of the cab. "The CO thought you might enjoy a tour of the facilities on your way in, Special Envoy," he said. "The place has changed a lot since you left."

She didn't care, not even a little tiny bit. They could have dragged Chichen Itza here from the Yucatan and restored it down to the last block and she would have said "BFD." She was here for one reason, and one reason only, and all she wanted to do was get on with it.

"Some other time perhaps," she said. "It's been a long day and I'm a little tired."

"Commander's orders, ma'am," Chavez said, with just a fleck of regret in his tone. "He thinks the ride will help you acclimate."

With that, the sergeant made two things perfectly clear. One: Special Envoy or not, her wishes were not the same as commands. And two: Shingo meant to punish her in a thousand and one small, plausibly deniable ways for returning to Farside. Especially for returning to deal with the Q. Her mandate, the official doc read. Her responsibility. And the only authority to which she was answerable was the TSC. She wasn't at all surprised that Shingo didn't like the terms of her residency. That's why she had insisted on getting them in writing. Too bad she hadn't thought to include a good-sport clause.

"Well, if you're going to insist," she said, and then swore as a synapse fired retroactively. "Thirteen months must be how long it takes to forget every good habit a body ever learned."

"Excuse me, ma'am?"

"I forgot to collect my gear," she said.

"No need to worry, ma'am," Chavez said. "It has to go through security first."

"Security?" she said, injecting a full measure of affront into the echo.

"Yes, ma'am. SOP. As soon as your gear clears, one of our people will make sure it gets where it needs to go."

The promise struck AJ as more sinister than reassuring. *I swear, ma'am, I don't know what happened to your equipment, it must've went walk-about.* "What if Val stayed here and helped out? He hasn't been gone that long, so he doesn't need a tour."

"After two weeks in a can," Val added, seemingly catching her drift, "I wouldn't mind working a few of the kinks out."

But their escorts wouldn't hear of it. "NCD, ma'am," Chavez said. "The CO said that the lieutenant is to be treated as one of yours rather than one of ours. And unauthorized personnel are not permitted in restricted areas without a clearance."

"I see," AJ said. And she did. Shingo meant to punish Val, too, for not committing hari-kari when he landed on her list of non-negotiables. What a cold bastard. "In that case, boys, let's get going. And just so you know, if any of my stuff turns up missing or broken, I'll be requesting you both for special assignment."

"Yes, ma'am," Kim said, and then slipped the crawler into gear. As they pulled away from the port, she switched back to the channel that she and Val shared. "Really?" she said. "Shuttleport security? What's the point?"

He shrugged. "Like the dude said, it's SOP."

"Seems a little—excessive—to me."

"Jesus, AJ, this is a military base now. The military is all about excessive."

Ooh, cranky Johnny. She had a feeling that he hadn't expected Shingo to turn on him. She had a feeling that he was just a little—hurt.

The crawler was rolling toward an unfamiliar gleam in the semi-gloom. A minute or two after AJ noticed it, Chavez got on the PA and began his song and dance. "Coming up on our right is the mining complex," he said. "The glow you see is from the processing plant, which is, as you know, where we separate the ice from the harvested regolith and store it as water. The water is piped over to the MF, where it's converted to hydrogen fuel. BTW, the MF's been operational for almost three months now," he added. "In that time, we've produced enough fuel to power this whole compound and then some. We expect to open our sub-orbital re-fueling station within the next thirty days."

"So the wind farm is already obsolete," she said, managing to skim all but a trace of bitterness from her tone. "A spinning junkyard."

"Oh no, ma'am," Chavez hastened to assure her. "The farm's still on-line, only on a separate grid. CO said we'd need a back-up system in case of disaster, industrial accident, or—" He lowered his voice as if he were afraid of being overheard. "Alien attack." They were driving past the processing plant now. It was big and boxy and all lit up like an ancient ocean liner, but instead of smokestacks, it had towering cylindrical storage tanks. AJ expected Chavez to regurgitate more TSC-approved trivia about the facility, but he was still yammering about the farm. "CO also thought it would be a good idea to keep the Free Zone on the other grid—you know, so the Union would have to pay to maintain it. Delgado wasn't happy about that, let me tell you—"

"Who?" she said.

"Heavenly Delgado," he said. "You know—the Space Union's enforcer? Lord of the Free Zones? Johnny Rocket's best friend?" Every time she shook him off, his tone grew a little more incredulous until finally he said, "I thought you said you used to work in space!"

She found his amazement more amusing than anything else, but to her surprise, Val took offense on her behalf. "Jesus, Sergeant," he said, "just how green are you? This woman was a RSO master chief. She lived and worked in the field in conditions harsh enough to make grown men cry. She made it possible for junior Johnnies like you to have a halfway decent life in deep space."

"OK, OK," Chavez said, in an aggrieved, back-pedaling tone, "I get it, LT. And ma'am, my apologies, I meant no insult. I was just surprised that you never heard of Delgado. I mean, he's like every space worker's godfather. You need something? He'll turn himself—and anybody in his way—inside out to get it for you. You got a gripe? He'll do his damnedest to make things right. Because of him, this Free Zone is going to have all the comforts of home. I hear he's even trying to get live entertainment out here for us on a semi-regular basis."

Kim sneered at that. "Yeah, right," he said. "And who's going to come all this way to do a show—the Stones?"

"Are they still alive?" AJ wondered, only to have everybody guffaw at her. "No ma'am," Kim said. "They're DNA-enhanced impersonators. They're all the rage back on Terra."

"Oh," she said, and felt suddenly old—old and tired and out of touch. She thought about turning her mic off and stealing a cat nap—nothing old-womanish about that, right? But even as she sulked, a dust-clogged corona out on the flats caught her eye. There was something beyond that, too—an array of saw-toothed silhouettes that hadn't been there thirteen months ago.

"What's that?" she asked, curious in spite of herself.

"That's the strip mine," Chavez said. "The dig's non-stop."

"And what's that going up on the far ridge?"

"Second seed stuff," he said, and then excused himself to answer a ping from Kim. As he moved to the front of the crawler, she went private with Val and said, "Is that the military term for an offensive installation?"

"Possibly," he said. "Could be defensive, too, or a little of both."

The crawler lurched forward, pressing AJ deeper into her seat, and then swerved sharply to the right. Prompted by a reflexive WTF rather than concern, she glanced over the sled's side. She didn't know what she expected to see, but she was fairly sure that the menu didn't include a mob of Q.

"Crud," she said, more to herself than to Val. "Look at them all. They look like a slick of gigantic catfish." Had Bob been that big? She couldn't remember, and before she could ask, one of the Q that she had been watching disappeared beneath the crawler's tracks. Two others met the same fate. And it was obvious that they had been deliberately overrun rather than accidentally run down. She was on the PA in a heartbeat.

"Hit the brakes, Sergeant!" she said. "Right now."

The crawler ground to a grudging stop. The surviving Q scattered into the semi-gloom. AJ did not observe their retreat. She was on her feet now, standing at Kim's elbow. All she could see was red.

"Really?" she said, struggling to keep herself from shouting into her mic. "Did you really just mow down a whole school of Q right in front of me?"

"It's no big deal, ma'am," Kim said, in a shrug-like tone. "Really."

A vein in her left temple started to throb as if it were trying to break free so it could then wrap itself around the man's throat and strangle him. "Do you know who I am, Sergeant?" she said.

"You're Special Envoy Johnson, ma'am," he said.

"And do you know why I'm here?" she said, refraining—just barely—from making any mention of her aborted retirement.

"No, ma'am."

His ignorance should not have surprised her. Shingo himself had been in the dark about her appointment until five days ago, when *The Bonhomie* cleared the APW. She didn't suppose that he'd be in any hurry to share that news—with anyone. Still, he should've said something. This was just another way of punishing her. Oh, well. She'd dug her own grave; now there was nothing to do but lie in it.

"Then let me enlighten you, Sergeant," she said. "I'm here to deal with the Q. And I don't see how I'm going to be able to do that if you keep running over them."

"It's not just him, ma'am," Chavez said. "Everyone does it."

"Oh?" she said, and stepped back so she could project a glare at both sergeants. "And how did so many people get the idea that killing Q is OK? Is that what you were told in orientation?"

"No, ma'am," Kim said. "The O-team told us repeatedly that the Q were not to be molested. Then we started working and saw how things really were."

"And then Guzman disappeared," Chavez added.

"What?" AJ said. "Who's Guzman?"

"He was the CO's science officer," Kim said, in the semi-hushed tones of a man telling a ghost story around a virtual campfire. "He went out to the perimeter two weeks ago to collect some samples and never came back."

Her first thought was: samples, my ass. That was quickly followed by: irony, anyone? But what came out of her mouth was more discreet. "Sounds like a walk-off to me."

"Yes, ma'am," Chavez said, "but apparently, it was Q. CO found the evidence himself."

"Evidence?" she said, her voice spiking with surprise. "What kind?"

"He didn't say, ma'am," Kim said. "And we didn't ask."

Naturally. These boys were here to follow orders, not ask questions. The surprise bled right out of her, leaving a cynical stain in its wake. She wondered if Shingo had planned the whole thing in advance or just seized the opportunity by the hair when it presented itself. Either way, the man was a friggin' genius.

"Since then," Chavez said, "the word in the field is—the less Q, the better. And nobody cares how you get rid of them."

"I care," she said, in a low, dangerous tone. "I care so much, I'm going to make Q abuse a flagging offense."

"But—ma'am!" Kim said, and even though she couldn't see his face, she could tell that he had gone pop-eyed with surprise and alarm. For good reason, too. A flagged jacket could keep a Johnny away from the highest-risk, highest-paying jobs. "They're incredible pests, worse than ship lice or even port vermin. You can't enter any of the outlying buildings without being met by their screeching. And when a whole bunch of them gets going, there's not a habby setting high enough to filter that racket out. If we weren't carrying zaps, they'd probably try to jump us like they do outside."

"What?" she said, an incredulous yelp, because the thought of a booger-y little blob taking down a full-grown Johnny seemed patently ridiculous—until she remembered Singer flat on his back with a face full of tentacles.

But that had been a one-time thing. And nothing bad had come of it. Right? She made a mental note to ask Val later.

Both men stiffened through the shoulders in response to her disbelief. "We're not talking about little Q here, ma'am," Kim said. "We hardly see any of those out in the open, and when we do, they're usually running the other way. But the big ones are a whole different story. Not only are they bigger, they're bolder—and they always travel in packs. A pack could take a man down easy. I've heard of it happening. They go for the legs with those tentacles of theirs and pull the guy down. After that, who knows? They probably eat like kings."

Again, AJ was dubious. Q didn't eat people. Right? And the fact that he had heard of Q-human muggings but never witnessed one firsthand smacked of extraterrestrial legend. Right? But thanks to that freshly resurrected memory of Singer, she kept this round of doubts to herself.

"Well," she said, "you've given me a lot to think about. Thank you for that, and for playing straight with me. As a gesture of appreciation, I'm going to forget what happened back there. But," she added, as their shoulders relaxed, "this is a one-time deal. If I even hear of you pulling another hit-and-run on the Q, you will suffer for it.

"Are we clear on that?"

"Yes, ma'am," both MPs said, and while AJ might've been imagining it, she thought she heard flecks of surprise and respect mixed in with their relief.

"Then let's start over with no hard feelings," she said, hoping to propagate the tiny bit of good will that she might have purchased for herself. "And if you could swing it, I wouldn't mind an abridged version of this tour."

"I'll do what I can, ma'am."

The crawler rumbled to life and then lurched forward. The motion rocked

AJ backward—right into the safeguard of Val's arm. In times past, she would've jumped all over him for trying to protect her from such knocks. Now she leaned into that support and even let it pull her closer to him. His proximity fortified and comforted her. She couldn't help but wonder what he was thinking. So she switched back to their private channel and asked.

"I'm thinking that flagging jackets for abusing Q is a bit harsh," he said. "The punishment has to fit the crime, AJ."

And just like that, his proximity lost its allure. She sat straight up and said, "Back on Terra, they would've been arrested for such blatant disregard for life."

"This isn't Terra, AJ," he said. "It's a frontier. Life's harder here."

"And sometimes," she retorted, "we make it harder than it has to be. But if it makes you happy, I won't make Q abuse a flagging offense." He reached for her as if to draw her back to his side physically as well as philosophically. As he did so, she added, "The flagging offense will be disobeying the Special Envoy's decree on Q abuse."

"Jesus, AJ," he said, in a dry tone that usually came with an eye-roll on the side. "You can be so stubborn sometimes."

"Slaughtering the natives isn't the way, Val," she said. "Trust me, I know."

"I trust you," he said. "I'm just saying." Then he folded his arm around her shoulder and they rode in companionable silence.

The tour took them through a section of the wind-farm. The visibility was better now, and the rows of turbines that they passed were all spinning at a drastically slower rate, but other than that nothing had changed. AJ was pleased her to see something from her first time here up and running. It was a vindication of sorts, moral assurance that those hellish three months hadn't been a complete waste.

"FYI, ma'am," Kim said, "this was Guzman's last known location."

"What was he doing out here?" she said. "I thought he was looking for—" The word dismayed and offended her, but she used it anyway. "I thought he was looking for samples."

"He was," Kim said. "For some reason, the Q seem to like this area."

"Interesting," she said, and made a mental note to find out why.

The road curved away from the wind-farm and took them into what should have been more familiar-looking territory. But everything seemed different now: darker, more foreboding, like the end of an adventure instead of the beginning, and a bad end at that. It took her awhile to grasp why this was so, and when she did, she blurted the realization out like a surprised child.

"The runner lights are gone!"

Val nodded. "That was Shingo's first order of business. He said they weren't appropriate for a military installation."

She supposed he had a point, but still—that friendly bit of color and flash had been like a lighthouse guiding tired minds home. In its absence, how many of those minds would lose hope and give up? The missing science officer was a perfect example. She'd had her suspicions before, but now she'd bet her whole pension that he'd walked off rather than been abducted.

"Hey," Val said, nudging her out of her thoughts. "Does that bring back any memories?"

He was pointing at a ramshackle Quonset hut with sand-pitted walls and double-wide doors. "Yeah," she said, recognizing their old garage immediately. "But it looks a little—neglected."

"Yeah, even more so than I remember," Val said, and then switched to an open mic to query their escorts about it.

"OB2 got torqued pretty badly in the quake that rumbled through here last month," Kim said. "But CO decided to abandon it even before that on account of all the Q activity."

"What kind of activity are we talking about?" AJ was quick to ask.

"Screeching, ma'am," the sergeant said, in a haunted tone. "Lots and lots of screeching."

Another artifact from her first tour of duty appeared on the horizon. It was broad and flat-backed, and sat deep in the sand like a brooding hen. The first time she had seen the shuttle from this angle, the mouth-watering aroma of Meli's roasted chicken burritos had come to mind. Now the sight triggered memories of S-rats and too much male musk. Her stomach lurched as if it were trying to play dead and then seized back up as a terrible thought struck her.

"Wait," she said. "That's not where I'm being quartered, is it?" Wouldn't that be just like Shingo?

"No, ma'am," one of the sergeants said. "OB1 was retired."

"Because if it is," she went on, "you can turn this thing around and take me back to the shuttleport."

"CO's got you in a VIP suite."

Ha-ha, was that what the bastard was calling it now? "Because there's no way I'm bunking down in that tin can again!"

"AJ," Val said. "Settle." The levelness of his tone snapped her out of her Shingo-inspired rant. "The only reason the shuttle is still out here is because we haven't got an APC big enough to tow it off to the junkyard."

"Ah," she said, a red-faced breath. Bad enough that Shingo could get the best of her when he was trying without her working herself into a froth over shit that he wasn't even trying to pull. "Did I mention that it's been a long day yet?"

"We're closing in on the Free Zone, ma'am," Chavez said. "With any luck, you'll be able to rest up a little before CO sends for you."

She liked the sound of resting up almost as much as she hated the idea of Shingo sending for her. As if she was here to beg a favor. As if he were capable of granting her wish. As if—

Settle.

A dusty aura rose up on the horizon and then blistered into a construction site. There were 'bots everywhere—ferrying module sections in, trucking regolith and refuse out. As she watched, a crane hoisted a huge, second-story panel into place and held it there while a swarm of welder 'bots went to work. AJ could not help but be impressed by the sight of so much frenetic industry. She also could not help but be a little bit dismayed.

"I thought you said this place was finished," she said.

"The Free Zone still needs a little work," Chavez admitted. "But the housing facility and dining modules are complete. I think you'll be comfortable."

"This is going to be the best Free Zone ever built," Kim chimed in. "We're going to have a casino, sim rooms, and a gaming deck. And the bistro-techs are going to serve born-again, not that synthetic crap."

"Somehow, I can't see Shingo signing off on that," she said. TSC wasn't big on stocking the frontier with 'recreational non-essentials.' Starship captains complained about the 'waste of limited cargo space.' COs worried about the 'potential for counter-productivity.' And then there was the expense. "It's a huge luxury item."

"It's not his call," Chavez said. "It's Delgado's. And Delgado says, 'The further from Terra a body is, the greater that body's need for earthly comforts. Without such comforts, the spirit shrivels and the will to survive declines.'"

"Sounds like a good deal for SU members," she said. "But you're military. You have a separate RNR facility, right?"

"Used to be," he said, after a pause that echoed his earlier surprise. *You used to work in space? Really?* "But the frijole-counters decided that wasn't cost-efficient since the average grunt would rather pay to play in a Free Zone than hang out on the base for free, so the military struck a bargain with the Union. Now we're issued quarterly Free Zone allowances to spend as we please. If we use up what we get before quarter's end, we have to pay as we go out of pocket, but no one really cares. Three years is a long time to go without the comforts of home."

AJ could not help but admire the set-up that this Heavenly Delgado had going here. Not only was the military picking up part of the tab for his Free Zone, it was also pitching in for the booze that it did not want its people to have and that it could not stop them from buying. And people of all stripes seemed to love him—with the possible exception of the local brass, ha-ha, Shingo, you bastard you.

She was still savoring the taste of Farside schadenfreude when Chavez popped in over the PA. "Begging your pardon, ma'am, but the CO just pinged. He's ready to receive you at the command center."

"Now?" she said, taken aback by the announcement. She wasn't ready yet. She needed a shower, some food, and a few years to ramp herself up. "But I thought you said I'd have—time."

"Plans change, ma'am," he said, in a semi-apologetic tone. "He wants to see you now."

She didn't bother to ask what the rush was, for it was clear that there wasn't one. This was just another power play, the schoolyard bully shoving the new kid around. She could either push back or let him think that the playground was all his. Both options had their charms.

"Ma'am?" Chavez prompted.

"Fine," she said, choosing to bide her time simply because it required less energy. "Take me to your leader."

The crawler swung wide of the Free Zone and then rumbled into what seemed like a dead zone. The only landmarks in the area were a sprawling junkyard and a squat, camouflaged dome that appeared to be their destination. The dome didn't look nearly grand enough for the likes of Shingo, but when she said so to Val, he assured her otherwise.

"Most of it is underground," Val said, "so it suits him well enough."

He stood up before the sled came to a complete stop and then helped her to her feet—a hand she accepted gratefully after sitting for so long. He probably would've helped her down from the sled, too, but Chavez stopped him before he could exit the vehicle.

"Sorry, LT," he said, "but he only wants to see the Special Envoy."

Although she couldn't see Val's face, she had no doubt that he was scowling now, an indignant grimace aimed at his former boss. She had elected not to push back for herself, but tired or not she was willing to move a small mountain for Val.

"You want me to insist?" she said. "It might be fun."

"Not likely," he said. "And there's no money in it so if you don't mind, I'll just wait out here."

"If that's what you want,' she said, and then added, "Just for the record, I think you're getting the better deal."

She climbed down from the crawler, ow-ow-oww-ing all the way, and then lamented her reconditioned knee as she stealth-hobbled her way over to the command center's main entrance. The airlock there was outfitted with the usual assortment of sensors and scanners plus a peculiar new device that had been installed at floor-level. It appeared to be a home-made trap, designed to capture Q. It looked like something Val might've dreamed up and come to think of it, she had a vague recollection of him talking about some such thing at some point during the flight back to Farside. He was such a clever man. She couldn't blame Shingo for being pissed about losing his LT. She'd be mad, too.

Speaking of his lordship, there he was, standing vector-straight in the foyer just beyond the security checkpoint. His jet-black hair was pulled back in a shogun's knot, and instead of a habby, he was wearing a fitted black robe. He looked powerful and sleek, and had the presence of a jaguar. A younger woman might've found him attractive. AJ saw nothing but trouble.

"Special Envoy Johnson," he said, offering her a formal bob. "Welcome back to Farside. Allow me to congratulate you on your—promotion."

Amazing how much he packed into that tiny pause: amusement, disdain, his intention to thwart her. All without raising his voice or even an eyebrow. She could not see his scorn, but she could feel it. And while she could not document his displeasure, she had no doubt that it was the flipside of his perfectly dispassionate façade. Crud. She was so out of her depth here. And out of steam, too. She was so tired, her thoughts were starting to hop like fleas on the hunt. Was it was too late to plead exhaustion and beg a rain-check? Probably. She just had to woman up and try to make old and erratic work for her.

"Thank you, Commander," she said. Then, prompted by a Meli microburst that urged her to be polite, she flipped up her face-plate. That first gust of cool, recycled air woke her up a little. "The council sends its regards."

"Of course," he said, and then motioned her past the checkpoint. "Please, join me in my office. We have much to discuss." As she closed the gap between them, he said, "May I offer you some tea?"

Ah, yes, the tea treatment—a page from their past. He would not have forgotten that. He was trying to psych her. Or was she doing his work for him again? Crud! She so did not want to be here.

"That would be nice, thank you," she said, and then on impulse, added, "If it's not too much trouble, I'd appreciate something to eat, too. My blood sugar is still screwed up from the switch back to S-rats."

"I will see what I have," he said. "In the meantime, please make yourself comfortable."

With that, he stepped into what she had assumed was a closet and disappeared from sight. In his absence, she popped her top and then strolled around the room, not snooping exactly, more like collecting impressions. His office was spacious but austere, an ascetic's retreat. It featured a glass floater desk that was set on low, a small futon, and an assortment of antique floor pillows. The plushest of those cushions occupied his side of the floater. The others were scattered on the opposite side. There were several objects d'art on display: an ancient holo-painting of Mt. Fuji from a time when the mountain was still snow-covered; an even older silk-screen of a pink-blossomed tree branch; and a semi-prehistoric, banjo-like instrument suspended in a C-Thru case. She was surprised to see these things—partly because she had assumed that he was like her when it came to decorating and partly because she would've expected someone so militarized to collect war memorabilia rather than antiques that evoked tranquility.

As she was contemplating this quirk in Shingo's character, he reappeared with a server float in his wake. "Ah, the shamisen," he said, when he saw where she was standing. "It is a beautiful instrument, no?"

"It is," she said. "Do you play?"

"Not for many years," he said, and then waved her toward the mound of pillows. "Please. Sit."

"This reconditioned knee of mine makes sitting on the floor a misery," she said, "so if you don't mind, I'll take the futon."

"As you wish," he said, seemingly more interested in the disposition of the tea. When he was done pouring, he split the server into two segments and sent one of them floating her way. Then he settled down in the pile of pillows with a geisha's studied ease. "To your good health," he said, raising a steaming porcelain cup.

"And to yours," she said, doing the same. But she was more hungry than thirsty at the moment, and so took only the semblance of a sip before turning her attention to the snack that he had sent over with the tea.

"They are called 'crazy fish,'" he said of the tiny desiccated sprat. "They are a delicacy."

AJ had never heard of such a thing, but that didn't stop her from spooning a heap of fish-mummies into her mouth and crunching away. She tasted mineral salts and fatty oils. She tasted the sea, a savor close enough to home to freshen her spirit. The tiny heads and eyes didn't bother her at all.

"I am glad you like them," Shingo said, as she went for another spoonful.

"They beat S-rats by a light-year," she said between one crunch and the next. Then, hoping to distract him so she could eat in peace, she pointed to the holo-painting of Mt. Fuji. "That's nice, too."

"Thank you," he said, studying her over the brim of his cup. "My father's great-grandfather, Hashimoto, created that. He was also a well-known poet in his time. Are you familiar with 'If I Were Your Emperor' or 'The Heart is a Sour Plum?'"

She shook her head, but he seemed to expect more from her. Crud. So she rinsed her mouth out with a swig of tea and then said, "I've never been big on poetry. It's too much work for too little return as far as I'm concerned."

"A pity," Shingo said. "The subtleties of a well-constructed poem nourish the soul." Then, in the same level tone and cadence, he said, "I will not permit the flagging of jackets for Q abuse."

She shouldn't have been surprised that he knew about that already—how long, really, did it take to boil water and spill fairy fish into a bowl? Nevertheless, he had once again managed to catch her off-guard. Would she never learn? "I will do whatever's necessary to protect the Q," she said. "If that means flagging everyone on this base, so be it."

"Ah," he said. "You are their protector then. Interesting. I thought you were here to figure out how to make them go away."

"Kind of hard to do that when you're having them killed on sight," she said. "Wouldn't you say?"

He shrugged, a gesture as eloquent as it was noncommittal. Just in case the visit was being recorded for security purposes. "How do you suppose the Q acquired their familiarity with our language?"

She matched him shrug for shrug. "My guess is that they learned most of it from the matrix that one of my guys built into our garage. OB2, I think you call it."

"Yes, yes," he said, "I am familiar with the building. We abandoned it after the last earthquake. Why do you suppose the Q ask only for you?"

"Beats me," she said. "But I'll bet you have a guess."

He extended the tea pot in her direction. When she shook the offer off, he refilled his own cup. As he did so, he glanced at her out of the corner of one eye and said, "I must admit that your apparent fondness for the creatures tempts me to think that you had a hand in their education."

Meaning—what? That she was some kind of traitor to her own kind? Her first impulse was to bristle and hiss. How about I give you a hand, butt-hole, right across the face? She could almost hear Val whisper, *Easy now*. Which made her wonder when he had supplanted her father as her inner voice of reason. Which stalled her pique and made her realize that Shingo was trying to make her angry to keep her off-balance. So she coughed up a laugh instead and then took him to task.

"You seem to have forgotten a few things about my last assignment here," she said. "One, I was fried going in. Two, I was given ninety days to get the job done. Three, my outfit consisted of a handful of Johnnies, a load of re-purposed gear, and a cache of compromised seed 'bots. So when exactly did you imagine me having the time or the energy to first tame and then teach a Q how to talk?"

"Yet from what I have seen of them," he said, "they cannot have learned such a thing on their own. They have no initiative and very little intelligence."

"Yet you credit them with the abduction of your science officer," she said, and caught him off-guard—enough to squeeze an unintentional blink out of him. Ha-ha! How do you like it, you creep? "What was the evidence you found that linked them to his disappearance?"

"I am afraid that is classified information," he said, demonstrating a cat-like capacity for near-instantaneous recovery. "I can, however, tell you that for some weeks now, gangs of Q have been targeting people who ignore warnings about coming and going alone on foot. It was only a matter of time before one of those gangs grabbed someone. Like they grabbed your man, Singer."

"There was only one Q involved in that instance," she said, trying to block the visual part of that memory. "And Singer wasn't taken."

"No doubt because you found him in time."

"More likely because we weren't flattening Q in droves with the crawler or electrocuting them with zaps," she retorted.

Shingo's eyes narrowed as if he were trying to see all the way through her. Then the corners of his mouth twitched—cat-like amusement. "Val told you quite a bit."

"He shared the basics," she said, aware on some level that she was trying to shield her second again. "I'm learning the rest as I go along."

His smile hardened into something more menacing. "I could teach you a thing or two."

The hair on her nape bristled, a reaction so visceral she had to resist the urge to squirm. *Easy now*. "I'm sure you could," she said. "But all I want from you is your cooperation until I can get the Q to stop popping up in places where they're not wanted."

"And how do you plan to do that?" he said, backing off but only a little.

"I'm going to ask them," she said.

CHAPTER 16

THE GARJ REMAINED DARK despite niji's best efforts to summon the companion lights. The matrix remained dormant despite niji's repeated attempts to rouse it. And while the uprights had not left the area, they had relocated all of the ulvarzi and stopped coming to this place.

Niji had to admit: this experiment had been a failure. And it had failed because niji had made a pervarz's mistakes. Niji should have given the plan more thought before proceeding. It should have contemplated possible outcomes and their possible outcomes. Most of all, it should have considered the ramifications of collaborating with an ul-nijit, even if that ul-nijit happened to be its own clone.

But, alas, niji had been blinded by ambition.

An emphatic outburst of high-pitched chatter disrupted the garj's silence. "Maytriks awn! Maytriks awn!"

Those were nijiti. Their chatter was the clone's doing. It had shared all of the knowledge that it had received from niji with every nijit that agreed to the infusion. When niji first learned of this indiscriminate redistribution, niji had nearly fallen out of the garj rafters that had become its preferred roost.

You did what? niji had pulsed, flushing a livid shade of disbelief. And when the clone gladly reiterated its misdoings, niji was so stunned, it could only pulse, *Why?*

You and I have been calling and calling, the clone replied, all but glowing with pride, *but zra has not responded. I have come to realize that that is because she cannot sense us, zra. The sounds that we generate are too small and diffuse for such a large, busy space. But just as two varzi are louder than one, many more will be louder still.*

Niji could not the deny that there was a certain logic to the clone's reasoning. But per had neglected to take the essential nature of nijiti into consideration. Instead of using their newfound knowledge to try and evolve, the clone's converts had passed their ill-given memories on to other nijiti. The result was this: an augmented super-swarm that regarded uprights and their things as a fabulous new source of thrills.

"Maytriks awn! Maytriks awn!"

As niji struggled to ignore this latest round of nijiti screeching, its clone came streaming toward niji's roost. Although per was uninvited, it approached confidently—like an equal. Niji reoriented, presenting its back-side to the pervarz, but per did not accept the snub. Instead, per settled down next to niji as if it had been summoned.

The swarm is getting louder and louder, it observed, pulsing instead of trying to make itself heard over the rest of the screech.

That is what comes of too much sharing, niji pulsed, making no secret of its unabated displeasure with the pervarz.

Once again, per refused to see the error of its ways. *Sharing is upright behavior,* it said. *Uprights are superior beings. Those who aspire to be more like uprights must do as uprights do. This was your belief before it was mine, zer.*

But nijiti do not aspire to be more like uprights, niji said, flushing with aggravation for having its reasoning twisted so. *They wish only to play at being upright. They wish to play with uprights—even though they know that uprights have no tolerance for such play.*

That is, per said, *the way of nijiti. But they are very loud now, are they not? Zra will come soon, I think.*

Perhaps, niji said, a curt pulse. Niji did not like discussing AyJay with the pervarz. Per presumed too much.

She will bring the ulvarzi back, too.

Perhaps not, niji said. Because the ulvarzi had a new burrow now, one that screeching nijiti could not infiltrate. Niji had been there several times and had considered relocating on more than one occasion. But tempting as living swarm-free was, niji could not bring itself to abandon the garj. This was where niji had first encountered zra. This was where niji would encounter her again.

A pod of nijiti skittered up a nearby support, screeching all the way. Niji loosed an azrum, an expression of pure contempt for their primitive predilections.

Perhaps they would calm down if you roused the maytriks, the pervarz pulsed.

I have tried, niji said. *But it seems to have entered a dormant phase.*

Could it be dead? per wondered.

I do not know, niji said. *It is hard to tell with ulvarz—*

A loud, violent shudder echoed through the garj, silencing the swarm and leaving niji ready to go aground if the shuddering evolved into a shaking. Frani-beats later, the duhbulwydz began to rise. Blue-white light flooded through the gap, then the tastes of ulvarzi exhaust. The next thing niji knew, the crawlyr was parked in the bot-bay. The ulvarz's back-end was heaped with containers. Uprights were emerging from its front-end.

Is it—zra? niji's clone pulsed.

Niji made no reply, but it was thinking the same thing. Was it her? Was it? It watched anxiously as one of the uprights moved toward a small box that was fixed to the far wall. That, apparently, was where the companion light slumbered, for as soon as the upright opened the box, darkness disappeared. The swarm let out a collective "Zhee!" and then began to slowly shadow-stream their way toward the uprights. The swarm was excited. The swarm wanted to play. And the swarm's favorite game involved collecting a sample from an unsuspecting upright without getting caught or frozen stupid—or killed. Niji grew anxious. What if one of those uprights was AyJay? She would not rebuff the swarm with lightning like many other uprights did. She would simply leave—and niji could not bear the thought of starting another wait before the last one had even ended. Until niji knew who those uprights were, there must be no games.

So niji shaped itself a set of sound-makers and issued an attention-getting buzz. The sound was so emphatic, it stunned most of the swarm into stillness.

"Doo not play wiz tha upryts," niji said, upright-style because sound was proving to be a surprisingly effective way of communicating with a super-swarm. "Leev zem be." Then, because nijiti required some kind of motivation to disregard their impulses, niji added, "I eet u if u tuch."

A micro-pulse zigzagged across the garj's upper reaches like serial lightning—a sure sign that the swarm had understood the message. But its comprehension did not necessarily guarantee its compliance. For while niji was the zernarz, most evolved and therefore dominant of all those present, niji had no authority to demand anything but sustenance from inferiors—and that only if no other sustenance was available. In all other ways, varzi followed their own dictates. Or at least they had back when they were solitary or semi-solitary beings. Who knew what these augmented, upright-crazed nijiti would do?

The micro-pulse dissipated. A buzz rose up in its place. "Maytriks awn!"

So. Crazed or not, they were in no rush to be eaten. That was good to know.

"Maytriks awn! Maytriks awn!"

The buzz grew louder and stronger. The uprights went very still for a short while. Then they began exchanging gestures. The larger one pointed at the crawlyr and then to the rafters and then to the duhbulwydz. In each instance, the smaller one responded with a zhrug.

What is this behavior? niji's clone said.

The larger upright wants the smaller one to leave the garj, niji said. *The smaller one does not want to go.*

Niji did not want the small upright to go, either, and so was very pleased when that one began removing containers from the crawlyr's flat-side. Moving things into a space was a good sign. Moving things out of a space—was not. The larger upright made a few more gestures that niji did not understand and then moved toward the pedwhey in energetic, ground-eating strides. The next thing niji knew, there was only one upright left in the garj.

Was it her? Was it?

The nijiti continued to buzz, louder and louder. The upright began delving into containers with a steadiness that suggested urgency.

What is it doing? niji's clone wondered.

I think it is looking for something, niji replied, and then congratulated itself on a guess well-made as the upright jumped up with something in its hand.

Before niji could figure out what it was that the upright had found, however, the upright went hurrying off toward the other side of the garj. Niji tried to follow with its eyes but failed and had to reorient its mass in that direction.

Where is it? the pervarz pulsed, for it was not as fast to react as niji. *Where did it go?*

There! niji said. *By the maytriks!*

Frani-beats later, the image-wall erupted into a scintillating display of sparkling white light dancing on blue-green water. The swarm screeched with wonder and then fell silent. Niji was instantly mesmerized, too, wistfully transfixed. Seeing these utterly foreign images again made niji feel strangely whole.

"OK, you little monsters," a familiar voice said. "You got the damn matrix back. What else do you want?"

Niji's rapture gave way to a sharper, clearer sense of triumph and near-bliss. It looked away from the image-wall to see the upright standing with her hands on her hips. Although her outer top-nob was still in place, she had pushed the shiny central patch back to expose her inner features. She looked darker and better hydrated. But there was no mistaking her for anyone else. That was zra.

"GeeZuz AyJay!" niji's clone said, an excited screech. The swarm was quick to copy it. "GeeZuz AyJay, GeeZuz AyJay!"

"Zhit," zra said. The swarm copied that, too. "Zhit, zhit, zhit."

Let us go and present ourselves to her, zer, the clone said.

No, niji said. *The swarm is too excited. If we try to contact her now, it will overrun her. She will not like that.*

But while that was true, it was not the only reason that niji wanted to delay contact. Zra was niji's territory, niji's ideal. When it made contact with her, niji wanted to do it alone.

I do not want to wait, zer, the clone said. *I want to make contact now.*

No! niji said—a vigorous, almost vicious pulse. *Your presence will offend her. You have not evolved enough. You are—unworthy."

I am as worthy as you are, per said, depositing an azrum for emphasis. *And if you do not wish to accompany me, then I will go to zra alone.*

Anger flared niji like an upwelling of magma. Challenging niji's superiority would have been reason enough for niji to dominate the clone. But challenging niji's exclusive claim for the zernarz's attentions was what prompted niji to act. After everything that niji had endured to find and impress her, it was not about to permit some other varz, especially a worthless ul-nijit clone, to offend and possibly drive her away. So niji loosed an azrum of its own—a distilled expression of the many discoveries and intellectual advances that it had made since it had created the clone. As soon as per sampled the marker, per turned a humbled shade of gray and flattened itself. Niji could have eaten the clone then, but had no appetite for stupidity. Instead, niji streamed on top of the clone and purged its digestive vesicles of the wastes from its last feed. Some of the waste was still coated with digestive juices. The acids began to degrade per's outer membrane.

Let the burns be a lesson, niji said, as the clone struggled to remain still. *You presume too much.*

I was excited, per said. *The excitement impaired my judgment.*

Then you had best go away until you learn self-control.

The pervarz tensed, a sign of apprehension perhaps or perhaps just pain. *Where would you have me go?*

I care not where you take yourself, niji said, *so long as you leave this place and stay away from AyJay.*

And if I refuse?

I could have eaten you, niji said, *but I chose not to. I will not make that choice again.*

The tension flowed out of the clone all at once, signaling its submission. *I will leave this place and learn self-control,* it said. *I will stay away from AyJay.*

Niji dominated its clone for a few more frani-beats and then removed itself from its mass. Per immediately reconfigured itself for traveling and fled the rafters, shedding digested zyl shells and acid droplets as it went. As soon as it was out of sight, niji turned its attention back to AyJay.

Just then, the ground began to shake.

CHAPTER 17

"ARE YOU SURE ABOUT this?" Val asked, as OB2's double-wide rumbled open. "Prejudice wasn't the only reason Shingo abandoned this place, you know. It really did take a hit in the last shake."

"What choice do we have?" she said, pointedly ignoring his mention of earthquakes. "I've been told that there's a science station in the works, but that it's a low priority project and months away from completion. In the meantime, we're not allowed to set up shop in any of the seed structures. Shingo is adamant about keeping those free of Q and I can even sort of see his point."

See? She could be reasonable, at least out loud. Privately, she was still of the opinion that the CO's security policies were designed more for her than the Q— anything to hinder or frustrate her. There were consequences for thwarting the local warlord.

"There's always the shuttle," Val said, for maybe the fourth or fifth time. "Shingo said we could have it. And we'd certainly have it all to ourselves."

She wondered why he was campaigning for the shuttle so persistently. Had he heard something? Or was he fussing out of habit? Not that it mattered, because she wasn't going back to that re-purposed piece of junk for love, money, or Terra. The mere thought of doing so left her dizzy and a little breathless. She didn't know why exactly. It was just too small and closed up and full of hardship memories. But even if the shuttle had been the most cherry site on the planet, she would've passed on it simply because she couldn't trust anything that Shingo wanted her to have.

Fortunately, she had a more PC excuse at her disposal.

"The shuttle has an airlock that Q can't operate," she said. "What's the point of having a base that our target audience can't access? Besides," she added, as he steered the crawler into the garage, "this is where the matrix is. Bob was attracted to it. My guess is that other Q will be, too. We won't have to go to them. They'll come to us."

"I suppose that makes sense," Val said, a supremely grudging concession, and then killed the crawler's engine with a gesture that looked resigned. "Welcome home."

The garage looked as run-down on the inside as it did from the outside. There was an odd slant to the overhead lights that she attributed to earthquake damage. Every surface that she could see bore a thick layer of dust. And the liquid-metal floor was so pocked with corrosion, it looked like Swiss cheese in some places. She nodded at one of the patches and said, "WTF?"

"Q-pie damage," Val said sourly. "When the garage was still in use, we used to patch the holes. Now that it's been abandoned—"

A strange screeching sound cut him off. It started off soft but quickly grew too loud to be ignored. The racket reminded AJ of cicadas screaming for love on a hot summer night. A whole army of cicadas.

"The wind?" AJ asked, even though it hadn't been blowing on the ride in.

Val shook the guess off and said, "That's the Q."

Until this very moment, she hadn't understood why everybody was so freaked out about a little alien chatter. Now she knew. "Un-fucking-real."

"The first time you hear it is especially mind-boggling," Val said. "I wanted to record it for you so you'd know what was waiting for you. But Shingo said that would be a security risk and wouldn't allow it."

"I could've listened to a million recordings and still not been prepared for this. I mean—just listen." At first, the screech had struck her as wild and chaotic and more than a little scary, but now that she was getting used to it, she could hear a distinct set of sounds being repeated over and over again. Mah-trykz-zahn. She was sure it meant something. But what? "It doesn't sound like they're asking for me."

"Just wait," Val said, which sent a little shiver scudding down her spine. "At any rate, it looks like you were right. This is definitely the place to find Q. Now what?"

"Let's start—"

He tensed as if stung and then forestalled her with an upraised hand. She knew a ping when she saw one, and she could guess who it was from by the way Val stiffened through the back and shoulders. So she wasn't surprised when the hand came down and he said, "That was Shingo. He wants to see me. Now."

"I guess you've been forgiven," she said.

"I'm your second," he said. "If you don't want me to go, I won't."

She dismissed the suggestion with a shrug. "You might as well get the unpleasantness out of the way now. While you're gone, I'll start setting up."

"He's going to want details about what we're doing," he said.

"So tell him," she said. "We haven't got any secrets."

"What about—us?"

"We're not breaking any rules or regs," she said, "so my official stance is that it's none of his business. But if you want to brag about banging an old lady, feel free."

He sputtered, an involuntary vent of exasperation. "You can be such a jerk sometimes."

She couldn't help but laugh, for it wasn't often that she managed to flush him out of his self-contained pocket. "And yet you continue to hang with me," she said. "Even when you have somewhere else to be." When he refused to take the hint, she nudged him with an elbow. "Why are you still here?" He shifted his weight from one foot to the other, and then muttered something under his breath. "What was that?" she asked.

He shifted again, folding his arms across his chest as if to form a bumper. "I said—I'd rather not leave you alone in here."

Her first impulse was to laugh again. Now he was afraid for her? Now? Talk about after the fact! Still, she could not bring herself to mock him outright. She liked that he worried about her, liked that he cared—even if she did have a hard time admitting that to him or anyone else. But there was no room for tender feelings out in the field. He could care, but coddling was not allowed.

"I can take care of myself," she said, even as the screeching grew more emphatic. "Now go and see what his lordship wants. On your way back, requisition a case of SBF. I think we're going to need it."

"You're the boss." He tossed her a mock salute and then headed toward the pedway with an exaggerated swagger. Over his shoulder, he said, "If you're covered with Q when I return, I'm going to let them have you."

"Yeah right," she said, and began off-loading the crawler.

"Mah-trykz-zhn! Mah-trykz-zhn!"

AJ didn't know when the screeching started to make sense. One moment it was a clamor that she was trying to filter out; the next, it was a demand that she knew how to answer. All she needed was a pack of mini-batteries. She rifled through the crates that she'd already pulled down from the crawler, but found only surveillance equipment: audio, visual, other. She had agreed to the monitors because they collected data without causing physical harm. But she'd put her foot down hard when TSC asked her to collect tissue samples, too, or if possible, a living specimen. NFW, she'd said, and promised to quit on the spot if she caught anyone trying to harvest Q or Q parts. The threat had prompted apologies, backpedaling, and documented reassurances of TSC's good intentions. She had no doubt that those reassurances would expire as soon as TSC had what it wanted, but she'd worry about that tomorrow. Right now—

"Mah-trykz-zahn! Mah-trykz-zahn!"

—she had more pressing concerns.

The battery pack was in the third-to-last container. As soon as she found it, she headed for the matrix, hop-scotching Q-pies and potholes along the way. Although she did not see any Q, she heard dry, leathery skittering all around her and so knew that she was being followed. It was a scary realization, but surprisingly exciting, too. What if she could settle everything right here and now and go home? The rational part of her recognized this as a fantasy, but ran with it anyway because hot-friggin-damn, wouldn't that be nice? She popped the matrix's power panel, snapped the pack in place, and then selected a program at random. As the chip clicked into place, she fired up the grid.

Paradise erupted across the dusty all-wall: blue skies, white sand, frothy turquoise water. She gasped, startled by the display, and then laughed. Nature porn—and one of her own long-lost chips by the look of it! Although she didn't believe in such things, she told herself that this was a sign, proof that anything could happen. Maybe she could settle everything right here and now and go home! It was certainly worth a try.

"OK, you little monsters," she said, pushing her face-plate back so the Q could see her. "You got the damn matrix back. What else do you want?"

The ocean-washed silence that had overtaken the garage lingered for a moment longer. Then the screeching started up again—a new, frenzied chorus. This time, she understood the message right away.

"GeeZuz AyJay! GeeZuz AyJay!"

"Shit," she said.

"Zhit, zhit, zhit," the Q screamed.

AJ was gobsmacked, totally blown away. Not only did the little monsters recognize her, they knew her name. But why? Why her? What could they possibly want with—

The ground jiggled —a fleshy little twitch that sounded worse than it felt. AJ had already dismissed it when the second jolt struck. This one lifted the garage right off of its foundation—and then slammed it back down again. The garage went dark and then started shaking in earnest. *Run, 'Nita!* Shit started raining down from the rafters: light fixtures, chunks of plastic, shadowy blobs. The floor buckled and then twisted into pieces with a shrill, liquid-metal groan. *Run!* AJ was already bolting toward the pedway, but it was—gone? No! The front wall was collapsing—her way. The adjacent wall was coming down, too. The only thing she could do was dive for the cover of a nearby workbench and hope for the chance to hear Val say, "I told you so."

An instant after she scrambled under the bench, the garage came crashing down around her. An instant later, something hard collided with the back of her head. Her helmet absorbed the worst of the blow, but even so it took her a moment to realize that the thing that had hit her was the underside of the bench. In that time-frame, the bench sank further into the ground and pinned her where she was sprawled. The floor beneath her was hard-pack rather than liquid metal, which meant that there was nothing to stop the bench from being driven completely underground—and crushing her in the process.

A voice erupted from her headset, loud as a thunderclap. "AJ! Where are you? Are you OK?"

"I'm in the—garage," she said, trying not to breathe and thereby lose that tiny margin of space. "It collapsed. I'm—" She couldn't bring herself to say trapped. "I'm stuck under one wall, maybe two. I'm gonna need some help getting—out."

"I'm on my way," he said. "Stay put."

She laughed just a little, ha-ha, who wouldn't in her habby? Mistake. The bench shifted, flattening her. The pressure on her backside intensified into pain. All she could do was grit her teeth and focus on an ending that did not involve being squashed like a flea. Her parents ghosted out of her memories. Meli looked worried. Her father was his usual no-nonsense self.

Good thing you're chipped.

He had the right of it, too. There was no way she was getting out of this alive. Gravity was going to finish asserting itself, and she was going to die. And the funny-sad thing was, the thought of Val finding her crushed disturbed her more than the prospect of her own demise.

Meli started singing in Cherokee. She motioned for AJ to sing along, but AJ couldn't breathe and her oxygen-starved brain was playing tricks on her. She thought she saw a face in the sand beneath her face-plate: a smiley, lump-nosed face with odd, bulging eyes. It sort of looked like—Singer. And it sort of looked like it was reaching out to her. She gasped, fighting against pressure and pain for a sip of air. Her thoughts were spiraling toward unconsciousness. The last thing she heard before blackness set in was, "Jesus, AJ, what's going on? Your loco-chip's gone loco."

CHAPTER 18

As SOON AS NIJI sensed the first shockwave, niji knew the ground-shake was going to be substantial and so fled the rafters. After the second shockwave hit and the companion lights went out, niji knew that the garj was likely to lose its shape. The last thing niji saw before it burrowed into the regolith for safety was AyJay. She was standing in front of the maytriks instead of moving in haste toward the pedwhey. Zhee! Did she not realize the danger? Or could uprights be frozen-stupid, too? Niji did not know how it was with her, but it intended to find out. So as soon as the shaking and groaning and crashing stopped, niji tunneled back into the garj.

Dark-warm-dusty was the first impression it collected. The floor was covered with debris and the rafters were much, much closer to the ground. The pedhway was now a jumble of ulvarzi metal, but niji started in that direction anyway because she would have gone that way if she had not been frozen-stupid. And niji did not want to believe that the supreme being had succumbed to panic. She must have been distracted or otherwise slow to react. And if she had not made it to the pedwhey, she would be somewhere near it. She would not be upright now. She would be on one of her flat sides, sealed up in her outer shell for protection. Niji wondered how much danger that shell could repel. Niji wondered if the shell could repel a whole garj.

As niji streamed through the wreckage, it sent frani ranging far and wide for markers so it could maintain its bearings in the dark. One sensor slid past a familiar-tasting overhang and then doubled back, drawn by the faintest of stirrings. Yes, there it was again! Movement! Niji probed deeper into the recess, expecting to find a sheltering varz. To niji's surprise and dismay, it found AyJay instead. It did not know how she had gotten into a space that was much too tight for her. It did not understand why she would choose to stay there now that the shaking had stopped. All it was certain of was her present danger. Little by little, the recess was being compacted by a great weight from above. She was being compacted, too. If she did not get out of there, she would be squashed like a varz beneath an ulvarz's treads.

Niji shaped itself a noise-maker and urged her to evacuate, but she did not seem to hear. It shaped itself a hand and tapped the back of her top-nob, but she did not seem to notice. She must be injured then, and in the sleep-that-heals. So the only way that she was going to relocate was if niji moved her. But niji did not have the strength to pull her from that recess. It was only strong underground and even then, it would not be able to shift her by itself.

But—what if it had help?

Niji began shouting upright-style. "GeeZuz AyJay Needz U Now!"

By ones and twos, nijiti began streaming forth from the the garj's detritus. Some had been damaged in the ground-shake, a few too badly to tunnel, but none could resist the lure of AyJay's name. As soon as the impromptu swarm came within range, niji absorbed its noise-makers and began communicating in micro-pulses so there would be no misunderstandings.

Hurry, it said. *GeeZuz AyJay is being crushed there beneath a great weight. We must join together and tunnel her to safety before her membranes burst.*

Pervarzi might have balked at the idea, for collaboration was swarm behavior. But nijiti had no such qualms. The thought of moving something other than themselves through the sand excited them. And knowing that that something was the supreme being multiplied the thrill. So without further urging, the swarm started digging. And niji was in the lead.

CHAPTER 19

AN IMPRESSION IMPINGED ON AJ's pain-spangled subconscious: movement; a headlong, horizontal passage through resistant, undulating darkness. It felt like birth—or maybe peristalsis. Either way, it felt like something for which she ought to be present. She thought she opened her eyes, but maybe not, for the darkness remained. As she stared at it, it seemed to develop texture, a coarse graininess that struck her as strangely familiar. She thought to confirm that impression with a touch, but her arms remained molded to her sides. When she tried to press the issue, she was punished with a bristling clap of pain.

So impatient, just like your father.

She played dead, hoping to fool the pain into moving on, but then her brain began playing tricks on her. It kept registering phantom sensations—pinpoints of pressure that were everywhere and barely there and never in the same place twice. Once as a child, she had watched a company of ants carry a dying grasshopper back to its hill. Now she thought she knew how that hopper felt. Like fresh meat for the colony. Was this what an out-of-body experience was like? Or was this all just a trauma dream?

Her trajectory went abruptly vertical. Toward the sky. Toward the stars. Toward Canis Major and the guardians. *Remember to save something for the second dog.* And then—release. No more pressure, no more movement, only pain and someone shouting her name. "AJ? Is that you?"

Something heavy landed on the ground next to her. Strong arms scooped her up. She recognized the feel, and the fit. This was Val. He'd rescued her.

"Jesus, AJ," he said, hugging her to his chest. "I thought you were dead."

"Me, too," she said. And although it hurt to talk, she absolutely had to add, "Thanks for getting me out."

She felt every muscle in his body tense. Uh-oh. "But I didn't. You were already out by the time I got here. This is where I found you."

"But—I remember being carried." She scowled, trying to bring the memory into focus, but the details remained just beyond the boundaries of recall. "I remember feeling—like shit."

"AJ, a garage fell on you! Who wouldn't feel like shit after something like that?"

"No, that's not what I meant," she said, but suddenly, she wasn't sure of anything other than the pain in her back and a sense of being put through a giant wringer. "Help me up, OK? I have to get some PK in circulation before everything stiffens up."

"How about you just stay put for a few minutes?" he countered. "I put a call into Dispatch said they'd send the next available float."

The thought of floating back to the FZ appealed to her. The thought of waiting out in the desolate semi-gloom did not. "We lose anything besides the garage?" she asked.

"I hear one of the power sub-stations took a minor hit," he said. "A second seed install collapsed, too—with personnel in it. That's where everybody is at the moment."

"Which means there's not going to be a float heading this way any time soon," she said, going by the needs of the many versus the needs of the few. And that was the deciding factor. "So help me up. I'm not going to lie here all day like roadkill."

He groaned—a long, aggravated belly-sound that jack-knifed into grudging resignation. Then he shifted her out of his lap, stood up, and then offered her a hand. Halfway to her feet, her entire back seized up. He scooped her up like a child as she collapsed and broke into a trot only to stumble and sputter, "What the—?" The next thing she knew, they were both on the ground again, and she was half-blind from the pain.

"I can't—believe—you—did that," she managed to gasp.

His only reply was a string of epithets—a hugely uncharacteristic response that set off all sorts of alarms in AJ's head. She rolled over, then pushed herself onto her hands and knees—an agonizing process that had her eyes streaming tears. She blinked to clear her vision and then blinked again as she spotted Val. He was writhing on the ground and clutching at his helmet like a crazy man. WTF? Had he brained himself on a rock when he fell? She crawled toward him, meaning to help in any way no matter the cost to herself. Then, as she closed in on him, she realized that he was clutching at his helmet because there was a big blob of flailing tentacles attached to it. Crud! She didn't even want to imagine what that looked like from Val's point of view.

"You OK in there?" she said, tapping into their private channel.

"So far," Val said. "But I think it's trying to pop my top."

"Mm, take-out," she said, but it was the pain talking. She was trying to control too many things at the same time. "Hard on the outside, soft and pink in the center."

"Not funny, AJ," Val said, and then groaned. "Jesus, it just jacked on my face-plate. This is—this is worse than the cheap seats at a Martian peep show. Get it off me already."

"OK, OK," she said. "But you're going to have to hold still. If you hit me, I'll pop your top myself. I won't care if you hit me by accident."

"My old man would've loved you," he muttered. But he did in fact go very, very still.

AJ dragged herself into a seated position, grinding her teeth all the way. Then, because she didn't have a clue as to what to do next, she went with the first thing she that came to mind—a polite little tap on what she fervently hoped was the Q's backside. Dozens of tiny new tentacles sprouted up from the point of contact. Some of these entwined to form a bulb-tipped stalk. The rest grew over the stalk, leaving only the knobby tip in sight. The knob split open along the meridian, revealing an eye that bore hints of green in its eerie, diamond-shaped pupil.

"Crud," she said. When Val asked what was going on, she added, "It's rearranging itself."

Another eye formed, identical to the first. A nose-like lump appeared next, then a broad gash with gelatinous edges that curled upward at the corners. She stared at the face, for that was what it was. She had seen it before—in a dream maybe. But it seemed more familiar than that. She could sense the answer lurking just beyond the pain.

"What's it doing now?" Val said.

"It grew a face," she said. "It looks a little like—Singer." Crud, that was it! Or at least some of it. She had a niggling sense that there were other pieces to this alien puzzle. "I think this is Bob. I think he's smiling at me."

"Great," Val said sarcastically. "Now get it off."

"Patience, Johnny," she said. Because despite the pain and the threat of shock setting in, she was surprisingly curious.

Bob's tentacles had all gone still. His eyes were ranging independently of each other—one up and down the length of her face-plate, the other forth and back. She wondered what he was looking for—a way in? She didn't think so. But the Q had attacked Val. Hadn't he? Crud. She didn't know what to think.

Bob continued to scrutinize her face-plate. Then, although his frog-like gash of a mouth didn't move, she clearly heard it say, "AyJay? OhKay?"

AJ remembered then. This was the face that she had seen rising up from the ground after the quake when she was trapped and out of breath and starting to die. This was the face that had saved her life.

"Yes, Bob," she said, utterly convinced. "I am OK—thanks to you."

The tentacles that had been resting on Val's face-plate stirred like a nest of AZ snakes and then began to slither her way. As they did so, they knitted and wove themselves into the facsimile of a hand.

"AyJay?" Bob said, reaching out to her. "OhKay?"

The sight spawned another realization. The Q wanted to touch her. She didn't know why, but he did. And despite her condition and personal misgivings, she was prepared to grant Bob's wish. It seemed like a small enough price to pay for her life.

But first, some house rules.

She pointed to herself and said, "AJ," then to the Q and said, "Bob," and then to Val and said, "Val." Then she pointed to herself again, hoping that the Q was as smart as he seemed to be.

"AyJay," Bob said. And when she pointed to Val, it said, "Vahl," with a distinct frown. Ha, thought so.

"Val is mine," she said, thumbing her chest. "AJ's. Bob no touch Val. Bob touch Val, AJ give Bob to vac. Now leave Val."

The exaggerated gestures that accompanied the commands fanned the pain in her back into full-fledged agony, but they had the desired result. Bob abandoned its perch on Val's face-plate without hesitation or a backward glance. Then it closed in on her, still sporting a hand and Singer's countenance.

"Now AyJay?" it said, reaching out. "OhKay?"

"Yeah, sure," she said, because she had promised. "Just don't get carried away, OK?"

She had visions of Bob latching onto her face-plate or probing her every nook and cranny. Instead, the Q simply took possession of her hand and held it, pulsating like a happy heart, until the EMTs showed up. Then, as they began prepping her for transport, he let go of her and started sinking or maybe melting into the sand. Just before his ersatz face disappeared, he said, "Zee U Zoon, OhKay?"

By then, the PK that the EMT had given her was kicking in and she thought she might be dreaming again. But she said, "OK," anyway because really, how could anyone refuse a pulsating heart?

CHAPTER 20

Niji was in a singular state, so self-satisfied that its outer membrane actually felt strained. *Hahpee* was the upright wrd for this condition. The sound seemed too short and taut for such an overfull sensation, but niji had been assured by AyJay herself that the shape of an upright sound did not always reflect its meaning. And AyJay was always right.

So niji was hahpee.

And why would niji be otherwise? Here it was, ensconced in *daboht*, engaged with a miniature maytriks that was much smaller and much smarter than the one that lived in the garj. *Pahd*, this new maytriks was called, and it contained vast stores of upright knowledge that niji was in the process of absorbing. The pahd also contained challenges that AyJay wanted niji to solve, but thus far, niji was not having much success. Mayzyz in particular mystified niji. Why would anyone try to navigate an extremely convoluted passageway when it could—

A shallow thud in the next compartment diverted niji's attention. It extended a cluster of frani in that direction, feeling for movement, and was rewarded with a faint shuffling: the sound of padded upright feet sliding across the floor. Yes! AyJay was finally emerging from her resting place. Niji was not allowed in there. And she needed a lot of rest. So niji was even more anxious than usual for her to make an appearance. Niji had to be careful not to display its anxiety, though. Uprights did not like to see agitation in varzi.

The shuffling transitioned into distinct footsteps: a cue for niji to retract its sensors. Niji had discovered that uprights did not care for the sight of undifferentiated frani, either. Niji shaped the retractions into a third eye which it embedded in the back of its top-nob and then watched for AJ. She entered the main compartment slowly, holding on to whatever presented itself in passing. As she moved, she bared her front teeth—a display that niji had come to recognize as pain. But her inner top-nob looked less faded than it had when she first started coming to daboht, and her respiratory processes were much less strained.

"Well," Vahl said, when he saw her. "Look who's up."

He rushed to her side and then helped her over to a roosting place. Although their contact was purely collaborative, it provoked an unreasoning pang of possessiveness in niji just the same. And although niji knew that AJ would not be hahpee if niji acted on the impulse, niji was visited by the urge to topple Vahl and express digestive vacuoles in his face.

"How are you feeling?" Val asked, as AJ lowered herself onto her roost, and it seemed to niji that he was deliberately blocking niji's view of her. "You look better."

Niji knew that its hunger to dominate Vahl was wrong. He might be inferior to AyJay, but he was still an upright and vastly superior to niji. But lowly or not, niji could not bear the thought of being separated from zra again. So when Vahl came between them by a lot or even just a little, niji wanted nothing more than to make him go away.

If only zra did not favor Vahl so!

"I'm OK," AyJay said. "I'm not crazy about sleeping in that tiny bunk in this condition, but it beats sleeping standing up."

"You could go back to the FZ for naps, you know," Vahl said. "You might even want to think about staying there for a few days. The bed in our apartment is comfortable enough."

"Cracked ribs are going to hurt no matter where I am," she said, "so I might as well be here where all the action is. The sooner we figure out why I'm here, the sooner I'm on my way back home."

Vahl's mouth puckered. Niji thought that was a signal for *unhahpee,* but it was still new at interpreting facial displays and could not be sure. "Let's cross that bridge when we get to it, shall we?" he said, and then touched her arm. "You hungry?"

"A little," she said. "I'll fix myself a bite after I check in with Bob." Niji flushed with pleasure, for 'Bob' was the upright wrd for 'niji.' If AyJay was tawkyn about niji, then AyJay was thinking about niji! Zhee! "How's he doing with the maze, by the way?"

"He keeps on trying to go over the walls," Vahl said. "But I have to admit— he's made more progress with the pad than I thought he would. He's definitely smarter than he looks."

"Isn't that what your father used to say about you?" AyJay said.

Vahl's mouth tried to pucker again but quirked to one side instead. Niji did not know what that display meant, either, and wondered if it would ever be fluent in that form of upright communication. Chemical expressions were so much easier to understand!

"Smart-ass," Vahl said. "Good thing I'm so damn fond of you. Otherwise, I'd abandon you to the Q in a heartbeat."

"Yeah, right," AyJay said, and then ran a finger down the underside of his chin as if she were collecting some kind of sample. "I'm rather fond of you, too. You know that, right?"

Vahl turned an interesting shade of pink and said, "Not in front of the alien, OK?"

AyJay started to expel a hahpee gust of air only to abruptly suck it back in. Vahl stiffened at that and tried to touch her again, but to niji's gratification, zra motioned him away. "It's OK," she said. "I'll be fine. But maybe I ought to get something in my stomach sooner rather than later after all. Would you mind fixing me some tofu and re-hydrated mango while I look in on Bob?" Frani-beats later, she added, "Please?"

"Yeah, sure," Vahl said then. "But only if he comes to you."

"Why disturb him when he's already settled?" AyJay said, as she lifted herself off of her roost. "I'm hurt, not crippled."

As soon as niji realized that zra was coming over for a visit, niji absorbed its third eye and refined its upright semblance as much as it could. Nothing less than its best efforts would impress AyJay, and impressing her was all that mattered. Niji tried to focus on the pahd as she approached, but it was too excited to do more than fondle its front-side. And when she lowered herself onto the roost next to niji, niji forgot about the pahd entirely. Without her outer top-nob, she was even more of a distraction than usual. Her exhalations were laden with water and intriguing oils. Her outer membranes exuded complex smells. And— the upper parts of her inner top-nob were covered with strands of frani-like insulation. Vahl liked to run his fyngrs through this covering. Niji yearned for a chance to do the same.

"Hello, Bob," she said, sending niji's longing back into hiding. "It's good to see you again."

"I hahpee you ar heer, AyJay," niji buzzed.

The corners of her mouth curved upward. That was encouraging, a good sign. She pointed at the pahd and said, "I hear you are doing well with this."

"Yzz," niji said, flushing with pleasure at the praise. "I want bee smart lyk uprytz."

Zra expelled a microburst of air through her nose. Niji did not know what if anything that was supposed to mean, but before it had a chance to consider the gesture in depth, AyJay tapped the pahd and said, "Work the maze for me."

The precursors of a panic sweat began to take shape in niji's protoplasm. For while niji could not refuse AyJay in any way, it had no desire to demonstrate its unworthiness to her, and its failure to comprehend mayzyz would surely do that. Niji thought about distracting her. A few loose frani would do the trick— especially if they caught Vahl's attention. But before niji had a chance to act on the idea or even think it through, the hach slid open and an upright strode into daboht. AyJay's attention turned toward the newcomer. Niji's panic precursors dissolved. Then the newcomer skidded to a stop and pointed in niji's direction.

"You're teaching that thing how to use a pad?"

"Commander Zhingo," AyJay said, in a voice that was sharp and cold like shattered ice. "How nice of you to drop in. To what do we owe the pleasure?"

As soon as niji sensed the sound 'Zhing-oh', niji oozed down to the floor and then hid itself in the shadows beneath AyJay's roost. For even the dimmest of nijiti were aware of this upright's existence and his extreme intolerance of inferiors.

"I was told that you had been injured in the quake, so I came to see how you were faring," Zhing-oh said. "Obviously, that report was exaggerated. You look quite functional to me."

"How nice of you to say so," zra said, although she did not sound very pleased.

"The ribs are still a little sore, but I'm managing."

"You appear to have a knack for managing things," Zhing-oh said. "Perhaps you could tell me how you managed to survive OB2's collapse all but unscathed. The report says that you were still inside when the structure came down, but that does not seem plausible."

"Plausible or not," zra said, "the report is true. I remember being trapped beneath a pile of rubble and being unable to breathe. I remember blacking out and thinking that I was dead. Then I remember waking up and finding myself outside. Everything else, however, is a blank."

"That seems rather—convenient," Zhing-oh said.

Zra's shadow stiffened. "Too bad you didn't send a crew to my rescue," she said, using that shattered ice voice again." A third party might have been able to provide you with a more complete story."

Although niji could have been mistaken, niji thought that Zhing-oh's shadow grew a little taller, too. "The quake caused an explosion in one of the second seed facilities," he said. "Twelve lives and some highly important equipment were at risk. Given the circumstances and the limited resources at my disposal, I chose to try and save twelve instead of one. I am sure you would have made the same decision in my stead.

"And let us not forget that it was you who insisted on occupying OB2 despite my urgings otherwise."

"Finally," AyJay said. "I thought you were never going to get around to dropping that I-told-you-so. Happy now?"

"Not at all," Zhing-oh said, and then shifted, an obvious attempt to look under her roost. His top-nob patch was up now. Niji caught a glimpse of narrowed eyz and a pinched mouth—a threat display if niji had ever seen one. Then he pointed directly at niji and said, "Why are you teaching this thing to use a pahd?"

Niji flushed a darker shade of shadow, hoping to remove itself from Zhing-oh's sight. As it did so, AyJay moved to block his view. Niji nearly went flat with gratitude and relief. Zra was truly supreme!

"It's the fastest way to figure out what he and the other kew want," she said.

"Why not just ask it what it wants?" Zhing-oh said. "You say they are smart. We know they have a primitive capacity for speech."

"Maybe so," AyJay said. "But how can we trust any answer we might get if we're not sure what it is we're asking? We need to establish a cognitive baseline."

"Show me."

"Excuse me?" she said.

"I wish to see what you are doing to establish this baseline," Zhing-oh said. "Show me."

"Sorry," she said, and even without seeing her facial display, niji could tell that she was not expressing genuine regret. "No can do."

Zhing-oh shifted again, seemingly trying to become more upright than AyJay. "I am the CO of this installation," he said. "I am responsible for its security. You will show me what you are teaching that thing."

"This thing," AyJay said, "is obviously afraid of you. And that, Commander, is the only thing we're going to establish as long as you're here. If you want answers, you'll take yourself elsewhere and stay there. I promise I'll copy you on every single report I file."

"I prefer reports that include supplemental documentation," Zhing-oh said, "for they are less likely to reflect the reporter's bias, unintentional or otherwise. What a shame that you lost all of your monitoring equipment in the collapse. Or was that, perhaps, the real reason that you were so adamant about returning to OB2?"

"What?" AyJay said—a harsh, nijiti-like sound. Val made an unfamiliar noise, too, and then said, "Jesus, Zhing-oh! Did you really just accuse the Special Envoy of sabotage? That has to be the most ridiculous—"

He stopped, silenced by the sound of the hach opening. All three uprights pivoted in that direction. All three then recoiled from the pock-marked varz that came streaming into view. Per had shaped itself a reasonably detailed head and face, but everything below its chin was a mass of writhing frani.

"Zra!" it buzzed, as it wriggled its way toward AyJay. "Zra!"

"Crud," zra said.

Vahl stepped in front of her. Zhing-oh pulled a lightning stick from a compartment in his outer membrane. By then, niji was already streaming toward the ul-nijit. Zhing-oh's presence no longer mattered. Neither did the prospect of being shocked. Keeping the clone away from AyJay was niji's sole concern.

I told you to be gone, niji pulsed, a microburst as livid as its flush.

The clone skittered to a stop, but offered no display of regret or remorse. *You told me to go away from the garj,* it said. *This is not the garj.*

This is the new garj, niji said, *and your presence offends me. Leave before you offend zra, too.*

To niji's utter astonishment, the clone remained where it was. *How can I be offensive if you are not?* it wanted to know. *I possess most of your memory strands. And I demonstrated my worthiness by finding my way into this place.*

How can you be offensive? niji repeated, injecting a full measure of contempt into the pulse. *You are ul-nijit, a thrill-seeker with forward-thinking strands. You lack comprehension. You lack perspective. You lack control.* As niji recounted the clone's failings, niji also adopted its likeness. *Despite all the knowledge in your possession, you have progressed no further than this. Look what I have learned to do.*

Niji shaped itself a neck and then a set of shoulders, a torso, and limbs. The arms were fitted with hands, but not elbows or wrists. The legs had no knees or ankles. Even so, niji was completely upright—an unprecedented accomplishment.

"Jesus," it heard Vahl say.

Niji had never felt more dominant. It looked down at the ul-nijit. Per's flush had turned a distressed shade of grey. Its upright features had become less defined.

As niji towered over it, per expressed an azrum.

"Damn," Vahl said, and then went hurrying off.

Niji did not concern itself with Vahl's departure. Niji was busy sampling the azrum with a feeler that stemmed from the bottom of niji's toeless foot. The marker tasted of submission and humility. The marker contained an offer to go away and never return. But niji no longer had any desire to be generous with its clone.

You will stay, niji pulsed. *I am hungry.*

The clone made no effort to dissuade niji or escape. Instead, per began to relinquish the remnants of its upright façade. *I am inferior,* it pulsed, as it changed. *I give myself up so you may continue to evolve."

Niji lowered itself onto the ul-nijit's unresisting mass, returning to shapelessness in the process. Per was too big to be absorbed, so niji started to engulf it instead. As it folded its leading edges over and around the clone, stretching and straining to enclose per's much larger mass, the uprights began to chatter excitedly.

"What is this behavior?" Zhing-oh said.

"Beats me," Vahl said. "This is the first time we've seen kew interact. But it looks like Bob is trying to wrestle with the other guy."

"That doesn't look like wrestling to me," AyJay said.

"I concur," Zhing-oh said. "Tell your Q to disengage."

"Why?" AyJay asked. "We're not here to interfere."

"I wish to see if it will obey you."

"Why?" AyJay asked again.

"Because I wish to know if it has the capacity to be compliant."

Niji's leading edges were on the verge of knitting together to create a giant vacuole. As soon as engulfment was complete, digestion would begin. It could already feel acidic precursors forming in its protoplasm. If niji had not been hungry earlier, it certainly was now. And after a feed of this magnitude, it was going to need a sizeable nap.

"Bob."

The thought of a lengthy jaza did not agree with niji. If niji was sleeping, it would not be able to attend to AyJay. And in its absence, some other ambitious ul-nijit varz might sneak in and try to claim zra's attention. Niji did not like that thought at all.

"Bob!"

Perhaps eating its clone here and now was not the wisest course of action—

"Bob!"

Zhee! Niji knew that sound! It was the upright wrd for niji. Zra wanted niji's attention! Niji hastily shaped itself an oculum and aimed it in her direction. Her mouth was pinched. The span of membrane above her eyes was bunched. She did not look hahpee. Niji wondered if she was in pain.

"Let that kew go," she said, and pointed at the gap between its leading edges.

Niji understood the wrdz. Niji understood their context, too. What it did not understand, however, was why she wanted niji to release the clone. Had she not been offended by its obvious inferiority? Could it be that she did not want it to go away or worse that she favored it over niji? That possibility made niji want to feed on the ul-nijit more than ever, no matter how lengthy the resulting jaza might be. But even as the urge tickled its leading edges, niji had another thought. What if, like niji, AyJay simply didn't think that eating the clone now was the wisest course of action?

Zhee! Niji was starting to think like an upright!

Niji disgorged the clone all at once and then distanced itself from the insensate mass. Niji was hungry but had no appetite. It was tired but had no wish to sleep. It wondered if this strange state was what came of surrendering a catch or if it was starting to feel like an upright, too.

"Interesting," Zhing-oh said. "What will you do with the other one now?"

"Given Bob's apparent dislike of it," AyJay said, "I'll probably ship it off to the detention center for relocation."

"As it happens," Zhing-oh said, "I am heading in that direction. If you wish, I can take it to QDC for you."

"Would it get to detention?" AyJay asked. "Or were you planning on putting it out of its misery somewhere along the way?"

"You have yet to prove to me that it is capable of misery," Zhing-oh said. "However, if you do not trust me with its transport, then by all means, find someone else to do it. I was merely trying to be of assistance during your convalescence."

"Thank you, Commander," Vahl said. "We appreciate the help. Give me a minute to pack it up for you."

The upright peeled the still-senseless ul-nijit up from the floor and then disappeared into the next compartment with it. When he returned, there was a container trailing behind him. *Floht*, this container was called. Vahl had first brought niji to daboht in that vessel. No doubt, the clone was now leaving in it. Niji was hahpee to see it go and wanted never to see it again.

"Thanks again," Vahl said, as he gave the floht over to Zhing-oh. Zhing-oh said, "I will be expecting your reports," and then started toward the hach with the floht on his heels. As soon as he disappeared from sight, AyJay slumped on her roost and let out a long exhalation.

"You OK?" Vahl asked.

"Yeah," she said—a flat, unenthusiastic sound. "I just wasn't expecting a visit from his lordship. That offer of tofu and mango still good?"

"On it," Vahl said.

As he withdrew, she turned her attention to niji. "You oh-kay, Bob?"

Her interest in its condition energized niji. It shifted back into its upright configuration, eyz first and then noise-makers, and said, "Yzz, AyJay. Oh-kay."

"Did you know that other kew?" she asked.

"Yzz," niji said.

"What did it want?" AJ said.

"It wahnt be ur fren, zra."

The upper part of her face bunched up again. "Why? Why me?"

The question flustered niji. It did not know enough wrdz to tell her about the obsession that she had inspired in niji or how niji had accidentally passed that obsession on to its ul-nijit clone, or how the clone had spread the infection afterward. And even if niji had been that fluent in upright, it was not sure that it wanted to claim such a disastrous cascade of events.

"You no hurt kew," niji said. "All kew no thiz."

"So if he was friendly, why did you—" She made an engulfing motion with her arms. "Attack him?"

Another complicated question! Was this another test? "Zhat kew not zo gud," niji said, wishing that it could express the answer in an azrum instead. "Zhat kew not gud nuf fer you."

Just then, Vahl reappeared with a thin slab in his hands. As he set the slab down in front of AyJay, he said, "Sounds like our BEM has a little daddy complex for you."

"Funny," AyJay said, and then began transferring jiggly white bits and glistening orange strips from the slab to her mouth-hole. Between transfers, she said, "I no hurt kew so you no hurt kew, oh-kay, Bob? We do not attack our friends. Understand?"

"Yzz," niji said, flushed with pleasure. For now it understood why she had interceded on the ul-nijit's behalf. She wanted niji to change—not just its appearance, but its behavior! With enough practice, even a nijit could look like an upright. But to truly evolve, niji had to assume upright ways as well. That meant doing things that did not come naturally—like being generous with and tolerant of other varzi, especially nijiti. It would have to stop feeding on inferiors, too, unless it was on the verge of—

No. There could be no exceptions. Where there were exceptions, there were opportunities for failure. And failures did not evolve.

CHAPTER 21

"So—ANY GUESSES AS TO what really prompted Shingo to visit?" AJ said.

"Curiosity," Val said, as he hit the Q-pie that Bob's rival had dropped with another shot of homemade neutralizer. "Not knowing how you got out of the garage alive has to be putting a serious strain on his anti-ulcer nanos."

He scraped the hardening glob off the floor, slung it in a haz-mat bag, and then treated the floor with an anti-corrosive. AJ crinkled her nose at the ensuing chemical stench and pushed her food away half-eaten.

"Gah," she said. "I think you've discovered a new appetite suppressant."

"Sorry," Val said, in a less than sympathetic tone, "but you're going to have to live with the stink until you find a way to housetrain your subjects."

"I'm working on it," she said. "Once Bob catches on, the others are sure to follow."

"So what part of Take It Outside do you suppose he doesn't understand yet?" Val said.

"Don't be such a—" Princess, she meant to say, but before she could get the word out, the hatch opened and two habbies rushed aboard. Crud, she thought, resenting the intrusion. She was never going to get anything done if people kept barging in on her. Then the dramatic nature of the entrance registered and she forgot about being inconvenienced.

"What's wrong?" she said.

The habbies flipped their plates in unison, revealing a pair of sweaty, wild-eyed men. "You gotta come—quick," one of them said, gasping between words as if he had just finished running his first marathon. "They—got someone."

She met his breathlessness with conditioned steadiness. "Settle down, Johnny," she said. "Deep breaths—in through your nose, out through your mouth. That's right. Now tell me who you are and what the problem is."

"Sorry, ma'am," he said. "I'm Little Del and this here is Danny Singh. We're grounders, up-shift. We were out on the west forty tagging turbines for maintenance when all of a sudden, the ground at our feet began to churn. The next thing we knew, there were tentacles everywhere. I'm talking hundreds here, ma'am, maybe thousands. We were all set to haul ass out of there, but then Danny saw the habby. It was caught in the middle of that mess. We managed to snag it by a boot, but the swarm dragged it back underground before we could secure it.

Luckily, I got a loco-strip on it before it disappeared completely."

"Was there someone in that habby?" AJ said, trying not to cringe as she asked.

Yes, ma'am," Little Del said. "It was definitely occupied."

"Was the occupant alive?"

"Fifik, ma'am," Danny said. "If he was alive, he wasn't putting up much of a fight."

"Who else knows about this?" she said.

"Nobody," Little Del said. "We were told to bring all matters regarding the Q to you."

Right. That might be the official policy, but she'd be willing to bet her lucky eye-tooth that Shingo had at least one live feed keeping him current on shit like this. All she could do was hope that he'd lie low and let her handle things.

"What kind of ride did you guys come in on?" she said.

"Scoots," Little Del said.

"No good," she said, thinking out loud. "We're going to need something bigger." She hustled both grounders back toward the hatch. "Scoot back to the garage and sign out a crawler with a tracking app. Meet us back here ASAP."

"But ma'am," Danny said, dragging his heels. "We're only authorized to operate scoots."

"Can you drive a crawler?" she said. When Little Del nodded, she let out an exasperated bark. "Then go and get one! If anyone gives you any guff, I'll vouch for you. My private channel is oh-one-nine. Now move it."

"Yes, ma'am," the two grounders said in unison, and then went bounding off.

"What about him?" Val asked, glancing at Bob as she went hunting for her helmet and an extra PK patch. "I'm not comfortable with letting him stay here while we're gone."

"Let's bring him along," she said. The thought shot straight from her brain to her mouth, bypassing all filters and filibusters. And as soon as she said it, she knew it was the right thing to do. "He might be able to help."

Val didn't like the idea. She could tell by the sour turn that his scowl took, and by the way he drew his shoulders back like he was getting ready to throw a block. She felt compelled to defend the decision.

"C'mon," she said. "He's harmless. You know that."

"Do I?" he said. "He behaves around you because you're some kind of idol to him. But he's jumped me twice already. And who knows what he'll do when he's back in the wild with a bunch of other Q."

"It'll be OK," she said. "I trust him."

He rolled his eyes—schoolyard sarcasm—and then pulled his own headgear on. As he snapped the collar's seals into place, he said, "I just don't want anybody, especially you, getting hurt. Again."

"Duly noticed," she said. "But I'm not going on safari without a guide."

"Suit yourself," he said, and then jerked a thumb toward the hatch. "I'll be outside, waiting for our ride. I'll leave it to you to tell those boys about our 'guide'."

She didn't take his surliness personally. He always got snarky when he was worried—especially when he was worrying about her. She'd make it up to him later. But first things first. She peered into the shadows, looking for Bob. He'd gone into hiding after their little talk about friends not hurting friends. She imagined that he was sulking or the alien equivalent thereof, but when she found him sprawled beneath a console with his pad, he seemed more focused than put out. Belatedly, she noticed that he was working on a maze. If nothing else, Q were most certainly persistent! She tapped the part of him that was closest to her. An instant later, he was out in the open and standing in front of her, human-style.

"Ay-Jay oh-kay?" he said.

"Yes, I'm OK," she said, and then pointed toward the hatch. "You go with me?"

Bob slumped as if he had been deboned. The reaction puzzled her until she realized that he probably thought that she was sending him away. "With me," she said, pressing a hand to her chest. "You go with me outside." He perked up, but only a little. Apparently, he preferred being inside—just like everyone else on this rock.

Val pinged in with, "Crawler's here." A moment later, he added, "Hurry it up, will you? These guys are jumpier than moon fleas."

"Sit up front with them," she said. "I'll ride in back with Bob."

"Yeah, that'll help," he said, and then closed the link.

Now that she was out of time, taking the sensitive approach with Bob was no longer an option. So despite her ongoing, deeply personal, and not entirely explicable aversion to direct contact with Q, she grabbed Bob's ersatz hand. "You Stay With Me," she said, as she marched him toward the hatch. "You No Touch Other Terrans. Understand?"

Yzzz!" he said, and plumped back into a more enthusiastic shape.

She hoped so. If this gamble went wrong on her, she wasn't the only one who was going to lose in a big way.

As soon as they stepped outside, a gust of wind slammed into them. AJ staggered back a step. Bob melted into a ground-hugging puddle. She shuddered, grateful for the privacy that her habby provided, and then motioned the blob toward the waiting crawler. Despite her resolve not to, she half-turned twice to make sure that he was following her.

Danny and Little Del barely reacted when she poked her head into the crawler's cab. But when Bob appeared a moment later, plopping into the cab without a recognizable feature to his name, the grounders sprang out of their seats like circus performers. "Sweet suffering mother!" Danny squawked. "Get the zap!"

"No!" AJ said, jumping onto the PA before either of them could move. "It's OK, he's with me."

"Are you shitting us?" Little Del said, radiating mortified indignation.

"No," she said, "I'm not shitting you. He's here to help us if he can. And I apologize for startling you. When I told him to follow me, I didn't think he was going to be so literal about it." *And why was that, 'Nita?* "Don't worry," she added, when they persisted with their circus poses, "he'll leave you alone."

"Damn straight he will," Del fired back. "Or else."

The two grounders grudgingly returned to their seats. As Little Del shifted the crawler into forward gear, Val's voice bloomed in her headset. "That went well."

More snarkiness. Sometimes it was harder to ignore than others. Sometimes, it got a little old. She glanced at Bob, who had taken refuge from the wind beneath one of the back-benches. What was so threatening about an ugly brown blob, really? Did humans have to fear everything that didn't meet a certain aesthetic standard? She resented the grounders for being so primitive—even though she knew she was just as bad in some regards.

"I got a loco-blip," Danny announced, after they had gone a few minutes in sulky silence. "It's coming from the south forty, upper quadrant. Looks stationary." A few heartbeats later, he added, "Profile matches. We're adjusting course to intercept."

"Do we know who we're looking for yet?" AJ asked, forgetting her resentment as quickly as she had embraced it.

"Guzman," Val said. Then, knowing that she probably wouldn't remember, he added, "The science officer."

"Ah," she said. "The walk-off."

She'd meant that for his ears only, but once again she had forgotten to switch off the PA and so Little Del felt free to jump in. "Carried-off is more like it," he said. "And I still don't see how adding another Q to the mix is going to change that."

"That's because you only see what you want to see, Del," she told him, and hoped that the same wasn't true of her.

"Blip is holding steady," Danny said. "Time till intercept is seven minutes. Then what?"

"I'll let you know when we get there," she said, another rose-colored hope.

In less than a blink, it seemed, a wind turbine sprouted on the horizon. Another appeared, and then dozens more. These were different from the Darries that she and her crew had installed: shorter and more compact, with straight blades rather than curved. She guessed that they were a little less productive than Darries, but also likely to wind up as windfall. They were probably a snap to install, too. A wave of ghost fatigue mixed with regrets washed over her as she recalled how hard she had pushed to get that damn farm planted. Only to hear: 'Priorities have changed'. The memory still griped her, although not as much as it used to. Time had absorbed some of the sting. And Val had broken up the scar. One of these days, she was going to have to get around to thanking him for that.

"ETA, three minutes," Danny announced.

"Let's start looking," AJ said. "Sing out if you see anything."

Danny climbed onto the cab's roof and began scanning the semi-gloom for signs of life. Val mounted a watch from the port-side window. Incapable of sitting and waiting while others worked, AJ positioned herself as the starboard look-out. As she peered out at the expanse of sand and turbines, she felt a gentle tapping against the back of her knee. When she looked down, she saw a pair of lidless eyestalks poking out from under the bench.

"Ay-Jay oh-kay?" Bob buzzed.

"Sure," she said, and then gestured. "You Come Out."

Bob came oozing forth from his hiding place, assuming human shape along the way. The sight both repulsed and fascinated AJ; it was watching water flow into an invisible pitcher. She could not help but marvel at how exquisitely detailed the Q's transformations were getting to be. In a dark room where everyone was drinking heavily, he might actually pass for a scrawny child at this point. She wondered if he knew how much more at ease people were around him when he was in Terran-form. She wondered if that had been his goal all along. If so, then maybe the others were right to be a little afraid of him and his kind.

"Cohld owt," he said. "No lyk cohld."

"You should dress warmer," she said—a flippant remark that coincided with Little Del's excited shout.

"There, to the right! By the TFM! I see something!"

The crawler dropped into a lower, slower gear. AJ shifted to port-side and searched for a turbine that had been tagged for maintenance. There! The area around the TMF was studded with rubble. Her gaze leapfrogged from one dark patch to the next: shadow, rock, shadow, rock, sha— Wait. That last rock had had a strange sheen to it. And the shadow behind it was long and solid-looking—like a body.

"I've got a visual," she said, and then ordered Little Del to hit the brakes. "We don't want to get too close until we know what we're dealing with."

The crawler lurched to a stop. She motioned for Bob to follow her. Val and the grounders fell in behind her as well. She thought better of the grounders for that, but ordered them to stand down just the same.

"The Q and I are going in for a look-see," she said. "As soon as I figure out what's what, I'll ping you with a plan. Until then, I want you to stay here."

Neither grounder argued with her. But Val did. "I'm with you," he said, blocking the exit. "I insist."

"No way," she said, equally adamant. "If there are other Q in the area, too many feet on the ground could spook them into doing something everyone will regret."

"I'll walk softly," he said.

"No, you won't," she said. "You're staying here."

He switched to their private channel and said, "Dammit, AJ! I don't like this. You're not even close to a hundred percent. Bob's an unknown. You should have back-up."

"Exactly!" she said. "That's why you need to stay here. If this thing goes wonky, I'll need someone to stage a rescue. You won't be able to do that if you're up to your eyeballs with me and I don't trust our grounders to make smart choices in a pinch."

His entire body tensed as what he knew to be right and what he wanted to be right vied for dominance within him. She knew which side won out when his shoulders sagged in defeat and gave him a consolatory pat on the back.

"I'll be OK," she said. "You'll see."

"I still don't like it," he said, grinding the words into a frustrated paste. "You be careful, you hear? Ping me if anything—anything at all—looks suss."

"Promise," she said, and then turned her attention to Bob.

"You And Me Go There," she said, gesturing at the TFM's surrounds. "You Look For Q. I Look For Terrans. You Understand?"

"Yzz," Bob said, and then oozed over the crawler's side like a giant gob of ectoplasm. As soon as he touched down, he tunneled into the ground and was gone.

AJ swallowed hard as she watched the Q disappear. For all she knew, she had just made a huge mistake. But no, that was Val talking, not her. She could feel his eyes boring into her back, willing her to turn around and admit that she was wrong. Instead, she climbed down the crawler's side and started toward the blip on her handheld. Meli popped in to offer encouragement: *have a little faith, 'Nita!* But Val's anxiety was infectious. All of a sudden, she found it harder to breath. Logic told her that it was just her ribs acting up as the PK wore off, but part of her didn't believe it. Then something grabbed the bottom of her foot. She started and nearly cried out loud.

That you, Bob?

Val's ping was immediate. "You OK out there?"

"Yeah," she said, perversely emboldened by his concern. "I just stepped on a Q-pie. They're all over the place."

The number of deposits supported Little Del's claim: *I'm talking hundreds here.* But— where were their makers? Val wanted to know, too. "Fifik," she said. "The crawler must've sent them into hiding." He started to ask another question, but she cut him off. "Ease off on the pings, would you, Johnny? I'll let you know when I find something."

He closed the link, but she could still feel his eyes on her backside. Was it any wonder she had the yips? She advanced gingerly, half-expecting to find tentacles or an eyestalk lurking within every shadow. All she found was grit and more Q-pies. The swarm must have fled, she told herself. But why would it do so and leave Guzman behind? She looked around for Bob, hoping to get a little insight from him. As she did so, an off-color flash caught her eye. That could only be light reflecting off a gold-coated face-plate! Her yips vanished. She forgot about her ribs, too. A short jog later, she was on her knees beside a mostly buried body.

"I got him," she told Val. "I found our MIA."

"How is he?" Val said.

"Fifik." She unearthed his torso, biting her lip as she worked, and then pressed a hand to his chest. "I think he's breathing, but it's hard to tell." She tapped his face plate—anyone home? Nothing. "If he's still alive, he's unresponsive. And his helmet releases are jammed."

"Any sign of Q?"

"Pies everywhere," she said, "but not a single blob in sight." She wondered about Bob's whereabouts in passing, but then decided to worry about first things firsts. "Bring the crawler."

"Roger that," Val said, only to swear a moment later. "The damn thing won't start."

"Typical," she said. "You want me to try and hump our guy out?"

"Negative," he said, a distracted auto-response rather than the sarcastic retort that she had been expecting. "Give me a minute to try and get the bus running. If that's a no-go, the two idiots who requisitioned a crawler that was in for maintenance will carry both of you out."

In the background, she heard Danny bleat, "It's not our fault. This is the only one the RO would let us have."

She rolled her eyes, thinking SOS. Then, because she had time on her hands and a need to keep busy, she started digging Guzman out. "Don't worry, Johnny," she said, as she scooped grit away from the lower half of his body, "you're OK now. We've got—" You, she was about to say but blurted, "WTF?" instead because the trough that she had just dug around Guzman's legs was filling back up with sand.

Val pinged in. "What was that, AJ?"

"He's sinking," she said, more to herself than to him. But why? Had something below him shifted, creating a patch of quicksand? It occurred to her to start digging faster. Before she could act on the thought, the ground around Guzman erupted and began to writhe. "Shit!"

"AJ? What's going on?"

There weren't hundreds of aliens, but there were at least that many tentacles. All of them were thrashing at the air, Guzman—and her. The sight triggered a memory. In it, she was pinned to the ground with the weight of a wall on her back. Her ribs were on fire. All she could see was compacted darkness.

"Answer me, dammit!"

But she could not talk; there was too much pressure and not enough room to breathe. As she struggled for stray molecules of air, a face emerged from the grit beneath her face-plate. An instant later, there were tentacles everywhere and she was being dragged underground like ant food on its way to storage. Fear flooded through her, pure and primal. She wanted to resist. She needed to be free. But her limbs were pinned to her sides and she could not break free.

"No!" she shouted, and then recoiled as that face reappeared in front of her. "Let me go!"

"Ay-Jay oh-kay?"

Just like that, the memory bottomed out, leaving her in the present. There were still Q everywhere, but none of them had a hold on her. And Guzman was still half-buried in the sand. She pushed herself up and into a sitting position, unaware until now that she had fallen from her knees to the ground. As she sat there, trying to collect her thoughts, Bob tapped her.

"Ay-Jay oh-kay?"

"Yeah, sure," she said, although her ribs were throbbing in earnest again. "Just a little disoriented. I guess I remember more about my extraction from the garage than I thought." Bob cocked his head at her, the seemingly universal sign for come-again. She let out a little laugh which her ribs protested and then started to put him off until later only to be distracted by the distinct sizzle of EM cannon-fire. An instant later, a coruscating bolt of concentrated electricity arced over her head and slammed into the ground a few meters to her rear. Every tentacle in the vicinity stiffened in the direction of ground zero. But Bob tapped AJ on the knee again and said, "We go now?"

"Yeah," she said, wondering WTF, and then started to stand up. As she did so, she caught sight of multiple oncoming flashes: a strike team armed with zaps. She looked at Bob and said, "Tell your friends to get out of here!"

It did not seem as if he had heard her or understood, but heartbeats later, pandemonium broke out just the same. Some Q plunged underground; others bolted, drawing zap fire. As AJ glanced this way and that, looking for a way to stop the attack, she saw one of the lead strikers take aim at Bob. She waved him off, shouting, "No! Stop," but it was already too late. The only thing she could do was step in front of the shot.

CHAPTER 22

Niji TUNNELED THROUGH THE regolith, sampling any and all nijiti spoor that happened into range of its frani. Niji finally understood why AyJay was so interested in this swarm. It had an upright of its possession, one that had gone dormant while out in the wilds. But niji had yet to figure out why zra wanted niji here. Given the choice, niji would have preferred to stay back in daboht with the pahd. It did not the cold, the feel of regolith—or the taste of swarm babble. Still, zra had been adamant about niji's attendance. Such an unprecedented show of favor could not be ignored or left unexplored. She must want niji to serve some purpose while niji was here.

If only niji knew what that purpose was!

A distant rumbling invaded niji's ponderings. It immediately recognized the sensation as ulvarzi shockwaves. If niji had been back on daboht, niji would not have paid much attention to such rumblings for ulvarzi were as thick as a fresh hatch of ice mites back on *zabayz*. But there was much less traffic out here in the near-wild, and those ulvarzi were coming this way in a very great hurry. It wondered if it should tell AyJay of their coming and then was struck by a sudden insight. Maybe that was why she had insisted on niji's presence. Maybe she wanted niji to serve as her leading edge!

The thought sent niji streaming toward the surface.

As soon as niji broke ground, it shaped itself a head and looked for the zranarz. Niji was not surprised to find her with the swarm's upright. It was, however, quite taken aback to see how rigidly she was holding herself. At first, it thought she must be in pain again. But then it saw the swarm playing all around her and blamed her tenseness on nijiti foolishness. Then she fell from her knees to the ground and niji did not know what to think. It raced toward her, meaning to drive the offending swarm off. But when it finally reached her side, it saw that she was still tense and twitching now, too.

"No!" she shouted, for no obvious reason. "Lemme goh!"

How curious! Niji tapped her top-nob patch and said, "Ay-Jay oh-kay?"

When she did not respond, it tapped her again. "Ay-Jay oh-kay?" She sat up, but did not otherwise respond, so niji tapped her again. "Ay-Jay oh-kay?"

Whatever had been holding her in its grip seemed to let go then, for she relaxed then and made reassuring sounds. Niji's relief was displaced by a sudden burst of odd sensations: first, the shallow vibrations of many upright feet on the run, then a highly energized, overhead sizzle, and then a plasma-shaking explosion. These activities unsettled niji. It tapped Ay-Jay once again and said, "We goh now?"

The next thing niji knew, she was on her feet and shouting. "Tayl ur frenz too get owt uv heer!" A frani-beat later, she pushed niji to her back-side. Then she convulsed and fell on top of niji. As she hit the ground, the remnants of an electrical charge passed from her to niji. It grasped the significance of that tingle immediately. Someone had struck zra with the little lightning! But why? She was not some witless nijit. She was an upright, the supreme being.

As niji grappled with the implications of zra's assault, the sensation of many feet on the run acquired a more coordinated feel. Several sets skidded to a stop beside the swarm's upright. Several more stopped beside AyJay. Then someone peeled her up from the ground, exposing niji to the taste of burnt ozone and the sight of crisped nijiti husks.

"Shit!" an unfamiliar upright said. "There's another one!"

"Stand down!" a second, more familiar-sounding upright said, moving to shelter niji's body mass with an outstretched arm. "And you guys get her back to base pronto. Don't worry," he added, "it's not going to eat you."

A pair of uprights rushed in in, hoisted AyJay's unmoving body onto a nearby ulvarz, and then rushed off again. Niji thought to follow, but before it could act on the impulse, Vahl grabbed it by the back of its half-formed neck and said, "You're coming with me, you little bastard."

CHAPTER 23

AJ WOKE UP WITH aching ribs, a tingling in her limbs, and a headache the size of Flagstaff. She had been dreaming of summer lightning strikes, the kind that used to ignite huge swathes of beetle-infested forest. Meli liked to hush her when such storms came boiling over the compound. 'The Thunder Beings are drawn to voices', she used to whisper. 'You don't want them to come looking for you, do you?'

"Crud," she said, fingering her ribs to pinpoint the sore spots. "I must've said something that pissed those bad old boys off in a big way."

That was when she realized that she wasn't wearing a habby. She bolted upright—a WTF, knee-jerk reaction—and then hissed as her body punished her for her temerity. Through a haze of tears, her surrounds came into focus. She was in her apartment. In bed. The only thing she had on was a cozy old housecoat. She felt bare-skinned and exposed like a fresh-hatched chick. She felt kind of rubbery, too—inside and out. When had all of this happened? The last thing she remembered was a coruscating flash.

As she sat there, trying to wring memories out of recycled air, Val strode into the room. The worried grooves that bracketed his mouth softened back into lines as soon as their eyes met. "Welcome back," he said, as he sat down on the pull-out next to the bed. "How are you feeling?"

"I'm confused," she said, blurting out the confession. "What the hell happened out there, Val?"

"You got zapped," he said, all hang-doggy like he was the one who had ordered it. "Your habby repelled most of the shock, but the shot knocked you A over T. Somewhere along the line, you picked up a concussion."

"I know I got zapped," she said, instantly irritated with him for leading with the obvious. "It's the why of it that's giving me fits. Why did it happen? Be specific."

"Two grounders came to us with an MIA sighting. We went to investigate. Remember that?" he said.

She nodded, flash-recalling a habby buried in the sand. The Johnny within had been—in trouble.

"How is he?" she asked, remembering nothing else about him. "Did he—make it?"

"Roger that," Val said, returning her nod. "The doc pumped him full of warm water and calories, then quarantined him for testing."

"Is he—responsive?"

"Wide awake and surprised as all hell to find himself still alive."

"You debrief him yet?" she asked.

He confirmed that with a head-bob, too. "Walk-off, just like you figured," he said. "He has no idea how he came to be with the Q in the west forty."

"I'll want to talk to him," she said.

"Of course."

"OK then," she said. "Moving on. Let's talk about how that EM cannon and strike team happened to be in the area at exactly the wrong moment."

His gaze wavered for a microsecond—a tiny, suspicious tell that provoked a realization as shocking as any wayward zap bolt. "Shit," she said, "you called Shingo in, didn't you?" When he averted his eyes again, a clear admission of guilt, she went from shocked to fighting mad. "What the fuck were you thinking, sending in an armed task force? I had everything under control."

"The hell you did," he said, jumping at the chance to return fire. "You were down, AJ. And you weren't returning my pings. From my perspective, it looked like the Q were about to abduct you, too. The grounders were afraid." Almost as an afterthought, he added, "So was I."

"So you OK'ed cannon fire," she said, refusing to let him off the hook just because he'd acted out of concern for her. "And a frigging strike force. Talk about overkill! Never mind that the EM round almost landed right on top of me and Guzman. Never mind that one of the troops zapped the shit out of me. What about the Q? How many of them were killed for being nothing more than a minor disturbance?"

"No one even bothered to count," Val said, a grudging admission that might've contained an undercoat of shame. "But just for the record, it was Shingo who authorized the attack, not me. I briefed him on the situation while you were still aboard the boat and asked him to send back-up after us just in case something went wrong. I didn't know that he was leading the back-up force until it got here. And I had no clue that he had a cannon with him until he fired that round."

"Did you tell him to fire it?" she asked, in a stropped tone.

"Negative," he said, an emphatic denial that came with full eye-contact. "I'll admit that I was squirming in my habby by then, but I urged him to stand-by until we had a clearer idea of what was going on."

"Will you swear to that?" she said. "For the record?"

"Of course," he said. "I've already entered my report into the incident log. Why?"

"Because his lordship willfully and with malice aforethought slaughtered innocent indigenes," she said, starting to bank her fury so it would burn colder and cleaner. "That's genocide. He also destroyed the one reliable link I had to the surviving indigenes. That's sabotage. When TSC hears about this, he'll be lucky if he just loses his command."

Val sucked in a breath between his teeth. "Jesus, AJ," he said. "Are you sure you want to go that way? Shingo's got a lot of pull. And he's not one to play fair in a fight."

But AJ's zap-induced headache was pounding like a Cherokee war-drum and she could not be daunted. "Thanks to him," she said, "I have to start all over with the Q. Thanks to him, I don't even have a place to start."

"I'm sorry about the way this incident played out, AJ," Val said, "Truly, I am. But on the bright side—"

"Don't you dare try to spin this for him, Val," she warned.

"On the bright side," he said, "you're not going to have to start all over with the Q."

She dismissed his ill-designed optimism with a sneer. In response, he stood up and left the room. Part of her wanted to snap, 'Good riddance,' after him, because she was nowhere close to forgiving him for instigating this fiasco. It appalled her to think that he had so little confidence in her abilities. And the fact that he had trusted Shingo to watch her back galled her even more. That would-be warlord didn't want her to succeed. Didn't Val get that?

As she stewed in her own bitter juices, Val returned with a mid-sized float in tow. "If that's a bribe meant to appease me," she said, "it's not nearly big enough."

"Don't be so sure," he said, then parked the float at the foot of the bed and popped the top. An instant later, an eye on a very long stalk snaked out of the hold and began a slow three-sixty. As it did so, AJ shot Val a wondering look.

"I figured you'd want to see him," he said.

"Yeah, but—" she said, consternated by the risk he'd taken. Smuggling a Q into the HF was the kind of infraction that could land a body in the brig—and not just for an overnight stay. But even as she marveled, a suspicion intruded. Feeling entitled and vindictive, she blurted it out.

"Shingo know about this, too?"

"No," Val said, taking the shot without flinching.

Bob was standing next to the float now. He had assumed his best human façade, but was ranging his eyes this way and that independently of each other like a chameleon. She wondered what he was looking for—a strike team wielding zaps? Who could blame him for being jumpy? He'd been given more than enough reason to question the trustworthiness of men.

"You OK, Bob?" she said. He didn't seem to be hurt, but then, what did she know about Q physiology?

His eyes snapped front and center with mind-boggling immediacy. "Yzz, Ay-Jay, I yam oh-kay," he buzzed, and then cocked his head at her. "You zawf-zhel now?"

For a moment, she was at a loss. Zof-zhel? Then her inner translator kicked in and she figured it out. Soft-shell! Of course! This was the first time he had seen her outside of a habby.

"Yes," she said. "I'm soft and pink in the middle just like everyone else." Then, realizing that he hadn't even come close to getting the joke, she shifted gears and said, "Don't worry. It's OK." When he continued to look at her askance, she bowed to expediency and made up a little lie. "It will grow back," she said, gesturing as well.

His head righted itself, but he still looked puzzled. "Lyl lytnyn mayk you zawf-zhel?"

Again, it took her a moment to translate. But this time, she skipped the flippant response and went straight to convenient half-truth. "Yes," she said. "In a way."

The Q buzzed, an unintelligible sound. His expression was unreadable, too. "Lyl lytnyn mayk kew dehd," he said. There was no hint of condemnation or even reproach about him. He seemed only to be comparing or contrasting the effects of a zap on their respective species. His objectivity puzzled AJ. Did he not care that a crowd of its own kind had been massacred? Or did he suppose that Terrans had not yet realized that the 'little lightning' was harmful to Q?

"What were those Q doing with that Terran?" Val asked, taking AJ's contemplative silence as an invitation to butt in. "Do you know?"

"Zwrm fynd heem zleepyn in za wyld," Bob said. "Wyld no gud playz too zleep zo zwrm dezyd too tayk heem to zabayz."

AJ arched an eyebrow at Val—a silent told-you-so. He pretended not to notice. "If that's so," he said instead, "then why did we find him off-base, buried in the sand?"

"Zhat awf-bayz playz got pach uv teenglee-warm," Bob said. "Zwrm lyk zhat pach very much. It mahk zhem veree hahpee. Awl zhey wan doo iz play."

"Doesn't explain why they buried Guzman like a bone," Val said, refusing to give the Q so much an inch.

But if Val was belligerent, then Bob was the epitome of cheerful compliance. AJ got the impression that the Q thought he was being tested and wanted to do well. "Zwrm berry heem zo heem ztay warm," he said. "Zhey no berry heem deep cuz heem no lyk zhat even azleep."

AJ could relate to that all too well, but Val remained unyielding. His scowl reminded her of something dug in, heels maybe or maybe a tick. Stubborn Johnny. He so hated to admit defeat. "How could you possibly know what those Q were thinking, Bob?" he said. "You weren't there when they were making their plans and I'm sure that's not the first thing you talked about when you finally caught up with them."

"I no frum zrumi," Bob said, and then glanced from AJ to Val as if he were looking for something. When AJ encouraged him with a nod, he expressed a Q-pie right there on the floor.

"Oops," she said, as Val swore. But while it was obvious that Bob knew that they were not pleased to see the Q-pie, he persisted nonetheless. "Zrumi lyk maytriks," he said. "Ful uv infermazhun. You tuch, you lurn zhingz."

"There were Q-pies all over the place out there," AJ said, in Bob's defense.

"That doesn't prove jack," Val said, as he dug a bottle of neutralizer from a utility pocket in his habby and started spritzing. "He could be making that stuff up to protect his friends."

"That seems unlikely," AJ said, "given that they're all dead now."

"Yzz," Bob said. "Zwrm dehd."

AJ interpreted that grim little statement as an attempt to revisit the subject of massacred Q. That surprised her. Maybe she had been too quick to label him as uncaring when it came to his kind. Maybe he had been using objectivity to distance himself from the horror of what had happened. Indifferent or not, though, he had a right to demand answers—and justice. And she fully intended to address those rights. But before she had a chance to boil her intentions into a phrase or two that the Q might understand, Val signed off on a ping that she had not seen him take and sputtered a curse.

"What?" she said.

"Shingo's on his way," he said.

"Here?" AJ said. "Now?" He nodded twice—curt little head-bobs that jump-started her grudge against the CO. "Excellent," she said. "That'll save me the trouble of having to hunt him down."

"AJ," he said, in a pleading tone, "don't call him out now. You're tired and sore and still a little concussed. Think about what you want to say first."

"I know exactly what I want to say, Val," she countered, and then glanced at Bob, who was waiting patiently for her attention. "You need go now," she said, motioning him back into the float. "You come back later." He did as he was told immediately, without ceremony or ado. "Nice to know someone around here trusts me to do the right thing," she said, as Val closed the float up.

He cast her a reproachful look. She repelled it with a bitchy half-smile, because he was still number two on her newest shit-list and he had a few more shots coming to him. "You had better scoot before Shingo shows up," she said. "If he finds out you smuggled a Q into the room, your days as anyone's second are over."

"What about that?" he asked, glancing at the denatured Q-pie.

"You can scrape it up later," she said. "I'll meet his lordship in the front room."

He scowled, willing her to read the reservations that were contained between the lines. She dismissed him with a wave of her hand instead. As he skulked off with the float in tow, she took pity on him and said, "We'll talk later."

As soon as he was gone, she eased herself out of bed, one leg and then the other, damn. Even with a fresh PK patch, everything ached. She stood up slowly, thankful that she was already dressed. The housecoat was an old favorite, too; they had both grown soft and worn in the same places. Only Val would have dressed her in something so comforting. He had a knack for getting the little things right.

Damn. What was she supposed to do with that man?

The housekeeper pinged, alerting her to a presence at the front door. The sound gave her a terrible thrill. It felt like a zap bolt's tingly residues. It filled her mouth with shocking words. She started out of the bedroom ready to discharge that hair-raising payload only to freeze in mid-step as the keeper pinged again to announce a presence in the apartment. An instant later, Val's voice rang out.

"AJ?" he said. "The CO's here. Do you want to meet him out here or in there?"

Questions lit up her thoughts like tracer-fire. What was he doing back so soon? What had he done with Bob? And WTF was he doing with Shingo? She didn't want to think the worst, but some small, paranoid part of her insisted on connecting the dots.

"AJ?"

"Coming," she said, and then reminded herself that trust was a commitment, not a feeling. She trusted Val. He had her back. He was his own man, and he didn't play his friends.

As soon as she stepped into the front room and saw Val standing shoulder to shoulder with Shingo, her confidence faltered. They were talking in an undertone—about her, no doubt. The float was nowhere in sight. That paranoid inner voice supposed that Val had handed it over to Shingo as a gift. She scowled, trying to squeeze off the internal dialogue, and then made her less-than-grand entrance.

"Sorry to keep you waiting," she said, as she hobbled toward the nearest pull-out, "but as you can see, I'm moving a little slowly." When Val made a move to come to her aid, she warned him off with the suggestion of a head-shake. "Fortunately," she added wryly, "it's just a flesh wound."

"Special Envoy," Shingo said, "again, despite reports to the contrary, you appear to be doing remarkably well."

"And again," she said, in a mocking tone, "that's no thanks to you. Care to tell me why one of your troopers zapped me?"

"It was," he said, perfectly deadpan, "a regrettable accident. Friendly fire, you could call it. Such things happen in the heat of battle."

"Battle?" she said, feeling her hackles rise. "What battle? I didn't see any Q shooting."

"Perhaps not," he said, in a tone which conceded nothing, "but they were holding you and Guzman. The team was there to extract you."

"We didn't need to be extracted," she said. "I was being—greeted. Guzman was being kept warm. The Q were being friendly. You loosed a strike team on unarmed non-combatants."

Shingo shrugged: the barest twitch of the shoulders, as if effort were directly proportional to significance. "My office received a priority call," he said. "We were told that two Terrans were being held by a crowd of hostile-seeming Q, and that that these Q were entrenched in a sensitive location." Then he smiled ever so slightly and added, "Since the call came from your second, I had no reason to question the information and so responded with enough force to secure the area and free the hostages."

She wondered if he had planned to throw Val under the galactic people-mover all along as payback for serving as her second or if he had done so extemporarily to accessorize his lies. Either way, she was happy to despise him.

"You know damn well that we weren't hostages," she said.

"In situations where human lives might be at stake," he said flatly, "I prefer not to take chances."

"Oh, please," she said. "Ambitious men like you take chances all the time. I believe you committed genocide, Commander, willfully and with malice aforethought. I'm going to say that in my next report to TSC. I'm also going to recommend that you be reassigned to a less sensitive post."

His nostrils flared. His eyes narrowed. These were the tiniest of tells, but together, they represented a huge, angry display. "That would be a mistake," he said. "The council knows my worth."

"Soon it'll know your worst as well," she said, and while she got a visceral thrill out of threatening him, it was not as satisfying as she thought it would be. Must be fatigue setting in again. "Your only hope of getting off with a wrist slap is to turn over a new leaf right now and make above-and-beyond cooperation your new policy."

They locked gazes, staring frost and murder at each other. Depleted as she was, she was determined to go the distance in this pissing match just so he'd know how serious she was. But even as she steeled herself for a raging case of dry eye, he ended the contest with that inscrutable quarter-smile of his.

"Special Envoy," he said, "perhaps we have been, as you suggest, working at cross-purposes. Perhaps we have let personal agendas become more important than our reason for being here in the first place. I want to protect Terra. You want to protect Terra. That's reason enough for us to regroup and make this situation work."

Whoa. She'd been expecting something direct, an alpha male play for dominance. Instead he had managed to sound rueful and remorseful and willing to reform. She didn't believe a word of it. But his advocates on the council would when they heard his report and then they'd use it in his defense—even though he hadn't actually accepted any blame for the massacre. Was that man slick or what? She looked like a denatured Q-pie by comparison. Nevertheless, she'd given him the out. Now she had to follow through and hope that there wasn't a people-mover with her name on it lurking in the wings.

"What's your idea of regrouping?" she asked.

"Send my office a list of areas where our cooperation has been unsatisfactory," he said. "Offer suggestions on how we can improve. You will have our compliance. This, I promise you." He was about to say something else when he got a ping. He listened for a moment and then did her the dubious honor of a crisp half-bow. "I am required elsewhere. Have your second arrange a meeting with my office if you wish to set further conditions for our new and improved alliance." He glanced in Val's direction—the first time he had done so since betraying him. A moment later, he was gone.

"Hard to believe I used to enjoy working for that man," Val said, scowling at the front door as if he expected Shingo to come ghosting back through it.

"He's definitely not my cup of tea," she said.

"Listen, AJ," Val said, swiveling toward her with an obvious ache in his eyes. "About what happened—"

She forestalled him with an upraised hand. "Not now," she said. "I need to sort through my thoughts first, and I'm too tired for that."

"Fair enough." He clasped that upraised hand and kissed it. The part of her that liked to hold grudges wanted to pull away, but Meli overruled the urge. *He was thinking of you, 'Nita.* "I'll get to work then. You get back to bed."

Him telling her what to do again. She felt compelled to return the favor. "I want you to go back to the west forty and do some investigating. Bob said something about the Q being attracted to some kind of 'tingly-warm'. I want to know what that's all about."

"Sure," he said, and she could tell by the sudden distance in his eyes that he was already thinking about how to approach the job.

"Speaking of, how'd it go with Bob?" she said. "His extraction, that is."

He blinked and then scowled like someone waking up from a dream too soon. "Oh, yeah, that. We cut it a little close—OK, a little more than a little close given that I ran into Shingo just as he cleared the entryway airlock. I told him I was on my way to the boat with some equipment that I'd scrounged, but he insisted that I return to the apartment with him 'for propriety's sake.' I had to leave the float anchored in the hallway."

"What?" she said, instantly swarmed with 'what-ifs.' "Shit, Val. Don't just stand there, go and bring Bob back in here!"

He disappeared only to return a moment later with a stricken look on his face. "He's gone," he said. "The little bastard's disappeared."

CHAPTER 24

Niji HAD MIXED FEELINGS about traveling in the *floht*. Niji liked getting from one place to another without having to move or keep itself warm, for that allowed it to focus its energies on processing information that it had absorbed elsewhere. And since niji never knew where it was going, its destination was always a surprise. Niji liked surprises. It did not, however, like being contained within the floht. The ulvarz's insides were much like the vac's had been: stuffy and dark, with no view of the outside. Niji could sense movement, but not what it was missing along the way. Niji did not like that, either. Given a choice, niji would have much preferred to travel by crawlyr. Nevertheless, when AyJay told niji to return to the floht, it did so immediately. Niji thought she was sending it on another excursion. It expected the trip to be as lengthy as the one that had brought niji to her jaza-burrow. So when the floht stopped shortly after lift-off, niji grew curious. And when no one came to let niji out, its curiosity turned into excitement. Perhaps this was not an excursion after all. Perhaps this was one of zra's tests—like the mayz without the pahd. Perhaps she wanted to see if niji could get out of the floht without help. Niji was hahpee to make the attempt.

A few clicks and jiggles later, niji emerged from the floht in full upright form, expecting to find itself in AyJay's presence. To its surprise, it was not even in her jaza-burrow. This space was very long and very narrow and possessed of many doors. Niji liked doors. Doors led to new places, new places led to new knowledge, and—zhee! That must be the reason niji was here. Zra was giving it a chance to explore a new upright place and learn what it would. Niji flushed with pride. Zra's confidence in niji was clearly growing.

As niji basked in self-satisfaction, a light above the door at the near end of the enclosure flashed green. On daboht, that meant incoming uprights. Niji supposed it meant the same thing here. The prospect was both exciting and unsettling, for while niji welcomed chance encounters with uprights, uprights tended to be much less enthusiastic about happening into varzi and niji had no desire to offend anyone's sensibilities—or be shocked out of existence for doing so. So niji dove into the gap between the wall and the float, and then compacted its body mass to fit the space.

Two uprights entered the enclosure. Niji could not see them in its current configuration, but it sensed their footfalls first and then their voices as well. They sounded very agitated.

"That's where she and the el-tee live, you know," one of them said. "She's probably in there now, recovering from the shot she took."

"Damn zap-happy jar-heads," the other said. "They could've killed her. Then we'd be right back where we started with them screeching her name from every rafter and ambushing unsuspecting field-workers. At least now she's got 'em doing something useful."

"Damn straight," the first said. "Though I gotta say, I can't imagine being carried out of no-man's land by a pack of Q."

"Neither can Guzman. Word is, he was all shades of confused when he woke up and found himself still alive. I also hear he's mad at the Q—and the Special Envoy for ruining a perfectly good walk-off."

"Jesus."

"Yeah, no kidding. Ungrateful bastard."

The two uprights passed the floht without breaking stride. Niji was more disappointed than relieved to be overlooked, for while it did not understand everything that they were saying, they sounded well-disposed toward varzi. Maybe they wanted to be frenz. Excited by the thought, niji streamed up the wall and onto the ceiling and then started after them.

"I can't want to knock back a born-again," one was saying now. "My mouth is watering already."

The other made a rumbling sound and said, "It took them long enough to get it here. Your brother said it was going to be on tap on opening day."

"Bitch at him if you want," the first one said. "I'm just happy he finally came through for us."

The uprights were approaching the far end of the enclosure. Niji tried to catch up with them before they ventured beyond the door, but gravity made traveling ceiling-side slow-going and the door opened and closed again long before niji got there. Niji loosed an azrum, detailing its disappointment. The prospect of making new frenz had been so tantalizing. It thought about staying where it was and maybe meeting the pair upon their return only to realize that they might not come this way again. Then another possibility occurred to niji. Why not go after them? Was niji not here to explore and learn?

The audacity of the notion left it giddy with excitement. Who knew what wonders might be waiting beyond that door? Who knew what adventures there were to be had? Niji oozed down from the ceiling with the recklessness of a nijit, changing as it went. Frani-beats after its leading edge hit the ground, its reconfiguration was complete. It patted the door with a new-formed hand, feeling for the sweet-spot that would cause the door to open. It was still searching for that trigger when the door slid open of its own accord. The next thing niji knew, it was standing nose to chest with a soft-shelled upright with obvious balance problems. He swayed from side to side and then peered down at niji with eyes that were as unsteady as its legs.

"Shit," he said, spraying flecks of warm, organic fluid from his mouth-hole. "When did they start letting kids on this rock? Naked kids at that."

"Whaz kiz?" niji said.

The upright blinked, shook his head as if to dislodge something that had gotten stuck and then squinted at niji's face. "Do that again."

Only then did niji remember that it was supposed to move its mouth-hole while making sounds. Being upright was such a complicated process! It repeated the question, this time with more attention to the details.

The upright shook his head again and said, "One of us is really fucked up, an' I'm not entirely sure it's me." Then he shambled off without a backward glance.

Niji scurried past the still-open door and then came to an abrupt, wonder-struck stop. For the space beyond was like nothing that niji could have ever imagined. It was one vast enclosure filled with many, many smaller structures that stood side-to-side and top-to-bottom. There were companion lights overhead, and on every wall. There were matrices flashing images and blaring sounds and possibly even radiating smells. Niji's senses began to swirl—a whirlwind of greed, hunger, and disbelief. It might have stood transfixed on the leading edge of this wondrous place until it expired if an unfamiliar voice had not pierced its rapture.

"Effin' Ay! Is that what I think it is?"

A swarm of uprights had emerged from a nearby structure. All of them were carrying some kind of cylindrical container in one hand. All of them were wearing that frozen, slack-jaw look that niji had come to associate with surprise. And all of them were looking right at niji.

"That's a kew, right?" one of them said.

"Yeah," another said. "What the fuck is it doing here?"

A strange new sensation arose in niji: acute discomfort mixed with a sudden desire to be elsewhere. Niji could not put a reason to this unease. Uprights always stared. It was accustomed to such behavior. But as long as they were not frightened or carrying lightning sticks, there was no call for excessive anxiety.

"Hey, kew!" an upright shouted. When niji looked his way, he waved. "C'mere. We wanna talk to you."

"C'mon Cowboy," one of the others said. "Remember what they told us in orientation? We're not supposed to approach them."

"Relax, Johnny," Cowboy said. "We didn't go to him, he came to us." He waved at niji again. "C'mon. It's OK. We won't hurt you."

Uneasy or not, niji could not resist an opportunity to meet new uprights and sample their society. So it took one last hard look at the swarm, searching for tell-tale signs of lightning sticks, and then started in that direction. It did its best to approximate upright kinetics—bend one knee, extend leg, pitch forward, repeat other side—but scores of frani on its reconfigured soles did all of the actual work. The uprights did not seem to notice that its feet neither quite left nor touched the ground. They were much more interested in its face.

"Too fucking weird," the one called Johnny said. "He kind of looks like a short version of a guy I used to crew with."

"Hel-ho," niji said, as it approached, remembering to move its mouth as well as both of its legs. "I am Bob," it said. "I am ur fren."

"You are one weird looking motherfucker," Cowboy said, and poked a bare finger into niji's shoulder, leaving a generous smear of body oils and essences behind. "Feels like a boob job," he said, and started to laugh only to go slack-jawed an instant later. "Shit," he said, and pointed at the spot where he had touched niji. "Would you look at that? His skin is crawling."

There was no mistaking the negative undertones in the upright's voice. He did not want niji to absorb the deposit. That made no sense to niji. Why leave it there if he did not want it to be processed? Confused or not, though, niji absorbed the offending frani. Its shoulder returned to being smooth and still.

"Crazy," one of the other uprights said. "Do it again."

The uprights crowded in, probing niji's outer membrane with pokes and jabs. Niji found the contact exciting. And the crush's synergistic heat was delectable. Niji flushed, savoring the sensations, only to be sobered by a thought and a splash of zervarzi caution. What if niji became heat-drunk and did something offensive? What if it lost control of its shape and became as lowly as a nijit in the swarm's eyes? It tried to ease its way into a less confined space only to be hauled back into the center of the swarm.

"Hey, Del!" someone shouted. "C'mere and check this out!"

Niji knew what that meant: more uprights on the way. That meant more poking, more jabbing, more heat. The precursors of a panic sweat beaded up on niji's membrane, an outbreak that amplified its anxiety. It did not want to go frozen-stupid in front of the swarm. The uprights would know the true measure of niji's inferiority if it succumbed to dwaza and then they would lose all interest in being frenz. Niji had to focus. Niji had to stay calm. But that was so hard in the midst of so much contact and heat!

As niji struggled to keep its chemistry from cascading, a voice that niji did not recognize boomed, "What's wrong with you boys? Step back and give the little guy some room!"

The crush immediately subsided. Frani-beats later, a draft of cool air enveloped niji and turned its sweat to dust. Niji flushed with relief and then looked around upright-style to see what had changed. The first thing niji noticed was it was still surrounded—the swarm had only backed away, not dispersed. The second thing niji noticed was the newcomer. He stood a head taller than the next tallest upright and was broader in the chest than any two uprights. And the mass of hair beneath his marvelously bulbous nose was even more impressive than his physique. The growth was so profuse, it completely hid his upper lip. If niji had a growth like that, niji would not have to remember to move its mouth-hole when it talked! It wondered if the uprights would notice if it shaped itself one now.

"You're a kew, aren't you," this newcomer said.

"Yzz," niji said, having decided that the uprights would definitely notice and most likely object to niji sprouting new features in front of them. "Kew."

"His name is Bob," the newcomer's much smaller companion said. "And he's not just any kew. He's the Special Envoy's protégé. He helped rescue Guzman."

"That a fact?" the newcomer said, never taking his eyes from niji. At his companion's enthusiastic nod, he broke into a grin that even his lip hair could not hide and extended a hand. "Pleased to make your acquaintance, Bob," he said. "I'm Hehvenlee Delgahdo."

Niji knew that the outstretched hand was an invitation to make membrane-to-membrane contact. *Shaykyn*, this was called, and until now, niji had assumed that it was a ritual exclusive to uprights. Pleased to learn otherwise and eager to experience the custom, niji extended one of its own hands. Hehvenlee grabbed the construct and pumped it with enough force to generate ripples in niji's protoplasm. Afterward, he gestured at his companion and said, "This here is my brother, Lil Del. But I think you two have met already."

Niji did not recognize the smaller upright immediately, but it offered him a hand anyway. As they shook, niji realized that he was one of the uprights who had prompted AyJay and Val to go out to the near-wild. He had not looked as hahpee to see niji then as he did now.

"You're the first kew I've run into," Hehvenlee said, when the introductions were over and done with. "How about we sit down and talk for a while?"

"Oh-kay," niji said, and immediately shifted its center of gravity onto the floor.

Hehvenlee stared at niji for a fran-beat, then let out a ha-ha sound as big as he was. "I'm not as flexible as you are, Bob," he said, "so if you don't mind, let's sit over there at one of those tables." As niji sprouted back to its former height, Heavenly turned his face to the other uprights and said, "The rest of you are welcome to join us, but only if you mind your manners. No poking. No crowding."

The swarm relocated, taking up positions behind Hehvenlee, Lil Del, and niji. Niji did not like having so many uprights at its back-side at first for it found all of their shuffling, slurping, shifting, and talking distracting. Then Hehvenlee said, "So what's it like to be a kew?" and niji forgot everything else. No upright had ever wondered about that, not even AyJay. She was more interested in what niji knew and the sorts of problems it could solve. Niji did not fault zra for her lack of curiosity about its essential nature; indeed, niji rather encouraged it. For to be kew was to be inferior, and niji aspired to be more in her eyes. However, niji had no such aspirations where Hehvenlee was concerned and so appreciated his consideration.

"Too bee kew iz too eat, zleep, ahn zhink," niji said. "Too bee kew iz too bee kold, too."

Lil Del made ha-ha sounds and said, "Of course you're cold. You're running around butt-naked. Try putting some clothes on."

The rest of the swarm laughed at that, but not Hehvenlee. His demeanor remained intently benign. "Fair enough," he said. "So what brings you here today?"

"Zhat dor," niji said, pointing toward the entrance, and then looked all around, trying to absorb the wonder of the surrounds. "Wat bee ziz playz?"

"It's called the Free Zone," Hehvenlee said. "But I like to think of it as a home away from home for all the people who wind up on this rock." He lifted a container halfway up to his mouth and then made a mildly un-hahpee face. A fran-beat later, he offered the container to Lil Del. "Go and get me another one, would you?"

"Sure," he said, and went bounding into the structure that the swarm had emerged from earlier. When he returned, he had two containers in hand. "I got one for Bob, too," he said, as he plunked one down in front of Hehvenlee. "If you think that's OK."

"I think that's up to Bob, not me," Hehvenlee said.

Lil Del plunked the second container down in front of niji. "There you go, old son," he said. "Your first born-again."

"Wat iz?" niji asked, eying the yellow liquid that was all but foaming over the container's rim.

"It's an ice-cold reconstituted beer," Lil Del said, as he settled back into his seat. "It tastes like the real thing and packs a better punch. You've never tasted anything like it."

"Well, of course he's never tasted anything like it," Cowboy jeered from the background. "He's a friggin' alien."

"Go on," Lil Del urged. "Try it."

Niji had already taken a sample by dipping the tip of a frani-tipped pseudo-finger into the container. The liquid contained alcohol and a variety of other carbon compounds as well as an abundance of gassy bubbles. But since the uprights clearly expected niji to imitate their way of experiencing beyr, it sloshed a bit into its mouth-hole. The beyr's coldness numbed the vacuole that niji had formed to contain it, and the hyperactive bubbles stimulated the formation of useless digestive acids. Zhee! What a repellent fluid! Under other circumstances, niji would have purged the vacuole immediately. But because niji wanted to please the uprights who were looking on, it internalized the vacuole for later disgorgement.

"So what do you think, Bob?" Lil Del said. "You like?" When niji did not reply right away, he said, "G'won, give it another try. The stuff grows on you."

Niji did not know what that meant, but Little Del seemed very excited by the prospect of niji sampling the beyr again so niji did so. The second experience made niji feel even worse than the first. For now, in addition to being cold and hungry, it was also bloated. It had never taken in so much fluid, not even when feeding from ulvarzi track slush. The distended vacuoles made niji feel wobbly—and unbalanced.

"Well, Bob?" Little Del said, persistent in his enthusiasm. But before he could press niji to sample the loathsome fluid yet again, Hehvenlee said, "Give it a rest, LD. Bob's not made the same way we are." Then he focused on niji and said, "So tell me if I have this right. A bunch of kew found a Terran out in the wild and decided to bring him back to the base. Somewhere along the way, they were ambushed by Shingo's thugs and killed. Is that right?"

Although niji did not know what *zugz* were, it got the gist of what Hehvenlee was saying. "Yzzz," it said. "Kew dehd."

"And did I hear that those kew were transporting the Terran underground?" Hehvenlee asked.

"Yzz," niji said, following the upright's gestures as well as his wrdz.

"Do kew like to move underground?"

Niji liked this upright and his priorities. Unlike AyJay, he did not seem to be excessively concerned with that swarm's demise. Unlike her, he was more interested in the doings of living varzi. Perhaps he shared niji's belief that those stupid nijiti deserved to die for stopping to play while in possession of an upright. Perhaps he was testing niji to see if niji was stupid, too. Niji meant to convince him otherwise.

Yzzz," it said. "Wrmyr unnyrgrohn."

"Ah," Hehvenlee said, and started to make another sound when a soft beep cut him off. He paused for a moment and then cocked his massive head at niji. "Sorry, Bobby," he said, "but I'm expected elsewhere."

He stood up. Niji went vertical, too, out of a reflexive desire to remain in the upright's presence. During the shift, its beyr-filled vacuoles sank into its midsection. Cowboy pointed at the resulting bulge and made ha-ha sounds.

"Check it out," he said. "Bobby's got a brew belly!"

The other uprights made ha-ha sounds, too. Even Hehvenlee joined in.

The anxiety that niji had suffered earlier surfaced again, filling niji with a excruciating sense of unworthiness. It was no better than a nijit to these uprights. If it were to expire on the spot, they would go on sampling beyr and ha-ha-ing as if nothing at all had happened.

"Ha," Cowboy said, as niji staggered beneath the weight of its own inferiority. "Can't hold his born-again!"

"Zip it, Johnny," Hehvenlee said, and then set a massive hand on niji's shoulder. "You OK, Bobby?"

On any other occasion, niji would have taken comfort and encouragement from upright contact. Now, though, Hehvenlee's hand was just another burden threatening the integrity of its configuration. "Muz go," niji said, desperate to leave before it lost control and changed back to its lowly varz form. "Tired."

"Happens to the best of us," Hehvenlee said, and then gently angled niji toward the exit. "C'mon, I'll walk you out. And just so you know, you're welcome back anytime."

Niji understood welkum bahk. But it was not certain that it had processed the rest of the wrdz correctly. "Welkum here?" it said, refusing to hope. "Here in za Free Zohn?"

"Hell yeah, here," Hehvenlee said. "You saved one of us. As far as I'm concerned, that makes you one of us. That means this is your home, too."

All at once, the weight that had been crushing niji's sense of purpose evaporated. For in the span of an upright's breath, it had gone from most unworthy to—one of us. And instead of a burrow, it now had a home.

This, niji thought, was what evolution felt like. And it could not wait to embrace the change.

CHAPTER 25

AJ EMERGED FROM THE bedroom to find Val all suited up and ready to roll. It seemed like he was always on the move these days, off to the boat or the field or some destination in between. For the most part, she appreciated him picking up the slack while she recuperated. But every now and again, she'd see him go and think—off to powwow with Shingo again, lover? She hated that bitchy inner voice and the grudge that it kept trying to fan. She knew that Val had her back. She knew that he would do anything to ensure her safety. Unfortunately, 'anything' included second-guessing her decisions and collaborating with her nemesis. She considered that undermining. He called it keeping all options open. This wasn't the first time that they had butted heads over their nonnegotiable positions. This was, however, the first time that she had been so slow to equalize afterward.

"So what's on your TDL this shift?" she asked, feeling a need to engage him.

He looked her way, semi-surprised by the question—and for good reason, she supposed, given how taciturn she'd become. "I'm heading out to the west forty to check some sensors that I planted earlier in the week," he said.

"What are you looking for?" she asked.

"The tingly-warm."

Ah, yes, the mysterious tingly-warm. If they could figure out what it was and why the Q found it so irresistible, they might be able to recreate it somewhere off-base and establish a new Q gathering place. Then maybe they wouldn't present such a threat to security in Shingo's eyes and he'd be able to wrap his head around the idea of peaceful co-existence. His lordship wasn't making any promises, but even he could see the merit in this line of investigation.

"Got any theories as to what it might be yet?" she said.

"Yeah," he said. "I'm thinking it's a leak in the grid."

"All grids leak a little," she said, mostly because it was true.

He managed a wry half-smile—the first she had seen in a while. Was it possible to miss things like that after the fact? "I'm not talking about a little leak," he said. "I'm talking about one big enough to create a localized sensation."

"Could be a cable failure," she supposed. "Or loose couplings. Given all the earthquake activity that the grid's been subjected over the course of its short history, I wouldn't be surprised if the cause was some combination of both." Then, suddenly hungry for another smile, she added, "Want some help checking those sensors?"

He arched an eyebrow at her. "Really?" At her nod, he asked. "Are you sure you're ready for a field-trip?"

"Just give me a minute to suit up," she said, and swiveled toward the SU with a spring in her step. Things felt right between them, like old times. Then he asked, "What about Bob?"

Her good feeling went a little cold. For the Q hadn't been the same since Val had stuck him out in the hallway. 'More aloof,' was how she'd described him in her last log-entry, but that wasn't right. When Bob visited the boat, he was his usual eager, engaging self. He simply didn't visit very often these days. She supposed he was feeling a bit disgruntled. And who could blame him, really, after being hung out like that? Anyone could have found him in that float. He could have been hurt—or killed. Fortunately, nothing like that had happened. He'd simply let himself out of the float and gone back to whatever hole he called home. Still—

"Bob's got his own agenda these days," she said. "If he shows up at the boat and I'm not there, he'll find something else to do and no harm done."

"Fine by me," Val said. "So go get ready."

"On it," she said. "I just need to find my Mars pullover. My habby hasn't seemed warm enough to me since I got zapped."

"There's probably a short in the insulation system," he said, as he joined the hunt. "You should send it to maintenance for an overhaul. We're talking about that red poly tunic with the retro zip, right?"

"Right."

"Where'd you see it last?" he said, looking in all of the usual places.

"I thought I left it on the boat," she said, "but it wasn't there when I looked for it a few days ago."

"Well, I don't see it anywhere here, either," he said. "It probably got sucked up by the laundry 'bot. I have a sweater you can borrow if—"

The housekeeper cut him off with a ping: incoming call. She glanced at the monitor, but there was no ID. "You expecting a call?" He shook his head. "Me, neither," she said, and tried to forward the call to her message center.

But the keeper kept on pinging.

"Crud," she said, "it's a bug." Which meant that someone knew exactly where they were and wasn't taking 'later' for an answer. "Fine," she said, as if the word were a curse. "Pick up."

A parade of digitized words goose-stepped into the room. "Commander Shingo requires an audience with—Special Envoy Johnson. She is to meet him at—her residence—at—oh-nine-hundred, first shift. Attendance is mandatory. This message will not be repeated."

"Friggin' drone-calls," she said, as she triggered the disconnect. "They're the ultimate in passive-aggressive bad manners. Figures Shingo would like them.

What time is it now?"

"Oh-eight-fifty," Val said. He had abandoned the search for her pull-over and was now reaching for his headgear. That bitchy inner voice of hers wondered why he was in such a big rush all of a sudden. But instead of holding that poison in so it could fester, she decided to let it out.

"You looking to catch his lordship at the airlock so you can have a few minutes alone?" she asked, with just a little arch in her tone.

"Negative," he said, looking her straight in the eye. "His lordship is rather pissed at me."

"Why's that?" she asked.

"We had words," he said, and she could tell by the set of his jaw that he did not intend to elaborate. "So if you don't mind, I'd like to jet before he gets here."

"And if I do mind?" she asked, allowing the arch in her tone to creep into an eyebrow—as if she'd been flirting all along.

"Then I'll have two people pissed at me," he said, and then headed for the door. "See you later."

"As soon as I'm done here," she said, "I'll catch up with you."

But he was already gone.

AJ stared at the door for a moment with a half-formed wish caught in her throat and then headed into the SU to don her habby—just so Shingo would know that she had other places to be. She was still working on the seals when the housekeeper announced the CO's arrival. She ran her fingers through her overgrown hair, thinking that it was time for a shave. But Meli wouldn't hear of it. *Val likes it that way.* The keeper pinged again. She headed into the common area and keyed the door. Shingo blew into the apartment like a bad wind.

"You do not appear to be convalescing," he said.

"Who said I was?" she retorted.

"Your second," he said, stressing the word like an insult. "He has blown everything about your accident out of proportion."

AJ kept a straight face, but only by the narrowest of margins. Leave it to Shingo to turn an incident into an accident and make it sound like everyone else had it wrong. But at least now she knew why he and Val were on the outs. His former 'ling had sided with her instead of him. Was it wrong of her to be inwardly gloating about that?

"Is that why you're here?" she said. "To complain about Val?"

He dismissed the possibility with a scowl—a rare, unguarded display of irritation. "We have a much more important matter to discuss."

"By all means," she said, "let's discuss it. Will you sit?"

"No."

"Would you care for refreshment?" she asked. "I can call for tea."

"No."

If he had been his usual inscrutable self, she might have continued to torture him with insincere offers of hospitality. But since he was already agitated, there was no point in trying to get a rise out of him—not when she could be out in the field with Val.

"Then let's just cut to the part where you tell me what's on your mind," she said.

"The Q must be removed from the base," he said. "All of them. Immediately. I insist."

Here we go again, she thought, resisting the urge to roll her eyes. But all she said out loud was, "Why's that?"

"They are criminals."

"Really?" she said, wondering if she was the only one who'd find that statement ironic. "What sort of crimes are they allegedly committing?"

"The very least of their offenses is thievery," he said, as if that charge could possibly compare to xenocide.

"Are you sure it's the Q?" she countered. "Because a degree of thievery is common on remote sites. It's a by-product of boredom and limited resources. What's disappearing—small stuff like clothing and mementos?" He nodded, a grudging concession. She used that to support her argument. "Typical RS pilferage. If I were you—"

"There's more," Shingo said, in a tone so caustic that it dissolved her train of thought. "Q are infiltrating restricted areas."

She sucked in an apprehensive breath. "The second seed installations?"

"No," he said, too proud of his hyper-secure facilities to lie about them being breached by a species as backward as the Q. "But they are turning up just about everywhere else."

"That's a statistical inevitability, Commander," she said, happy to hear that it was nothing worse. He would have been able to ride a black box breach a long, long way. "More Terrans plus more Q in the same finite space equals more interaction."

"You don't understand," he said. "They are—co-mingling."

"Sounds like whisper campaign material to me," she said, refusing to get worked up over such a vague accusation, no matter how creepy he made it sound. "I'm going to need specifics."

"It would be better if you saw it first-hand," Shingo countered.

Irritation welled up within her. She didn't want to play mind games with this man today. She wanted to be out in the field with Val, repairing the bonds between them. But it was obvious that she wasn't going to get her wish until she granted his. So she resigned the match with a sigh and said, "OK," she said, "you win. Let's go and see what's got you in such a tailspin."

"I cannot go with you," he said. Before she could insist otherwise, it being his pain-in-the-ass idea and all, he added, "I have no access to the Free Zone."

Ah. Free Zones were owned and operated by the Union. In addition to being recreational complexes, they were sanctuaries of a sort, places where rank-and-file Johnnies could indulge in their preferred pastimes without fear of being monitored or reported. Officers were only allowed on the premises at certain times and only with a special pass. TSC objected to this policy, calling it 'exclusive', but whenever the council attempted to delete it from a contract, the Union called a general strike and brought all walks of space industry to a halt.

"You understand my predicament," Shingo said.

"I do," AJ said, although she was struck more by the irony of it. Here was a man who had barged into a potentially superior race's space without blinking an eye but would not step inside a structure on his own outpost for fear of provoking a group of neo-Teamsters. "But if you haven't been in the FZ, then how do you know there's something amiss going on there?"

"I have my sources," he said, reverting to his usual unrevealing self.

Her bitchy inner voice had a name for that source: Val. Strangely enough, though, the ire that accompanied that naming was all for Shingo. "All right then, Commander," she said. "I think we're done here."

"Are you going to investigate?" he said.

"Absolutely," she said.

"When?"

"Problems are researched in the order that they are received," she said, semi-imitating a digitized drone-call. "There are currently several ahead of yours."

"Special Envoy," he said in a tone that might've seemed mild if not for the calcified glint in his eyes. "You were the one who asked—no, demanded!—that I leave all matters pertaining to Q to you as a condition of our reconciliation. I have attempted to honor those terms by coming to you with a matter that could threaten the stability of this outpost. If you do not see fit to address my concerns in a timely fashion, then I will attend to them myself and be justified in doing so."

Although it galled her to the core, she had to admit—Shingo was right. Never mind that he only played by the rules when they were in his favor. Never mind that she couldn't trust him even then. If she was going to dictate terms, then she had to honor them, too.

"Point taken, Commander," she said, with as much humility as she could muster. "Thank you for the reminder. I'll look into this matter right away."

"Excellent," he said, and then adjourned the session with a curt nod. "I will leave you to your work. I look forward to receiving your report."

An instant later, he was gone and she was tapping out a message to Val: *Something came up, see you later.* An instant before she hit 'send', though, she wondered if she should call him in to help investigate Shingo's complaint. Four eyes would cover more than two, and the Free Zone was a very big place. But even as she entertained the notion, her conscience got the better of her. She wanted Val's company, not an extra set of eyes. And he was already working on something important. So she dispatched the note, then grabbed her helmet and headed out. She could've left the lid—and the habby—behind, for there were no hazardous spaces between here and the Zone, but since she was suited up already, she decided to stay that way. If she chilled down, which was likely these days, she could always seal the suit up to get warm. Plus, it offered more protection than loungers in a pinch. And who knew where her search for illegal goings-on was going to take her?

She only wished she knew what she was supposed to be looking for!

As she made her way through the apartment complex, she began compiling a list of the less-than-savory activities that went on in a FZ: drinking, drugging, brawling, gambling—ooh. Bored spacers would make book on almost anything that moved. Maybe a few entrepreneurial ne'er-do-wells were rounding up Q and racing them. Or pitting them against each other. And—ooh. Maybe the culls were being sold on the black market as pets. *Can we keep him, Chief?* The Q were so contact-hungry, they'd probably go peacefully, possibly even happily.

At the entrance to the Free Zone, she flipped up her face-plate to be scanned. The retinal reader ID'ed her as SE Awinita Johnson, and listed her access as unrestricted. That surprised her, for she'd been expecting at least a partial exclusion.

"Guess I'm even less important than I thought I was," she said, and then forgot all about her dubious status as the door slid open.

The Farside FZ was a modular, multi-leveled mall, a space-age adult entertainment mall with enough bells and whistles to shake even the most sensory deprived Johnny out of his shell. But while it looked much the same as every other FZ that she had ever frequented, there were a few stand-out differences. The stale reek of spilled synthetic beer was missing—an absence that she belatedly attributed to the newness of the air scrubbers. And instead of hyper-loud music and holo-deck ads, the prevailing sound was—surf? Yes. Water crashing into land over and over and over like a Viking lullaby. And as if that weren't weird enough, the nearest all-wall displays were of palm trees, sun-washed beaches, and water. WTF, she thought, even as she fought back a pang of longing. Had FZs changed that much over the past quarter-century? The one on Mars had been a roughneck's paradise. She'd embraced the lifestyle with a newbie's abandon, intent on ditching her earthquake-shattered past. She gambled. She drank. She went on party safaris instead of LTL. Then one day she woke up and realized that her memories were packed in fuzz. Panic set in. All of a sudden, she wanted everything back—even the pain. That was the epiphany that changed her life. Instead of forgetting, she focused on forgiveness. In time and in turn, she forgave her parents for dying, then Terra for killing them, and finally, her own self for surviving.

An outburst of laughter elbowed AJ out of her bittersweet reverie. She tracked the sound back to a nearby bistro-tech. A crowd had assembled out on the patio. Most of the revelers were wearing topless habbies, but a few had opted for loungers instead. The center of attention seemed to be a woman in a red caftan. She was small, almost child-sized, and had a distinct pot-belly. As AJ watched, the woman said something that the others must've found funny, for they all laughed and thumped her in that manly, good-one sort of way. The woman endured the thumping without complaint even though she seemed to shrink a little with each blow. One of her companions—

Wait. That caftan looked familiar. AJ blinked, not believing what she was seeing, but a second glance confirmed the first. That was her missing Mars pull-over. She should have realized that someone had swiped it. In her insular little world, however, theft was one of those things that only happened to other people. The question now was: how should she proceed? She could barge over there and interrogate the would-be thief. But in doing so, she would call unwanted attention to herself and possibly compromise the overall investiga—

Oh, crud. The woman was looking in AJ's direction now, staring as intently as AJ must have been. AJ expected her to bolt as guilty people often did. Instead, she raised a gangly arm and waved.

"Zra! Hell-o!"

For one dumbstruck moment, all AJ could do was gape and think: WTF? Then, as her initial shock thinned out, her thoughts began scrabbling for traction. Bob? That was Bob? Crud! What was he doing here? How did he get in? No wonder Shingo was in vapor-lock.

The Q was heading toward AJ now. At first it seemed like he was actually walking, but then she noticed that that neither of his feet ever quite left the ground. Still, he was doing a first-rate job of impersonating a Terran—the best, most cohesive effort she had seen yet. She expected his facade to lose its polish as he drew closer, but while a few flaws did in fact appear, she had to look hard to see them. His facial features were stable and highly detailed. His body, though small and slight, was convincingly humanoid. And the pull-over completed the illusion. By the time he came to a stop in front of AJ, she was no longer surprised that she'd mistaken him for a woman.

"Hello, Bob," she said. "I wasn't expecting to see you here."

"I lyk Free Zohn ver-ee much," he said, flushing with pleasure.

"I see." Then, because her cover was already blown and she didn't know what else to do, she gestured at the pull-over and said, "Where'd you get this?"

"I fown onza floor in daboht," he said, preening a little. "Iz ver-ee worhm."

"It's also mine," she said. "And I don't remember telling you that it was OK for you to take it. Taking without an OK is called stealing. Terrans do not approve of such behavior."

The preening came to an abrupt stop. His expression flickered like a holo running low on power. "You leev," he said, "I tahk. Iz wat kew doo."

"I see," she said—or at least she was starting to get an inkling.

Then one of Bob's pals peeled away from the group and converged on them at a pace that only looked casual. He was an enormous man, a presence and a half. His face was all lumps and pits, and the mustache that he wore like a wrap did nothing to hide his homeliness. But while AJ noticed the man's looks first, it was his eyes that held her attention. They were deep-set and dark like an osprey's, and she knew instantly that they saw everything.

"There a problem here, Bobby?" he said, as he inserted himself into their midst.

"No problem," the Q was quick to reply. "Zizuz AyJay."

"Awinita Johnson," AJ said, offering the man a hand. He gripped it with just the right amount of force. Any more, and it might've hurt. Any less, and she would've been offended.

"Special Envoy," he said, acknowledging her title without blowing it out of proportion. "So glad to finally meet you."

"And you are?" she asked.

"Heavenly Delgado," he said. "At your service."

Ah. The patron saint of Free Zones. She should have known, even though they'd never met or even crossed paths. He had the look of a legend about him. "Chief Delgado," she said, paying him the same kind of respect that he had paid her. "What a surprise."

"OK, you call me Heavenly and I'll call you AJ," he said, offering her a smile that was as crooked as it was engaging. "And before we go any further, allow me to congratulate you on your work with Bobby. He's quite the character."

AJ glanced at the Q out of the corner of an eye. He was watching a jungle travelogue on one of the all-walls. His complexion now had faint green undertones. On a human, such a shade would have suggested sickness. On Bob, however, it seemed more like—reverence.

"He's one surprise after the next, that's for sure," she said. "And I have to admit, I'm a little shocked to find him here—hobnobbing with a Union overlord no less."

Heavenly laughed, a mountainous sound. "Yeah, well," he said, "you're not alone in that regard. Jaws have been dropping like express elevators ever since he started showing up here."

Since? Crud, she hadn't seen that coming, either. Exactly how far out of the loop had she fallen? "So he's a—regular?"

"Pretty much," he said.

"And no one's complained?"

"Oh, I wouldn't say that," he said, with a dark gleam in his eye. "At first, we got a fair share of whingers. Some even huffed off, thinking they'd be missed. But that's mostly old news already. Fact is, most Johnnies are more curious than scared of Bob. Once they realize he's not going to suck their brains out through their noses, they're OK with him." He reached over and poked the Q in the side. "Right, Bobby?"

Bob started, a reaction that prompted a smattering of tentacles to pop up from his pseudo-comb-over. "Yzzz," he said, as the strays settled back into place. "I yam—oh-kay."

"But—" Her gaze shifted from Heavenly to the Q and back again. Talk about strange bedfellows! "You know he's not supposed to be here, right?"

"Says who—that tea-sucking sneak Shingo?" he scoffed. When AJ betrayed the CO with the faintest of shrugs, he scoffed again. "His lordship knows better. Union turf, Union rules. And the Union has no problem with Q being on its turf. If that bothers Shingo—" His smile returned, more crooked than ever. "So much the better."

OK, it was official. AJ liked this man. Unfortunately, that wasn't going to make her job any easier—unless she could convince him to work with her. She liked the idea. She liked the odds, too—two against Shingo. She could even pitch it that way. But even as she decided to do just that, Bob distracted her with a curious chirping sound and then tugged at her habby.

"We zhud goh, zra," he said, pointing at the nearest exit.

AJ took a reflexive step in that direction and then hit the brakes, thinking, first Val and now Heavenly. Maybe it was a compulsion. Maybe it was possessiveness or some weird alien instinct. Whatever the official term was, the Q definitely had a problem with her spending time with alpha male types. And that simply would not—

The floor began to shake ever so slightly.

"Goh now, zra," Bob said.

EBS alarms started blaring. An instant later, bubble shelters began popping up from the floor. AJ clenched her fists and stood her ground.

"C'mon!" Heavenly said, shouting at her over the sudden din. "There's no telling how secure the overheads are."

"You go on," she shouted back. "I'm done running from Kisin." When he gaped at her, radiating disbelief, she waved him after his erstwhile companions and said, "Go on, take cover."

His disbelief narrowed into disapproval. An instant later, he was gone.

The now-shuddering all-walls went dark. A moment later, the overheads winked out, too. The entire Free Zone trembled and creaked and groaned. AJ stood through it all, daring the god of earthquakes to do his worst. She was tired of being terrorized—tired, fed up, and exasperated beyond all fear. Kisin had already made her an orphan. He'd battered her, bruised her, and buried her alive. If he had something else in store for her, then he could either bring it on now— or else leave her the fuck alone!

As abruptly as it had started, the shaking stopped. A moment later, the alarms went mute and the overheads flickered back to half-strength. AJ knew that was the generator kicking in and wondered if the power station had taken another hit. Probably, she thought, and then gave herself a quick once-over by the FZ's grainy, gray light. Her knees were quivery, as was her gut. Nothing was broken, though. She wasn't leaking anywhere. Her legs felt heavy, but only because Bob had wrapped himself around them. She found his presence oddly comforting.

"Thanks," she said, and gave him a friendly pat on the whatever. "You can let go now."

A series of gummy pops broke the post-quake silence—the sound of bubble shelters being blown. Moments later, Heavenly came tearing toward her like a guided missile. "Fuck a duck, lady," he said, as he approached. "What in hell is wrong with you?"

"Long story," she said, and then turned her back to him so she could take a ping from Val.

"You OK?" were Val's first words.

"Yeah," she said, happy to leave it at that. "You?"

"Ditto," he said. "But the west forty took a hit. Turbines are dropping all over the place."

"Shit," she said, and her gut started quivering in an entirely different way. "You're out of there, right?"

"Working on it," he said, and now that she was listening for it, she could tell that he was running by the way he was breathing. "Wind kicked in just as—the shaking started. I'm—having a hard time—finding the crawler."

"Use the loco," she urged.

"Didn't bring it," he said, and then swore—a surprised yelp. "Ground's collapsing!" he shouted, in response to her WTF. "I can't—I can't outrun it! Send—"

She waited for him to fill in the blank. The link went dead instead. "Val?" she shouted anyway, as if she could reach him through sheer desire. "Val?" No response. "Shit!"

"What is it?" Heavenly asked, getting right in her face. "Who's Val?"

"My second," she said. "He's in trouble."

CHAPTER 26

Zhee! Niji was going on another excursion with AyJay and Hehvenlee and some of niji's Free Zohn frenz! At first, niji thought that niji was going to be left behind, for all of the uprights started moving in great haste in the same direction. But then zra stopped and pointed Hehvenlee back toward niji.

"We might need him," niji heard her say, before she continued on her way.

The next thing niji knew, niji was folded over Hehvenlee's shoulder and jouncing to the urgent beat of his footfalls. Although the upright had his outer top-nob on now, niji could sense him talking to other uprights as he raced along. "Bring a crawler to the FZ's main entrance, stat," he said. Frani-beats later, he added, "Screw the weather report. We got a man down." After that, he said, "You get that friggin' transport out here or I'll rip out your heart the next time I see you."

Although niji did not understand all of the words, there was no mistaking the force with which they were issued as anything but an attempt at domination. That surprised niji, for while it considered Hehvenlee to be first among its frenz, it also considered him too big to be a dominant, and indeed, the upright had never shown any interest in exerting force before now. Niji wondered if he had ul-nijit-like ambitions, and was trying to overcome his inferior predilections. Or maybe, when it came to uprights, size was not a conclusive indicator of superiority.

As niji pondered the mysterious ways of uprights, Hehvenlee entered the airlock that led out of the Free Zone. As soon as he stepped out of the structure, nazza tried to blow him back in.

"Sumbitch!" he said, tightening his grip on niji. "Where did this bitch of a wind come from?"

Niji could have told him. The Season of Storms was returning to this region. Nazza was returning along with it, and so was the cold. Niji could feel the temperature dropping with every step Hehvenlee took. The transition was always abrupt, but this one seemed more sudden than usual—possibly because niji had been paying more attention to the uprights than the weather's nuances.

A crawlyr spanned out of the windblown darkness and then rumbled to a stop. AyJay was the first one to climb aboard. Niji knew it was her because she was the smallest, and even though her face-plate was down, it knew that she was agitated because she used abrupt, insistent gestures to communicate with the upright who boarded after her. Hehvenlee and niji caught up with her in the crawlyr's cab.

"Move!" niji heard her shout at one of the other uprights, and then, "Punch it, damn you!" When the upright gestured at the world of swirling grit beyond the crawlyr's face-plate she hit his arm and then tugged on it as if she meant to displace him. Niji did not think that she would have succeeded, for that upright was much bigger than she was, but Hehvenlee pulled her away before the contest could produce a winner on its own.

"Let him do his job," he said. "We can't help if we don't get there."

"But we're going too slow," AyJay said, and then abruptly removed herself from the cab.

Although niji had no desire to be outside in the plummeting cold, it would have followed zra just the same in the hope of learning more about her agitation. But even as niji shifted toward the door, Heavenly held niji back. "Let her be for now, Bobby," he said. "She won't appreciate the company."

So niji stayed in the cab. Heavenly and the other upright stared at the crawlyr's face-plate, but niji oozed under a seat and reconfigured itself into a heat-conserving ball. The last thing niji heard as it started to drowse was, "The wind's starting to let up."

The next thing niji knew, AyJay was back in the cab and shouting, "There! Over there!"

Niji shifted out of its repose and back into upright form to see zra and Hehvenlee pointing at something beyond the crawlyr's face-plate. Zra was very agitated. Curious as to what all of the commotion was about, niji extended its neck in that direction. The only thing it sensed, however, was a rather unremarkable jut sticking up from the sand in the near distance. At first, niji thought it was a boulder, but as the crawlyr drew closer, niji realized that its dimensions were too regular to be natural and deduced that it must be an upright construct. But— the only constructs out in the near-wild were the whoozhing ulvarzi. And there wasn't a single one of those in sight.

As niji scrutinized the jut, it tipped sharply to one side. Frani-beats later, a colossal dent appeared in the terrain. The crawlyr jerked to a stop and then started moving rapidly backward. As it did so, the jut vanished. Zhee! Now niji understood why there were no whoozhing ulvarzi in the vicinity! A sinkhole the size of an ice-field had swallowed them all up.

Sinkhole or no sinkhole, zra did not want to retreat. She kept shouting, "Stop, dammit!" until the crawlyr finally came to a halt. Then she began shouting other things. "Hehvenlee," she said, "tell your Johnnies to buddy up, grab a loco, and move out. Team one goes east; team two goes west. You and I will head due north."

"AyJay," Hehvenlee said.

"Val was heading for his crawler when we lost contact," she said, "so we can triangulate on the last set of coordinates I have for that and—"

"AyJay!"

"And go from there. C'mon, you guys," she added, when Hehvenlee and his frenz did not move, "get cracking. There's no telling how long this break in the wind is going to last."

Hehvenlee folded his arms across his chest and said, "Sorry, AyJay. No one's going out there until I'm sure the ground is stable."

She stood before him on the balls of her feet as if trying to tower over him. When he did not submit to her immediately, she shrugged and said, "Stay here then. I'll go."

"No, you won't," he said, and then grabbed her by the arm when she tried to shoulder past him. "It's too risky. I'm afraid your second is on his own."

She made a sound that resembled a small version of nazza at its worst and then began to pummel him with her fists, feet, knees, and elbows. Although the blows seemed quite insistent, Hehvenlee refused to release her. Niji did not understand why its two most favored uprights were abusing each other. Were they vying for dominance? Why? Could Hehvenlee not see that zra was the superior being? What he was doing was ill-considered!

"Bob!" AyJay said, as she struggled for extract herself. "You—have—to help!"

Niji needed no further prompting

"What the—?" Hehvenlee sputtered, as niji raced up his back-side and onto his top-nob. Frani-beats later, he added, "That's disgusting!" and then let go of AyJay so he could attend to the azrum that niji had deposited on his face-plate. Niji thought AyJay would evacuate the cab after that. Instead, she gave niji's leading edge an urgent tug.

"Bob," she said, in an equally urgent tone, "quit messing around and get down from there. I need your help."

That confused niji. What did she think niji was doing if not helping? Still, it abandoned its roost on Hehvenlee's top-nob to stand before her in upright form. "How help?"

"I need you to find Val!" she said.

That inspired more confusion. Why did she want Val? How would his presence improve this situation? "Vahl not here," he said, hoping that she was a little confused, too, after struggling with Hehvenlee.

"I know that!" she snapped, and then gestured in the direction of the sinkhole. "He's out there! The ground swallowed him up. I don't know where exactly. That's why I need you. You know your way around underground." When niji did not respond, she made an effort to contain her agitation and speak slowly. "I want you to get Vahl out of that sinkhole. Understand? I want you to find Vahl and bring him back to me."

Niji continued to balk—not from a lack of comprehension but rather a lack of desire. It did not want to search for Vahl. Vahl treated niji like a nijit more often than not. Vahl was frenz with Zhingo. Worst of all, Vahl was zra's most favored. If Vahl remained lost, then perhaps she would start favoring niji instead.

"Please, Bob?" AyJay said. "I—can't do this without him."

Despite its reservations and secret ambitions, niji could not refuse her—

and not just because inferiors deferred to superiors. The need to please her had embedded itself in its being. So whatever she asked, it would strive to do—even if that meant finding the one upright that it wanted to stay gone. "I goh," niji said. "You leev crawlyr thrumyn zo I no weyr feyn you."

"Sure," AyJay said, scooting niji toward the lip of the cab. "anything. Just find Vahl."

"Good luck, Bobby," Hehvenlee said, just before niji plunged over the side.

Cold-and-getting-colder was the first impression niji registered when niji hit the ground. The second was the crawlyr's thrumming. Niji knew from experience that the vibrations would travel a long way. Niji hoped they would attract a few varzi along the way—despite the cold-and-getting colder. In that unlikely event, niji left an azrum urging all comers to follow its lead. Then it dove into the regolith.

The ground tasted like the place where niji had first felt the tingly-warm. That delectable sensation was gone now—swept away by the sinkhole, no doubt, just like everything else in the area. Niji stretched its frani in all directions, searching for an inkling of Vahl's whereabouts. All it found, however, was loose, slushy sand.

How was it supposed to find Vahl when it could not even find a trail?

Niji expressed its frustration in an azrum. Then, at a loss for a better approach, niji began to tunnel through the regolith in an ever-expanding outward spiral. Shortly afterward, its leading edge bumped into something solid. Vahl? A flash of excitement warmed niji's extremities only to die back down as the details from that contact registered. No, not Vahl. This mass was long and thin and made of upright metal—part of a whoozhing ulvarz, niji guessed, and chose to be encouraged because finding something was better than finding nothing.

More ulvarzi parts cropped up in niji's path, pieces for which it had no name or interest. It was growing numb and discouraged and ever more frustrated. The conditions were impossible! How could AyJay expect niji to know something that remained a mystery to her?

As it languished beneath the weight of zra's expectations, a pod of zyl swarmed up from the depths and began to feed on the crystals that were starting to precipitate from the surrounding regolith. Only then did iti realize that the conditions were becoming even worse than impossible. The slush that the earth-shaking had created was freezing back into ice. And instead of reverting to its former particulate state, it was forming slabs. Eventually those slabs would coalesce into a single mass. If niji was still searching for Vahl when that happened, then both of them would be lost. And niji did not want to end its existence frozen in the grips of a nascent ice field. It angled its leading edge toward the surface as if it were trying to far-sense AyJay's thoughts. Surely she would understand if niji abandoned the hunt. Surely she knew that some tasks simply could not be done. Yet even as niji tried to convince itself to quit, niji pressed on. It had to keep moving to keep its protoplasm from turning to slush. Zhee! How it despised the cold! When this excursion was over, it was going to acclimate to warmth all over again and—wait, what was this? Another piece of metal? This piece was too big and too dense to be part of a whoozhing ulvarz. This one tasted of burnt hydrocarbon residues.

Zhee! This must be the missing crawlyr!

Instinct urged niji to look for Vahl in the cab. Since niji did not know where the cab was relative to the rest of the crawlyr, it began following the ulvarz's contours. In its eagerness to find the upright and conclude this increasingly miserable excursion, niji tunneled swiftly and without caution. So niji did not realize that there were hazards present until something pierced its leading edge. Ice, it supposed at first, but the taste was all wrong. The splinter embedded in its membrane was made of metal. How curious. Niji extruded the sliver and sealed the wound, then resumed its headlong race only to be punctured again. Only then did niji realize that the surrounding regolith was riddled with metal fragments. Some shards were membrane-thin, others were huge; most of them were sharp. Under other circumstances, niji might have wondered how such a shatter-field had come to exist. Now, though, it merely wanted to avoid further injury. But even as niji shifted course, niji came upon the ruins of a whoozhing ulvarz. The remains seemed to be embedded in the crawlyr's flatbed. And somewhere in the vicinity of this convergence, something was leaking. The seepage was carbon-based; rich in iron and oxygen; organic. That was no ulvarz fluid. It had to have come from an upright!

Niji loosed an ecstatic azrum. AyJay was going to be so pleased!

Abuzz with the false warmth of excitement, niji followed the half-frozen gradient around the wreckage and to the crawlyr's undercarriage. There, tangled in a length of broken track, niji found Vahl. There was a rippled dent in his face-plate and a small tear in the middle section of his outer membrane. The tear was the source of the iron-rich seepage. When niji probed the gap with a cluster of frani, it sensed a deep wound that bore the shape and residues of a metal shard. The wound itself was sticky and cool and no longer oozing. Niji did not know how to close such a puncture and so tapped on Vahl's face-plate to get instructions from him. Vahl did not respond. Niji tapped again, more insistently. When Vahl remained unresponsive, niji decided that he had gone into the upright version of fwaza and set out to free him from the track.

He was entangled in two places: ankle and upper body. Niji was able to extricate his foot because it was caught in a loose, tail-end loop. But the greater part of the track had coiled around Vahl's shoulders and held him fast. Niji tried to pull him free, but he was too heavy. So niji had to loosen the track instead. Ice was forming on its surface—slick crystals that compromised niji's grip. Crystals were forming on Vahl's outer membrane, too. Instinct began urging niji to give up and get away before it was covered with ice, too! Niji was tired, and so very cold. All niji wanted to do was return to the surface and get warm.

But AyJay had asked, so niji persevered, and soon the burgeoning layers of ice began to aid rather than hinder niji's efforts. The more slippery Vahl became, the more the track yielded, until finally the upright was free. There were patches of ice throughout the regolith now; some were already starting to coalesce. Niji knew it had to get Vahl topside fast, but he was heavy, so heavy, and niji had never felt so sluggish. It did not want to be underground any more. It wanted to be—

It wanted to—

It wanted—

You have chosen a perilous place to drowse, zer.

The pulse nudged niji out of its stupor, but its frani were frozen and it could not get a feel for the sender's identity. The only taste that registered was that of its own self. One of its wounds must have broken open and started oozing protoplasm, it supposed. The thought did not concern niji. It started drifting off again only to be troubled by another pulse.

You must move now, zer.

The upright is too—big, niji pulsed sleepily. *I cannot—*

Where one fails, many may succeed.

The sender was close now. Niji could sense that much. It extended a brittle fran. The varz that niji contacted was much warmer than niji, but the taste was again all self. Confusion swirled through niji; it felt like oblivion's tug. But even as niji started to surrender to that pull, it made a connection that jolted it back to near-consciousness.

You! it said, an incredulous pulse. *How?*

We followed your azrumi, niji's clone said simply, as if there were no bad experiences between them.

But— niji said, struggling in vain to clear its thoughts. *You are ul-nijit—*

Did you think you were the only one capable of evolving? the clone said. *If you can assist with the upright, join with us. If you cannot, hang on to him.*

Us? There were other varzi in the area? Why? Did they not realize that this kind of cold could freeze their memory strands? And what was this thing-that-was-not-a-varz that niji found itself attached to? It reminded niji of a slab of rock or ice except for the fact that it was moving. Why would a slab be moving? And why did niji seem to be frozen to it?

The next thing niji knew, niji and the slab were topside. Nazza was blowing, but niji could not bring itself to stream to the slab's underside to hide from the wind. It was senseless from the cold, so senseless that it did not even twitch when something heavy dropped onto the ground next to the slab.

"Jeezuz," nazza groaned. "Izzat you, Bob-bee?"

Niji had the niggling sense that it should know what the wind was saying, but could not bring itself to care. It wanted warmth and it wanted sleep. Nothing else mattered. So of course it did not care when the wind started screaming, "No-o-o-o-o!"

Warmth and sleep. Sleep and warmth. Nothing else mattered.

PART III

CHAPTER 27

"AJ? SWEETIE?"

AJ kept her eyes shut and her breathing steady in the hope that the voice would go away even though the sugary ones never did.

"Ah-wi-neee-tah." See? "Wakey-wakey."

When AJ continued to fake unconsciousness, a hand gripped the knob of her shoulder and shook—much harder than necessary. That was typical of sugary types, too. "C'mon, Sleepy-head, time to get up. You've got a visitor."

"Tell whoever it is to fuck off," AJ said, even though she knew that wasn't going to happen, either. "You should feel free to do the same."

The aide chuckled. "There's my grumpy girl. C'mon now, let's sit up and make you presentable." More clutching ensued, unwelcome contact. AJ batted the aide's hands away as if they were malarial mosquitoes and then sat up of her own accord—oops, too fast. Her thoughts swirled like water circling a drain. She grabbed the railing of her deluxe bunk to steady herself.

"That's what happens when you rush into these things," the aide told her, sing-songing his critique.

What did he know? She glared at him, trying to recall his name. Gassy? Grabby? No, no, it was Gabby—short for Gabriel the Archangel, or so he claimed. Short for obnoxious butt-hole as far as she was concerned.

"But everything just has to be your way, doesn't it?" he went on, unable to resist goading her.

"Used to be," she said, and then batted his hands away again as he tried to smooth away the creases in her expensive retro-cotton loungers. "Now my way is whatever way you want it to be. I don't have a say in anything."

"Maybe that's because you said too much when you first came back from Farside," he said. "That's the general consensus up here, anyway."

That was the general consensus just about everywhere, she thought. And just this once, she had to admit that Gabby was right. She had said way too much, once too often.

It had started at her TSC exit interview. The council had come at her in an avuncular way, wondering if Remote Site Fever might have been a factor in her decision to resign her position as Special Envoy— 'Abandon her post' in their words. She should have said sure, whatever, or kept her mouth shut. But she'd been insane with grief over Val. Insane and bitter and eager to fertilize the universe with her pain. So she said, "I didn't abandon the post, I tapped Heavenly Delgado as my replacement and then quit." No one was happy to hear that, no, not at all, but they pressed on through too-tight smiles and wondered why she had handed the job to a money-grubbing union Jack instead of someone who'd be more inclined to put the Q's interests first—someone like one of Shingo's lieutenants perhaps. She should have said that she hadn't considered the matter from that angle or kept her mouth shut. Instead, she said, "Heavenly will do his best for the Q. Shingo or one of his 'lings would've done their worst." More huffing and hawing ensued, almost all of it in defense of Shingo: a hard man in a hard place at a hard time.

Desperate measures, right?

Then the council came at her again, urging her to go back.

Terra needs you on Farside.

Your presence is vital to the installation's success.

Just until we get the Q situation sufficiently sorted out.

"No. No way," she said, even when they threatened to revoke her island privileges. "I'm not going back. Ever."

And deep in her delusional heart, she actually believed that the council had gone as far as it intended to go. When it realized that it had her absolute final word on the matter, she thought that it would dismiss its collective disappointment with a shrug and allow her to keep what they had previously granted her. So when she woke up the next day in a landlocked TSC retirement commune on the outskirts of Fargo, ND, she went over-the-hill berserk. Instead of complaining through official channels or leaving town with her mouth shut, she called a multi-media press conference and spilled every single bean she had about the Q.

That was how she wound up at the orbiting gulag known as Gateway, at the mercy of overzealous watch-dogs like Gabby.

"Personally, I admire what you did," he went on, persistent as a monkey in his attempts to groom her. "I mean, it's their world. And it's kind of exciting tending to a celebrity—even if you are a pain in the ass."

Celebrity? Ha! Try prisoner. In the aftermath of that ill-conceived press conference, TSC had taken her passports away for jeopardizing global security. It confiscated a giant chunk of her retirement funds, too—a fine for violating the non-disclosure clauses in her contract. It probably would have voted to make her disappear, too, if her story hadn't gone viral and made her famous. Everybody knew about the Q Lady. And everybody wanted to talk with her. So instead of having her killed, TSC installed her in this swank cis-lunar Free Zone—to better support and protect her mental health, the official documents read. But she knew the council had put her here so it could control access to her—and charge her visitors handsomely for the privilege to boot.

"How about you let me give you a skin and muscle tone anti-age nano-booster?" Gabby said. "You'll look twenty years younger. The Johnny who's here to see you will think you're his sister instead of his mother."

"Like I give a shit," she said. There was only one Johnny whose opinion had mattered enough to make her want to nano-up. And she just couldn't think about him. Could not. Would not. "Tell whoever it is to fuck off."

"Not even at gunpoint, sweetie," he said, managing to spritz her with some kind of faux-lavender reek. "This guy's important."

She rolled her eyes—a jaded BFD. Her visitors had included princes and religious dignitaries, politicians, media stars, and Nobel prize winners. Important was a relative term.

"I wish you'd grow your hair out," Gabby went on, as he brushed the pillow impression out of her salt-and-pepper stubble. "This style makes you look like a death-row crone."

She grunted, her opinion of his opinion. She didn't like talking anymore—not to this jerk, not the other aides, and not especially not to visitors. All she wanted was to be left alone.

"There," he said, stepping back to admire his handiwork. "At least now you look semi-presentable. Do you want to receive your visitor here or in your sitting room?"

"Fuck off." She was tired, played out, empty. The only visitor she wanted was dead.

"Sitting room it is then," Gabby said. "Do you need a float or can you manage on your own?"

As if he didn't know that she insisted on walking everywhere—no matter how tired or achy she was. "Just go and fetch whoever it is already," she said, waving him off yet again. "The sooner this is over, the sooner I'm rid of you."

"It's good to have goals," he said, and then departed, leaving her to stew in a cauldron of long-simmering resentments.

Swank or not, she loathed everything about this resort—the way it looked and the way it smelled and the way it made her feel, locked up and warehoused like a spent plutonium rod. She wanted to see palm trees, taste a fresh-picked mango, feel warm salt water splash over her feet, and hear Val gripe about man-eating fleas.

Damn, how she missed that man. And damn, how she hated him for that. If he hadn't happened to her, she'd be knee-deep into her retirement by now and enjoying a private, solitary life. Val had ruined everything. Everything. And the worst of it was—

Her housekeeper pinged, announcing a new message. She would have ignored it until it degraded into static, but Gabby had bugged it to play no matter what she did.

"On our way," the drone said. "Get your fanny in that sitting room now!"

AJ yowled, an upwelling of visceral frustration. Shi-i-it! She was tired of being a circus attraction: see the Q Lady, ask her a question if you dare! She had said as much to TSC, but the council ignored her complaints. Publicly, it explained her irascibility as a long-term after-effect of RSF. Privately, they didn't care what her problem was—especially since the visitors kept on coming regardless of her disposition. And when she tried to escape by withdrawing into herself, her so-called caretakers tormented her until she started talking again. This was the price she was being made to pay for blabbing TSC secrets. The council could not have chosen a more terrible punishment.

The keeper pinged again. "Almost there now."

Insufferable scrote.

Nevertheless, she shuffled out to her luxurious sitting room. Dead woman walking, she thought. It felt that way, too. She was always tired—not just weary of her situation or worn down by grief, but profoundly exhausted. When she got to her padded, high-back chair, she was glad to sit down. Was this what old age felt like? She didn't know. Neither of her parents had lived this long. She used to think that was a tragedy, but now she wasn't so sure.

The door to her apartment slid open—without a knock or ping beforehand. She hated that. What was the point of having a door if anyone could walk through it?

"This way, gentlemen," Gabby said, almost gloating as he ushered a pair of strangers into the room. "She's been waiting for you. Awinita," he went on, downshifting into a more coercive, condescending tone as he glanced her way. "Can you say hello to these nice people?"

"Help me," she said instead. Because sometimes she just had to push back. "I'm being held prisoner." Gabby clucked like a nervous hen, but before he could refute her claim, she hastened to exaggerate it. "Call Amnesty International. Tell them where I am and—"

The larger of her two visitors snorted—an amused sound that broke her concentration and drew her ire. She stopped staring at a point just beyond his head and focused on his face. It was enormous, pock-marked—and familiar. Even demented, she would've recognized the elaborate mustache.

"Heavenly," she said. "Heavenly Delgado."

"Hello, AJ," he said, breaking into a ten-gallon grin. "Been a while, hey?"

But the thrill of seeing someone who had known her as something other than the Q Lady was gone already, dispersed by disappointment—wrong Johnny—and then suspicion. In lieu of a greeting, she said, "What do you want?"

"Awinita," Gabby said, as if he were scolding a child. "That's no way to talk to such an impor—"

Heavenly cut him off with a look that only pretended to be friendly. "I think we're good here, hombre," he said. "Why don't you run along and attend to your other duties?"

Gabby flushed as if stung. His expression was disinclined. "I, uh, usually stay for visits," he said. "You know, in case she needs help."

"This woman was running deep space RSOs when you were still an itch in your daddy's space diaper," Heavenly said. "I'm pretty sure she can manage this little sit-down without your assistance."

"But—"

"Would you rather that I didn't ask nicely?" Heavenly said, and while he did not move a muscle, everything about him suddenly seemed larger. Gabby stiffened like a man at knife-point and then raised his long, thin hands as if to fend off the attack.

"Just leaving," he said, back-pedaling toward the door. "If you need anything, just ping." AJ snickered at the hastiness of his retreat. He narrowed his eyes at her, promising payback. A moment later, he was gone.

"Bloody hell," Heavenly said. "Why do you put up with that officious little prick?"

"What makes you think I have a choice?" AJ said.

He snorted again. "You're Awinita Johnson. You have choices."

"Really?" she said. "Then get out."

"Not just yet," he said, smiling his way around the contradiction. But she called him on it anyway.

"See?" she said. "Choice is just another empty word around here."

"Could be worse," he said—as if he had a clue. "At least they put you in a seven star facility. Lot of Union nabobs live here at Gateway."

"Why?" she said. "They have faulty impulse control, too?"

He laughed aloud at that, even though she hadn't been trying to be funny. "Feisty as ever," he said. "I'll never forget how you stood out in the middle of the FZ during that killer quake. It was like you were daring the whole place to come down on your head."

She wondered what he was thinking, bringing up that temblor. Nobody got on her good side like that.

Val, make him go away!

"And now you're the Q Lady," he went on, seemingly oblivious to the chill that she was projecting. "I wish you could've seen Shingo's face when he heard that you had forced TSC into investigating him for possible abuses of power. He went cherry-red! It's not a good color on him, either. But—you'll be happy to know that things have been getting better for the Q ever since."

"Your doing, not mine," she said, refusing to let him further inflate her already overblown legend. "That was a brilliant move on your part, by the way."

"What was?" he asked.

"Bringing the Q into the Union," she said. "Giving them their own Chapter. They get protection; you get control over local assets. And Shingo gets a poke in the eye two ways." The thought gave her a pang of visceral satisfaction. "A plan with something for everyone. I wish I had thought of it."

"Didn't you?" he said. "Why else would you have picked me to take your place?"

She flashed back to that moment: her on her knees beside Val's unmoving body, willing him to be alive so she could say the things that she needed him to hear. Things like: I love you; thanks for always being there; please don't go. But even as she tried to resurrect him, Heavenly pulled her away. She had hated him so much at that moment, she'd thrown the worst punishment she could think of at him. 'Since you're so tight with the Q these days, you can be their goddamn advocate from now on.'

"I picked you," she said, "because you were there."

The memory left her tired and heart-sore. What little appetite she'd had for this visit was failing fast. "So now that we're all caught up," she said, trying to hurry things along, "why don't you tell me why you're here?"

"As it happens," he said, "I've got face-time with the council today. SWU asked for the meeting so we're hosting it on our turf."

"Hope your meeting goes better than mine did," she said, and then noticed his companion for the first time. He was much smaller than Heavenly, both in height and in girth, and delicately featured. His caftan and headscarf were the same color as Heavenly's habby. Although AJ didn't recognize this individual, there was something familiar about him, something substantial that she couldn't quite put her finger on.

"Who's that?" she said, almost grudgingly.

"What?" Heavenly asked, in a teasing tone. "Don't tell me you don't recognize your old friend, Bobby."

"No," she said, possibly out loud. But even as she denied it, she realized that it was true, this would-be retro-drag-queen was Bob! Heavenly motioned for the Q to approach. He did so demurely, smiling Singer's smile and looking perfectly human. Unbelievable. She never would have guessed.

"Hel-lo AyJay," he said, with only a slight buzz. "Itz good to zee you."

"Are you out of your mind?" she said, talking to Heavenly though her gaze kept darting back and forth between him and the Q. "This is—" She couldn't find a word strong enough to contain her astonishment. "You shouldn't have—"

"Shouldn't have what?" he said, wide-eyed as a virgin at a porn-fest.

He was faking, right, Val?

"This might be a cis-lunar facility," she sputtered, "but make no mistake. This is Terran territory—Terran only. When word of this gets out, every single regulatory organization on the planet is going to chew you up and spit you out. You'll lose everything: your job, your pension, your citizenship."

"Relax, AJ," he said. "It's OK."

"No," she countered, torn between a whisper and a shout. "It is not OK. The people on yonder planet have spent trillions upon trillions of credits in the hope of keeping aliens out of their solar system. Now you've smuggled one into their thermosphere. You'll be lucky to spend the rest of your life in the apartment next to mine. TSC is going to want to vent you into the APW."

Heavenly caught her hands and caged them against his chest as if they were panicked birds. "AJ," he said, "it's all good. I cleared everything in advance with the proper authorities. Furthermore, this facility is Union-owned and operated. Bob has as much right to be here as any other brother. So be a sport and say hello to him already. He's come a long way to see you."

"You should've cleared this with me beforehand, too, Heavenly," she said, jerking free of his tender trap. "I'm stuck in this subspace dungeon because of those—" Things. Blobs. Stupid useless pests that let Val die. She turned to the Q, meaning to savage him with a look and maybe leave him as raw as she felt.

He was watching her intently, as if he had been born with those eyes instead of masses of spaghetti tentacles. Un-fucking-real. He had changed so much since the last time she saw him. It was like he was a completely different creature—a strange, fantastical being that she could not quite bring herself to hate.

"Oh, hell," she said, surrendering her grudge. "Hello, Bob."

"AyJay," Bob said. "You are displeazed?"

"Not displeased," she said. "Surprised. I don't like surprises."

"I do," Bob said, shriveling a little.

Heavenly gave her a discreet nudge, and in an undertone, said, "He wants to be just like you."

It took her a moment to realize why the man was telling her this and then hastened to say, "Enjoying surprises is a good thing. Don't stop on my account." Because only a monster would let such an inquisitive soul believe that surprises were something to be transcended.

The Q's features plumped back up and into a perfectly happy expression. "Still learning," he said. "Alwayz."

"Maybe," she said. "But you've come a long way."

Further than she would've ever thought to guess.

"Your outer membrane iz loose," he said, glancing at her neck and then her hands and then her face. "Are you dehydrated?"

"It's called age, Bob," she said, trying to sound dignified and blasé. "This is what happens to Terrans as they approach the far end of their life-spans."

"Have you budded yet?"

Was she supposed to know what that meant? She couldn't remember. And when she tried to peek under the scab that had grown over the past, the only thing that seeped up under 'budded' was spring: plants, bushes, and trees all wrapping their reproductive potentials up in the prettiest packaging possible. Val would have deplored the season. Too messy, he would have griped. Too much pollen and too many bugs.

"Basically," Heavenly said, "Bob wants to know if you're planning on making little AJs."

"I figured as much," she said—or would have, eventually. "I'm simply not interested in discussing my plans for posterity with you or anybody else. I'm also getting tired of socializing, so why don't we just scroll down to the part where you tell me what you want and then call it a day?"

Bob just stood there beaming at her, but Heavenly did a very good job of looking hurt. "What makes you think I want something?" he said.

"No one visits me 'just because,'" she said. "I'm the Q Lady, and a royal pain in the ass to boot. Furthermore, no one transports an ET all the way into Terran space just so that ET can drop in, unannounced, to say 'Howdy!' to a former advocate. The higher the risk, the higher the stakes. So what's your game here, Jack?"

He studied her for a leisurely moment, taking in details and giving nothing back. His smile calcified. His eyes narrowed. She wondered what he saw. "I like straight talk," he said at last. "I don't get a lot of it, and I don't always go that way myself, but I like it when I hear it and imagine that you appreciate it, too. So I'm going to forget that you went viral with the last big secret in your care and let you in on another one." He leaned in close like a confidante. In spite of herself, she gave him an ear. "TSC is going to abandon Farside."

Farside was a hellish place—cold, windy, treacherous. The news shouldn't have shocked her. She shouldn't have cared. Even so, her head snapped back as if she'd been sucker-punched and her thoughts began to spin. All that work—for nothing. Val, dead—for nothing. "Why?" she said, a sound between a mewl and a croak.

"Seismic activity is increasing," he said. "Originally, the council had hoped to relocate to a more stable piece of Farside real estate, but we have since determined that the planet is entering a prolonged period of geological instability. There's not a seed facility on the market that can handle that much shaking. So Recon is looking around for a more hospitable planet."

She snorted, a derisive sound. "Let's hope they do a better job this time."

"Farside wasn't the worst mistake they could've made," he said.

"I'm not sure the Q would agree with you."

"Why don't we ask?" he said, and then grabbed the Q by a shoulder and drew him close like an old drinking buddy. "Hey, Bobby," he said, "what do you think about Terrans coming to Farside?"

"Best event ever," Bob said, glancing from him to her and back again. "Terrani brought knowledge. Knowledge iz gateway to evolution."

"And how do Q feel about Terrans leaving Farside?" Heavenly said.

Bob flushed a distressed shade of purple. "Q are ah-fraid. We have changed. We know zo much more. When Terrani leave, zeyr light and warmth and knowledge will go, too. Farzyd will be cold and empty again. Zhat iz not enough for Q anymore. When Terrani leave Farzyd, Q want to go wiz zem."

Right. And she wanted Val back. She glanced at Heavenly, expecting him to share her cynicism. To her surprise, he supported the idea. "It's only fair," he said. "Once you've shown someone the light, you can't just snatch it back away again."

"I'll bet TSC doesn't share that sentiment," she said.

"They have been a little slow to warm to the idea," he admitted. "But once they see Bob for themselves and realize that he's no threat to them or the planet, they'll change their minds."

AJ sneered. She couldn't help herself. The council had dropped her with a sledgehammer for talking about aliens. It wasn't that hard to imagine how it was going to respond to an alien in the flesh. "I hope you like tofu," she said, "because that's all we get to eat up here."

"C'mon now," he said, "don't be such a negative particle. Bobby here is appearing before the general assembly in less than an hour and I'm sure he could do with a few encouraging words or even some advice from his idol."

"Is that why you brought him here?" she asked, intending to abuse him if he confessed.

"Coming to see you was his idea," Heavenly said. "I just made it happen."

"Out of the kindness of your heart," she said.

"Something like that," he said cheerfully.

But she could not let the matter slide. She simply had to know what his game was. "I'm not buying it," she said. "There has to be something in this for you. Nobody goes this far out on a limb just to feed the birds."

"You did," he said, and the soft-spoken sincerity of the accolade stopped her in her tracks. If he was trying to play her, he was doing a damn good job. "And if it means anything, I'm sorry for where it got you. But attitudes have changed since you first dropped the Q-bomb. People are starting to get used to the idea of having company in the cosmic hot tub. A significant percentage of Terrans believe that interaction with aliens is inevitable. And the fact is, Q have the potential to be very useful allies."

You hearing this, Val?

"They're intelligent, trainable, and loyal to a fault. They tolerate some extremes better than we do, and require less care. Deploying them to frontier construction sites would be fast, cheap, and safe. Everyone would win."

"Everyone but the spacers who lose their jobs to your ET labor force," she said.

He scoffed at the point. The sound drew a curious tendril out from under Bob's headscarf. Heavenly drew the Q's attention to the stray with a casual gesture, as if it were a bit of tofu stuck in some Johnny's teeth. Then he jumped right back into the conversation with AJ.

"Do you know how many times TSC has met its quota for field hands, remote site or otherwise?" he asked, and then hastened to fill in the blank for her. "Never," he said. "Not even once. And finding field hands who are OK with being posted beyond the APW is an even more daunting task. So nobody needs be worried about Q taking Terrani jobs."

"So TSC gets the frontier fortified faster and the Union reaps the rewards," she mused, impressed with his thinking in spite of herself. "That's going to look good on your CV."

He held out his hands as if to show that they were empty. "It looks good already, Sister Spitfire. That's not why I'm doing this."

She decided to take his word on that simply because she didn't have the strength to keep on badgering him. She was fatigued again, spent. All she wanted to do was go to bed and dream of walking on her beach, hand-in-hand with Val. *You'll never guess what Heavenly told me today.* They'd stop for a mango along the way and maybe catch a fish for—

Something thready and dry tickled the inside of her wrist. She started out of her drowse with a gasp. The first thing she saw was a headscarf. Then Bob's face phased into view. He was standing in her personal space, waiting for her attention. Like always. She wanted to recoil. She ached to forget. But her aversion to the Q was tempered by grudging admiration. He had come so far, and looked so human. It didn't matter that he was small and slight, or that there was a hint of fluidity to his features. He was convincing. What did such a profound transformation mean? Was it flattery—or camouflage?

"What do you want?" she said, because he clearly expected something of her.

"I would like to vizit you again," he said. "Would zhat be OK?"

"Sure," she said, because he deserved some kind of concession for his unrelenting devotion. And it was a safe enough bet, really. The council could take years to make a positive ruling on alien visas, decades even. Who knew where she'd be by then? "Good luck with the council. Try not to spook the old poops."

He cocked his head. "Spook za poopz?"

Heavenly rumbled her name, a subsonic plea to keep the council-bashing to a minimum. She pretended not to hear. Since Bob had come seeking advice, she meant to give him some that he could use. And if Heavenly didn't like it, tough titty. Maybe next time he'd think twice about surprising her.

"That's right," she said. "They're not comfortable with the idea of sharing the universe with non-Terrans, so you'll have to convince them that you're not a threat. Let Heavenly do most of the talking. And try to look a little less Terran-like. They'll need to be able to recognize you as a different life-form. No! No tentacles!" she went on, as snaky tendrils began slithering out from under his caftan. "That will only freak them out. Try a different skin color, light green if you can manage it. Green is a very relaxing color."

"I like green," Bob said, taking on a springtime hue. "Itz a happy color."

And just like that, he became the little green man of B-movies and urban legends. How could the council be afraid of something like that? "Perfect," she said. "I think you're good to go."

"AyJay? May I?" he said, and reached for her hand. She nodded in spite of herself. An instant after he made contact, an eruption of tiny filaments scoured her palm. The hair on her nape stood on end, but she resisted the urge to pull away. "Heavenly teach me about gratitude," he said, looking up at her with earnest, Singer-esque eyes. "Zo I want to zay thank you."

"For advising you to go green?" she asked, joking to keep her mind off the creepy-crawly sensations that were shooting up her arm.

"Yez," he said, oblivious to her humor. "Alzo for making it pozzible for me to be more zhan I waz."

She didn't know what to say. She'd never been good with the oral form of gratitude. And gratitude from an alien that she had rarely been kind to struck her as exceptionally misplaced. But if Bob thought that she had been good to him, then who was she to burst his little extraterrestrial bubble?

"All right then," she said. "Glad I could help."

"You ready to zip, Bobby?" Heavenly said, glancing at his keeper. "We've got a meeting to catch."

"OK, Heavenly," the Q said, and then nodded to AJ. "I never forget you again, zra."

"Don't get up," Heavenly said, "we'll see ourselves out." Then he leaned in close as if to give her a brotherly peck on the cheek in farewell and whispered, "Thanks for being a sport, AJ. You'll never know how much this visit meant to him."

"Whatever," she said.

Moments later, she was alone again. She wasn't sorry the visit was over, but surprisingly enough, she could not put it out of her mind. *Never forget you again.* When had she not been the epicenter of the Q's attention? The first time she left Farside, he had thought so much of her that he found a way to call her back. This time, he had traversed the APW to visit. Even at her worst, he had idolized her, and put her needs before his own.

And in return for his steadfast devotion, she had abandoned him.

Shame flared across the flats of her cheeks as the memory crept out of hiding. It wasn't Bob's fault that Val had come back to her DOA. Bob wasn't to blame for Val being out on the west forty in the first place, either. The only thing that the Q was guilty of was a desire to please her. At her behest, he dove into a sinkhole and retrieved Val's body. Apparently, he nearly froze in the process. And she repaid the Q with outrage and indifference, leaving him to live or die in Heavenly's hands. After that, she never looked back, not even once—until now.

Never forget her again? Damn straight! She deserved to be immortalized as a Terran to be avoided at all costs.

Her keeper pinged—a gentle tone that nudged her out of her thoughts without startling her. "Unidentified visitor at the door, state desired course of action."

"Tell whoever it is to away," she said, in no mood for more company. But the pinging continued, growing louder and more urgent.

"Visitor refuses to depart."

"Visitor refuses to depart."

"Visitor refuses to depart."

She cursed the existence of obtuse people and then slung herself out of her chair. "Shut up already," she snapped, as she hobbled across the sitting room "I'm coming."

She smacked the access pad as if it were someone's face. The keeper fell quiet, the door slid open, and in staggered Bob. The Q was still a springy shade of green, but it looked wrong on him now, like a fungal overgrowth. And his features were as wobbly as his ersatz legs. She gaped at him for a WTF moment, mental gears stripped, and then shut the door in a hurry.

"What are you doing here?" she said. "Where's Heavenly?"

The Q's legs deconstructed. The rest of him hit the floor with a gelatinous plop and then disappeared within his suddenly shapeless caftan. Moments later, his head popped back out of the neck hole. His eyes were rolling around in their sockets—independently of each other. His lack of coordination reminded her of a drunk fresh from a binge. That impression was so strong, she even sniffed for alcohol. But all she smelled was recycled air and a whiff of silicon.

"Bob," she said, in a tone sharp enough to cut through his daze. "What's going on? What happened to you?"

"Zra," he said, making an effort to focus on her. "I zpookd za poopz."

"What?" she said, struggling to make sense of his semi-coherent buzzing.

He turned a lurid shade of orange. "Azzem-blee room very hot. Many Ter-rahn-ee zheyr. I get too much egg-zytyd ahn looz controhl uv my shayp. Ter-rahn-ee get up-zet."

Surprise, surprise, she thought wryly. But what she said was, "What happened then?"

"Ter-rahn-ee try put me in floht, but I con-fuz and no wanna go. I get away and come zee you."

"What about Heavenly?" she asked, glancing at the door. "Where was he during—"

The keeper interrupted with a ping. "Unidentified visitor at the door."

Speak of the devil, she thought, and moved toward the access pad. Before she got there, the door opened of its own accord and a half-dozen Terrans in sealed-up habbies stormed into the room.

"There it is!" one of them said, pointing at Bob. "Just where Delgado said it would be."

"Damn," someone else said. "It looks like a giant wad of chewing gum."

"What's going on here?" AJ said, as the men formed a circle around the Q. "Who are you guys?" A small float drifted in through the still-open door. "This is a private residence. You can't just come barging in."

"Zip it, sister," the team's apparent leader said, and then gestured at one of his 'lings. That bravo darted in and latched onto Bob's arm. Bob offered no resistance. Nor did he provide any. When the man pulled on the arm, meaning to sling the Q into the float, the arm went limp and stretched proportionally.

"Shit," one of the others said, "would you look at that?"

"C'mon," AJ said, tugging at the leader's elbow, "you don't need to manhandle him. He's traumatized enough as it is."

The man shoved her into the unready arms of another 'ling. "If you're smart, you'll shut up and let us do our work. You're in enough trouble as it is."

"What?" She broke free of the hands that were holding her and got right in the leader's face. "I haven't done anything! I've been here all blasted day. Do you hear me? Are you even listening?"

She gave the blockhead a push, trying to jar a response out of him. He stumbled forward a step and swore. "You want to play rough, bitch? Fine, we'll play rough. Junior, light her up."

The next thing AJ knew, electricity was coruscating through her. Her last thought before she blacked out was, WTF?

CHAPTER 28

"DON'T WORRY, I CAN fix this."

That was the first thing AJ heard as she roused from a very deep and vaguely disturbing slumber. The words didn't register at first, for she had a serious case of cotton brain. Nothing but static was getting through. She also felt as if she had been beaten with a crowbar.

"How are you feeling?"

She lolled her head in the speaker's direction, but saw only a massive blur. Whoa. She scrubbed the film from her eyes with the back of a very dry hand and then looked again. The blur sprouted a familiar, mustachioed face.

"Heavenly," she said, but her relief immediately gave way to confusion. "What are you doing in my—?" Bedroom, she started to say. But that wasn't right. This room was smaller than her gulag boudoir, and more Spartan. It reminded her of a—surgi-center recovery cell? But that couldn't be right. She had only talked about having her knee reconditioned again. Right?

"Where am I?" she said, running a bit of discreet recon on herself. "What's going on?"

"I've been wondering the same thing myself," Heavenly said, with what seemed like forced cheer. "At first, I thought you were having a bad reaction to the zap—"

"You zapped me?" she asked.

He threw up his hands as if to deflect the accusation. "Not me," he said. "A TSC security agent. He lit you up for interfering with his arrest."

"What?" She didn't understand how she could have taken part in such a dramatic event and not remember a shred of it. "Who was he trying to arrest?"

"Bobby," he said.

I zpookd za poopz.

That short-term memory fragment attracted other bits and pieces: men in haz-mat suits, a little shoving match and then: '*You want to play rough, bitch?*'

"Shit," she said, twitching as her body recalled the shock that had taken her out. But none of that shed any light on why she was in a recovery cell. The last time she had been zapped, she had woken up in her own bunk—with Val by her side.

"I'm still confused," she said, as if Val were with her now.

"I'm not surprised," Heavenly said, capsizing the fantasy with his outsized voice. "The jolt you took from that agent fried a bunch of your nanos. And as luck would have it, you were fighting off the latest cis-lunar flu at the time. When your nanos tanked, the virus wiped you out. But it took my techs a while to figure out what was going on."

"Your techs?" she said, bewildered anew. "Since when did my health get to be any of your business?"

His smarmy bedside manner acquired a sudden, distressed rigidity. He swallowed hard, like a man with lock-jaw, and then said, "Since they shipped you back to Farside."

She bolted upright, propelled by a resounding "What?" that blew out of her like cannon-fire.

"I know," he said, as a second disbelieving salvo stuck in her throat, "you're upset. And rightly so. But the good news is—it's a mistake. A terrible, regrettable mistake. And like I said, I can fix it."

An urge to punch him reared up in her—wham, one shot straight to that big smug mug of his. Fix that, meat-bag. She might've acted on the impulse, too, if she hadn't just spent what little strength that the flu had left her on sitting up. Crud. Every time she thought she had plumbed the depths of feebleness, something new came along to drop her even lower.

"This sucks," she said, and went prone again—her choice, but just barely.

"Of course it does," Heavenly said. As if someone that aggressively robust would know. "But I'm going to take care of you—Johnny's honor. And I'm going to start by getting you some grub. You're bound to feel better with a little ballast in your belly. What sounds good to you at this point?"

"Mango," she said, translating the growl that rose up from her gut. "And lots of water." As he tapped the order into his handheld, she added, "While we're waiting for the delivery-'bot, you can tell me how someone winds up on the far end of a wormhole by mistake."

He tucked the handheld into a pocket, then drew a pull-out from the wall and sat down—a hint, perhaps, that the telling was going to take a while. "It was more of a fubar than a regular oopsie," he said. "And it started at the general assembly."

"But I had nothing to do with that," she said.

"You didn't," he said, "but Bobby did. He had a mega-meltdown in front of the council and all of its invited guests. One moment he was a little excited and twitchy. The next, he was falling apart. First, he couldn't talk. Then he couldn't stay on his feet. Then he started changing shapes and colors as if he were auditioning to be someone's psilocybin trip. I still have no idea why he went so haywire."

"It was the assembly room," AJ said softly, recovering another fragment of memory. "He said it was too hot."

Heavenly scowled. "Didn't seem warm to me."

"You were wearing a habby," she said, "so you could have been sitting in an inferno and not noticed. I happen to know that most of the council members live on Terra. Grounders aren't comfortable unless they're sweating."

"Whatever," Heavenly said, dismissing the council's predilections with a shrug. "The long and short of it is, Bobby went native and everyone wigged. I think you know the rest."

"Yeah," she said archly. "I got zapped and sent back to Farside." Then, realizing that the Q could have suffered a far worse fate, she lost the attitude and asked, "They didn't zap Bob, did they?"

Heavenly erased her fears with a shake of his head. "When Security dropped you, he sort of froze up and checked out. Stayed that way for most of the trip back to Farside, too. He's fine now, though, back to his usual happy self. He doesn't even realize that he's being held."

AJ's head swirled: another round of incredulity eddying up from her bowels. "You're holding him?" she asked. "For what—disrupting a general assembly?"

The big man heaved a sigh that was both dramatic and convincing. "I wish it was that simple, AJ," he said. "Unfortunately, Bobby violated anti-terrorism laws when he fled custody. The laws weren't written with the Q in mind, but he met all the right requirements at the right time, so the hammer came down. Now the process has to run its course."

"Meaning?" she asked, projecting disgust now as well as disbelief.

"The 'incident' is being investigated," he said. "Bobby has to remain in my custody until the charges against him have been resolved." In an undertone and almost as an afterthought, he added, "So do you."

She was being held as a terrorist? After a lifetime of service and sacrifice? In her younger days, she would have gone off over that like a block of Z-4 and let the body parts fall where they would. But she was old beyond her years now, and her detonator had been broken by desperate times and measures. All she could manage was a sneer.

"The thanks from a grateful planet just keep on coming, don't they?" she said. "What are the charges?"

"Harboring a fugitive," Heavenly said, looking a little hang-dog, "and interfering with an arrest."

"And what about you?" she said. "You're the one who brought the Q to the station in the first place."

He made a sour face. "Believe me," he said, "I've endured more than one grilling on the subject. Fortunately, I had a substantial paper trail to back up my—" A buzz from his pocket cut him off. He triggered the door by remote, saying, "That would be your breakfast."

A servo-'bot in a frilly French maid's uniform came zipping into the room. At least, AJ thought it was a 'bot until she realized that there was nothing mechanical about it. By then, the Q was poised at the foot of her bed with a tray in its hands. She couldn't tell if it was a he or a she. The costume was feminine, but the face was all Singer.

Damn, this day just kept on getting weirder and weirder.

"Iz honor to zerv you, zra," it said, in a buzz that was both high-pitched and cheerful. "You wan more, you call, I get."

When AJ just laid there and stared, Heavenly relieved the Q of the tray and said, "That will be all for now, nija. Zra is tired."

Nija stretched her faux lips into a froggy smile and then reversed course. As she departed, Heavenly set the tray on AJ's lap. But she wasn't interested in slivers of reconstituted mango at the moment. She was still trying to process what she had just seen.

"Please tell me the uniform wasn't your idea," she said at last.

"I had nothing to do with it," he said. "Seriously," he went on, when she arched a dubious eyebrow at him. "She probably saw the outfit in an old vid and ordered a scaled-down version from one of the Free Zone merchants. Dressing retro-Terrani-style is all the rage with Q these days."

"That must make Shingo crazy," she said, blurting out the first thing that came to mind.

"Strokish, actually," Heavenly said, allowing himself a wicked smirk. "And as long as the Q stay out of secure areas, there's nothing he can do about it."

"He must not be too happy about me being here, either," she said.

"An understatement," Heavenly said. "He did everything in his power to ship you back to Terra before your shuttle even touched down here. But the council wasn't having any of it. They wanted you here."

"And why is that?" she said, as she picked at the mango shavings. The fruit was stringy and under-ripe, but she could not seem to resist it.

"The council wasn't exactly forthcoming with its reasons," he said, "but I got the distinct impression that it thought you could do less damage here than on Gateway." When she scowled, despising the whole lot as cowards, he laughed. "That's what you get for embarrassing a bunch of politicos, Q Lady. Now eat up. When you're done with that, you should probably grab another nap. If you wake up feeling energized, there's fresh loungers and even a habby in yonder closet. You're free to roam the FZ and other unrestricted areas."

Same privileges as the Q, she thought. BFD.

"I want to go home," she said, only to remember that that was off-limits to her, too. Same as the Q.

"You'll get there," he said, "just not today." Then, in one fluid motion, he stood up and pulled his handheld out of its pocket. "I gotta jam for now, AJ. See you later."

"Not if I see you first," she said, an automatic comeback. He laughed as he left the room, which was a relief, really, because Heavenly was the only friend she had at the moment and she needed to stay on his good side.

[∗∗∗]

"You're looking much better this shift, Chief."

Her first impulse was to grump at the aide as she had grumped at Gabby. But before she could act on the urge, Meli stepped in with one of her favorite old saws. *You'll catch more flies with honey than vinegar, 'Nita.* Val came back with, *Who in hell wants to catch flies in the first place?* But her mother's point had been made. She didn't have any rank or influence on this rock anymore. If she wanted support, she'd have to cultivate it. And support was a very good thing to have when you were stuck at the wrong end of a wormhole.

"Thank you, Miguel," she said, trying her best to be pleasant. "I'm feeling better, too. In fact, I'd like to do a little walking this shift if I may. If I don't exercise regularly, my knee stiffens up on me."

"You're in luck then, Chief," Miguel said, "because you have an appointment with the CO this shift. One of his 'lings is on his way to escort you to his office. I was just about to tell you."

"An escort?" she said, resenting Shingo's excessiveness. "What for? I can find my way around the HF. It's not my first time here."

"The CO prefers a Q-free environment," Miguel said, "and so conducts all of his business from the CP now. Perhaps he believes that you do not know where that facility is. Or, perhaps he simply wants to know where you are at all times."

She harrumphed. "Fat lot of good that did him last time."

"Yes, ma'am," the aide said, and while it could have been her imagination, she had the sense that he was on her side. His sympathy, real or not, gave her a morale boost.

"Guess I'd better get suited up then," she said. "We can't keep his lordship waiting."

"What's he going to do if you're late?" Miguel retorted. "Deport you?"

An excellent point. When TSC swept her island privileges off the table, it eliminated the only threat that could've guaranteed her table manners. The only threat except— "He could keep me here."

Miguel laughed out loud—a lively, mocking sound that extinguished any lingering doubts that she might have had about his true colors. "Not likely, ma'am," he said. "Rumor has it that he took a crowbar to a crate of illegals when he heard you were coming."

Indignation welled up within her, hand-in-hand with disgust, and the few regrets that she had entertained about blindsiding Shingo like she had turned to toxic dust. Only a monster would turn a temper tantrum into an excuse to abuse the weak and defenseless. A bar beating probably wouldn't kill a Q, but it would certainly inflict damage and distress. She should've tried harder to have the bastard de-commissioned!

"I was under the impression that Q were being treated better around here nowadays," she said.

"They are," Miguel said. "So long as they belong to the Union. Shingo may be brutal, but he's not stupid. He preys on unregistered wildies—so-called transients." She arched an eyebrow, urging him to say more. He needed no further prompting. "Transients caught in restricted areas are supposed to be trucked back to the wild. But while Shingo makes a great show of crating the detainees up, they don't always go out. Sometimes, they just—disappear."

"How do you know?" she asked. "Has someone filed a complaint?"

"No, ma'am. There's no point in filing a complaint without proof and proof is particularly hard to come by where wildies are concerned. They're all pretty primordial-looking, so there's no way of distinguishing them visually, and they aren't registered so there's no way of keeping track of them. And if the local Q notice when a wildie goes missing, they sure as hell never say so."

"Really?" she said, surprised to hear that. "Have you talked to Bob?"

"Big-Shot Bobby?" he said, surprising her all over again with the sneer. He's supposed to be a Union liaison now, but he doesn't like to associate with other Q when he's not on the clock. If he can't hang with Terrans, he'd rather be alone."

That assessment seemed rather harsh to AJ. She thought of Bob as gregarious, both with Terrans and his own kind, and on two stand-out occasions, she had personally benefited from his association with other Q. Then again, she had not been in any condition to observe the nature of those associations on either of those occasions. And overall, she had been more concerned with more fundamental matters: was he friendly, was he smart, did he like the taste of Terran brains? Miguel and his fellow Johnnies didn't have to worry about such basics, so it stood to reason that they would know him better.

And if Bob could learn gratitude from humans, then why not snobbery?

"I'd like to see him," she said. "Can you arrange a meeting?"

"I doubt it," Miguel said.

"Is communication between detainees forbidden?" she asked. But what she was thinking was, *Sometimes they just disappear.*

"No, ma'am," Miguel said. "It's just that we'd have to find him first."

"I thought he was in custody."

"He is," the aide said, sounding utterly unconcerned. "But the FZ is a big place, and as you know, Q can fit into some mighty tight spaces. We could look for hours and never find him. But don't worry, he'll turn up—sooner or later. He's gotta have his Terran fix."

"You make it sound like he's addicted to us," she said.

"I think he is."

The thought intrigued her, but before she could pursue it, the keeper announced a visitor. Her escort, she presumed. "Keep him busy while I suit up," she told Miguel. The aide scowled as if she'd just saddled him with latrine duty, but then waved her toward the SU and went to answer the door.

"About time," was the first thing the escort said when she finally made her appearance. The name-tag on his camo-habby said, 'Bondo', and he didn't show her the courtesy of flipping his face-plate before marching her out the door. On the walk through the HF, he kept giving her three-fingered nudges in the back instead of asking her to step lively. Finally, she rounded on him and said, "Next time you do that, I'm going to rabbit-punch you right in the nuts."

"A Q could outrun you," he grumbled, but quit with the poking. She maintained her snail's pace with passive aggressive glee.

They stepped out of the airlock and into the calm semi-gloom of Farside summer. There was a transport waiting for them in the loading zone. She hadn't been expecting that. Crawlers reminded her of Val. She averted her eyes as she climbed into the cab, but even so, she caught a glimpse of his battered, forever-still ghost in the flatbed. Bile surged into her mouth. The threat of tears stung her eyes. She had never been more glad of the anonymity that a habby guaranteed.

Jesus, AJ, it was an accident, get a grip already.

The crawler lurched forward, knocking her into her seat. She webbed herself in and then focused on the world beyond the windshield—anything to escape that smart-mouthed phantom. With no wind-blown grit to obscure the view, she could see much of the installation—and what a depressing sight it was. Modular buildings dominated the foreground like active, well-lit termite mounds. A jagged sprawl of smokestacks in the distance pumped steam into the perma-grey sky. There was 'bot traffic everywhere, APCs mostly, most of which were transporting ice ore from the unseen strip mine to the processing plant. And everywhere she looked, she saw junk: refuse piles, slag heaps, worn out 'bots, broken turbine parts. The Q should have been thrilled to learn that humanity was packing up and moving out. Clearly, they didn't realize that this sort of blight would spread to every exploitable corner of their world if Terrans stuck around.

"End of the line," Bondo announced, as they came to a stop in front of an unremarkable, single-story construct.

A bad end at that, she thought, still working through her mortification. This was exactly what humans were afraid the Un would do to Terra.

Bondo slung himself out the cab and then waited for her to disembark without offering to help. She repaid him by climbing down very slowly, wishing that doing do was more a matter of spite rather than necessity. When she finally hit the ground, he started to give her a three-fingered nudge toward the CP only to reconsider when she openly balled her hand into a fist.

"That way," he said, pointing instead.

They passed through a high-security airlock and into the main foyer. The checkpoint there had a dock for a security 'bot, but at the moment, the station was being manned by—his lordship. Although he was sealed up in a habby, she recognized him by his vector-straight carriage. Same old Shingo, she thought. Still playing head games. But she wasn't interested in playing along.

"What's it going to be, Commander? Retinal scan or strip search? Personally, I'm hoping for the strip search. Bondo here seems to really know how to treat a woman."

Shingo gave his head a slight and hopefully sour shake. "In your case, neither procedure is called for," he said, and then waved her through the checkpoint. "This way, please."

"Sure," she said, and then gave the tiger's tail another little tug. "I have to admit, I didn't expect to see you again."

"A mutual expectation, I assure you," he said, and then ushered her into what was clearly his office.

"Don't mind if I do," she said, when he motioned her toward the seat that had popped up on the visitor's side of his desk. That little walk had left her appallingly fatigued. "I've been sick, you know."

"Yes," he said, as he sat down across from her. "I know."

He flipped up his face-plate. She did the same, expecting him to recoil just a little—that knee-jerk, oh-shit fear-of-infection that all spacers shared due to their immuno-isolation. He did not so much as blink. She stifled her disappointment. Was it so very wrong of her to want him to be afraid?

"It is my sincere wish that you will soon be back on Terra, recuperating at your leisure," he went on. "Until such time, however—"

Here it came, she thought, the reason for the summons. And before the filter in her brain could engage, the next thought popped right out of her mouth. "What? No tea first?"

To her surprise, he acknowledged the quip with a twitch of the lips that could have passed for amusement on someone else's mouth. Then he continued in his usual monotone. "Until such time, I urge you to remember that you are here uninvited. You have no special status, no security clearances, and no purpose. Under no circumstance are you to involve yourself in any aspect of this station's business. Do I make myself clear?"

"Absolutely," she said, only to have another thought slip past the filter. "But what's the point? Heavenly says this installation is being phased out."

He stared her for a long moment—sizing her up, it seemed. As if he didn't already have a complete set of blueprints on her. "You and Delgado have something in common," he said. "You both like to talk about sensitive matters in public. But I realize that you have a special interest in this place—for multiple reasons. Out of respect for those reasons, I am going to disregard SOP and confirm what you have heard. TSC has found a suitable alternative to Farside and is in the process of seeding it. As soon as the seed is completely germinated, we will withdraw from this planet."

Whoa. Forthrightness from the Lord of Locked Lips? She never thought she'd live to see the day. It had to be a trick. But that suspicion didn't stop her from exploring the boundaries of that unprecedented exception.

"The Q don't want us to leave," she said.

"That is no concern of mine," he said.

"You still think they're vermin," she said, marveling at his intransigence.

"I think they are disgusting," he said.. "I think they are profane. The sooner we cut off contact with them, the better off everyone will be."

"Heavenly thinks otherwise," she said. "He's petitioning TSC on their behalf."

Shingo's nostrils flared—a shocking display of agitation. His lordship was becoming downright demonstrative in his old age. "You approve of his actions," he said. "You think he is trying to do what is best for the aliens."

She shrugged off the accusation. "What's wrong with giving the Q a chance?"

"A chance at what, I wonder?" he said. "He claims to be their friend, but he is not. He is not your friend, either. You would do well to remember that."

AJ was stunned. Advice now—on top of everything else? WTF was going on here? "Why do you say that?" she asked.

His keeper pinged, cancelling any response that he might have made. He glanced at the message and then favored her with another of his twitchy quarter-smiles. "Josiah Woo is on his way here," he said. "I would prefer that you be gone when he arrives."

"Josiah Woo?" she echoed. "The biographer to the stars?" He had pestered her for weeks for permission to document her life, saying history needed to know about the Q – Lady. She had been forced to threaten him with a restraining order to get him to back off. "How did he find out I'm here?"

"He is here to interview me," Shingo said. "Apparently, the public's interest in frontier figures has reached a new all-time high thanks to you and your misadventures with the media. Woo believes that history needs to know my side of the story. I am anxious to set the record straight."

Spoken like a true xenocidal tyrant.

For once, she managed to keep a thought to herself. "Thanks for the update," she said, as she headed for the door. "Give my regards to Josiah."

"Remember what I said," he said in parting.

As if she was likely to forget. Indeed, almost every part of their conversation came back to haunt her on the ride back to the HF. The Woo interview in particular bothered her. Instead of getting Shingo decommissioned for massacring aliens, she'd turned him into a frontier celebrity. He'd probably wind up making zillions in royalties and franchise rights. *Thanks to you.* Perhaps that was the reason behind that new mouth-twitch of his—the irony of it all would have left an indelible smirk on a stone. And perhaps that was why he'd been so effusive. *Delgado is not your friend.* Shingo never offered advice. Or issued warnings. And she certainly hadn't done anything to endear herself to him. Except create his fan-base.

As the crawler closed in on the HF's main entrance, she got her first good look at the building. It had not weathered Farside's wind well. Its synthetic façade had a dull, pitted look, and a significant number of insulation cells were missing. Normally, those cells would have been replaced as soon as they disappeared. But nothing got repaired on a soon-to-be-abandoned base. By the time that alternative seed was operational, this whole installation was going to be a dark, decaying dump—a parting gift from Terrans to their hosts.

And the Q would no doubt think them generous.

How pathetic was that?

"End of the line, lady," Bondo said. "Un-ass it so I can get back to work."

"OK," she said. "Since you asked so nicely."

"And just so you know," he added, as she prepared to disembark, "I think the council should've vented you for ratting on the CO. You got off lucky, Q-lover."

"Fat lot you know, Johnny," she said, and then shut down their link so she wouldn't have to suffer any more of his opinions on her way down to the ground. *Q-lover.* That would be funny if it weren't so damn sad. She didn't even like Q all that much.

As soon as AJ was clear of the crawler, Bondo sped off. She thought about taking a walk, but then decided that a bite or two to eat sounded better and headed inside. As she made her way toward the FZ, she thought about Bondo and what he'd said. His attitude ticked her off, but at the end of the day, he was right. She shouldn't have ratted on Shingo—leastwise not out of pique or desperation or deep personal grief. She should've done it because it was the right and honorable thing to do. If she had it all to do over again, she might—

"You OK, zra?"

She was standing at an entryway to the FZ. She couldn't say when she had gotten here or how long she had been waiting for the door to open for her. There was a large Q standing next to her. It was dressed in a black trench-coat and a retro-fedora. *What can I say? They like to dress up.* Its hands were thrust in the coat's front pockets. Its face has half-hidden beneath the hat, but she could still make out Singer's jawline. Its skin seemed to be heavily pitted.

"You know me?" she said.

"You are zra," the Q said. "Everyone know you. You go FZ? OK I go wiz you?"

"Yeah," she said, wondering if this situation would seem weird to anyone else. "Why not?"

She submitted to a retinal scan and discovered that she still had unrestricted access to the FZ. She made a mental note to thank Heavenly for the courtesy later and then headed inside. The Q glided in beside her, making no pretense of walking. She liked that, even if it did remind her of something out of an old antique vampire vid.

"Where you go now, zra?" it asked. When she pointed to a nearby bistro-tech, it said, "OK I join you?"

"Why not?" she said, and then hit the brakes as a swarm of pint-sized Q came scampering out of the premises. They were as colorful and noisy as island parrots, and seemed to be flocking her way. But even as AJ braced herself for a close encounter, they let out a collective squawk and reversed course. A moment later, they were nowhere to be seen.

"What was that?" she said, wondering out loud.

"Terrani call zhem nee-hah or she-kew," her companion said. "To uz, they are ni-ji-tee. Idiotz, you would zay."

"Where did they go?" she asked, furtively glimpsing into corners.

The Q shrugged as if it had been born with shoulders. "Who can zay?" it said. "They are eazily diz-tracted."

She took a table on the patio—the first one she came to. The instant after she sat down, the muscles in her legs began to twitch, telegraphing a close call with collapse. As she scrolled through the pop-up menu, she glanced at the Q and said, "Want anything?"

"I have no hun-gyr," it said.

"Me, either," she said, clicking on the links for braised tofu and lemonade. "But I have to eat anyway to build up my strength."

"Be-cuz you been zik, yzzz? Ev-ree-one knowz," it went on, before she could ask. "Can you zhow me how to be zik? I wud like za experienz."

"It's not an experience," she said, "it's a condition. And trust me, you don't want to know what it's like. Not everything Terran is a good thing."

"How will I know," the Q said, "if I do not experienz?"

A server-'bot came zipping out of the café with her order. The lemonade looked good; the tofu, not so much. But she started eating just the same. The Q watched her intently, as if it meant to memorize everything about each and every bite.

"Why would you want to experience things that aren't good for you?" she said, hoping to distract the weirdling or perhaps just herself from its scrutiny.

"Experienz creates knowledge. Knowledge generates change. If there iz no change, there can be no evolution, and this iz all I will ever be."

"Is that such a bad thing?"

"It iz when you want to be more," the Q said.

AJ's head swirled—a sense of unreality as disorienting as vertigo. Was this some kind of post-flu delirium? Or was she really trading philosophies with a shape-shifting alien over a plate of braised tofu at a café on the far side of a wormhole? She pinched herself. Nothing changed.

Jesus, AJ. Just relax and enjoy it.

The Q's eyes bulged in their ersatz sockets as if it were straining to see through her. The scrutiny collapsed her link with Val's ghost.

"What?" she said, though what she was thinking was, please don't go.

"I zee happy and sad together on your face," it said. "I do not know what ziz means."

"Ah," she said, waxing melancholy. "I was thinking of someone I used to know."

Normally, she would've left it at that. Normally, she would've suppressed the ache that was welling up within her. But there was nothing normal about this moment and she couldn't stop herself from saying more.

"His name was Val," she said, imagining him as he had been back on her island. Wind-tousled hair. Notched eyebrow. Bug-bitten everywhere. "LT, some called him. He was—" My friend, she started to say, but that wasn't enough—not now or ever again. "I loved him. I miss him. I wish he was here now."

"Like ziz, zra?"

She looked up from her thoughts—who wouldn't? But as soon as she saw the face that the Q was now sporting, she wished that she had gone blind instead. That scarred eyebrow, the slightly jowly cheeks, the thin Johnny Rocket mouth turned down at the corners, *told you these things were bad news.*

"Damn," she said, strangling on a sudden upwelling of grief. The eyes were all wrong. But oh, the jaw, those lips. Her heart was imploding all over again. "Lose that face now."

"I do not understand," he said. "Iz ziz not za face you wanted to zee?"

Of course the Q didn't understand, how could it? But she didn't care. The Q had made presumptions like a human. Now it could suffer the consequences like one, too—her pain and rage rushing right at his misappropriated face.

"No, blast you," she said. "That's the face I'll never see again! Now get away from me. Go on!" she shouted, when he hesitated. "Go away!"

The Q's face shimmered for a moment and then went completely blank. An instant later, it shrunk into the folds of its trench-coat and slunk away. As soon as it was gone, AJ started to cry.

CHAPTER 29

"HEY, JAH-NEE!"

The sound startled AJ out of her weepy funk. She didn't know how long she had been crying. The tears just kept flowing—a lifetime of built-up grief streaming from the chambers of her heart. She cried for her parents. She cried for her island. But most of all, she cried for Val because she'd just seen his face and it wasn't fair, dammit! Everything that she had ever wanted to love had been stripped from her like so much sunburned skin.

"You oh-kay, jah-nee?"

She looked up to find herself surrounded by the flock of she-Q that she had seen earlier. Up close, they seemed less like parrots and more like sidhe or a flight of Broadway imps. Some had adopted Singer's facial features. Others resembled celebrities from bygone eras—Liberace, Mae West, Marilyn Monroe, Cher. Others still had taken the aspect of cartoons. None of them was bigger than a bag of habby juice, but they were all well-formed and wildly dressed.

"You lown-lee, jah-nee? You wan com-pan-ee?" said a would-be fairy complete with dainty dragonfly wings.

"No," she said, in no mood for these Terra-formed aliens and their weirdly suggestive costumes. "Go away."

But the flock closed in instead. "We like you," a she-Q in a flamboyant purple evening gown said. "You like us?" Another Tinkerbell darted in and lightly tapped the ridges of AJ's scowl. "No do," it said. "Not gud for ur owdr membrayn."

The next thing she knew, she was being mobbed. There were she-Q on her back and in her lap and wrapped around her legs. She could feel them poking and prodding—pinpoints of repetitive pressure that felt almost like a massage. The contact would've been pleasant if it had been welcome. But AJ most definitely didn't want to be touched—leastwise not by a swarm of aliens in drag. So she brushed herself off: arms, lap, legs. As soon as she stopped moving, the Q swarmed her again like hungry sand-fleas. Their tenacity drove her to her feet.

"Dohn go, jah-nee!" they pleaded. "We be nice. Promiz!"

"Let the Ter-ran be!"

The flock immediately dispersed and then regrouped to AJ's rear—as if they were hiding behind her. She half-turned to see Bob pseudo-striding toward them. He was at least three times the size of the largest she-Q, and dressed in a black caftan. As he approached, he said, "When a Ter-ran wantz you to go away, you go away. Otherwize, Zhin-go will come and hit you with hiz lightning stick."

An agitated buzz rose up from the she-Q. AJ wondered at the sound for a moment and then snickered as realization hit. Shingo had become the Q's boogeyman!

Her amusement drew Bob's attention. He looked at her as if to say, 'Why are you still here?' An instant later, recognition hit. His look of surprise was exquisitely human: wide-eyed and slack-jawed, a classic WTF. Even his mortified flush was the right color.

"Zra?" he said. "They were swarming you?" His color darkened, and he seemed to grow taller. The she-Q huddled quietly in their finery as he turned his attention back to them.

"Thiz iz zra," he said. "She iz the zupreme Ter-ran. If you approach her again, I will tell Heavenly to zen you back to the wild without your clothz." The threat provoked another agitated buzz and several Q-pies. "Clean up thoz azrumi," he said. "Then go and look for Terrani who want your company."

The she-Q let out a collective squawk and then scattered. As soon as the flock vanished from sight, Bob returned to his former size and sandy coloring. "I am happy to zee you, AyJay," he said. "Are you leaving? If zo, may I keep your company?"

Now that the she-Q were gone, she was in no great rush to relocate. "I'm good here," she said, sitting back down at the table. "You're welcome to join me if you wish."

"Thank you," he said, and sat down across from her.

She was struck by the Q's poise. She had never seen him so confident, so in control of himself. And so different from that flock of she-Q. As she marveled at the deference that they had shown him, a thought occurred to her. Could Bob be the Q's supreme being? His Royal Q-Ness? Now seemed like a good time to ask.

"Do all Q do what you want them to?" she said. "Are you their leader?"

"I do not know what that means," he said.

"A leader is someone that others follow and obey," she said. "Do the Q follow you?"

"No," he said, with a totally natural shake of his head. "Q all go their own way zo there is no following."

"Then why do those she-Q do as you say?"

"They have learned new shapes," he said, "but are still nijiti. They do az I zay because I am more evolved than them. And I only tell them what to do to please Heavenly. He zayz I am a supervizor. He wantz me to keep nijiti focuzed while they are jobbing."

"Working," she said. "While they're working."

"Yes," he said, "working. They belong to the Union, zo they must work."

"So that would make you their boss," she said. "That's your job."

He shrugged, a deliciously human response. "I belong to the Union, too."

"Next thing you know," she teased, "you'll be telling me what to do."

His face flattened for a second—a brain-boggling sight. At the same time, his coloration went from beige to a ghastly shade of gray. "No," he said. "You are zra.

I am inferior."

AJ was tempted to tease him further simply because it had been forever since she'd seen the humor in anything, but the Q's obvious distress persuaded her otherwise. "It's OK, Bob," she said, as he continued to diminish himself. "I was kidding. Joking. You know what humor is?"

His stress levels dropped immediately, and just like that, he was his beige, composed self again. "Yes, I know of humor," he said. "It brings the ha-ha sound. Heavenly enjoys joking very much. But he says I am humorlez."

"Why's that?" she asked.

"What goes ha-ha-plop?" the Q said. In response to her shrug, he said, "A man laf-fyn his head off." When she stared at him, waiting for an explanation, he said, "It makes no zenz to me, either. But Heavenly lafs very hard whenever he hears this."

There was just no telling about some people.

A crew of Johnnies went strolling by, clearly on the look-out for a place to land and party. As they passed the café, the flock of she-Q descended on them, buzzing, "Hey, jah-nee!" To AJ's immense surprise, the Johnnies made no effort to shoo the flock away. Instead, they laughed as the Q clamored for their attention, and actually seemed to enjoy all the touching and tugging and tickling.

"Well," she said, as the two groups drifted deeper into the FZ, "things have certainly changed since the last time I was here."

Bob was watching the goings-on, too—making sure that the she-Q weren't making pests of themselves, no doubt. Big-Shot Bobby, Miguel had called him, and that shoe seemed to fit. But the part about him being indifferent about other Q didn't play all that well. He was clearly very interested in what that flock was doing.

"How come you're so much bigger than they are?" she said, out of random curiosity.

"It is not to their advantage to be large in this environment," he said, still keeping tabs.

Before she could ask the Q why that was, a giant shadow engulfed their table. An instant later, a mountain of a man sat down next to Bob. Although he was fully suited up, there was no mistaking him for anyone but Heavenly Delgado.

"Heavenly!" Bob said, doing a splendid job of looking both surprised and delighted. "Good to zee you. Want I buy you a born-again?"

"Good of you to offer, Bobby," Heavenly said, "but this isn't a social call. I'm here to see AJ." Then he turned to her and said, "Would you mind flipping your plate down, Chief?"

"Sure," she said, guessing that the FZ was experiencing some kind of low-grade scrubber malfunction. It wasn't a common problem but it did happen. But then he flipped his plate up and confused her clear to next week.

"What's up?" she said.

"Remember me telling you how my techs had a hard time figuring out what was wrong with you when you first arrived?" he said, all grave-faced and concerned.

Delgado is not your friend.

"Yeah," she said. "I remember. I had an influenza virus. What of it?"

He swallowed hard, clearly distressed. And his distress was clearly for her. Now she knew why Shingo had said such a thing. He didn't want them to bond and possibly double-team him. Divide and conquer. How like his lordship to go for the preemptive strike.

"Actually," he said, "it was a mutated influenza virus. And it didn't attack you, it attacked your nanos. We thought the zap had cooked them, but it was the virus."

She scowled, trying to wring some sense out of what she'd just heard, but the statement remained stubbornly nonsensical. "You're telling me I had a nano-virus? That's absurd. There's no such thing."

"There didn't used to be," he said, "but there is now. I had my techs double-check their results. And we're not talking 'had' here. AJ. It's 'have'. You're infected. Apparently, you have been for quite some time now."

Her jaw worked, but no words came out. She was so stunned, she didn't know what to say. And before she could cobble a coherent thought together, he said, "I'm afraid there's more." *Not your friend, not your friend, not your friend.* "There's a growth on your thyroid. Your nanos must have been suppressing it until they started failing. It's—it's cancer, AJ. That's why you've been so tired."

The news hit her like a one-ton wrecking ball. She felt flattened; leveled; too crushed to breathe. Cancer? Really? No one had cancer anymore. No one but her, apparently. *That's why you've been so tired.* And she had been tired for a very long time.

"We don't have a surgical facility here," Heavenly was saying now, though she could barely hear him over the sudden roaring in her ears. "But my techs tell me that they can control the growth short-term with bio-chem therapy. And cleared or not, you're leaving on the next ship that comes through the APW. The council will have to let you back on medical—"

"HEH-VEN-LEE!"

The screech jarred AJ out of her self-absorbed bubble. She returned to the here-and-now to see Heavenly being overrun by ecstatic she-Q. He seemed to enjoy the attention. He grabbed one of the flock by the nape and set her on his lap as if she were a cat. He permitted another to wrap herself around his neck like a stole. The rest fluttered and fussed around him, jockeying for contact. The sight disturbed AJ, but she couldn't say why exactly. It just looked too friendly. But that was probably because she wasn't feeling too friendly herself at the moment.

It's cancer, AJ.

"I need to go and lie down now," she said, pushing herself to her feet. "My head feels like it's going to explode."

"I hear you," he said, absently stroking the she-Q on his lap. "Something like this would knock anyone for a serious loop. But before you go, there's one more thing. Shingo knows about the nano-virus; I had to tell him. He's ordered you to be quarantined. So from now on, you have to be sealed up when you leave your room. And while you're not required to wear a habby when you're at home, any and all visitors must be suited up. I know, that sucks, but it's the best I could do for you. Shingo wanted to throw you in isolation."

The rational part of her understood Shingo's reasoning. If this nano-virus was contagious, it could shut down all space-based operations plus a big chunk of Terra. Nanos corrected genetic disorders like diabetes, ALS, and MD. Nanos quelled diseases, repelled parasites, and neutralized toxins. An NV pandemic would probably fall short of the apocalypse, but was definitely wrath of God material. AJ understood all of this—and still bristled. She deserved better from Shingo and the universe.

"Thanks for taking on his lordship for me," she said, too numb and weary to rail against the unfairness of it all. "I appreciate it."

"Sure thing," he said, and then laughed as the she-Q around his neck nuzzled an earlobe. "Now go and get some rest. I'll check in with you later."

"OK if I walk with you?" Bob said, as she started away from the table.

She shrugged, too demoralized to object. The Q was at her elbow in an instant.

"We're going to have a lot of Johnnies in for a three-day at the end of this shift," Heavenly said. "I'm going to need you here, Bobby."

"I will return," Bob said.

"All right then. Have a nice walk," Heavenly said, and then let out a laugh. "Ooh, you saucy little imp!"

AJ didn't look back to see what had prompted such a declaration. And it didn't take her long to regret that decision. Maybe it was her subconscious clamoring for a distraction. Maybe it was just a feeling that something wasn't right. Whatever the reason, she found herself becoming more and more curious about the she-Q as she made her way out of the FZ and through the HF.

"Are you tired, zra?" Bob said. "Do you want to stop and rest?"

The question startled her. The Q was so quiet, she had forgotten that he'd decided to join her.

"No," she said, "I'm OK. I was just wondering—what kind of work do the she-Q do for the Union?"

"Heavenly calls them entertainerz," he said. "Their job is to make Terrani happy."

"I see," she said, though she didn't like the image that was forming in her head. "And how do they do that?"

"Mostly by touching," he said. "Lot of Terrani like being touched by she-Q. Some like touching so much, they make donations to She-Q Accessories Fund so she-Q will always have pretty cloz to wear."

"And does your job as supervisor include finding Terrani for the she-Q to entertain? Do those Terrani give you their 'donations'?" When Bob nodded once and then again, she heaved a sigh that sounded a lot like, "Damn," and then lapsed into dyspeptic silence. No wonder Delgado was so pro-Q. The dumb ones were turning tricks for him while the smart ones served as pimps. How naïve she had been to trust him with such eager-to-please beings! How galling to think that she had actually told the council that he would do his best for the Q

He is not their friend.

Shingo had known better all along! And that was the bitterest capsule of all to swallow.

"You are unhappy," Bob said, surprising her out of her thoughts.

"You are getting very good at reading people," she said. Sometimes.

"Are you unhappy with me?" he said. "Zhould I leave?"

"No," she said, "it's not you. It's—" She paused, held up by an internal debate. A primal part of her was reluctant to expose Delgado for the shit-heel he was out of—what, loyalty to her own kind? But her spanking-new sore spot insisted that she speak up. "It's Heavenly," she said. "He's exploiting you. He's exploiting all of the Q."

"What means this?"

"It means 'taking advantage,'" she said, trying to make the words sound as unsavory as they felt in her mouth. "It means misusing someone else's ignorance or innocence for fun and profit. In this case, Delgado's using the she-Q to—"Jerk off Johnnies, she would've said, if she had been talking to Val. But for some odd reason, she couldn't bring herself to talk frankly about sex with a Q. "He's using them to make money for the Union. That's wrong."

But Bob didn't get it. "She-Q only touch Terrani who want to be touched. How iz that wrong?"

"Terrans consider such activity to be degrading when it's done for money or favors," she said. "To degrade someone is to diminish them and their status. That's wrong."

"But she-Q are nijiti," Bob said. "Nijiti do not care about stature. They are thrill-zeekerz. Touching Terrani iz a very big thrill."

Her frustration levels spiked—a poke that roused Val's ghost. *Why try to graft human morals on an alien race, AJ?* The Q weren't being forced to do anything they didn't want to do, so there was nothing illegal going on. Maybe she should just shut up now and forget she'd ever said anything. It was a tempting suggestion. Looking the other way would certainly be the easier course of action. And really, what was she trying to protect: the Q's innocence or man's sordid alter-ego? It was already a bit late in the game for both teams. She knew that. But she also knew that the game might never have started in the first place if she hadn't walked away when Val died. So tired or not, dying or not, she knew she had to press on because that was the honorable thing to do. And honor was what kept Terrans from turning into less advanced versions of the thing that they feared most.

"Eventually, the thrill will disappear," she said. "What will the she-Q do then?"

"Iz hard to predict what nijiti will do," the Q said. "But when they are no longer thrilled by a thing, they uzually move on."

"So you don't care what happens to them," she said.

He responded with one of his exquisitely human shrugs. "There is no one sure path to evolution, zra. We must all find our own way."

That's right, she had forgotten; evolution was the Q's religion. And if she understood correctly, salvation was not a collective pursuit but rather a personal one—Q nirvana. Bob saw humanity as his next stop on The Great Wheel. But she was willing to bet that he didn't realize that humanity was a spectrum. And that was just the hook she needed.

"OK," she said, "let's talk about you then. The work that Delgado has you doing for him is called pimping. That makes you a pimp. Pimps have a terrible reputation. Terrans don't admire or respect them. In fact, unless they're looking for the sort of entertainment that the she-Q are offering, Terrans generally avoid pimps."

Bob shrank into his caftan a little, and his complexion darkened. "I did not know this," he said. "Heavenly did not tell me."

Big surprise there. *He is not your friend.* But she did not say that aloud. Now was not the time to muddy those waters. It was more important for Bob to realize that he was shinnying up the wrong evolutionary tree. "Well," she said, "it's true. If you're going to model yourself after a Terran, at least pick one with a good reputation."

"Like you," he said. "I want to be like you."

She bit her lip so she wouldn't laugh at the irony. Her reputation had been sterling at one time, but now it was shot—thanks to Q. "I appreciate that," she said. "But I'm not a pimp. I never have been and never will be. I won't be friends with a pimp, either."

His features flickered as if he'd been struck by static. She felt bad for distressing him, but he had to know what his choices were and that the choosing came with consequences. "You need to decide who you want to be, Bob," she said. "Until you do, stay away from me."

Then she turned her back on him and walked away. She was tired, so tired, and not just because she had cancer.

CHAPTER 30

AJ WAS IN BED. Val was there beside her. She kept burying her nose in the hollow of his shoulder and sniffing. She couldn't get enough of the smell: man-musk mixed with deodorant and pheromones. Likewise, she had a fascination for his arms. How was it that she had never noticed how well-muscled they were? "You were tired," he told her. "And you had other things on your mind."

"Excuses," she said. "I should have paid more attention."

"You have a visitor," he said, in a strangely melodic voice. "How do you wish to proceed?"

"What?"

He repeated himself, throwing a chime in at the end for good measure. An instant later, he was out of bed and receding into a featureless background. His eyes were tender; his mouth, sad. "How you wish to proceed?"

"Wait," she said, reaching for him. "Don't go."

But it was too late. He faded away like the Cheshire Cat, his sad mouth last of all. She was still reaching for him when the keeper pinged again.

"You have a visitor," it said. "How do you wish to proceed?"

"Tell whoever it is to piss off," she said, aggrieved to find herself awake. She had never had such an exquisitely vivid dream. It could've killed her and she wouldn't have cared. Her few mourners could have taken comfort in the fact that she had died in her sleep.

"Visitor refuses to depart."

"Replay the quarantine message," she said. "I'm not wearing my habby."

"Visitor is exempt from quarantine restrictions."

She cursed, the only option left to her. What was the point of having a door if it couldn't keep people away? At least this SFB didn't just barge right in—although that would probably be his next move.

"What does the visitor want?" she asked.

"Heh-ven-lee zend," a distinctly Qish voice said. "He want me zhow you to kemo."

"Oh." She hadn't been expecting a Q. Or a chemotherapy session, for that matter. She had to give Delgado credit in one regard: when he said he was going to do something, he didn't waste any time getting it done. Such a conscientious pimp-master. "Wait there," she said. "I have to suit up."

She thought about calling for something to eat, too, but then decided that habby juice was probably the smarter way to go. According to the little bit of research that she'd done, bio-chems could cause unpleasant side-effects like dizziness, headaches, and vomiting. She had hurled into her suit more than once over the course of her career and it wasn't an experience worth repeating. So she climbed into her habby hungry and then went to meet her escort.

The Q waiting in the hallway was dressed in a red, sequined sheath and matching faux-feather boa. Her tiny face was a cross between Mae West and Singer, and her platinum beehive wig looked like the real thing.

"You ready, zra?" she said, in a chipmunk-y kind of voice. "I take you where Heh-ven-lee want you go."

"Sure," AJ said. "Take me to my liter."

The she-Q set an almost lackadaisical pace—not because she was worried about wearing AJ out, AJ quickly realized, but because she was fascinated with the HF. The Q's head and eyes moved constantly as she glided along. She tickled the wall with her fingers. And the tentacle-like filaments that lined the bottoms of her Lilliputian feet flicked at the floor like tiny snake tongues. When they came to the entryway to the Free Zone, she turned and took a last look at the way they had come.

"Heh-ven-lee zayz Terrani be gone zoon, I no wanna mizz a zingle tayzt."

The FZ had a deserted look about it. The overheads were on half-power. The all-walls were a muted gray. Nothing seemed to be open or moving.

"Looks like we're the first ones up," AJ said.

"This zec-zhun clozd for cleenyn," the she-Q said. "Heh-ven-lee lyk zhingz cleen."

Two levels and numerous turns later, they came to a walk-in clinic. It was a low-profile, back-alley doc-shop that provided discreet care for ODs and other typical down-time injuries. A tech met them in the lobby. "Chief Johnson, I presume," he said amiably. "I'm RK." To the Q, he said, "You can go now, nee-hah. I'll ping Heavenly when she's done here."

The she-Q departed without so much as a backward glance.

"I apologize in advance for the somewhat primitive conditions," RK said, as he led her down a hallway and into a tiny, white-walled room. "But in our defense, you took us by surprise. We've never treated a cancer patient. And your infection is—unique." He motioned her toward the only piece of furniture in the cell: a black vinyl lounger. "We borrowed it from the spa next door," he said, as she settled into it. "Heavenly told us to make you as comfortable as possible." He clicked a remote. A float bearing an IV and a mish-mash of monitors came drifting out of a storage cell. "Here's what's going to happen," he said, as he anchored the float behind the chair. "This bag of bio-chemicals is going to enter your bloodstream, one drop at a time. The chemicals are going to migrate to your thyroid and start killing cancer cells. You shouldn't feel any pain. However, there might be other side-effects—"

"I know," she said. "I did some reading."

"Excellent," he said. "Then you know the side-effects are usually mild and short-term." He snapped on a face mask and then a pair of gloves. "Again, my apologies," he said, "but we have no idea how contagious that nano-virus is. I'm going to put the IV in your neck. You can pop your top if you'd like. Or you can stay lidded up and I can run the feed past your face-plate. We're probably going to seal this room off either way."

"I'll keep the top on," she said. "I'll stay warmer that way."

"Thanks," he said, and then motioned for her to flip her plate. "Now turn your head this way. A little more. Good. You may feel a pinch now—" It felt more like a vampire bite, but she didn't bother to quibble with him. "OK, slowly now, turn your head forward again." When she did so, he gave her an approving clap on the shoulder and then pressed her plate down as far it would go without constricting the tubing. "OK, you're set. You want a pad or something to pass the time?"

"Thanks," she said, "but my lid has a music app. I'll be fine."

And oddly enough, she was. The comfortable chair, the soft music, and the habby's self-contained warmth conspired to relax her. Her breathing slowed down. Her eyelids grew heavy. She grumbled something about being woken up early. The next thing she knew, the tech was gently shaking her by the shoulder.

"Hey, Chief," he said, "you're good to go." As she fluttered awake, he added, "How do you feel?"

She ran a quick check on herself. Aside from that ubiquitous sense of fatigue, she felt OK. No headache, no queasiness, no pain. "Not bad," she said. "I guess I lucked out."

He handed her a cup of cold sludge and encouraged her to drink it. When she balked at the noxious-looking offering, he said, "It's a protein shake with supps. It promotes strength."

"If you insist," she said, and tried to knock the shake back in one quick gulp. But it tasted just as bad as it looked: orange-flavored yeast lees mixed with fish oil and pharmaceuticals. And it did not go down fast. "Meh," she said, after she choked the last of it down. "Next time, you get to drink while I watch."

"Aw, c'mon, it wasn't that bad. Was it?"

"You'll find out next time," she said menacingly, and then flipped her plate down. But when she tried to stand up and make an aggrieved escape, an invisible hand knocked her back onto her butt.

"Whoa," RK said. "Maybe you ought to give yourself a little more time to equalize."

"I'm fine," she said, refusing the suggestion like she should've refused the shake. She could feel it pooling in her guts like quick-set. If she heaved now, she'd blow bricks. "Really," she said, when RK continued to hover. "I just needed to catch my bearings. Which way's out?"

Instead of pointing, he guided her out to the lobby. The Mae West she-Q was waiting there. As soon as she saw AJ, she got all fluttery and excited. "You feel better, zra?" she said. "You want zum fun?"

"You are to escort Chief Johnson back to her room," RK told the Q. "She needs rest, not fun."

AJ didn't know who she resented more: the Q for making the suggestion or the tech for forbidding it. "I can find my own way back to my room," she said.

But the she-Q wouldn't hear of it. "Heh-ven-lee want I tayk you. Heh-ven-lee want, I do."

Although AJ did not share the she-Q's desire to please Delgado, she had to admit that her sense of direction was a little muzzy at the moment. She weighed the possibility of getting lost in the FZ against her contentious urges, and then grudgingly surrendered to practicality. "All right then," she said, "let's go."

The she-Q gave her boa a happy little twitch and said, "Ziz way, zra!"

The Q seemed to move much faster on the flipside of their trek—possibly because AJ was feeling crummier by the minute. The knot in her gut had tightened into cramps; the brain-fog was spiraling toward vertigo. She tripped over her own feet and then berated herself for being clumsy. She couldn't afford to fall down, not while this part of the FZ was still shut down. She might not be found for hours.

Maybe you should go back to the doc-shop. Or ping for help.

That was Val. But he didn't understand. She didn't know where the clinic was from here. And she simply couldn't bring herself to broadcast an SOS. If she did, Delgado would send help and she'd be even more indebted to him. The next thing she knew, he'd have her turning tricks, too. No. No way. She'd rather tough this nasty little wave of side-effects out.

Then sit down before you fall down.

That was Meli, and AJ could almost feel an invisible hand steering her toward a nearby bench. Just for a minute, she thought, as she sat down. Just until her head stopped spinning and her gorge settled down.

The she-Q was closing in on the mouth of a service alley. When she realized that AJ had fallen behind, she came flitting back to hurry her along. "Ziz way, zra," she said. "You come wiz me."

"I don't think so," AJ said, panting as she tried to breathe around a sunburst of abdominal pain. "That's—not the way we—came."

"Heh-ven-lee zay tayk you ziz way," the Q trilled.

AJ pitched forward, doubled over by a vicious stomach spasm. A fireball of fish oil, bile, and partially digested protein surged up her esophagus and into her habby's catch-all. The spew's stink made her vomit again. As her guts emptied, the pain migrated to her head.

"We go now, zra?"

"No," she said, folding into a fetal ball on the bench. "I can't move. You're going to have to go and get help."

"Help?" the Q said, sounding confused.

"Yes!" AJ said, shouting over the sudden pounding in her ears. "I need—" Delgado, Val wanted her to say. But even now, she could not, would not, force the name past her lips. So she blurted out the only other one that came to mind.

"Bob!" she said. "I need Bob. Go and get him. Now!"

The she-Q went fluttering off—toward the alleyway.

Idiot, AJ thought, and then closed her eyes to block the slivers of light that were stabbing at her forebrain. The next thing she knew, she was being jostled out of a shallow, semi-delirious drowse. She waved the jostler off, a childish dismissal. She didn't want to open her eyes yet; the FZ had just stopped spinning.

"Zra."

The sound sparked a spangle of recognition. Bob? She cracked one eyelid. The other rolled back of its own accord. The Q standing in front of her face-plate was not Bob. This one was much bulkier, and wore a black trench coat and matching fedora. The outfit struck her as familiar, but she could not attach a time or place to the oddly pock-marked face, only a vague sense of unhappiness.

"Thiz iz not a good playz for you, zra."

"I know," she said, in slightly more than a murmur. "I sent a she-Q for help. Have you—seen her? She's wearing a red feather scarf."

"The nee-hah went there," the Q said, pointing toward the alleyway. "It will not be back."

"Why not?" she asked, confused by his certainty and the niggling sense that she somehow knew him. "I sent her to get Bob."

"That nee-hah wuz not your fren, zra," he said. "Why you want Bob?"

Not your friend. Damn. More déjà vu. "I need him to take me to my room," she said. "I don't know where it is from here."

"I will take you," the Q said. "Iz not far."

"You know where I'm staying?"

"You are zra. Everyone knows," he said, and then stepped back to give her room to stand up. "We zhud go now. Terrani will be looking for you."

Had she been MIA that long? It seemed like she had only sat down a few heartbeats ago. But that was the tricky thing about being sick: minutes passed like hours while hours passed like minutes. She sat up and didn't suffer for it. But when she pushed to her feet, she got light-headed again and clutched at the Q for support. As she steadied herself, she felt his insides pitch.

"Whoa," she said, startled by the intensity of the shift. "What was that?"

"Zumzin I ate," he said, and then pointed to an elevator bay to her rear that she had failed to notice earlier. "Ziz way, zra."

She glanced back at the alley once and then again, stammering in her confusion. "But—the she-Q said that way!"

"I tol you, zra," he said, "that nee-ha wuz not your fren. We go now, OK? People looking for you."

She did not have the energy or wit to resist him as he guided her over to the elevator and into a car. She did not have the impetus to hold the door for the trio of maintenance workers who urged her to do so from across the concourse. And by the time the elevator spilled them onto the main level, she was damn near exhausted. Fortunately, this level was open for business again and there were floats for hire. The Q flagged the nearest one down and then helped her aboard.

"That's OK," she said, when he started to board after her. "I can manage from here."

"Iz best if I go with you, zra," he said. "You might need help again."

She didn't remember inviting him to help in the first place, but she was too far gone to stop him from riding along if that was what he wanted to do. And her condition went from bad to worse as the float skimmed through the Free Zone and into the HF. Her guts began to percolate again. An unnamed fear began to clutch at her lungs and heart. She tried to deflect the anxiety. No. Not now. Not in front of the Q.

And the tactic seemed to work. When the float scudded to a stop in front of her room, she felt stable enough to climb out of it without assistance. And when the float scooted away with her credit info in its memory bank, she felt strong enough to send the Q away.

"Zhat iz not a good idea, zra," he said.

Then a blob oozed down from the ceiling like a mass of ectoplasm. As it bellied toward the ground, it changed shape from the bottom up like water being poured into an invisible vase. The next thing AJ knew, the blob was gone and she was looking at Bob. His presence confused her.

"Did the she-Q tell you to where to find me?" she asked.

"I do not understand what ziz means, zra," he said, and then turned his attention to her self-appointed escort. "Why do you zhadow her?"

"It was—nezezzery," the other Q said. "Zhere are zhingz you do not know."

"Explain," Bob said.

"Wait," AJ said. "You two know each other?"

"He iz my clone," Bob said, and then thrust a foot into the Q-pie that his clone had just expressed. A snake's nest of tendrils erupted from Bob's blunted toes and began probing the goo. The sight tickled her gag reflex. She looked away only to do a double-take as a bright red splash snagged a corner of her befogged brain. Was that—blood? No, couldn't be. Q didn't bleed. Then it dawned on her: the she-Q's boa had been that shade of red. And as soon as her thoughts turned in that direction, that splash took on the semblance of a feather. She glanced at Bob's clone. His hands were cradling his bulging midsection.

Zumzin I ate.

AJ's stomach clenched, refusing to be denied any longer. In her hurry to get into her room and be sick in private, she tripped over her own feet and fell. The landing knocked the breath out of her and filled her windpipe with vomit. She coughed, but couldn't dislodge the blockage. She gasped, but couldn't draw air.

"Zra? What iz wrong?"

She flipped her face-plate up, but still could not catch a breath. Her vision flared capillary red and then start to decay. The last thing she saw before the world went dark was a stampede of wormy tendrils heading her way.

CHAPTER 31

AJ CAME AWAKE WITH a drowning man's gasp. She was lying on her back, which confused her as she distinctly remembered hitting the floor face-first. She remembered choking on vomit, too, and then nothing else. But—there was nothing stuck in her throat now. And the catch-all in her habby was empty. Except for the sour taste in her mouth, there was absolutely no proof that her own body had tried to suffocate her.

"You OK, zra?"

She rolled her head in the direction of the sound. Bob was parked beside her on the floor, not sitting exactly but not standing, either. It could've been her imagination or maybe a little bit of projection, but he seemed tired to her. Were Q susceptible to that condition? She didn't know, and suffered a pang of shame for her ignorance.

"You OK now?" he asked.

"I think so," she said, taking quick stock of her woes. The nausea was gone. So was the headache. Even her fatigue seemed less devastating. "I guess the chemo must be working." She eased herself up and into a sitting position. Her upper back was a little sore, but other than that, the only lingering after-effect from her face-plant was that tiny sliver of amnesia. Good thing Bob was around to fill in the blank. "So what happened here?" she said. "What happened to me?"

"When you fall," the Q said, "you stopped breezyn. I know Terrani need to breeze, zo I probe you."

Her memory disgorged an image—Singer writhing on the ground with a pulsating blob plastered to his face. Then she remembered something new: tentacles skittering across the floor at eye-level. She would have been happy to dismiss the recollection as a last-gasp hallucination. Now she had to believe that it was Bob scampering for the cookie jar. Again. She was appalled, repulsed, outraged. A chorus of inner voices wanted the Q punished for his presumption and oh, the violation! But Meli didn't see the problem, given that AJ would've certainly died if Bob had not probed her.

What do you say when someone saves your life, 'Nita?

"Thank you," she said, struggling to project gratitude rather than dyspepsia. "I appreciate what you did for me."

To her surprise, her appreciation seemed to distress rather than please him. He turned an uneasy shade of gray and random strands of his pseudo-comb-over began to fidget. "What?" she said, forcing him to look her in the eye. "What's the matter?"

"I zhould have withdrawn after I cleared your breeze-way," he said. "But I was curiouz about your zickness, zo I probed deeper and then releezed some vytzi."

"Some what?"

"Hunter-probes," he said.

Her immediate reaction to this confession was horrified distress. Now she had some kind of alien predator prowling around inside of her? Out of the fat and into the fire, her father would have said. But Meli urged her to keep an open mind. *You never know, 'Nita. Bob hasn't hurt you yet.*

"Did these fitzee find anything?" she asked, trying to sound casual.

"Yez," he said, and pointed to her neck. "You have wrongnez in zhere."

Have, he said. Not had. But she couldn't stop herself from asking. "Did you— make it go away?"

"No," he said, and what had she been expecting, really? He was an alien, not a doc. "It iz very big and haz lotz of frani." He could not help her. "The vytzi could not dizlodge it." No one could. "They making it smaller, though." She had a cancer and it was going to kill—

"Wait," she said, backtracking as fast as she could. "Did you just say that you made my cancer smaller?"

"Not me," he said, "the vyzti."

"How?" she said, refusing to hope.

"Rightnez and wrongnez taste different, zra," the Q said. "When I know what 'right' taste like in you, I make vytzi that know, too, and then releez them in you. They make themselves very small and pass through your inner membranez. Your body fluids carry them to the wrongnez—" He started to point at her throat only to freeze and then shrink a little when it made eye contact with her. "You making the frown face becuz you are unhappy wiz me?"

"No," she said, unaware that she had been scowling. "Not unhappy." 'Unnerved' was more like it. And who wouldn't be a little freaked after learning that there were alien gunships conducting war-games in their bloodstream? "It's just that I'm not comfortable with the idea of having foreign probes in my body."

The Q cocked his head like a confounded spaniel. "But I zenzed many such probez in you, zra. None of them appeared to be active, but they were there."

She suffered another WTF moment, thinking, 'What now?' and 'Why me?' only to be bitch-slapped by a sudden realization. "Not probes," she blurted. "Nanos."

"I do not know thiz nanoz," he said.

"I'll explain later," she said, still trying on her new perspective for size. She'd lived with nanos throughout her life. They were so common and so beneficial, it was easy to think of them as natural. But they were in fact foreign objects—just like the vit-zee. Did origin make that much difference?

Damn straight it does, Val was quick to say.

But AJ wasn't so sure.

"Tell me more about these vit-zee," she said. "How are they making my cancer smaller?"

"Digestive juicez," Bob said.

The significance of that statement hit her with the force a rabbit-punch to the solar plexus. An instant later, Val popped up again. *Told you!* He had always worried that the Q might harbor a taste for human flesh. And wasn't that every Terran's secret fear—to be eaten while still alive? As she struggled to block out the thought and its attendant horror flick images, Meli entered the fray. *If the Q wanted you dead, he could have made it so several times over already.* That point resonated with AJ, but Val remained unconvinced. *Maybe what he wants is a lunch truck!* And since her inner voices couldn't come to any kind of consensus on the matter, she decided to face her fear head-on.

"So you're—eating the cancer," she said.

Bob's face went a little flat, a sure sign of distress. "Thoze vyzti hunting for you, zra, not me," he said, "zo I get nozzin from them. They feed a little on the wrongnez cuz they need to eat zumzin to funkshun. But mozly, they excrete digestive juicez to break down canzer. Iz chem-iz-try."

Well. When he put it like that, the goings-on didn't sound so awful. In fact, they sounded a lot like chemo. Biochemicals were biochemicals, right? She thought of Singer again. After his 'therapy session' with Bob, he had gone from wrecked to ready in the span of a few short hours, a truly remarkable recovery. Of course, he had had a flare-up of Pigeon Pox rather than cancer, but—oh. They shared the same underlying problem. Oh. Their nanos were bad.

Oh, shit!

"Bob," she said, "did you release any vit-zee in Singer when you were—you know—on him?"

"Yez, zra," he said. "He had no canzer, but the inner chambers of hiz head were filled with wrong-nez." He flushed a dismal shade of red, and added, "I fed on some of thoz proteinz, zra. I could not stop myself. I was very hungry and very excited and Zingyr was zo warm and full of newnezz. I have more zelf-control now, zra. I am—"

"It's OK, Bob," she said, a perfunctory reassurance intended to shut the Q up while she worked through this second bombshell of an insight. It could not be coincidence that Singer got sick because of bad nanos. They had spent too much time in close quarters and shared too much recycled air. He had to be infected with nano-virus. And if he was, then the entire crew from that first Lazarus operation probably was, too. That meant that the NV had been circulating for quite some time now. That meant that it had probably already made its way to Terra. If the virus gained a toehold there, all sorts of pathological horrors—genetic, biologic, and otherwise—were going to start popping out of the woodwork. And that would only be the beginning of a shit-storm of biblical proportions.

TSC needed to know about this ASAP. She had to get the news to—

"Zra?" Bob said. "Are you tired again?"

"I have to talk to Shingo," she said, completing her thought out loud, and then laughed nervously as the Q shrunk toward the nearest patch of shadows. "It's OK. Really," she said, and then ordered the keeper to connect her with the CP. When the responding robo-secretary told her to leave a message, she said, "Connect me with the CO immediately. This is an emergency."

"Commander Shingo is in a—meeting—and does not wish to be disturbed," the 'bot said. "Your claim of emergency has been—rerouted to and—rejected by the FZS monitor, which reports—no unusual or suspicious activity in your area. If you wish to pursue this claim, you are advised to—contact the FZS directly. CP out."

That brought AJ to her feet faster than a shot of B-12. "If I wanted to talk with Security," she snarled, "I would've called Security. C'mon. Let's pay his lordship a visit."

Bob recoiled again. "I do not like that idea."

She snorted. "Don't worry. He's not going to hurt you."

"My concern is for you," the Q said.

"I know I was a little wobbly earlier," she said, happy to skirt around that frost-heave in her memory. "But I'm feeling better now." Much better, in fact. Almost bouncy. She didn't know which form of chemo to thank for that. Maybe it was a combination of both. Maybe it was just a respite between storms. In any case, she was going to take advantage of it while she could. "I'll call for a float if you think I need one, but I think I can manage a walk to the nearest exit and then a crawler-ride. I'll call for the crawler now."

"No!" Bob said, the first time he had ever raised his voice in her presence. "Thiz iz not a good idea."

"Why?" she said, forcing herself to be calm despite the inner voices that were clamoring for immediate action.

"People are looking for you," he said.

A distorted recollection stirred beneath the frost-heave: somebody urging her toward an elevator, saying the same thing. Or was that a false memory—chemo-induced déjà vu? It didn't matter either way, she supposed. Bob's concern was real enough.

"Why is that a problem?" she asked.

"They want to damage you," he said, and then turned ashen again as her keeper chimed. "Incoming call from Heavenly Delgado. How do you wish to respond?" Pick up, she thought to say, but before she could get the words out, the Q raised his voice a second time. "No! Do not answer!"

"Why not?"

"The people who want to damage you are Heavenly's frenz," Bob said. "He sent them."

The keeper chimed again. "How do you wish to respond?"

Crud! There was too much coming at her from too many directions. She couldn't process everything at the same time. "Tell him that I'm recovering from my chemo session and will get back to him later. Take no messages and accept no other calls."

The chiming stopped, but that came as no relief. The ensuing silence had a foreboding feel. She turned her attention back to Bob, who looked tired and deflated. "Heavenly knowz where you are now," he said.

"He knew anyway," she said. "If I had been out, the keeper would have gone straight to message. But if he thinks I'm sick, maybe he'll stay away for a while."

"Or maybe he will zend his frenz here," he said, "thinking that it will be eazier to damage you while you are not well."

She had to admit, he had a point. She wondered when he had gotten so good at thinking like a Terran. She also wondered where he had gotten his information.

"So I guess I'm going to make a run for the command post after all," she said. "Before I go, though, tell me how you know about Delgado and his friends."

"My clone zhowd me in an azrum," he said.

Disbelief deepened the furrows of her scowl. She was on the verge of running for her life on the basis of a Q-pie? Really? It wasn't that she distrusted Bob. How could she after everything he'd done for her? But asking her to accept a goo-bomb as a credible source of information was a near-deal-breaker. She was tempted, so tempted, to cancel the red alert and let her cortisol levels start creeping down toward normal. But even as she wavered, one of her inner voices whispered, *He's not your friend*, and that was that.

"You should probably find a place to hide until all of this blows over," she said. "I don't want you getting hurt because of me."

But the Q ignored the suggestion. "I will go with you," he said. "I know of pazzagewayz that are free of Terrani eyes."

His unflagging devotion humbled her. She might have expected such fidelity from Val or a crewman—one of her own kind. But from an alien? No way! Was that because she needed an excuse to be faithless in turn? Damn. She hoped the Q never became that human.

"OK," she said, and then flipped down her lid. "Let's go."

He led her back to the FZ's main concourse and toward the nearest alleyway. The sight unearthed another shard of memory—a blonde she-Q in a red feather boa saying, "Heavenly say we go this way." She gulped back the queasy feeling that came with the flashback and pressed on. The alley was on the narrow side, but very clean and uncluttered thanks to Delgado's zero tolerance policy for filth and grime. It was also a cul-de-sac. She assumed that they had taken a wrong turn, but before she could say so, Bob made a beeline for the service portal at the far end of the alley and pressed a palm full of writhing tentacle tips to its access panel. The hatch slid open—no alarm, no hesitation, just whoosh.

"This way, zra," he said, urging her into the FZ's substructure.

She wasn't surprised that he knew about the service tunnels. He had a long history of getting into places that weren't meant for him. What took her aback was how technically savvy he was. The portals might be unmanned, but they weren't unlocked, and it would take more than a physical jiggle to get past the safeguards. *See, Val?* Q were a lot smarter than either of them had ever suspected.

The FZ's servo-network was teeming with 'bots. Some were sorting incoming garbage into piles for recycling or the dump. Others were loading the sorted trash into carts which they then sent rolling down a designated track. Others still were cleaning up the residues and stenches that came with refuse. Happily, the portal that AJ and Bob had come through serviced a strip of shops rather than cafes, so the garbage was mostly dry. And interestingly enough, they were not the only non-'bots present. There were Q everywhere: picking through the trash, playing with it, possibly even studying it. They let out a collective buzz when they saw AJ and seemed to orient themselves toward her. Then Bob made a sound that she didn't understand and they returned to their former preoccupations immediately. The scene troubled AJ for reasons that she struggled to name. Was it the sight of Q rummaging through Terran refuse? She didn't think so. Garbage was garbage, and clearly no one was forcing them into the tunnels. It was something about the Q. And the 'bots. And—

All at once, she knew what the problem was. The realization made her laugh out loud.

"You OK, zra?" Bob said, swiveling an eye in her direction.

"I'm fine," she said. "Just feeling rather alien at the moment."

"Is that humor, zra?"

"Just a little irony," she said.

"I do not know what that meanz," he said, and before she could come up with a suitable explanation, he added, "How will I learn about such thingz if Terrani leave uz alone, zra? How will I evolve?"

"I don't know," she said. "I'm sorry."

He led them over to a cart that was nearly full. "This one is ready to go. Can you climb into it?" She managed—not gracefully and not effortlessly, but without help. Afterward, as she sat on the flat side of a broken down container, quietly trying to catch her breath, the Q joined her, oozing rather than climbing over the cart's side. For the first time ever, she found herself wishing that she could do that.

"You muz get down," he said, as he settled deep into the trash. "Cartz get a cover when they are full."

An instant later, a stat-o-tarp came sweeping out of the gloom. She ducked. The tarp skimmed across the top of her helmet and then electro-snapped into place. She heard a loud clang. The cart shuddered and then began to roll.

"You seem rather familiar with this process," she said.

The Q shrugged or at least that seemed to be the intent. His body didn't have shoulders at the moment. "Knowing the wayz out of a place iz az important az knowing the wayz in," he said, "ezpezially when you are on re-ztrik-zhun." Then, as the cart began to accelerate, he said, "I need more than ziz, zra. Can I go with you when you leave?"

More irony. Him coming to her for sanctuary was what had landed her in this mess in the first place. But this time she didn't laugh. "I don't think Shingo will let that happen," she said.

"Maybe you could per-zuade him," Bob said. "Tell him I need be wiz Terrani."

Amazing. Despite the steady stream of abuses that he and his kind had endured since humanity had parked itself on their doorstep, Bob still perceived Terrans as good guys, role models, an evolutionary goal. Was that optimism? Or astounding naiveté?

"I'll try," she said, because she owed him that much. Then, because she owed him much, much more, she added. "But you might be better off asking Delgado to get you another audience with the council. He's out to get me, not you."

But the Q dismissed the suggestion with a shake of his slightly flattened head. "After you zent me away," he said, "I went to Heavenly and asked him to ztop exploiting the nijiti. He zay he waz not making them to do anything they did not want to do. I told him they wanted nothing for the doing other than the experience. He zay that waz not the Terrani way. He zay they had to pay their way, zaym az everyone else in the Union. I zay I mean to tell them to do other things to make pay. I zay I mean to do other things, too, and not pimp for him anymore. He got very red in the face and told me to keep my mouth zhut. He told me to tell you to keep your mouth zhut, too, and keep your nose out of matterz that do not concern you."

"I see," she said. And she did. The peasants were on the verge of revolting, and Delgado thought she was the one who was rallying them against him. She was happy to take the blame for that, but in truth, it really hadn't occurred to her that Bob would go all Cesar Chavez when she told him to choose what kind of Terran he wanted to be. "I guess he decided to shut my mouth for me."

"I dohn underztand, zra," Bob said. "Why iz Heavenly zo angry?"

"If you and the she-Q stop 'entertaining' for him," she said, "he's going to lose a lot of extra income. And apparently, he's greedy."

"Ah," Bob said. "Like nijiti."

"Worse than nijiti," she said. "Because he's willing to hurt others to get what he wants. You need to steer clear of him from now on. And—"

The cart lurched to a sudden stop. Her first thought was that they had been caught and things were about to get very unpleasant. She pushed at the tarp, thinking that she'd rather see what was coming than be surprised, but Bob stopped her before she could pop the seal.

"Not yet, zra," he said. "The out-door iz not open yet."

Since he was familiar with the way these garbage runs worked, she cancelled the red alert. But it suddenly seemed like a good idea to contemplate their next move. "Where does the cart go from here?" she asked.

"Thiz one will go to the recyclyn ztazhun," he said.

"Does it stop anywhere else between here and there?" she said.

"No, zra."

She checked the admittedly sketchy map in her head and decided that the walk to the CP would be shorter from here than the RS. As she did so, the cart started rolling again. She pushed at the tarp again, saying, "Let's get out here."

As soon as the seal broke, the Q squirted through the resulting crack like a fresh-shucked oyster. Unfortunately, AJ needed a larger gap. She could've used a few extra hands as well—one to hoist her out of the garbage, another to keep the tarp from closing back up as she climbed out of the cart, and another still to help her hang on until she was sure her ride had cleared the servo-door. Then, with a wordless prayer to any gods that might be listening in, she flung herself to the ground. She didn't realize that she had closed her eyes until the shock of landing knocked them open again. She laid there on her back staring at the perma-gray sky and trying not to think about the bruises that were rising up on her body until Bob turned up at her elbow.

"You OK, zra?" he said. As if she were not a middle-aged woman who had just pitched herself from a moving vehicle.

"I think I would've been better off letting Delgado's thugs find me," she said. But she had to admit, despite the aches and the overdose of excitement and the recent chemo session, she didn't feel nearly as horrible as she ought to.

"You need I get help?" he said.

"No. Thank you," she added a moment later, and then pushed herself up and onto her butt-bones. As she did so, she noticed the ground for the first time. It was covered with grayish, semi-sticky, semi-crunchy crud. "What's this stuff?"

"Zyl larvae," Bob said. "They come to the surface after hatching to collect energy for the season of stormz."

"Yuck," she said, brushing herself off as she stood up.

"Yzz," he said. "They do not taste good in thiz phayz." Then he looked up at her with his hands on his hips and said, "What now?"

He sounded just like Delgado. Under other circumstances, it might have been funny. Now it just reminded her that she needed to keep moving. She pointed in the direction of the command post and said, "I'm going that way. It might be better if you followed underground. Anybody who sees me will think I'm a grounder and shine me on. But a Terran and a Q traveling together could invite unwanted scrutiny."

"I understand," he said. And just like that, he began shrinking. His soiled caftan folded around and over him like a magician's cape, and then fell empty in a heap. The only sign of him was nascent bump in the sticky, crackly ground.

AJ picked up the tunic and started on her way. Although she was much more comfortable with Bob's companionship these days, she was happy for a little time alone. She had so much to ponder, so much to process. Yet to her surprise and initial dismay, her mind refused to cooperate. She found herself entertaining other thoughts, like how good it felt to be walking and how semi-tolerable Farside was when that infernal wind wasn't blowing and there was a hint of light in the sky. If she shut her eyes and listened to the crunch of her footfalls, she could almost imagine that she was back on her island, walking along the beach with Val by her side—

"AJ?"

Val disappeared. The beach became a desert. And the inner turmoil that she had managed to forget for a microsecond came boiling back into her frontal lobe. Crud. She had forgotten to switch off her comm link.

"What are you doing up and about?" Heavenly asked. "You're supposed to be resting."

"I woke up hungry," she said, "so I stepped out for a bite to eat."

"Liar," he said, in a tone like a grin. Crud. She'd forgotten about her locator, too. "You wouldn't be trying to do a walk-off, would you?"

"Would you be sorry if I was?" she said. The CP was in sight now, maybe five minutes away. She could go that distance easy.

"Of course I would," he said. "I like you, AJ. You've got spunk. But you had no call to turn the Q against me. I'm their friend."

"You're their pimp-master," she said. "There's a difference. All I did was point that out."

"Don't be like that, AJ," he said. "You're here as my guest. I've gone out of my way to be nice to you. Come back to the FZ so you, me, and Bobby can talk through this. He needs to know that he misunderstood you."

"I think you're the one who's confused here, Delgado," she said. "And the only one I'm interested in talking to at the moment is Shingo."

"He can't help you, AJ," Delgado said, in a softer, more sinister tone. "Only I can. So just stop where you are and take a breather. I'll be there to pick you up in just a tick."

As he said this, a pair of high-pitched whines intruded on her awareness. She recognized the sound of scoots being pushed to their limits immediately. She broke into a shambling trot.

"Run if you want," he said, and now the grin was back in his tone. "But Shingo's going to kick you out as soon as he sets eyes on you. When he does, I'll be right outside waiting for you. And then we can explore your suicidal tendencies in more detail."

The CP was steps away now. Even without looking back, she could tell that Delgado wouldn't catch up in time. She shuffled to a stop, then half-turned and dropped the caftan over the molehill on her heels. The garment began to squirm like a sack of feral cats. A moment later, Bob was standing beside her.

"Fuck you, Delgado," she said, and then strode into the CP's airlock with the Q. As soon as the door shut behind them, though, she realized her mistake. Crud! Did every single step of the way have to be an uphill struggle?

"This lock is fitted with a Q-trap," she said. "It's not going to let you in."

"I will paz," Bob said calmly. "Do not be concerned."

To her massive surprise, he was right. The hatch slid open without so much as a ping of alarm, admitting them into the main foyer. Bondo was manning the checkpoint. As soon as he realized who she was, he started sputtering. "What—? I thought you were with—" He glanced over his shoulder at Shingo's office. "How did you get out?"

"I don't know what you're scatting about, Johnny," she said, "but you'd best save it for later. Right now, you need to call Security. Have them detain the two scoot jocks who followed me here. Then tell Shingo I'm here. He'll want to hear what I have to say."

"I'm calling Security," Bondo said, "but it's you they're going to drag away. The only thing the CO wants to hear from you is, 'Sayonara!'"

"Regrettably, 'want' and 'need' are two different things, Sergeant."

At the sound of that all-too-familiar voice, all eyes turned toward Shingo's office. He was standing in the doorway, looking tired and not at all pleased to see her. "See if there's anyone out there," the commander said. "If there is, tag them and send them on their way." Then he gestured at AJ. "This way, please."

But she didn't move. "I know you have your rules," she said, "but Bob has to come, too. He's the Q who—"

"I know who he is," Shingo said, already turning on his heel. "If he wishes to join us, he may."

Really? Just like that? She couldn't believe that his lordship had made an exception to his Q-free environment without raising so much as an eyebrow. Or that he' had actually admitted to knowing who Bob was. And the surprises didn't stop there. Someone else was in the office with Shingo. He was wearing a trench coat. His matching fedora was parked on Shingo's desk. Bob's clone flowed to his feet as AJ entered the room and offered her a respectful nod.

"Zra," he said. "It iz good to zee you. You look OK."

Her gaze darted from him to Bob and then on to Shingo. Everything that she thought she knew and understood turned into a swirling vapor cloud of confusion. She did another double-take. Then another. But no matter how hard she tried, she could not make sense of what she was seeing. She was so baffled, all she could do was say so.

"I don't understand," she said, addressing the clone simply because she didn't think Shingo would answer her. "What are you doing here?"

The Q cocked an eye in the commander's direction. Shingo nodded. Permission? Really? "I am a 'ling, zra," he said. "I am reporting."

Her confusion went nova: a brilliant, soundless explosion that made her blink repeatedly and stammer. "But," she said, focusing on Shingo in spite of herself. "But—" *Jesus, AJ.* "You're anti-Q. A scourge. How is it that you have a Q for a 'ling?"

"Think back to your time as an envoy," the CO said. "Do you recall being approached by a large, pockmarked Q?" She shook her head as if to dislodge the memory. "Val was there," he went on. "So was I."

"OK," she said, finally making the connection. "The two Q fought. I broke the fight up at your urging. You supposedly took the other Q to the DC."

"That was Eirian," Shingo said. "And instead of detention, I took him to an abandoned outbuilding so I could question him. He offered no resistance. He said he wanted to learn. He said he wanted to serve. I must admit, I was intrigued. I decided to see what he could do. When he proved himself capable, I made him an aide. Now he goes places where I am not welcome or allowed and sees things that would otherwise not get back to me."

AJ stared at the Q, trying to put him into context with her memories. He had turned up at her elbow on several occasions. She hadn't given much thought to those appearances at the time because all sorts of things popped up on this miserable rock, but now she saw them for what they really were.

"You were following me," she said.

He offered her a curt bow, a distinctly Shingo-esque gesture. It was then that she realized that he was much slimmer than he'd been the last time they met. It was then that she remembered that Q-pie laced with blood. No. Not blood. A red boa feather.

"You ate that she-Q, didn't you?" she said.

Eirian bowed again. "Yez, zra."

She turned to Shingo, radiating disdain. "I have to admit, I didn't see this coming." she said. "I probably should have. But I didn't."

The CO looked at her askance, as if she had just started speaking howler monkey. "What are you talking about?"

"Your homegrown death squad," she said, glancing at Eirian again. "If you can't kill 'em, recruit 'em, right? And then let them do your dirty work. Your hands stay clean and the transients disappear."

"There is no such squad," Shingo said.

"Is Josiah Woo still around?"

"Zra?"

"Because I think he should hear about this."

Zra."

"Your would-be fans should know—"

"Zra!"

She rounded on the two Q with an exasperated, "What?" Eirian went a little flat in the face, but Bob held his ground and his shape. "Eirian did not eat the nijit for Zhingo," he said. "Eirian ate it for you."

A shorter, sharper, "What?" burst out of her—pure indignation that such a crime would be laid at her feet. She focused her shielded glare on the clone and said, "Why would you do such a thing?"

"Zra," he said, "the nijit was leading you into—" He struggled with a word, once and then again. Then he looked to Shingo, who obliged with the elusive word.

"The she-Q was leading you into a trap. Delgado's people were waiting for you at the far end of that alleyway."

She had always assumed that a jaw could only drop so far. Yet hers felt like it was in a slo-mo free-fall toward the center of the world. "You know this?" she said, although she wasn't entirely sure who she was asking. "How?"

"Eirian told me," Shingo said. "That is what we were discussing when you arrived."

"And how do you know?" she asked the Q in turn.

"I asked the nijit," Eirian said. "It revealed all in an azrum."

"And then you ate her."

He shrugged, a gesture he could have gotten from Val via Bob. "The nijit was very eager to pleez Heavenly and would not dizregard hiz inztrukzhunz. So I azzerted my zuperiority and ate it." He paused for a moment, and then asked, "Do Terrani not eat lezzer Terrani?"

"I can't say it never happens," she said. "But it's not common or acceptable behavior. Those who do resort to it usually only do so out of desperation, to avoid starvation."

"I waz hungered when I ate the nijit," Eirian assured her.

"Whatever," she said, reminding herself that she wasn't a missionary and it wasn't her job to impose her values on their culture. But she signed off on one distasteful subject only to jump right onto another one. "So," she said to Shingo. "You knew Delgado was gunning for me?"

"Not until Eirian told me," the CO said.

"Then why were you having me shadowed?"

"Trouble seems to follow you wherever you go," he said. "I thought it prudent to do the same."

While she didn't appreciate the sentiment, she had to admit that it had probably saved her life. It felt very weird to be grateful to a man whom she had spent years despising, so she decided to feign indifference and thereby spare them both a ration of awkwardness. "So now that you know about Delgado," she said instead, "you're going to arrest him. Right?"

"I cannot," he said, turning his palms up as if to show that his hands were empty. "I have no proof. There is no proof."

"You have Eirian's statement," she said.

He dismissed the suggestion with a shake of his head. "Unfortunately, Eirian consumed the only direct link to Delgado that we might have had. Anything that he learned from the she-Q would be considered hearsay. And hearsay is inadmissible in a court of law."

"But you didn't hear it from her, did you?" she said to Eirian. "She told you in an Q-pie, right?"

"Yez, zra," Eirian said.

"And as I understand it, Q-pies are like memory chips," she said. "They can be uploaded and downloaded repeatedly without losing their integrity. Is that right, Bob?"

"I do not know what thiz meanz, zra," he said, so she bit back a burst of impatience and tried again.

"It means that you can pass any given thought or memory to another Q in a Q-pie and that Q will remember it exactly as you do. Yes?" Bob exchanged a look with Eiran and then nodded. "And if that Q shared that thought or memory with someone else, he would remember it exactly as you do, too. Right?"

"Yzz, zra," Bob said. "Memoriezs are the only thing about forward-thinking varzi that do not change."

She turned to Shingo, arms spread wide in a what-more-could-you-want pose. But he was less than impressed. "A jury would still have to be able to examine the evidence for themselves," he said, "and that could only happen if the jury was all Q. Do you think the SWU would permit such a thing?"

"Well—"

"Zra."

She had never been chipped for law as she had never seen the need. But— there had to be a way around this legal roadblock, some Qish solution that she had thus far overlooked. It had to be floating around in her head somewhere. All she had to do was—

"AJ."

Crud. She wanted to snap at the Q for distracting her, but stifled the urge because nothing about this situation was his fault. "What is it, Bob?" she said.

"We zhould go now," he said.

Moments later, the CP began to tremble.

CHAPTER 32

THE FIRST SHOCKWAVE ROCKED the building. The second killed the lights. AJ hit the deck, a classic duck-and-cover, and Bob rolled into a ball by her side. She had no idea what Shingo did, although she thought she heard a meaty thud over the rumbling. Seconds passed. The shuddering slowed to a quiver and then stopped. Moments later, the emergency overheads flickered on.

"I hate this friggin' rock," AJ said, as she flipped over and onto her butt.

"I am inclined to agree with you," Shingo said, already climbing to his feet.

A moment later, Bondo barged into the office. "We got damage reports coming in, Commander," he said.

"How bad?" Shingo said, squaring his shoulders as if he were facing a firing squad.

"Mixed bag so far," Bondo said, scowling at his hand-held. "Sub-station One went down again. A new sinkhole opened up—out on the junk flats, looks like. It got two garbage carts and a length of track. The mine is reporting injuries, none of them serious, and oh—this just in. There's an SOS out on Heavenly Delgado. Looks like the sinkhole got him, too, and his brother. A rescue team is on its way, but Delgado's not responding to pings so it doesn't look good."

A chill skated up the length of AJ's back and released an image of Val's lifeless body from cold-storage. In her mind, she leaned over and pressed her lips to that fractured face-plate, then whispered, 'It's OK, my love. You can go now.' And just like that, the chill was gone.

"Zra?"

"What is it, Bob?" she said, and now the image of Val's body was gone, too.

"You OK?" the Q asked.

"Yeah, sure," she said. "Why do you ask?"

"Eirian and I would like to help look for Heavenly," he said. "But we will not go if we are needed here."

Shingo met and held her gaze. Although his expression remained neutral, there was no mistaking the message that he was sending her: all she had to do was tell the Q to stay put and Delgado would be out of everyone's hair for good. Frontier justice, this was called. And there was no doubt in her mind that he would've done the same to her. Yet despite his ruthlessness, despite her desire to see him gone, she simply couldn't wish death-by-sinkhole on anyone, not even her own worst enemy.

"Go ahead," she said. "I can manage by myself."

The two Q departed immediately, without so much as a backward glance. Shingo arched an eyebrow, inviting her to disappear, too, but she shook her head and held up a forefinger to let him know that she still had one big-ticket item left to discuss. He slumped ever so slightly, then gestured for Bondo to continue. He did not look at AJ again until his 'ling was finished with the report and gone again with a long to-do list.

"They will find Delgado, you know," he said, as he pulled out an electric tea kettle out of storage space. "The Q are surprisingly good at search and recovery."

"I know," she said. "Hopefully, it won't matter. Hopefully, he's dead."

"Feeling as you do," he said, "why did you allow the Q to go after him?"

She hesitated, afraid to let her guard down. Would he understand that she had passed on her chance for an easy kill because of Val? Or consider her weak? Her doubt hissed and sputtered like his now-steaming kettle and left her with a boiled-down version of the truth.

"The Q aren't familiar with the concept of revenge," she said. "I didn't want to be the one to teach that to them."

"They do learn surprisingly fast," he mused, and then suddenly looked her in the eye as if he'd made up his mind about something then and there. "I am considering training a select few to run a modified version of this installation in our absence."

The confession, so casually divulged, stupefied her. First a Q 'ling and now a few select Q to take over when the last boat-load of Terrans lit out? Who was this man? "You called them 'profane' and 'disgusting'," she said. "You threatened to exterminate them if I didn't make them go away. No offense, but you're not given to sudden changes of heart."

Shingo expelled a long breath. He looked tired, tapped out. The look wouldn't have been surprising on anybody else, for Farside excelled at sucking the life out of people. But for him to show weakness, especially to her was just plain unnerving.

"We need a buffer zone against the Un," he said. "If Terrans cannot man the frontier, then someone else must do it for us. The Q are available. They are willing. Necessity demands that we utilize them if we can."

Just like that, the universe became a more familiar place. Pragmatism was driving the CO's new attitude, not a newfound appreciation for other life-forms. What a relief! For a few moments there, she thought she had fried one circuit too many.

"Chief Johnson?"

He was holding a steaming porcelain teacup out to her. She declined the offer with an upraised hand, saying, "I've been quarantined. Remember?"

"You are exempt in my presence," he said, and offered the cup to her again.

As he did so, the cup began to tremble. AJ gritted her teeth, thinking aftershock. An instant later, she corrected herself. The ground wasn't shaking. Shingo was. He tried to set the cup down, but couldn't make his arm work. Tea splashed everywhere. Shards of porcelain followed as the cup hit the floor. He tucked the trembling hand under his armpit and then gazed down at the mess he had made.

"That cup was a family heirloom," he said mournfully. "It endured ten generations before me."

"Not a bad track record," AJ said, and then glanced at his holstered hand. "What was that? Do you need me to get the doc?"

"There is no need," he said, and then one-handedly poured a second cup. He breathed in the tea's scented steam, admired its light green color, and then finally tasted it. In the aftermath of that perfect sip, he let his afflicted hand drop to his lap. It wasn't shaking anymore. Everything about him looked normal. Everything but the bittersweet crook to his mouth. She could not stop herself from calling him on it.

"So what was it?" she said.

"It is called multiple sclerosis," he said. "It is an autoimmune disease. It, too, has been in my family for generations."

AJ sucked in a scandalized breath. This shouldn't be happening. Genetic disorders like MS were easily suppressed. Then it hit her: Singer had sailed with Shingo, too. *You are exempt in my presence.* "You're infected, too," she said. When he confirmed the guess with a nod, she asked, "Does TSC know?"

He nodded again. "The outbreak is more advanced than we had hoped. Worse, the virus appears to be a designer."

Of all the shocking things that had come out of his mouth today, this was by far the worst. When she finally reeled her jaw back up from the floor, she said, "Who would do such a thing?"

"Most believe Terran terrorists are responsible," he said wearily. "A few blame the Un. Whoever engineered it did a very good job. So far, our techs have been unable to find a way to disable or even repel the virus. Nano-technology as we know it is being burned to the ground."

"Who would do such a thing?" she said again, stuck in a stunned loop.

"It does not matter who launched the virus at this point," he said. "What matters is what is happening now that the virus is starting to have an impact on the general population. People of all persuasions are falling prey to illnesses and diseases that the docs have forgotten how to treat or cure. Trade is being disrupted. Off-world colonies are experiencing shortages. RSOs are being shut down because infected spacers don't want to be bombarded with cosmic radiation."

A coppery taste crept into AJ's mouth—shock laced with outrage. Every fear that she had ever had about this miserable planet was coming true. "What about Farside?" she asked. "Is TSC going to evacuate us?"

"Only as a very last resort," he said, in a tone as flat as a death knell. "The frontier must be held as long as possible."

The knot in her gut from spread to her lungs, for she knew too well what Shingo wasn't saying. Holding a frontier was one thing; supporting it was a whole different animal. If a solution to the NV epidemic wasn't found posthaste, Farside's supply line would surely collapse. There'd be no warning. The supply ship would simply never show up. Eventually, big Terrans would start eating small Terrans to survive—just like Q. And eventually, there would be no Terrans left. That was why Shingo wanted to train Q to run the Farside installation.

"So all that talk about relocating to a new planet was just talk," she said.

"No," he said. "There is another planet. But it has not been seeded yet. And the shift from here to there has been put on indefinite hold."

"Seems kind of mean to dangle something like that in front of everyone," she said. And by 'everyone', she meant her.

Shingo set down his cup and tucked his hand under his arm again. "What would you have me do instead—make it known that we could be marooned here? The resulting emotional turmoil would most likely open the door to anarchy. Does that seem less mean to you?"

"No," she said, conceding the point. "I can see the need for discretion. In fact, I'm rather stunned that you've been so open with me. What brought that on?"

"You chanced to observe one of my—secrets," he said, with a sly, sideways glance at his imprisoned hand. "And I know you can be circumspect when it suits you. Although you may not believe it, I am human, too. And some burdens are impossible to carry alone."

Whoa! Now he was showing his vulnerable side? This day just kept getting crazier and crazier.

Shingo's keeper pinged as if to second the thought. He responded immediately. "Yes? What is it?"

"The Q found the Delgado brothers," Bondo reported.

"And—?"

"Both DOA."

The corners of Shingo's mouth twitched ever so slightly. "Have the bodies brought to cold storage and inform Delgado's 'lings of his demise. No doubt they will want to conduct a ceremony of some sort before we cremate the remains. Encourage them to be quick about it."

"Will do," Bondo said, and signed off.

"Well," Shingo said, "it appears that fate has interceded on your behalf."

"Fate or Farside," she said. "But given the way my luck runs, the Q will probably bring the bastard back to life."

He blinked hard as if stunned by the thought. "They cannot do that, can they?"

How was it that absolutely no one knew when she was kidding? "Relax," she said. "I was only joking. The Q can fix what's ailing you, but they can't—" Wait. "Raise the dead." That was it, the solution to chaos. And it had been staring her in the face all along. "Shit."

"Are you unwell?" Shingo said, taken aback by her outburst.

"No, no," she said, hyper with sudden excitement. "I'm fine. Really. Did you hear what I said? The Q can fix what's ailing us. This could be our way out!"

"Babble," he said, recoiling slightly as if he thought she'd come down with a contagious form of madness. "I fear the day's events have overwhelmed your sensibilities."

"No," she said. "Listen! On my first go-around on this planet, one of my crewmen had an attack of Pigeon Pox. Bob made the flare-up go away."

Shingo's expression hardened—a resistant cast. "There was nothing of this mentioned in any report."

"Yes, well, I didn't see the relevance then," she said, white-washing over the rest of her reasons for the omission. "I figured he'd gotten sick because a wonky nano-booster. I've since realized that the NV was to blame."

"Speculation," Shingo said, giving the word a millipede's prickly legs. "It means nothing. You should go now."

He stood up, meaning to escort her to the door. She refused the invitation to move. "He helped me with my cancer, too," she said. "It's getting smaller."

"That is the chemo," he said, and then gestured for her to vacate her seat. She ignored that, too.

"The chemo made me sick," she said. "Bob made me feel better." Shingo's hand closed around her upper arm. "He might be able to help you, too." His hold on her didn't relax, but it didn't grow any tighter, either. She could feel suspicion radiating from that grip. It was mixed with reluctance, uncertainty, and underneath it all, a single, uncontestable grain of hope. "What do you have to lose," she said, "besides that tremor in your hand?"

He tensed—one last spasm of resistance. Then he let go of her and said, "What would I have to do?"

She considered candy-coating what-all was involved but opted for full disclosure instead because this was not a time for surprises. As she filled him in on what he could expect, his back stiffened and then the set of his shoulders. By the time she was done, the cords in his neck were taut, too.

"Do you truly expect me—or anyone else—to tolerate such an—invasion?" he said, his nostrils flaring at the thought.

"I know, I know," she said, sympathizing because in her heart of hearts— OK, not even that far down—she felt the exact same way. "It's not a glamorous prospect. It's not appealing in any way. But if it works, it could keep you and the rest of Terra in space." When he continued to balk, she said, "Desperate times call for desperate measures. How desperate are you?"

He swallowed hard and then seemed to go still from the inside out, as if he were listening to voices that AJ couldn't hear. *He's got a mother, too, you know,* Meli said.

"I will try it," he said. "And then we will see."

CHAPTER 33

"So," AJ said, as she paced the confines of her FZ apartment for the last time, "any second thoughts now that your wish is coming true?"

"I have many thoughts, zra," Bob said, looking dapper and quite serious in his black caftan. "Which one would you like to hear?"

She knew better than to pose figurative questions to this literal-minded Q. She'd done so anyway because she was nervous and excited and brimming with an inner effervescence that she hadn't felt in years. "Tell me how you feel about leaving your homeworld," she said. "Are you scared? Uncertain? Reluctant?"

"I am eager, zra," he said. "I want to zee new places and experience new things."

"Won't you miss being around your own kind?"

"I am not the only Q making this journey," he said. "But even if I were, I would not care. I am not nijit. I do not crave the society of other Q."

"Not even Eirian?"

The Q shook his head like a puzzled parent. "My clone seeks evolution in a different direction."

His bafflement was understandable. She didn't know what to think about Shingo as a mentor, either. The Q were so—impressionable. And his lordship never strayed far from his own agenda. She could imagine Eirian learning all the wrong things from him. Then again, the Q had been snacking on each other without remorse long before the CO ever set foot on Farside so it was quite possible that her concern for their sensitivities was misplaced.

"Well," she said, "at least he knows he has other options." She patted the security pouch that she had attached to her habby. It contained a strongly-worded recommendation from Shingo along with some before-and-after results that they had compiled while waiting for *The Bonhomie* to arrive. "When the council sees these docs, it'll revoke the ban on Q travel in a heartbeat."

"Is that good, zra?"

"Yes, Bob," she said, "that is very good."

"Zhingo told Eirian that hearts are bad," Bob said.

AJ could see Shingo saying something like that, the heart being the seat of all emotion. In his world, control trumped feeling. And that was exactly the sort of disinformation that—

"He said that waz why Heavenly died."

Wait. "What was that?"

"He said Heavenly died because he had a bad heart."

Ha-ha, OK, she got it—bad as in weak rather than bad as in evil. She should've known. His lordship didn't have a poetic bone in his body.

"Shingo was right," she said, words she never thought she'd hear herself say. "Delgado's heart was bad. It stopped when the sinkhole swallowed him." Then, because there was poetry in her on her mother's side, she felt compelled to add, "That doesn't mean that all hearts are bad."

The Q turned a distressed shade of gray. The change confused AJ. She'd been expecting a more positive reaction to the revelation—relief at the least, maybe even some form of happiness. Her puzzlement seemed to compound his distress.

"What?" she said. When he balked, she pressed. "Tell me."

His coloring paled even further—more apprehension. But even now, after all he had done for her, he still felt compelled to do her bidding. "I failed to save Heavenly," he said.

Her response was immediate. "So?"

"When I failed to save Val, you got angry and went away," he said. "Now you are leaving again."

"Yes," she said, "but you're leaving with me this time. And I'm not angry."

His face plumped back out. His complexion returned to a mottled shade of sandy brown. Then he said, "Why?"

"Why what?" she said.

"Why were you angry about Val but not angry about Heavenly?" he said.

The question gave her serious pause. How was she supposed to explain love to an alien when she barely understood it herself? She could tell him that it was hormones. She could say it was need. But there was so much more to it than that.

"My anger then was illogical," she said, "a violent reaction to a loss that I couldn't bring myself to accept. It was wrong of me to blame Val's death on you, Bob. Farside killed him, not you." His eyes goggled slightly—him encouraging her to go on.

Even aliens know when you're beating around the bush.

Sometimes, Meli was too smart for her own good. But both she and the Q were right. AJ was avoiding the meat of the matter. It was just so hard getting some things right. She had to try, though. Because if he continued to associate with Terrans, somebody would surely introduce him to hate. And it would be better if he knew about love first.

"OK," she said, and then took a deep, bracing breath. "Val was the most precious person in the universe to me. He was my best friend and my partner. I would have done—anything for him." Bob goggled at her again. Crud. "He was—" She groped for a word that the Q might understand, a word that captured a singular feeling without getting all sticky and sweet. And just like that, it came to her. "Val was my zra."

"Zhee," Bob said, and she could almost see him rearranging the Terran pantheon to suit his altered perception. "I understand."

"Good," she said. Which was her way of saying, Now we never have to speak of it again. Meli chuckled at her squeamishness. As she did so, the keeper pinged.

"The transport to the shuttle pad has arrived," it said. "Please proceed to the loading dock with all carry-on baggage."

"That's us," she said, and then glanced at the regolith-filled float that was to be his home during the cruise back to Terra. "Are you sure you want to do this?"

"I am sure," he said, and glided toward the container. "I cannot imagine anything more exciting than probing the unknown. I want to be an explorer like the Terrani."

The declaration tickled her curiosity. "What makes you think Terrans are explorers?"

"Heavenly told me," he said, as he climbed into the float. "He said Terrani came through the sky-mouth to zee what was on the other side. I want to do the same."

Someone else might have let that impression slide without comment, for it did contain a romanticized nugget of truth. And 'explorer' had a sweeter ring to it than inter-galactic thug. But AJ wanted Bob to know the whole truth. He had earned that much.

"Terrans have been explorers throughout the course of our history," she said. "But that's not the reason we came through the sky-mouth. We came looking for aliens."

Bob flushed jungle green, a display of delight. "For Q?"

She dispersed his joy with a shake of her head. "You were a surprise," she said. "We were expecting to meet a more advanced race."

"More evolved than Q," he said, taking his race's place on the cosmic totem pole for granted.

"No," she said. "More evolved than us."

"Zhee! Such beings exist?"

"We're not sure," she said, "but we think so."

He went green again—not the color she had been expecting. "This iz very exciting, zra!" he said. "When you find them, could I meet them, too?"

This wasn't the first time that she'd been struck by the Q's outlook. It was, however, the first time that she found herself admiring, and even envying it. How nice it must be to perceive the unknown as an adventure to be had rather than a threat to be intercepted prior to its arrival in the neighborhood. Could I meet them, too? And really, who was to say that aggression was the superior approach? Terrans had only encountered real-life aliens once—just like Q. In response to that encounter, Q had aspired to become more than they had been. Terrans had nearly turned into the thing that they feared most. If that had happened, they would have lost their best hope of stemming a civilization-crushing pandemic.

"Zra?" Bob said. "Have I offended?"

"No," she said, reassuring him with a smile. "Not at all." Even now, with a world's worth of leverage at his disposal, he wanted nothing more than to stay in her good graces. Amazing. "I was just thinking, is all."

Everyone involved assumed that the Q would benefit more from their unlikely alliance with Terrans. Everyone assumed that humans would be the instructors and Q, the students. But AJ believed that the Q had a few things to bring to the table, too. They could teach Terrans how to share the universe and embrace the unknown. They could reshape the meaning of fearlessness in their own eager, elastic image. And everyone would be the better for it.

Could I meet them, too?

Why the hell not?

"You ready to go adventuring, Bob?" she said.

"Yzz, zra," he said, with an all-too-human smile.

"Then let's go," she said, and closed him up in his float.